Daniil Granin

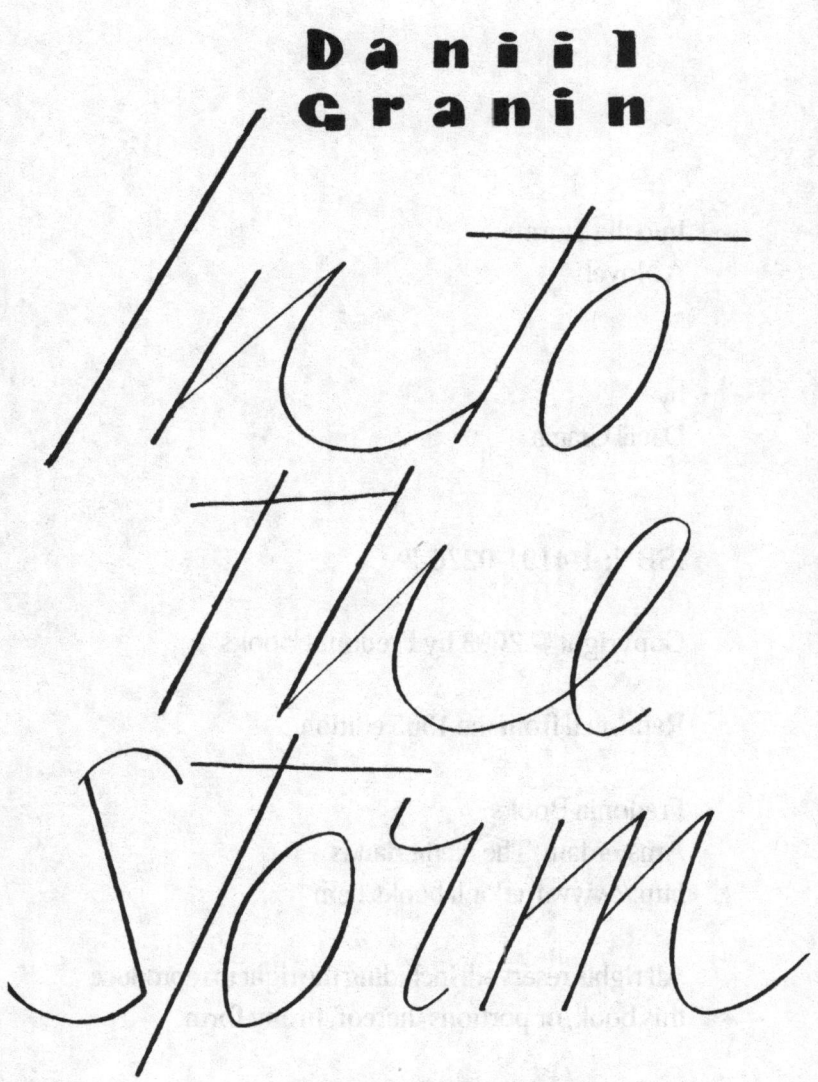

Into the Storm

A NOVEL

Fredonia Books
Amsterdam, The Netherlands

Into the Storm:
A Novel

by
Daniil Granin

ISBN: 1-4101-0226-2

Reprinted from the 1965 edition

Fredonia Books
Amsterdam, The Netherlands
http://www.fredoniabooks.com

CONTENTS

Part One 5

Part Two 92

Part Three 176

Part Four 281

PART ONE

Chapter One

The wizard flew into Moscow on May 6, at eight in the morning. He was the first off the plane, running down the swaying ramp to the concrete of the airfield. Eyes followed him, but only for a moment; no one was impressed by the slim sunburnt young man in his fashionable sports jacket.

He walked through the crowd, leaving behind him kisses, laughter, flowers, and the unnaturally loud voices that people have for the first few minutes after landing, while they are still feeling slightly deaf.

His only luggage was a leather briefcase, in which a toothbrush and a soapbox rattled occasionally among the papers.

Thirty minutes later a taxi brought him into town. He stepped out into the morning stream that surges round the doors of underground stations, pedestrian crossings and news-stands. Moscow was hurrying to work and he hurried with it.

Trolleybuses that seemed higher than usual with their new blue-glass tops floated aquarium-like upon the glittering flood of traffic. The flower sellers at street corners, their green-painted tubs afoam with blossom, were doing a brisk trade. A small donkey, plastered all over with circus bills, clip-clopped amid the growing roar. It was ten minutes to nine; people were no longer walking but running.

His glance lingered on a girl in a shop window holding a roll of printed cotton.

A dummy? No, she moved. He stopped to smile and commanded the girl to smile back at him. She turned obediently and looked him over and her lips moved soundlessly, then she laughed and her mouth opened very wide, as though she wanted to show him all her small pearly teeth at once and couldn't quite manage it because there were so many.

He pursued his way with many strange changes of direction, now slowing, now quickening his pace, turning off down quiet sun-drenched side-streets, then swinging back on to the main boulevards.

In Pushkin Square he halted before a newspaper pasted on a hoarding.

Moscow Welcomes Boxing Champions.

Kremlin Reception for Delegates to Astronomical Congress.

New Building Exhibition.

Academician Likhov Decorated.

He read the paper with the special zest of the new arrival who suddenly finds himself with all Moscow at his command, who only has to make up his mind which congress or exhibition he wants to attend.

This time his coming would pass unnoticed. It wouldn't be in today's papers or tomorrow's either. There had been no reporters at the airfield to meet him. Yet, surely, wizards didn't come to Moscow every day. Somewhere, sometime there would be a newspaper with his photograph in it. He could see himself, a smiling figure among the flowers. No, better not to smile, better make it tired, slightly embarrassed. "Moscow welcomed today Oleg Tulin. In a talk with your correspondent, he said. . . ."

No man can predict what will one day be in the newspapers. But that is what wizards are for. Even now he could feel the page, still fresh and damp with printer's ink, and see his picture squarely in the middle of it.

From Kamenny Bridge he had a view of the Kremlin's gilded domes. On the right, in sunlit mist stood a skyscraper, pompous and gross, a red surf of lesser roofs swirling at its base, and tower cranes riding the surf like the masts of a huge fleet.

With the eye of a general he surveyed this city that he was to conquer, that was to acknowledge him, and that as yet had no suspicion of his presence.

The idea was so pretentious he had to curl his lip ironically to keep his self-respect.

He paused at a corner, deciding which way to go. He was not usually undecided, but in this state of unstable equilibrium a pull one way or the other would be enough to make up his mind for him.

The wind nudged him on and he went where the wind went. At the end of the street was a park. Every path had its procession of prams, but the park still retained the morning stillness. Here and there on the benches sat students—blank-faced sleep-walkers engrossed in their lecture notes. Surely *he* had never taken his exams that seriously?

A waitress was setting out chairs under a striped awning. He sat down at a table overlooking the pond. The waitress handed him the menu.

"The lot. Start from the first line and work down. I'll say when I've had enough."

The waitress smiled. She had dimples in her cheeks.

The wind ruffled his hair. It was fair and wavy and he made no attempt to push it back. He could see she liked it that way too. His southern tan marked him out among the pale-faced Muscovites. Tulin took off his jacket and hung it over the back of a chair, then he pushed back the sleeves of his woollen shirt and started on the salad, yoghourt, fried eggs, and sausages. He drank a glass of coffee, then went on with a cheese sandwich, a ham sandwich, and a sausage sandwich in quick succession, and once again he felt like a wizard.

"So you were just bragging," the waitress said when he paused. "I thought this was only the first course."

He looked at her.

"A man always promises more than he can give."

"That's true," she said, and laughed without turning her eyes away.

"I don't want to seem greedy or you'll change your opinion of me."

"You think you know what that is?"

"I know everything. I know you're sick of the sight of guzzling men. You see nothing but guzzling men all day. The only man you could love would be one who didn't eat anything at all."

He had an overwhelming desire to charm everyone he met; this waitress, too, must yield to his spell.

He looked past her at the sky and said: "Take in the tablecloths, it's going to rain."

"Is it really? How do you know?"

"I told you I know everything."

Then he was walking along beside the pond, staring up at a bluish-grey cloud bulging out of the sky. The waitress watched him go. Yes, she was a nice girl. He would have liked to take her for a walk in the park one evening, but he was leaving tomorrow, so he could make no promises. He felt her disappointment and reflected how difficult it was to bring joy, pure joy, untinged with regret.

At a boat-hire station he ran up the steps of an ivy-clad shelter. The cloud was spreading over the blue sky like a huge ink blot.

In this still sunny and carefree park he was the only person who had any serious thought about what was happening overhead. He knew that the sky was spoiled.

The dark belly of the cloud sagged lower and lower. Ominous wisps curled from its silvery edges. Shadows crept over the earth; the wind hid among the trees, playing like a cat with the soft leaves.

It grew dark. With the oppressive sultriness came a hush that could be felt even amid the roar of the city.

A few heavy drops pattered down. The first shots, just a warning. The swans on the pond glided swiftly to their wooden pen.

Standing on the steps, Tulin raised his hand.

"Now!" he commanded softly.

As his hand cut the air there was a flash of lightning and a rumble of thunder. It struck again and again and the park was wrapped in a noisy deluge.

People came running to the shelter from all sides. Shaking themselves and laughing, they peeped out to admire the first storm of the year. Water was gushing off the roof. A steel-blue fork of lightning pierced the sky and its cold metallic gleam was reflected on thousands of wet leaves.

"Good!" said Tulin.

An explosion of thunder overhead made the onlookers gasp. Tulin lifted his dripping face to the echoing sky. The next moment he found himself reciting poetry, an old, majestic iambic that fitted perfectly with the booming accompaniment of the storm. He shouted the words, scarcely able to hear himself above the rising cannonade:

> *Whence come these hostile forces that attack*
> *The sky? And what imperious hand*
> *Doth gather up the clouds in vapours black*
> *And send its storms across the land?*

In a sudden lull a voice from the shelter asked sarcastically:

"Well, have you found out?"

"Yes, I have," he replied sharply, not turning his head.

He hated being laughed at.

"What it means to be a poet! Are you one?"

It was a woman's voice, low-pitched, rippling with suppressed laughter.

"And why not?"

"But that's fascinating! Do go on, please. I'm dying to hear more about your storm."

"Oh, leave him alone," another woman's voice intervened, and added something in a whisper. There was a combined giggle, then the mocking voice went on:

"I've never seen a real live poet before, specially one that's so wet. How do you write your poetry?"

"I use coils and condensers."

"Oh, yes. And what do they look like?" It was like somebody encouraging a small boy who is trying to make up a story. He tried to parry in the same vein.

"Well, I'll try to put it simply. It's something halfway between a vacuum cleaner and a bicycle."

"More robots!"

Then the other voice:

"I think it's a fridge."

"Or a condenser-tipped corkscrew!"

Now both voices were competing to make a fool of him.

"For your information. . ." Tulin burst out heatedly, but a salvo of thunder made him jump. He could never forgive himself for that afterwards.

There was a peal of laughter from behind him.

"Don't be frightened, poet. Only very prominent objects get struck by lightning."

At this he turned round. Two faces showed up faintly in the shadows of the shelter. He climbed to the top step and leaned over the railing.

"What a lovely pair of know-alls," he said. "Do you believe in miracles?"

"Are you a miracle-worker?"

"Think it's a joke, do you?" said Tulin. "That's extremely unwise on your part. It was I who called forth this storm. I command the lightning."

"And can you stop it?"

"Not yet," he replied seriously. "Come back in a year's time and I'll have everything under control."

He heard the more serious of the two say: "They're all a bit batty."

"How'll you manage it?" asked the other.

"Just fly up to the thunderhead and destroy it. You don't believe me? Give me your hand."

She put out her hand boldly. The small cupped palm was cold and wet.

"Going to tell my fortune?"

"Look up at the sky," he said.

Under the low, heavy layer of grey, even greyer, almost black shreds of dissolving cloud were jostling, spinning and floating away.

"A year will pass," he said solemnly, "and one small hand like yours will be able to control these rebellious elements. I don't expect you to believe me, I just want you to remember today's thunderstorm and what we've been saying."

The rain was slackening. The storm, its violet pall still torn by whitish lightning flashes, was rumbling away to the west.

The two girls had pulled aside the ivy and were looking at him. One was tall and dark, with a severe expression on her face; the other, in a little plastic hood, had deep brown eyes with an expression of wonder in them that would not be easy to forget.

"Which of us held out her hand?" she asked suddenly.

"You did," Tulin replied. "You're Zhenya?"

"That's not fair. You were eavesdropping!"

"Fourth-year student. Dying for practical work. Adores Yevtushenko. No intention of marrying...."

Raindrops were pattering down under the trees. The park was still stunned, but the air was sweet with the scent of grass, and sunlight and shadow were showing themselves timidly on the sandy paths.

Tulin stepped into a foamy yellow puddle. The girls laughed and quickened their pace. They were late for a lecture.

"I know what you're thinking," Tulin said. "I know your wish and I can make it come true."

"Have a try."

"You wish you hadn't got to go to a lecture and could stay here and walk with me in the park."

"Nonsense," the tall girl said severely. Her name was Katya. "You're much too sure of yourself."

Tulin glanced at Zhenya and said quickly:

"If you want to be original, be honest. Why not be original? Give yourself a break. You'll regret it afterwards if you don't."

Zhenya laughed. Her teeth were so white they seemed to light up her whole face.

But he didn't even smile. There was something in his self-assured tone that gave all this chatter significance. Zhenya's big brown eyes had grown serious.

"Never mind, we have a date for a year's time from now." Tulin squeezed her fingers.

"I think we shall meet before that."

"We're late," said Katya.

It was a long way to the trolleybus-stop and a trolleybus was overtaking them. Tulin stepped out into the road and raised his hand. With half-closed eyes he enjoyed the magician's sense of generosity in dispensing miracles. The trolleybus skidded to a halt a few feet from his chest. The driver shook his fist, then his face broke into a grin and the door of the bus snapped open. The girls jumped in. Tulin waved to them.

He glanced at his watch. He still had an hour and a half to kill. Someone ought to invent a bank where people could deposit their spare time, to be drawn on demand.

He brushed down his jacket and set out for the institute, knowing almost for certain that this was the one place where he ought not to be going.

Chapter Two

That morning in No. 2 Laboratory was no different from any other morning. The lab was stuffy. The men were working in their shirt-sleeves. Bochkaryov had brought in a bunch of lilies of the valley and put them in a retort for Zinochka, the senior laboratory assistant.

The atmosphere men had picked up a storm approaching from the north-east at a speed of twenty kilometres an hour. Matveyev had switched on the recorders.

The morning was bustling on as usual, quite unprepared for any emergencies.

Golitsyn turned up at the laboratory unexpectedly at half past ten. A wave of hasty improvisation swirled ahead of him from room to room. The men pulled on their jackets. Zinochka put her flowers away in the cupboard. Richard crammed all the rubbish that accumulated so quickly around him—the hanks of wire, the boards, the old circuits—under his table.

Golitsyn marched in waving an enormous briefcase, the skirts of his unbuttoned raincoat flapping like wings.

"Rubbish!... Balderdash! Conferences and meetings—bah!" Leaving the polite "good mornings" unanswered, he dumped his briefcase on Krylov's desk and fanned himself with his hat. Krylov's offer of a chair evoked another roar.

"Has anyone ever worked out how many hours I've spent at conferences in the past ten years? Just an approximate estimate?"

Krylov just stood there, long arms dangling, embarrassed, gloomily thoughtful.

"Well, I have—at this idiotic meeting I've just been to! Three thousand three hundred hours! And three thousand of them served no purpose whatever. You don't care, of course. No one bothers *you*."

From a distance Agatov smiled cautiously while Golitsyn rumbled on.

"You can just go on with your graph-making. But I've only another six thousand working hours left. With my health! No more, I can assure you!"

Golitsyn's thin grey hair was disarranged, revealing a tender pink bareness. He glared round fiercely at his assistants and fastened his gaze on Krylov.

"It doesn't matter to you, of course," he resumed with triumphant malice. "In fact, I don't really know what does matter to you. Where have you been all this time?"

Krylov's eyes remained sleepily unresponsive.

Golitsyn rounded on Matveyev.

"No good at all! Do it all over again! Do you call this a result?"

At times like this, one avoided arguing with Golitsyn. He could be unjust, capricious, anything. Matveyev muttered something inaudible and retreated.

"What's wrong with it?" Krylov asked suddenly, still looking as withdrawn from the world as ever. "You can't be any more accurate than that on the fluxmeter we've got."

Matveyev's small puckered face cleared and he nodded gratefully to Krylov from a distance.

Golitsyn spluttered.

"Who says it's wrong? Am I not allowed to speak? You'd better get a move on with your own work!"

"I'll adjust the fluxmeters," Agatov said.

Charts, photographs and spools of tape flashed through Golitsyn's fingers. After a stab at them with his noble, aquiline beak, he alighted unerringly on the chart Krylov had been hiding from himself and pulled it out. He eyed it appraisingly, turning it this way and that at arm's length.

"How much longer are you going to mess about?"

Behind Golitsyn, Agatov cleared his throat.

"I've been trying to make Krylov work a little faster. I've warned him the plan will suffer." His spare figure, the white face, the square jaw were a picture of controlled regret. "As for that meeting, Arkady Borisovich, you could quite well have sent me. I'd have stuck it out. You don't value your time yourself."

Golitsyn waved him aside impatiently with the chart. Krylov stared at Golitsyn's tie.

She must have known perfectly well that the faster we worked the sooner we'd have to part. We simply tried not to talk about it. What a pair of idiots. Two desperately conscientious idiots. She could have found any number of excuses for holding up the work. I wonder whether she thought of that. What was the date when we made out our last chart? The lake ice was cracking up under our feet. What did she say about the ice? Yes, the instruments were almost under water, and she made that wonderful remark about the ice. . . .

"Excuse me," Krylov said. He reached across the table for the chart. His gesture was clumsy, almost rude.

"Really! . . ." Golitsyn drew himself up majestically, so that everyone should see what an ill-mannered oaf Krylov was, and, when this had sunk in, he let his shoulders droop and turned into a crotchety, malicious old man. "Look at him! The fellow's a hermit! How much longer are you going to ruminate over your ideas? We shall have to force you out of this daydreaming."

Bochkaryov and Richard exchanged glances.

"The old man is out for blood today," Richard whispered.

Bochkaryov shook his huge gnome-like head.

"No, it's not that—wait a minute. . . ."

But Richard was already confronting Golitsyn.

"Why do you say you have only another six thousand working hours left, Arkady Borisovich? On what grounds?" His pale mobile face wore a valiant smile. "In that case, you ought to restrict yourself to one hour's work a day."

"Who's this, butting in? What do you know about old age? It's a dull occupation, getting old."

"It's the only known way of staying alive a long time."

Bochkaryov handed Golitsyn a letter from a would-be inventor who suggested making use of the sensations in rheumaticky joints as a means of forecasting the weather. The laughter was loud but rather forced. Bochkaryov stepped in between Krylov and Golitsyn, took the old man's arm affectionately and led him off to inspect the new apparatus.

"Falling over yourselves to cover up for him, aren't you?" Golitsyn grumbled.

A respectful procession followed Golitsyn to the test benches in the new room.

Krylov smoothed out the crumpled chart. It was dated March 12. Two figures and a few words written in a fine sloping hand. He tried to remember what kind of day it had been. Had they been taking readings on the lake? Or were they finishing their inspection tour of the forest?

Sometimes Natasha would come in late and we would work on far into the night. Yes, it happened when we had been working late. It was getting dark, but for some reason neither of us got up to turn on the light. Eventually it got too dark to write. We both laid down our pens and Natasha sat in her chair without moving. The Antonovs were out and we were alone in the house. I had thought of that. Yes, I know I thought of that. I got up and went over to her and suddenly she clung to me. I had never expected it to be so easy and good. I woke at dawn with the same feeling of surprise. Natasha was still asleep. She was smiling. It was a smile of complete trust, as if she had no more doubts. Her lips were puffy and her pencilled eyebrows were smudged but it only made her more lovable. All of a sudden she said without opening her eyes: "Don't look at me."

When we went out on to the front steps, the snow looked warm in the light of the rising sun, but the walls of the house were draped with long icicles. Soon the whole house began to tinkle as they thawed. I saw her off as far as the bus-stop. All the time she had that expression of trustful admiration in her eyes and it worried me. I wanted everything to remain just a pleasant incident, nothing serious. I wasn't ready for anything serious and I didn't want her to take it seriously either. It would be the wrong thing for both of us.

The mere sight of a chart filled in Natasha's handwriting was enough to lead his thoughts astray. Sometimes he would sit staring at nothing, his mind full of memories. No one suspected what an effort it cost him to make himself work. There were times when the people round him seemed as mute and two-dimensional as the figures in a silent film.

Golitsyn was returning with Richard and Agatov at his side; the others were following close behind.

"...don't the philosophers claim that theory is grey, but green is the eternal tree of life?" Richard was saying. He was about the only person in the institute who dared argue with Golitsyn.

"You're a very erudite young man," said Golitsyn. "I wonder if you can tell me what philosopher said that?"

"One of the ancients."

"Ancient! Of course, he thinks everything that happened before the Revolution is ancient. For your information, young man, it was Goethe. That 'ancient' poet! And he wrote a play called *Faust*, and those words were spoken by Mephistopheles to evoke doubts in Faust's mind." Golitsyn surveyed Richard critically. "And Faust was a scientist, not just a post-graduate. I would even rank him an Academician. You, Richard, haven't even tried your lance yet. You merely argue. You will surely stay very green, if you go on like this."

Agatov laughed and patted Richard on the shoulder.

"How very apt!"

He laughed, just as he spoke, always with a purpose. Bending towards Golitsyn, he made his progress report. The smooth forehead over the fair eyebrows and steely eyes was furrowed in concentration. Since the last head of the laboratory had left, all organisational matters had fallen almost automatically to Agatov, and it was taken for granted that he would eventually occupy the post.

Golitsyn frowned with annoyance. He disliked the dull routine of reports, plans and applications. Agatov, of course, was in a difficult position. Bochkaryov wanted to work on a subject that had not been officially approved. Because Krylov was late with his report the seminar could not begin.

"But this is anarchy!" Golitsyn exclaimed. "We can't go on like this."

Krylov smiled.

"Not long ago this ice was a wave itself," Natasha had said. *"And now it's choking the waves."*

Did she say "choking", or was it "crushing"? No, she used another word, something more exact. How quickly one forgets these things. That yellow plush armchair she liked to work in with her feet tucked up under her. The feel of her shoulder, always breath-taking, always as if I had felt it for the very first time. When she saw me off she was wearing a red coat and red mittens, and we talked about crocodiles. Nothing else, just crocodiles.

"You think it amusing!" Golitsyn was saying. "You're wrong, my friend. You won't get away with it this time. I'll make you work."

If only I could turn into a crocodile this minute, Krylov thought. Come crawling out from under the table, a great big crocodile.

Imagine their faces! Zinochka would scream and the Old Man would say: "Stop this impudence. You ought to be ashamed of yourself!"

Golitsyn picked up his briefcase and hat and, in the same grumbling voice, said: "Sergei Ilyich, put in your application for the vacancy."

Krylov stared at him obtusely.

"What are you goggling at me for?" Golitsyn exploded. "Put in your application for the post of head of the laboratory!"

There was a stunned silence. Everyone looked at Agatov. His lips had drawn together in a thin, almost invisible line. For a moment it seemed almost as if Agatov himself had disappeared, as if only his severe dark-grey suit was left.

Only Golitsyn pretended not to notice anything. He stumped over to Richard.

"Mind you've read *Faust* by next Monday. I suppose you're mad about Hemingway and the rest of them."

"Why, I'll . . . I'll learn it by heart!" Richard declared delightedly.

Golitsyn grunted. "What are you so overjoyed about?" Without turning he jerked his thumb at Krylov. "He's another one with his head full of nonsense, but there are a few ideas there." He closed one eye and squinted at Agatov. "Hare-brained though they are. . . . And he'll learn how to draw up plans. All this red tape, all these clips and drawing-pins—what we need are ideas! That's where the shortage lies. The late Professor Obolensky used to do all his accounts on cigarette packets."

As always, at awkward moments he put on his crotchety-old-man act. He screwed up his eyes short-sightedly and screeched as if he were deaf. No use reasoning with him. He was sixty-five, sclerosis was taking its toll.

The easiest explanation was that Krylov had been stunned by his good fortune and had no words to express himself. His gaze was still dreamily remote. Everyone could see this and everyone felt ashamed of him.

Bochkaryov nudged Krylov surreptitiously and hissed at him as if he were a small boy.

"Say thank you."

"Oh . . . er, yes. Thank you," Krylov said.

Now he had remembered what Natasha had said about the ice, he realised there was something else he ought to remember, but he couldn't think what. He watched Golitsyn's wrinkled lips moving, caught the gleam of a gold-capped tooth; then he noticed Richard's full fresh lips, Zinochka's lipstick-painted, the moustache that covered Matveyev's. They were all standing there moving their lips. It was like dubbing a film; he could put any words to it he chose.

Golitsyn signalled to the others to move away.

"What's the matter, Sergei Ilyich?" Golitsyn asked when they were alone.

Natasha said: "Why are we parting? I understand, I understand everything. But what are we doing?"

"Don't let it worry you," Golitsyn was saying. "Everything will be all right. There's nothing whatever to worry about."

The thing Krylov would have enjoyed most at that moment would have been to crumple all his papers into a tight ball and stuff it into the Old Man's mouth.

Chapter Three

The upper backstairs landing was their clubroom. The smell of tobacco, the buckets and mops of the charwomen and a few old litter baskets provided a comforting informality. No other laboratory had such a nice little corner. The corridors in the main building were much too clean and bright and the huge lounge, full of new furniture, was not the kind of place one could relax in.

While Krylov sat on the banisters and smoked, Bochkaryov speculated on what had prompted the Old Man's unexpected offer. It was not long since Golitsyn had at last decided to launch an attack on Academician Denisov, a move both Krylov and Bochkaryov fully supported. Perhaps he wanted to make that support more effective by putting one of them in a position of responsibility? Or perhaps he was just thinking of a successor?

"You make the perfect heir to the throne," Bochkaryov said. "Master's degree in physics. A promising young man. What are we waiting for? Take the job and get on with it!"

"But what's the point?"

"The point! The point is that any lab needs a scientist in charge of it, and ours needs a physicist. And the Old Man knows it."

"The Old Man!"

Despite his foibles they respected Golitsyn. He deserved his reputation as one of the pioneers of atmospheric electricity. A typical representative of the old school, he knew the problem as a whole better than anyone, though his knowledge was that of a meteorologist rather than a physicist. He had breadth but lacked the depth that comes with specialisation.

"You'll have to make sacrifices, that's inevitable," Bochkaryov said. "The total gain is what matters."

Krylov spat into the well of the staircase.

"Otherwise you'll be leaving the road clear for Agatov."

"Is that so terrible? He's a good organiser."

"Yes, I know. Many people think so. But surely not you! He's not creative, he's got no spark. And that's as dangerous as gangrene. No wonder he's after the job. Our last lab chief but one was the same—not a clue. We were all glad when Agatov got him kicked out, but even then I felt Agatov had his own axe to grind. Then they sent us Parkhomenko, Dr. Parkhomenko, as smart as they make them. That was more than Agatov had bargained for. It may have seemed to you that Agatov thought the world of Parkhomenko. Not a bit of it! He was trying to get rid of him all along, and this time he kicked his rival upstairs. My God, how blind you all are!"

"I think you're exaggerating. After all, if Agatov wants the job so badly he'll be good at it. And I don't want it. I've got work of my own to do. Why should I waste time managing the rest of you? I'm no good at that kind of thing anyway."

"You'll learn. Didn't Ophelia say we all know what we are but not what we may be."

"I can't go by Ophelia. No one asked her to take charge of a laboratory. I've got my own subject and I want to get it finished. I'm not interested in anything else."

"Are you interested in having a lab full of mediocrities?" Bochkaryov burst out angrily. "That's what will happen!"

With his natural ability for analysis he traced the regrettable consequences of Krylov's refusal.

"Why don't you take on the job yourself, if you're so keen on self-sacrifice?"

Bochkaryov was thought highly of as a specialist in measurement techniques. It had often been suggested that he should stand for a Doctor's degree, but he had shrugged off the idea. What was the point? Would he know any more merely because he had a Doctorate? This was not affectation. Bochkaryov was a hunchback with a huge, bald, egg-shaped head. Krylov had watched him muttering and whispering to himself over a circuit, and he knew there was nothing in the world Bochkaryov enjoyed more than his work.

Golitsyn would tease him about it: "Oh, King of Experiment, there's more in science than the deviation of the needle, you know." All Bochkaryov would say in defence was that a lot of things could be made of flour, but the grain had to be ground first. He simply couldn't work any other way.

He strode about the landing, kicking over the pails.

"Be head of the lab with a mug like mine! This may sound silly, of course, but I did have to deputise for Golitsyn once.... I had to preside over a meeting and I felt everyone was staring at me and laughing the whole time. It's agony for me to appear in public. I feel like Quasimodo."

His huge mournful eyes were intolerably bright. Krylov was so used to Bochkaryov's deformity he no longer noticed it, but suddenly he remembered how Bochkaryov kept in the background at meetings and could never be persuaded to speak. He had never been to an institute party. Nothing could shake his conviction that he was a freak.

"Don't give a damn for anybody," Krylov said. "And don't withdraw into your shell. If there's a murmur from anyone, give 'em a taste of your brain-power. Talent's the rarest kind of good looks a man can possess. And you've got it written all over your face."

Bochkaryov shook his head listlessly.

"When I was a kid someone told me that all hunchbacks were vicious. I've been afraid of getting vicious ever since. It'd be so easy."

Richard appeared in the doorway.

"I've been looking for you!" he exclaimed joyfully. "Congratulations, Sergei Ilyich! What a knock for Agatov, eh! That was quite a performance the old boy gave us. Now, look out!"

He submerged them in plans for reorganising the laboratory and new subjects for research. He let his imagination run. Television satellites, control of the weather. It didn't even occur to him that Krylov might not want to be head of the laboratory. While he talked, he kept stretching himself, limbering up and doing pull-ups on the step-ladder, making faces in imitation of Agatov or Golitsyn. He was bubbling over with the desire for action.

"Well, you individualist, can't you hear the voice of the people?" said Bochkaryov.

"You're individualists yourselves," Krylov replied. "But there are a lot of you, so you call yourselves a collective instead."

Richard gaped.

"You mean you don't want the job, Sergei Ilyich?" His eyes, hands, eyebrows, every limb and feature expressed surprise. Even the white buttons of his faded sports shirt stared in astonishment.

"I want to work," Krylov said. "You can all go to the devil! I'm just beginning to see daylight."

"We're always saying give the young men a chance, bring new blood into management," Bochkaryov reminded him.

"And when the chance comes, we prefer to stay on the side-lines!" Richard added. They both talked at once.

The translucent ice of the lake gave gently underfoot and they could see the white air bubbles being flattened between water and ice. The wind was strong enough to knock them over. Sometimes their feet went through, but luckily the water was shallow and they didn't get the instruments wet. Soaked and half-frozen, they only just managed to make their way to a little fishing village, where they sat for a long time in the local refreshment room trying to get warm. They ate beetroot salad and drank vodka. An old and ponderous cat padded out from behind the counter. He licked Natasha's wet slacks and miaowed sonorously.

"This cat's enchanted," Natasha said. "Don't you believe me? Want to see him eat a salted cucumber?"

Krylov laughed and said no cats ate cucumbers.

Natasha tossed a yellow cucumber skin on the floor. The cat sniffed at it and began to crunch....

"... the man at the top always knows best," Richard was saying, "getting to the top is the best way of improving your intelligence."

"Agatov wanted to make the lab bigger. What I think is—it ought to be smaller. I think we ought to cut down on contracts from outside," Bochkaryov insisted.

Richard stuck his hands on hips and punctuated what he was saying with bows to right and left: "Concerning the problem of inter-pretation—of the methods—of observing thunderstorms—in the Tula Region—in the second half—of the nineteenth century...."

"Yes, Agatov's got to be neutralised. He's dangerous."

"We'll fix him," said Richard. "Surely you're not afraid of him, Sergei Ilyich?"

"I'm not afraid of anyone, but, for God's sake, chaps"—Krylov put his hands on their shoulders and smiled guiltily—"give me a breather, will you?" And he walked out.

"What's the matter with him?" Richard asked.

"It started after he got back from Ozernaya," said Bochkaryov.

When Richard left, too, Bochkaryov strolled about the quiet landing and stared at his reflection in the shiny nozzle of the fire hose. In the crooked mirror his face appeared almost normal.

Krylov walked through the rooms of the laboratory, looking with fresh eyes at the familiar test benches, the apparatus and the men who worked with him. Suddenly he was aware of the ticking, click-ing and humming of the instruments, of recorders that tirelessly traced the development of invisible storms raging somewhere in the black depths of the universe, of eruptions on the sun, of showers of cosmic particles. These fine quivering lines spelled out the life of the tiniest particles, the breathing of the globe itself, its rain and thunder—all that went on in that clear blue sky and warm spring air. Green zigzags on the flickering screen of an oscilloscope indicated a thunderstorm moving across Africa.

Matveyev called him over to show him how a tracking system had been installed. It looked a simple, reliable piece of work, but Matveyev always showed Krylov anything he was doing, although Krylov knew less about such things than he did. Matveyev had no degree and he was diffident in the presence of any engineer.

As Matveyev turned a disc, Krylov noticed that the cuffs of his overall coat were frayed, and realised he had never seen him wearing a decent suit. For want of that wretched degree Matveyev was still stuck as a senior laboratory assistant. Yet he was a first-class research scientist in his own right and someone ought long ago to have arranged a proper salary for him. It ought to have been proved to the authorities that such a person should be judged not by degrees, or the lack of them, but by what he was and what he could produce.

Krylov was about to say so, but suddenly he realised he no longer had the right to be merely sympathetic or indignant. Now he had to promise something, or else say nothing at all. And this unaccustomed feeling of constraint came as an unpleasant surprise. Zinochka ran over to him, showed him an oscillogram and asked him to mark the peaks. Then she pressed up close to him and whispered, "Let's go and sunbathe on the tower. We're all going up there in the lunch-break."

Krylov scratched the back of his head.

"So you're too high and mighty already," she said.

He was stuck for an answer and felt a fool because only the day before he had stretched himself out on the tower platform with the others, playing cards and keeping a look-out in case one of the firemen appeared. The old tower was strictly out of bounds.

Krylov walked past the accumulator room and headed for the computer department, but turned back. In the corridor he saw Pesetsky.

"Sergei," Pesetsky said, "N equals minus two."

There was a copy of *l'Humanité* sticking out of his pocket.

"What's the news?" Krylov asked.

"Horrors of capitalism. Girl of eighteen just poisoned eleven of her relatives." Pesetsky thrust several sheets of paper covered with figures in Krylov's face. "N equals minus two," he repeated.

"I'm not keen on taking over the lab," Krylov told him. "It'll be curtains for our subject."

"Probably," said Pesetsky. "D'you know how I worked it out?"

"It's not my kind of job. I won't be able to cope."

"Don't worry, you'll have the support of the masses. Now listen.

I got it out by using the subcortical centres. Just switched on the old subconscious!"

"I've been thinking about it and I've realised I wouldn't be able to be myself. I'll be afraid of saying the wrong thing, of making some colossal blunder."

"Turn it down then."

They went into the room where the students worked. Pesetsky chattered on about his new method. If you couldn't solve a problem, the best thing to do was change over to something else and let your subconscious do the work for you. That was how the great mathematician Poincaré had worked. Once the subconscious motors were functioning the solution would occur to you by itself. One fine day it would just pop up from the dark depths of the subconscious mind.

"You've only got to tell the subconscious what to do," he ran on. "After that you've nothing to worry about."

"What about the spinal cord? Is that any good?" Alyosha Mikulin asked quite seriously.

Krylov had gone over to the window and was standing there with half-closed eyes. He said crossly: "N must be more than zero. Otherwise the clouds will be struck by lightning from earth."

"That's their worry," said Pesetsky. "My job is to solve an equation."

"But it has no physical meaning."

"Is there any meaning in lightning? I've been trying to compute static for six months. What's the sense in it? There is none." He flung his arm round Krylov's shoulder and whispered: "Stop worrying. It'll solve itself. Everything solves itself."

And having thus comforted Krylov, he became even more enthusiastic over explaining to everyone he met how to exploit the subconscious.

Chapter Four

He climbed the iron spiral staircase of the radar tower. The operators were out on field work and the apparatus room was in darkness, except for a slim golden cylinder of sunlight that pierced the blinds like a bamboo rod. Krylov held out his hand and the beam fell on his palm and made it luminescent.

The gentle warmth seeped through him and the unaccustomed tenderness of it made him feel sorry for himself.

In the long months since his return he had lived in a state of torpor, conscious only of a dull ache of longing that grew all the time. And now the moment of decision had come he was seized with disquiet. He felt that the trouble was not so much Golitsyn's offer as reluctance to make his position clear, to examine himself, to act. But even this was not the main thing. The main thing was a sense of foreboding, of expectation—expectation of what? Curiously enough, this was just the thing he didn't want to think about.

Cautiously he ran the tips of his fingers along the tangible, dusty surface of the sunbeam. He would have liked to break off a piece and send it to Natasha instead of a letter. A length of a sunbeam, in a long carton. Why didn't she answer his letters? He knew the reason but invented others.

He pushed his face into the beam and closed his eyes.

"Natasha!" he said aloud.

At the far end of the room someone chuckled. Krylov gave a start and groped along the wall for the light switch.

There was a shout of warning and, as the light went on, he saw Agatov seated on a box at the end of the room, his arms muffled in a black bag for loading film. "You nearly exposed my film for me! Doesn't matter, you needn't put it out now."

"Sorry," Krylov mumbled.

Agatov eyed his burning face with amusement, and Krylov realised that he had been watching him from the darkness for some time. The best thing would have been to apologise and leave at once, but Krylov stood there becoming more and more embarrassed, and the longer he stood there the more impossible it was to go.

"I forgot to offer you my congratulations." Agatov paused to enjoy his helplessness. "How did you manage to get round the Old Man?"

"I've no idea...I assure you, I..." Krylov faltered, becoming even more confused.

"Of course, you'll say you had nothing to do with it," Agatov said condescendingly. "But I've just been watching your antics of delight."

Krylov shifted his feet miserably.

Agatov shook his head. "What a dark horse, eh! You fooled us all very cleverly, I'll grant you that. And I had all my own papers ready. I had even had official copies made. Funny, isn't it?"

"Oh, come..." Krylov began to remonstrate sympathetically and suddenly blurted out: "I haven't made up my mind yet."

But Agatov was not listening. He went on, thinking aloud: "See what Golitsyn thinks of me? Tidy. Efficient. Good at filling in forms. But Agatov has no ideas of his own. That's the trouble apparently. Of course, the fact that I've been pushing his ideas doesn't count, does it? Not even if I completely agree with them?"

The fixed smirk on his face put Krylov completely at a loss. He didn't know what to say.

For two pins he would have cut in with a "Why ask me? Go to the Old Man and have it out with him!" But he was still tingling with shame and, besides, he didn't want to kick a man who was down. He realised that Agatov was deeply hurt, mortified, crushed.

"You can't trust anyone in science," Krylov said. "The Old Man is trying to mould us all in his own image. He can't help it. But we mustn't give way to him. For his own sake. It's a paradox, you see. Each of us has to stick to his guns. . . ."

Agatov didn't let him finish. "A moral smokescreen to cover your tactics, eh? But I can see through it. D'you think I don't know what opinion you all have of me?"

That relentless smirk made Krylov's frank reply sound absurd. Why in hell's name should I feel guilty, Krylov asked himself. If there were a number of attitudes to choose from he always chose the one least favourable to himself. Without fail. No one else had such a knack of making things awkward for himself. It was something he had never got used to, but at least he had learned to laugh at his own embarrassment.

"Golitsyn has let me down. I know I was misrepresented to him," Agatov was saying. "But I'm not going to leave it at that."

Krylov looked at him with curiosity.

"Are you really so put out about it? After all, it's only a position."

"A position. . . . No, Sergei Ilyich, it's more than a position for me." Agatov's voice hardened suddenly. The arm that had been squirming in the black bag became still. "I want recognition. Let's be frank. There're no witnesses here. This is just between you and me. Golitsyn himself let it out in front of everyone today. And you know it perfectly well yourself. I can make it quite plain, if you like. Would you like me to?" He leaned forward and his beady grey eyes bored into Krylov's face. "There are people who believe I have no scientific ability. You, for instance, are supposed to have talent, but not I. Isn't that so? You needn't be afraid. I've got nothing against you personally." He pulled his arms out of the bag and stretched his fingers vigorously. "Now, suppose I agree with that description of my character." He stood up. His lips were twitching, as if trying to throw off the smile they were forced to wear. "What can I do about it? Is it my fault? I just didn't happen to get the right set of genes from my parents. So what am I expected to do?"

There was a slight tremor in his voice, but it was cool and business-like. His eyes, though darkened with bitterness, were very clear;

this was his moment of truth. Krylov had never seen Agatov like this before, but it came to him in a flash that this was the real Agatov.

"No, Sergei Ilyich, you've dealt with me too easily. What if I have another kind of talent? Everyone has his own field...." Agatov broke off suddenly, staring hard at Krylov. "Just a minute, you mean you really haven't made up your mind? Why should you take this post? You won't make a go of it with Golitsyn. He'll want his own way, you admitted that yourself. And you've got a lot of character, you don't know how to adapt yourself. What'll be the result? The job will suffer, you'll land on the rocks and nobody'll have a good word to say for you. Yes, I'm trying to talk you out of it, but not just for my own sake. Refuse before it's too late." He tried to control his voice, but failed. "What will you get out of it? Direction of research? We don't get a look-in there anyway—you know that as well as I do. It hasn't yet dawned on Golitsyn that he'll find things much easier with me. So will you, so will everyone else. He'll soon regret his decision."

Krylov smiled trustingly.

"Well, I'm not a bit keen!"

Agatov began to stride round him in circles.

"No, I know exactly how it is. The head of the laboratory is his own boss. He comes and goes when he likes. He doesn't have to ask anyone's permission. Freedom means a lot, of course. But I can promise you that with me to shield you you'll have even more freedom. As soon as Golitsyn started giving me jobs to do, everyone decided I had no talent. No manager is ever credited with having any brains. You'll be classed among the dead-beats as soon as you take over."

Tired of standing in the middle of the room, Krylov edged away towards the curtained window.

"It seems to me there are certain other issues at stake, Yakov Ivanovich," he said gently. "You must agree we've got to make a start on new subjects." Agatov nodded vigorously. "We're wasting time on small stuff. The Old Man insists on statistics. He's making you measure the charges of moisture drops. Don't be offended, Yakov Ivanovich, but I'm afraid mere laboratory testing won't get us anywhere. And on the other hand, we steer away from the problem of active intervention."

"Exactly!" Agatov exclaimed. "We even..."—he hesitated for a second and gave a quick glance at Krylov—"turn our backs on it."

"The Old Man fights shy of modern physics. How do you expect to get round him on that?"

"We'll manage it by degrees. Do you think there's no way of coping with him?" Agatov was quickly recovering his assurance. "You needn't worry on that score. Just go ahead with your work. You'll be entirely your own master, I'll see to that. As for subjects of research, I quite agree, but it all depends how they're presented. We don't know how to sell ourselves, that's the trouble, Sergei Ilyich. Give the same subject the right build-up and you can have all the funds and equipment you want. Believe me, it's far better for the group as a whole if the person in charge has no specific scientific interests of his own." He lifted his hand to forestall the objection. "I know, I know. I know Bochkaryov and his gang are egging you on. Don't listen to them. They're all out for themselves. Actually I don't blame them. A real scientist has to be an individualist. Otherwise he'll never get anywhere."

His flat face was damp and shiny. He was working hard. He displayed his plans before Krylov, each more tempting than the other. He had it all thought out.

He knew everything there was to know about management, about the higher administrators, the fine points in the relations between them; he could list the works of members of the Academy, he knew their hobbies, what make of car they ran; he knew that the best way of contacting Likhov was at a concert at the conservatoire, that Academician Denisov's secretary's daughter worked in No. 5 Laboratory.

Krylov could not bring himself to interrupt. He lifted a corner of the window-blind and looked down at the sun-drenched met station below.

The students were working at the white-painted instrument screens. Matveyev and Zinochka were fitting out a radiosonde.

How nicely things could work out, he thought regretfully. And he'd still be able to sunbathe with them in the lunch-hour.

He heaved a sigh and cleared his throat once or twice before Agatov paid any attention to him.

"I'm sorry, Yakov Ivanovich, but you're missing the point somehow," he said.

"How do you mean?" Agatov was taken aback. "You have your own conditions to make? By all means, make them. . . ."

Krylov writhed inwardly, but he had to speak out.

"I don't like the sound of what you've been saying."

"But we can always come to terms. If you state what you have in mind, I'll be only too glad. . . ." He seemed very short all of a sudden as he looked up at Krylov with a timid readiness to agree.

"I haven't anything particular in mind," Krylov confessed.

Agatov eyed him questioningly.

"We ought to get Matveyev a proper salary," Krylov added lamely.

"I can fix that in five minutes," Agatov rushed on. "But can't you explain what holds you? Have you anything against me? I've never done you any harm. Why don't I suit you? Why?"

Krylov spread his arms guiltily.

"I suppose you want the job yourself," Agatov said suddenly, convinced by Krylov's diffident smile and even more so by his embarrassed silence. "Of course, why should you let the chance of power slip through your fingers! And I opened my heart to you...."

Krylov came to himself.

"You only say that because you're offended, Yakov Ivanovich. I'm grateful to you for being so frank. But I've got to think things over."

Agatov's shoulders sagged and he went back to the box where he had been sitting, picked up the black bag and busied himself for some time with the drums, his face to the wall. Eventually he got up and walked to the door. As he passed Krylov he halted. His smooth face had recovered its usual expression of cool politeness. Once again he was alert and fully in command of himself; there was not even a crease in his well-pressed suit.

"I'm doing my best to co-operate with you," he said stiffly. He did all he could to muster a polite smile.

The iron staircase rang with his footsteps.

"Now puzzle that out," Krylov said aloud, as though someone could hear him. He stared despairingly at the baggy knees of his own recently pressed trousers. Then he put out the light and waited. But the beam of sunshine had gone and he couldn't recover his mood. The need to take a decision annoyed him. He didn't want to decide anything. In any case, whether he refused or accepted, he would lose something. But decisions could never be taken without loss.

He didn't feel like going downstairs and sitting in the same room with Agatov. He felt as if he had been burned by the heat of this man's inner feelings. For a second the hidden depths had been revealed and Krylov had seen the quivering molten mass that had yet to form. Who knew when and where the turning point came in a man's life? When something was in ferment, about to coalesce, a word was enough to mould a man's life. It occurred to Krylov that it was men themselves who made one another bad or good.

Bochkaryov, Richard, Golitsyn, of course, they were all guided by their integrity as scientists. Krylov was sure of that. But to Agatov this seemed, on the contrary, the greatest injustice. Nature had cheated him of talent, so he was bitter, frustrated, envious, all the things that mar a man. But what could one do to help him? Was such injustice inevitable? The others were right too; there should be no place at the top for the untalented. The untalented never admitted their lack of talent. They didn't suffer, they envied and nursed their grudges. Yet everyone was in some respect lacking in talent.

Chapter Five

The shelves were stacked high with dusty volumes of scientific reports going back to the day of the laboratory's inauguration.

Somewhere near the ceiling were the old-fashioned bindings with sides of reddish marbled paper and gilded backs. Lower down came the cheap blue or rusty-looking cardboard of the war years, the dates and titles written in faded ink, and lower still, the more recent records in thick brown imitation leather.

The sight of these shelves put Tulin in an ironic mood. All the illusions of past generations turning to dust. . . . What a burial ground of lost hopes! How much wasted patience and effort! And these papers on Krylov's desk, would they not be similarly buried in the next volume?

Tulin picked up a chart showing total field intensity. In a month or two this sheet would be printed and attached to a report, which would be glanced through by some senior scientist before it took its perpetual place on the shelves.

He had been waiting for Krylov at least fifteen minutes. With a quizzical look on his face he scribbled dancing skeletons all over the chart and wrote underneath: *"Carthage must be destroyed!"*

While he was writing Richard came up behind him and looked over his shoulder.

"Terrific! Reminds me of Goya. You an artist?"

Tulin drew back and surveyed his handiwork.

"Anyone who can draw is an artist. Art isn't a trade, it's a talent."

"Isn't talent a rather vague concept?" Richard retorted. He loved arguments of this kind. "There must also be education, you know."

"And what is education?" Tulin asked, and without waiting for an answer proclaimed solemnly: "Education is what is left when everything we learn has been forgotten."

"Not bad. But you've made a mess of Krylov's chart."

"Never mind. Even if it goes into the file as it is it won't be discovered until the next century."

Richard tried to defend Krylov's work but Tulin waved him aside and pursued his own ideas, ignoring all objections.

"You, archive-suppliers, who work in this graveyard in the name of the nibbling criticism of mice."

"Oh, terrific!" Richard exclaimed delightedly.

"Marx said it, not I."

Other people in the room had begun to take notice and Tulin raised his voice. Keeping up the attitude of the carefree loafer, he took delight in stirring up this ant-hill, observing with amusement the consternation and resentment caused by his unconventional remarks.

The first to object was Matveyev. Instead of tackling Tulin directly, he tried to remonstrate with the delighted Richard. Didn't Richard value the honour of the team?

"That's just phrase-making," Richard retorted. "I can't bear phrases. What do you mean by the 'team'? What do you mean by 'honour'?"

"Now, look here," said Matveyev. "The majority of people in this laboratory are honest, conscientious people and they put all they've got into their work. You can't make light of that."

"Progress in science doesn't depend on honesty!" Richard flared back at him, but Tulin came in unexpectedly on the other side.

"No, honesty does count. I'm quite sure most of the people here are the soul of honesty. The trouble is that you honestly desire one thing and just as honestly do exactly the opposite, and the result is neither one nor the other. While the whole country is in a state of ferment and change you appear to be living on an enchanted island."

Now Matveyev felt he must argue with Tulin himself.

"For your information, this laboratory is well thought of; last year we overfulfilled our plan of research."

A knowing smile spread over Tulin's face and he became the weary cynic.

"Yes, indeed, thanks to your enthusiasm the report was placed on this shelf about a fortnight before schedule. I am sure you have used every penny of your allocations."

Matveyev looked horrified.

"Do you realise our department is run by Arkady Borisovich Golitsyn, a Corresponding Member of the Academy of Sciences?"

"But of course I do!" Tulin replied. "Lomonosov's favourite pupil. Do you still stand in awe of authorities? Some people just can't do without them, can they? No, I have a better opinion of you than that. I believe you're simply afraid to say what you think. But I'm not." He gave them a general wink. "I'm from a different Ministry...."

"What are you, an Academician or an inventor?" Zinochka asked.

Tulin's eyes appraised her figure before he said mysteriously: "Some people can be understood on close examination, others reveal themselves only from a distance." He glanced at his watch. "Time, space, motion. . . . This was the date that was not kept. I fear I must leave you, martyrs of science."

Richard saw him out of the building.

"Do you like Goya?" he asked again. "What about abstract painting? What do you think of astrobotany?" He fired questions at the stranger, delighting in his casual, aphoristic replies. "What's your profession? Let's introduce ourselves," he suggested, mentioning his own name.

"That's an unusual first name you have," Tulin replied questioningly.

Richard told him eagerly about his seaman father, who had drunk to brotherhood with Bo'sun Richard Cleb, an Englishman and a Communist, and named his son after him.

At a turn in the corridor they ran into Krylov.

"Sergei!" Tulin cried, throwing out his arms.

Krylov nodded absent-mindedly and walked on. Tulin's sunburnt face flushed hotly. Richard lowered his eyes. When he had gone a few paces Krylov turned round, let out a gasp and ran back to seize Tulin by the shoulders.

"Oleg!"

Gasping and laughing they slapped each other's backs and exchanged news. Alla Krivtsova had married a second time, no one had ever found out who nailed all the galoshes to the floor at the last institute party, Anikeyev had been transferred to Moscow, and on it went. Tulin remarked upon Krylov's smart shoes and the handsome pallor which was quite out of keeping with his homely snub-nosed face. Krylov declared that Tulin had the air of a footballer doing pretty well in the Second Division. How could any of his staff take him seriously when he looked such a spiv?

He had suddenly woken up and was beaming with pleasure because Tulin had specially called in to see him. He had not expected such attention. Since their student days together he had hero-worshipped Tulin and longed to be like him—gay, hard-working, sociable and brilliant. No matter which way he was going, Tulin always seemed to have the wind behind him. The taxis he hailed were always empty. All the girls smiled at him, all the men envied him—except Krylov. Krylov only admired and was proud of him, and now, too, he listened delightedly to Tulin's story of the new work he was doing and why he had come to Moscow.

Yes, of course, Krylov had read his article in the April issue. It was dazzling. Tulin's latest research opened up all sorts of possibilities. Of course, strictly speaking, the evidence was rather thin and Krylov tried to say so, but Tulin pooh-poohed the idea.

"You crusty old Academician. Is that what matters?"

In a few sentences he shattered Krylov's doubts. The idea was tremendous, of course, and soon it seemed to Krylov that he had long been thinking along the same lines.

"You know, I think I'd be afraid to take on a thing like that," he confessed despondently. "It makes me scared to think of it. And what about the actual flying into a thunderhead, isn't that dangerous?"

Tulin roared with laughter. Of course it was. But he had thought of a way out of any danger—simply not to be afraid.

"Are you sure you'll get permission?"

Tulin whistled expressively.

"I'll get it somehow. There's no other way."

The shadow of a frown crossed his face but the next moment he winked at Krylov. "It'll work out all right. Well, how is life treating you?"

Krylov realised suddenly what a good thing it was that Tulin had arrived. He could advise him what to do about Golitsyn's offer. His analysis would make everything clear.

"Manage this tomb?" Tulin stared disappointedly at Krylov. The message in his eyes was: "So you're glad, are you? Delighted you've climbed the ladder! It won't be long before they make you into a staid and comfortable official, entirely suited to this establishment where nothing ever changes."

He said: "Does the Old Man still fight over every figure and imagine he's advancing science thereby?"

"You shouldn't say that. He's basically progressive."

"Progressive? In this day and age! I know he's offered you promotion, but that alone is not progress. The level of his ideas is about.... Well, he believes in the abolition of serfdom. That's about where he stands, hovering somewhere between Aristotle and Lomonosov." Tulin was up to date on all the laboratory's publications. Apart from a few papers by Bochkaryov and Pesetsky, it was a lot of scholastic rubbish, a mere toying with trifles. "Somnambulant eunuchs wandering round doing sums...." He let his tongue have free rein.

They walked round the laboratory and Tulin made fun of the whole set-up, from what they produced to the grave expressions on the faces of this stable of ichthyosauri. When Krylov tried to argue, Tulin heaved a sigh. "We'll soon be in opposite camps, I see."

Agatov was busy with his apparatus.

"Still dripping?" Tulin greeted him. "Remember measuring drops on this instrument when we were students, Sergei? I wonder how many theses have dripped through it since then!" Still talking, he nudged Agatov aside, put his eye to the eyepiece and turned the adjuster screw. "You'd do better with circular laminae. They make it easier to compensate. Elliptical ones would be even better. Then you'll be able to fit a recorder."

He had no idea that quite casually, with a rich man's generosity he had given Agatov an idea he had been seeking for a month.

Agatov smiled his gratitude.

"Don't thank me, you're welcome," Tulin said. "You'll be getting it right within a ten-thousandth soon!" And laughing uproariously he passed on to another section. He seemed to have the laboratory in the palm of his hand, like so many slides to be put through a toy projector. At the door, Krylov turned round and saw the glance Agatov had thrown at their backs. It was a good thing Tulin hadn't seen it.

On the staircase some workmen were handling cases of instruments. One of the cases had been left in the passage. Tulin sprang over it without even taking a run and Krylov reflected that even if Tulin were head of the laboratory he would still jump over packing cases, wear spivvy ties, and go off with Zinochka and the boys to sunbathe on the tower. And to everyone it would seem quite natural and a new note of gaiety would be felt in the work of the laboratory.

He pushed the case aside with his foot and caught up with Tulin.

"What do you think I should do, Oleg?" he asked.

Tulin waved the briefcase he had been carrying under his arm.

"If I don't finish everything today, I'll spend the night at your place." He looked at Krylov. "Poor old chap.... So they want your fresh blood, do they? The energy of youth. A scientist, still capable of working himself, takes an administrative job. Unheard of! Don't look so fierce. But the idea of you as an administrator—well!"

Krylov returned his rueful smile.

"Still, you're as good as the next man, aren't you?" Tulin went on. "Someone's got to be in charge. Better you than some stick-in-the-mud. Have a try at climbing the ladder of fame, maybe you'll like it." He winked and made everything easy and amusing. "What the hell!"

He wagged a warning finger at Krylov.

"Remember, he who doesn't want to be boss is against the bosses."

Richard had appeared from somewhere.

"So you're Tulin! This is fine! I've read your article and I completely agree. Are you leaving? You handled Agatov beautifully. He just goes on dripping and dripping...." He laughed happily. "It's enough to reduce you to tears."

Krylov frowned.

"What do you know about it? That's not the way to talk."

Richard flared up. "Yes, it is! Just what he deserves. Show principle, I say. No mercy!"

"Ah, I see I have supporters here as well as opponents," Tulin said. "You'd better move over to our place, Richard. You'll be able to fight real thunder there, not just Agatovs."

They stood in the entrance hall and watched Tulin striding across the square, where the sparrows were twittering furiously in the dazzling sunshine.

Richard uttered a sound in which Krylov detected both enthusiasm and regret for the faded image of the institute that Tulin had left behind.

"It'll be a good thing if he manages to push it through," said Krylov.

Richard gave a shrug and a short laugh that indicated the total foolishness of doubting Tulin's ability to succeed in everything he undertook.

Chapter Six

The general's name was Yuzhin. Tulin knew hardly anything about him, so he made no attempt to plan the conversation and relied entirely on luck.

As he watched the pilots and engineers coming and going in the large waiting room he decided his attitude must be challenging and different in some way from the usual run of visitors who besieged Yuzhin from morning to night.

The general's room turned out to be huge and as devoid of individuality as any other government office. An absolutely empty desk, a switchboard, several telephones, black-shrouded maps on the walls.

Yuzhin took Tulin's report out of a drawer and began to reread it, pursing his lips.

Tulin watched his face and came to the conclusion that physiognomy was a useless art. The fleshy nose, the rough, permanently weathered cheeks could have belonged equally to a jovial character or a hardened bureaucrat. What qualities of mind were indicated by the stubbly grey hair, the tattooing on the back of the hand? The cordial manners might be mere good breeding, they might mean respect for Tulin, or perhaps they were merely a habit developed to cope with visitors.

A light glowed on the switchboard. The general picked up one of the telephones.

"I'm busy. . . . In about ten minutes."

He placed the report on his desk and weighted it down with a piece of fused metal.

Tulin was the first to speak, forestalling the general by a second. He had sensed that he must somehow seize the initiative. It was always easier to persuade than to dissuade. Once a man said no, his self-respect would depend on that no.

"You have flown. You must know what a thunderstorm is."

Yuzhin nodded.

"A man who flies doesn't write poems about the beauty of thunderstorms in early May. Don't you agree?"

He smiled and the general smiled back and said yes. Let him get used to saying yes.

Tulin did not go into the technical or scientific aspects of the problem. He knew from experience how easily the layman could be put off by figures and diagrams that could not be immediately understood. The expert rushes on confident that he is making himself clear and encouraged by the nods he receives from his listener, though the latter is merely going over in his mind a prepared statement of refusal. Tulin had had dealings with various kinds of inventors; they were like a wood grouse wooing its mate; in the heat of passion they heard nothing but themselves and imagined a finger drawing in the air was enough to make any diagram comprehensible.

Yuzhin was new to the Board and Tulin had to go back over the facts of the case. Investigation of thunderstorms had been in progress for several years and Tulin's previous chief, Professor Chistyakov, had enjoyed the support of the previous head of the Board. His research team had been loaned aircraft for research purposes. They had been fitted in to a general programme. But now the work had reached a stage when the group needed its own aircraft, its own programmes and complete independence. They had come to the vital point where they might be able to obtain an understanding of the conditions required for controlling or dispersing a thunderstorm. Tulin did not labour the point. He said it almost casually and went on at once to relate how they had had to raid a warehouse at night for oxygen cylinders, and several other amusing stories. While the general laughed, Tulin returned to his problem. The task that faced them now was to find the centre of a thunderstorm. If they were to have any influence on a thunderstorm they must be able to find its centre. Sooner or later one has to give up experimenting on mice and dogs and deal with people.

He slowed the pace of his argument to give the general time to get used to the idea of the inevitability of flying into storms.

With the candour of the victor he even mentioned some of the disappointing failures in their experimental work, the fiasco of the first thunderstorm detector, for instance. He expressed his own surprise at the strides that had been made in the past eighteen months. The instruments were ready, the methods had been worked out, a carefully considered programme had been drawn up.

Not once did he lapse into a cap-in-hand attitude. Leaning back in his leather armchair with a charming airiness he placed on Yuzhin all the burden of the forthcoming decision. Here you are, General, here are our results, our instruments, these are our prospects of success, the rest depends on you.

"Well, good for you, but, er. . . ." Yuzhin rubbed his bristly head in perplexity. "As you know, flying in thunderstorms is forbidden. Devilishly dangerous! Have you ever been in the belly of one of those thunderstorms? Well, I got caught in one once. Br-r-r-r!" The memory of this terrifying experience made his flesh creep. "Couldn't tell earth from sky, thrown about like a matchbox. Only managed to land the crate by the skin of my teeth."

So he was trying to talk Tulin out of it, frighten him with horror-tales? That meant he was on the defensive and Tulin had won the first round. He had the initiative and he must use it to full effect.

"Ack-ack fire's a lot pleasanter, honestly it is," Yuzhin was saying. "At least you can tell what's going on."

Tulin smiled sympathetically.

"But the ack-ack never stopped you. You went through with your operation, didn't you?"

"Now don't give me any of that. War's a disaster."

"So are thunderstorms. Particularly for aircraft. Isn't that so?"

Yuzhin, who had been in more air accidents than he cared to remember, calmly agreed, but drew an unexpected conclusion. Even veteran pilots drew the line at thunderstorms. How could he possibly allow any aircraft to fly right into the centre of one, and certainly not a transport aircraft with a group of scientists on board?

The general, it turned out, was by no means an easy customer to deal with. One by one he tore to shreds the flight plans that had been submitted with the report. Now he was on the offensive, and Tulin realised that he had only to make one move in self-defence and all would be lost.

"How do you expect to be able to fight thunderstorms if you run away from them?" He paused just long enough to make it clear that there was no answer to the question. "The proof of the pudding, you know"—he patted his stomach—"is in the eating."

Yuzhin chuckled.

"In Siberia we say that if you want to know whether the ham's high you don't need to eat the whole of it. Of course, that's just a saying. Our hams are first-class. They'll hang for a couple of years without spoiling." Glad to relax for a moment, he launched into a hearty description of how to smoke hams.

Tulin decided he was playing for time. In a moment he would glance at his watch and make a polite gesture.

"What exactly do you propose?" Tulin asked sharply. "Shall we go in for smoking hams?"

With energetic strokes Yuzhin marked out possible zones of operation on the flight plans. His voice had become dry. Other groups made do with less than this. They worked in large cumuli while they were forming.

Mastering his annoyance, Tulin replied that no one else was actually trying to control thunderstorms.

"No one?" And Yuzhin with a certain relish referred to Denisov's experiments with anti-aircraft guns and the work of other institutes performed on the ground and involving no risk.

Tulin foresaw what was about to happen. He just wants to palm me off on another department. Everybody likes anti-aircraft shells. It doesn't matter that the results are doubtful, that the principles and methods are different. The main thing is that there's no worry attached. He would have enjoyed telling Yuzhin this but there were risks that he didn't want to take either. The best thing was to explain the advantages of the new approach. The methods used up to now offered nothing really reliable.

"All these methods are based on chance. No one knows whether we are breaking up thunderstorms or merely accelerating them, letting them off the leash. An unstable process may spill over in any direction."

In this field Tulin had the advantage and could confront Yuzhin with all the complex and variable factors in the mechanism of storms.

But Yuzhin simply evaded the argument.

"Well, you seem to know everything. Surely with a brain like yours you can think up something that doesn't entail stepping into a deathtrap?" He made a vague gesture with his fingers and his face dissolved into a meaningless smile, but the glance under his lowered lids was alert.

What was he after? Why didn't he put an end to the discussion with a flat refusal? Perhaps he wanted Tulin himself to make concessions, change his line of research, give up.... If so, there must be something preventing him from simply saying no.

"Look at this"—Yuzhin tossed the fused lump of metal in his hand—"this is what was left of one aeroplane that strayed into a thunderhead." He took a wad of photographs out of his drawer and spread them out in front of Tulin.

Twisted chunks of wreckage. Splintered, uprooted trees. Charred, misshapen bodies. The glossy surface of the photographs seemed to give off the stench of the smouldering remains.

Tulin felt Yuzhin's glance upon him.

"That may stop you but it spurs me on," Tulin said, accepting the challenge. "I don't want aircraft to go on crashing. I don't want pilots to be afraid of thunder. I want them to be masters of the sky. Surely that's worth taking a risk for, even a big one?"

"Aha, so there is a risk!" Yuzhin exclaimed. "So you're not sure! You give us no guarantee."

"Anything new always involves risk. If you cut out risk, you cut out the new."

"I know, I know. In a moment you'll be accusing me of playing safe and all the rest of it. But why should I trust you? You've been poking about at this for three years. Where are the results? You can't even give us an exact forecast of thunderstorms. You say you'll be able to break them up. Wouldn't it be better if you first learnt to forecast accurately? All this field research! The state has spent millions of rubles on you! You've pranged a good many crates too!"

The question of forecasts was a sore point with him and Tulin was quite unable to impress on him the fact that their work had nothing to do with weather forecasting. He simply wouldn't listen. He was completely browned off with these jokers who undertook to do something for the air force, bamboozled him with a lot of new-fangled terms, were given large sums of money and produced nothing but another scientific monograph.

He took a tattered flight manual out of his drawer and brandished it in front of Tulin.

"Read this! I'm not allowed to break these rules and you can't give me any guarantee."

"But what's this got to do with forecasts?" Tulin laboured on.

"You want me to shoulder the responsibility!"

"Ah, so you're afraid of responsibility!"

"Responsibility for your lives? No, I don't want to be responsible for them. How can I be? Will it be enough for me to get a repri-mand?"

"...because you don't want to go to the root of things!"

Yuzhin looked away and wiped his forehead with a handkerchief. They both stopped talking at once. Yuzhin folded his handkerchief neatly.

"That was a nice little slanging-match," he said amiably. "We don't often get two people shouting at once in here. It's usually a case of one shouting while the other listens. Two's better. Tests the voice. Now listen. There's no point in reproaching me. I'm not an expert in your subject. But I can't take things on trust."

Tulin said nothing.

"So what else can we do?" Yuzhin said. "Shall we ask for an expert opinion? Do you agree to that?"

"Whose? Somebody on your side?"

"Now why take it like that?" Yuzhin continued amiably. "Who do you regard as an authority? Academician Denisov?"

"Denisov's wrapped up in his generators and anti-aircraft guns. He doesn't recognise anything else. He's completely intolerant and a monopolist."

"I see. What about Zhiltsov?"

Tulin shrugged.

"Zhiltsov is a sceptic. He's against anything new. He's a professional hatchet man."

"Any other suggestions?" Yuzhin asked patiently. "Give me an idea. Perhaps Lagunov would do?"

"Surely you know Lagunov is one of Denisov's creatures. He's no scientist."

"You seem to be surrounded by opponents. Have you no supporters?"

Tulin wondered why he didn't suggest Golitsyn. Perhaps because he was not sure of support from that quarter?

"You see, Comrade General," he said, "every new theory has to win its supporters. At first it's hemmed in with opponents. Facts are the only thing that will convince them. And the facts are up there, in the thunderclouds. That's the only place I can get them from."

"You're in a spot, aren't you? What do you want me to do? I'm expected to break the rules, go against the opinion of experts for the sake of something I don't know much about and haven't much faith in. I suppose you think here's a Blimp I've got sitting in front of me and he's the man on whom progress depends. But it's the easiest thing in the world for a Blimp to quote regulations and give a flat refusal. I haven't done that, though you've been pushing me that way."

His logic was impeccable and he had reached the point when there was nothing further to wait for, but still Tulin waited.

"Who's left?" Yuzhin asked. "Perhaps you're counting on Golitsyn?"

Tulin hugged himself. Yuzhin himself had come to his rescue by mentioning Golitsyn. This in no way committed Tulin and, as there was no other alternative, he had not sacrificed any principles. Tulin smiled ironically—a necessary precaution.

"Well, Golitsyn is an expert. You've got to give him that. He's one of the old school, of course."

"It's up to you," Yuzhin said.

"How long shall we have to wait for his opinion?" Tulin asked uncompromisingly. He thought of Krylov. We might get away with it, he told himself.

Yuzhin glanced at his watch.

"We'll have to wait about forty minutes."

"But how. . . ."

"As soon as I got your report a week ago I requested an opinion from Golitsyn." Yuzhin smiled subtly and Tulin realised that he had been led like a child. The general knew his business.

Now he couldn't afford to make the slightest slip. A show of temper would make his foolishness complete. He was going to make no presents of that kind. With perfect calm, as though merely out of curiosity, he asked why Yuzhin had chosen Golitsyn in preference to the others.

"I've known Arkady Borisovich for some time. I respect him. Would I be wrong in thinking that our opinions appear to coincide?" There was only a trace of slyness in Yuzhin's voice.

It was no use at all hanging about the waiting room. It would have looked far better to come back for the answer the following day and fill in the time by calling on the Gosplan and his editors. But he knew he would be incapable of work until he received an answer. Until now it had never entered his head that he might be refused. He had never allowed anyone in the group to hint at such a thing. When he had boarded the plane for Moscow he had known he would get what he wanted. How, he had no idea, but it could not be otherwise. And now, too, as he sat in the waiting room, his mind rejected all thought of defeat. Golitsyn should give him some support at least. Only a little was needed. It would be quite enough for the conclusion to be somewhat vague. The rest could be squeezed out of Yuzhin; it had not been an entirely fruitless conversation. Yuzhin had been forced to yield on some points.

He suddenly realised there had been a purpose behind his visit to the institute. All the time he had sensed that Golitsyn would have to come in somewhere. He should have warned Krylov; Krylov would have helped. Instead he had talked big, strutted like a peacock, mocked their way of doing things.

What if he were to telephone Krylov now? It was too late. He would never have done it anyway. He could ask anyone a favour but not Sergei. Vanity? Perhaps it was. Or perhaps it was pride, foolish pride. Confess that he needed Sergei's help? Never! Perhaps it was superstition, but it would mean their roles had been reversed.

Chapter Seven

Back in the laboratory he saw those familiar rooms through Tulin's eyes. Yes, it was a depressing sight. Should he take the plunge? He imagined himself as head of the laboratory.

The walls yielded obligingly to his touch. He lifted ceilings, pulled down partitions, rearranged the lighting, threw out rubbish that everyone was tired of. The rooms became well lighted, spacious. There were fewer people in them. Only the highly competent remained. Of course, the weeding-out process would be tricky. He would run into trouble there. The trade union committee and all kinds of other committees would want to know his reasons. Finding first-class men was hard enough, but it was even harder to shake off the weaklings. But wasn't it worth it? Why be afraid? What had he got to lose? No, this was no tomb. There was room here for action— plenty of room! A joint campaign could be launched from all sides against the mechanism of thunderstorms. There would be a co-ordinated plan of research, bringing in the Institute of High Pressures, the active intervention labs, the Academy itself. Their forces would be correctly distributed. He would have to be up to date on every aspect of the work. It would be his job, as head of the laboratory, to take snap decisions, ferret out mistakes, produce ideas, foresee difficulties. He must have his own style of work. He didn't have to be a Tulin. Each man should have his own style. He would do better as the unhurried serious type. No words wasted, but when he said a thing he meant it. With a good-humoured sociability to back it up. The kind of gentleness and courage that one associated with Hemingway or Fidel Castro. And like all the really great men of science, never be afraid to say: "I don't know."

He felt he must do something at once, take some decisive step. He gave orders for the monitor counters to be moved out on to the working site. He had been intending to do that for over a month but other things had intervened. Then he went over to Agatov.

"It's about time we did something about the generator," he said. "The thing's got no power at all."

"We have a spare one. We could connect up the two in parallel," Agatov said.

"They're not worth it."

Agatov gave him a quick look.

"You're probably right."

"And the rectifier is no good either."

"Yes, you're quite right."

"Look, Yakov Ivanovich, the theoretical side is becoming much more important nowadays. We shall have to review our programme. What it boils down to is—I'm going to accept the Old Man's offer."

An invisible hand seemed to rub every feature off Agatov's flat face with an eraser. Gradually the surface became perfectly white and smooth.

"I see," Agatov said tonelessly. "Was it Tulin who inspired the decision?"

"Yes—yes, he did, partly," Krylov went on happily. "I hope you and I, er.... You have a lot of experience on the practical side. I'm sure you'll be able to help."

He was trying to soften the blow, to offer Agatov some consolation. But why the rush? Couldn't he have chosen a better moment?

"I'm sorry things have worked out like this."

Now he was making excuses. Never mind, it might help Agatov a little.

Agatov switched off his apparatus and rose to his feet.

"I have always done all I could," he said. "It's easy for Tulin to criticise, when he's not involved."

"No, he's quite right about a lot of things," Krylov said eagerly, glad now to have got it over and to have somethinig else to talk about.

Agatov listened attentively, nodding his assent, but Krylov realised the other man had no time for his frank outpourings. The new job was proving tough from the start. Surely he wouldn't have to go on like this, smashing other people's hopes, stepping over them, deciding their lives for them? Was there no alternative? Must he always try not to notice, not to think about it because this was the only way of doing things?

Outside Golitsyn's room Krylov glanced at his reflection in a window and scratched his chin. From now on he would have to shave every day.

"What's he want me for? Why the urgency?" he asked Ksyusha.

She wanted to congratulate him and to know whether his life had "entered a new phase".

Ksyusha was one big mass of make-up—hair, nails, lips, eyebrows, eyelashes. A heavy necklace glistened on her lemon-yellow blouse.

"Yellow suits you," he said and smiled complacently at his own urbanity.

Ksyusha spoke into the telephone.

"Do you mind ringing later? He is engaged." With her eyes she motioned Krylov to his chief's door.

Krylov read the paper Golitsyn had given him when he entered the room, but his mind refused to take it in. He was thinking that he was a pig and that he ought to have thanked the Old Man properly.

"The testing of the hypothesis that has been proposed more than once in recent years requires extensive experimental data, data that can be collected only by an extensive programme of laboratory research over a period of several years...."

The Old Man had helped him at a very critical period in his life. He had forced him to defend his thesis. Things had been pretty sticky in those days!...

"Do you think I've made myself clear?" Golitsyn asked.

Krylov forced himself to concentrate.

"This idea is merely another project...." What idea? *"...Tulin's irresponsible, completely unjustified project...."*

What had Tulin got to do with it?

Golitsyn's fingernail was tapping the glass top of his desk impatiently. There was a silver signet-ring on the finger.

Krylov went back to the beginning and read the whole paper again.

"Well, now you know what it's about, kindly take our opinion to General Yuzhin at the Board. He's waiting. You'll be able to answer any questions he may have."

"But I...."

"It's time you got used to it, my dear fellow. There's nothing to be afraid of; it'll do you good to get around a bit."

"No, I don't mean that," Krylov said. "I mean this opinion. This means you're virtually closing down Tulin's project."

"So much the better—it'll make him get on with something useful. Drop in when you get back and we'll have a chat about the future."

Golitsyn put on his spectacles and opened a British technical journal. Krylov went out to the secretary's office.

"Everything okay?" she said. "I always believed in your lucky star."

For a few minutes Krylov stood at her desk.

"Ksyusha, this is impossible," he said and went back to Golitsyn.

"I can't do this," he said from the doorway. "There's no proof."

Golitsyn looked up in surprise.

"You still here?" He tossed the journal aside. "What did you say?"

"There's no proof," Krylov repeated. "I'm sorry, Arkady Borisovich, but I don't see where Tulin is wrong."

"An opinion of this kind doesn't have to contain detailed proofs. Have you read Tulin's articles, my dear fellow?"

"Yes, I have."

"Well, what do you think of them? Are his arguments valid?"

"Some of them are controversial, but. . . ."

Golitsyn frowned. "Now, look here, young man, are you trying to teach me my job? Do you expect me to give Tulin my blessing for his hare-brained scheme? You surprise me."

"It's not a hare-brained scheme. His arguments may have certain weaknesses but that gives him all the more reason for wanting to test them."

"It does not!" Golitsyn shouted. "A real scientist has no right to be so rash. Let him gather his facts and we'll consider the matter. So far he has nothing but self-assurance."

"But how long can one go on accumulating facts? There must come a time when. . . ."

"A hundred years, a thousand years, as long as is necessary! No intelligence is needed to pick the fruit before it's ripe." He went on more calmly. "You know, I have nothing against any method of active intervention, Tulin's included—when its time comes. It's too early yet. We still don't know enough. This project requires very thorough preparation or we shall simply compromise the whole idea." The feeling that he had been so tolerant made him almost paternal. After all, he had been through all this himself. Obstinately knitted brows, lowered head, confronting an old and cautious professor—how strangely life repeated itself!

"It was exactly the same when I started," he went on. "We demanded action. We were quite sure we could tame the skies, subdue the gods of thunder." He closed his eyes to look back into the past. "Rebellious youth . . . sweet, rebellious, questing youth. It all seems so easy, so simple. You young people, you just soar in the clouds and can't be bothered with details. But you'll get over it, you'll understand one day."

Krylov knew what was coming. In a minute Golitsyn would be talking about Gridnev. "In that case," he began "there's all the more reason to. . . ."

"Old men like Gridnev or Obolensky seemed to us. . . . I wonder how I seem to you now? A fossil? An old fogey, eh?"

"Why. . . no!" Krylov blushed, and Golitsyn suddenly gave one of his short, penetrating little laughs.

"I understand and I don't blame you, not for a moment. I can even understand Tulin. And understanding, you know, is halfway to forgiveness. I have no patience with scientists who never make mistakes. Wild ideas are useful, but only"—he raised a warning finger—"as long as they don't block up the main stream."

The door opened a little and Agatov's head appeared. Golitsyn nodded, and Agatov entered. He slid into the room and stood with his back to a bookcase, giving as much leeway as possible to his chief, who by this time was pacing up and down, hands behind his back, as he did on the platform during a lecture.

"In the 11th century Alhazen discovered refraction and calculated the altitude of the atmosphere. Unfortunately, these discoveries were of no use to science until five centuries later, when Torricelli had to discover them all over again. Scientific ideas must keep in step with the age." The history of science was his favourite subject. He could hold forth about it for hours.

Krylov offered Agatov the report.

"Have you read this?"

"What about Alhazen?" Agatov asked loudly. "Was his work wasted?"

"Indeed it was," said Golitsyn. "It has only recently been unearthed."

Krylov looked at Agatov, then at Golitsyn.

"Arkady Borisovich, surely you didn't write this report yourself?" he asked suddenly.

Golitsyn stopped short.

"Why do you ask?"

"It doesn't sound like you. These aren't your expressions. 'Adventurism', 'pseudo-scientific argumentation'...."

"Oh, all's fair in love and war," Golitsyn said with a somewhat embarrassed belligerence.

"There's no need to be diplomatic in scientific controversy," Agatov said.

Golitsyn turned towards him.

"But we're sending this to a somewhat different quarter, Yakov Ivanovich."

Agatov said firmly: "Clear-cut statements are exactly what the military need."

"Possibly so. Anyway we can't compete with Yakov Ivanovich in that field. And I don't see why we should—as long as the meaning is there.... Now, what was I saying? Oh, yes, let us suppose that some hundred years hence Tulin's idea is brought to light and some historian or other writes about this daring project that was not appreciated at the time. Somebody by the name of Golitsyn called Tulin a dreamer, didn't understand him, didn't appreciate him. How that historian will execrate us, hold us all up to shame!" And with a final flourish of pride he added: "You see, I'm quite impartial."

"Yes, you're impartial," Krylov said slowly. "But to whom?"

"Really!"

Golitsyn knew how to deal with any affront to his dignity. At such moments he became as aloof and inaccessible as the portraits of Franklin and Lomonosov on the walls of his study, as the dark oak-panelled room itself, in which nothing had changed since he took it over years ago.

"For your information, Sergei Ilyich, there are no personal relations whatsoever between Tulin and myself. And he is no competitor of mine." His nostrils twitched arrogantly. "I hope that is clear? And anyway, it's time I was thinking about the other place, as they say."

"You seem to be the one who is not impartial, Sergei Ilyich," Agatov said, detaching himself from the bookcase.

"I?"

"You're a friend of Tulin's. He asked you to do what you could for him."

"But this is nonsense!" Krylov exclaimed.

Agatov shook his head reproachfully.

"I think that is rather untoward, Sergei Ilyich. Tulin called on you today for that express purpose."

Golitsyn gave them a startled look. "What? Was Tulin here today?" Krylov, his cheeks burning, tried to explain, but Golitsyn ignored him. "So this has all been going on behind my back. And after that you demand impartiality! What an old fool I was to think of you as. . . ."

"But Tulin didn't say a word about this!" Krylov burst out desperately, although he realised his explanations would be lost on the old man.

"What are you actually trying to achieve, Sergei Ilyich?" Agatov asked significantly and accusingly.

"Achieve by what?"

"Do you realise what you are asking Arkady Borisovich to do? You insist on a different opinion. But that opinion won't be yours. If anything goes wrong, it will be Arkady Borisovich who bears all the responsibility. Is that what you want?"

"Don't talk rubbish," Krylov said. A sudden thought struck him: "Wait a minute, Yakov Ivanovich. You said yourself you were in favour of this kind of research. We were discussing it only today."

Agatov was not in the least taken aback. On the contrary, he seemed to welcome Krylov's remark. "I think we had better leave today's conversation out of this," he said.

"But why? I don't see. . . ."

"So you insist? Very well. Arkady Borisovich, far be it from me to hurt you in any way," Agatov began solemnly, "but my words have been misrepresented. . . ."

Golitsyn made an impatient gesture. "Oh, leave me out of it."

"No, this is something you should know. Today Krylov and I were discussing the laboratory's plans. Krylov stated that we were working on subjects that were of no use to anyone. I won't quote any of the improper remarks that were made. Krylov believes this is due to poor leadership and the hampering of initiative. Am I representing you correctly, Sergei Ilyich? Your words, if I remember, were that Arkady Borisovich fights shy of contemporary physics? You think he's behind the times, incompetent and so on. As for this report, you can scarcely accuse me of holding the opposite view, when I prepared it myself at Arkady Borisovich's request."

"Quite so," Golitsyn affirmed, all the spirit gone from his voice.

"It's not for me to criticise you, Sergei Ilyich, but you really ought to be ashamed of yourself."

Krylov was stunned into silence. With dull curiosity he noted that Agatov's voice was trembling with perfectly sincere emotion, and that his eyes had suddenly become large and reproachful in his pale face.

"Better the truth, however bitter, than a syrup of lies, Arkady Borisovich. I hate backbiting. If Krylov had been honest, straightforward. . . . I know, of course, he is your protégé and I shall suffer for this, but at least my conscience will be clear."

Agatov leaned towards Golitsyn.

"Allow me to take that report to Yuzhin myself."

"Yes, I think you'd better. Thank you," Golitsyn replied. "Take it now."

Krylov did not recover till the door had closed behind Agatov.

"Arkady Borisovich, this is all wrong——"

Golitsyn remained silent, his lips pursed in disgust.

"Agatov can go to the devil for all I care," Krylov went on. "It's not that I'm worried about——"

"After all I've done for you——"

"What it amounts to is that you've shut down a whole line of research that had real prospects. Is that how scientific controversies ought to be solved?"

"It's only what I deserve. But how could I have been so mistaken!"

They went on oblivious of one another; Krylov raised his voice in annoyance:

"Tulin may be going too fast over some things, but to clamp down like this—I can't let it go at that, I can't understand it."

"There appear to be other points of difference between us, besides Tulin," Golitsyn said. "We apparently have different codes of behaviour."

Krylov made a sound of strangled indignation.

"Yes? Do go on."

Krylov joined his hands firmly behind his back.

"This intolerance will make things very difficult for me," he said, choosing his words and trying to speak with restraint and clarity. "If I am to assume you are always right, I shall have no alternative but to turn myself into an Agatov and play up to you all the time. All the pleasure will go out of my work."

"Scientific inquiry is not solely a matter of pleasure," Golitsyn rasped.

"Perhaps I didn't put it very well. What I mean is that my value as a scientist will disappear."

"It will disappear if you take up Tulin's delirious ideas. But of course it's beyond me to tell you anything. There was a time when you considered me your teacher; now I'm behind the times, a drag on progress, I fight shy, I steer in the wrong direction—"

"I always respected you for allowing us to argue with you."

"The purpose of argument is to arrive at the truth. But you, Sergei Ilyich, did not argue, you intrigued. Yes, intrigued! It was you, you who displayed intolerance. You told Agatov things behind my back, but he has turned out to be more honest than you. You ought to be ashamed!"

"You have no right. . . ."

"Silence! You young upstart! To hear this, after I pulled you through the way I did! Go away! I've had enough!" Golitsyn was shouting, his hands were trembling, and Krylov shouted back, desperately trying to make himself heard.

"Don't count on me to run your laboratory for you! I refuse your offer!"

"Are you threatening me? Me! Do you think that after—" Golitsyn suddenly clutched the arms of his chair and slumped back heavily. Krylov rushed to him in alarm but the old man brushed him aside in disgust, opened his drawer, took out a phial of heart tablets, tossed one into his mouth, closed his eyes and, after drawing a deep breath, gave a gleeful titter.

"Tut-tut-tut! How could you deprive us of your kind services? What a misfortune for us, poor creatures, to be abandoned so!" Then he stopped laughing and said with soft malice: "If I were in your shoes I wouldn't have anything to do with tyrants like Golitsyn. Keep your principles to the last."

"Nothing will please me better," Krylov retaliated. "I'm getting out of here."

"For God's sake do. I'm not keeping you. Get out today if you like."

Krylov reached the door in a few strides and flung it open.

"Just a minute! Golitsyn's shout brought the secretary to her feet in her office. "I won't let you resign. I'm firing you. And remember this: it's not me you're leaving, it's science!"

Pesetsky had a corner of the lab to himself. It was partitioned off by a bookcase stuffed with reference manuals and detective stories.

"May I come in?" Krylov asked.

Keeping very still, Pesetsky replied cautiously, trying not to listen to the sound of his own voice: "Please—in the sense of for God's sake—stay out of here."

Krylov sat down on a stool. Pesetsky scribbled mechanically. He had the angry, intelligent expression of a man who is dissatisfied with himself. Eventually he threw down his pencil and stretched his arms.

"You still here? Now what's your opinion? Could a paralytic kill sixteen people? If so, how? Why don't you read detective stories? Keep yourself in training. Want me to give you one? *Death in a Cage*. Marvellous! What are you looking so down in the mouth about? Feeling the burdens of office already?"

"I am."

"Incidentally, much though I hate to admit it, N equals plus three and three-tenths."

"What did I tell you!"

"Must you gloat?"

They discussed the data that had at one time been obtained by Fyodorov and the station on Mt. Elbrus. The equation spread itself over half a page, but Pesetsky was delighted with it, called it a "peach" and claimed that even the doorman would be able to solve it now.

The equation was, indeed, an elegant piece of mathematics and Krylov sensed that it was absolutely correct. They admired it together, as they would a finely wrought ornament.

"Mathematics! Queen of the sciences!" Pesetsky boasted. He despised experimenters burrowing in their circuits like moles underground, considering the reading of the needle the supreme arbiter of all disputes. "If only I had a behind like Agatov, the things I would have achieved! My trouble is that I can't stick to anything long enough. Or rather, I won't. I'm in the same spot with women. I see through them too quickly. They bore me. I'm hampered by my own powers of reason. But it looks as if you'll drag me to the finishing post. You're a tough customer to deal with."

"I'm leaving the institute," Krylov said.

Pesetsky gave a whistle.

"You're joking?"

When he had heard Krylov's story he looked depressed.

"You're the only man in the department who knows anything about mathematics. Perhaps you'll change your mind? Just ignore the whole thing. It's all so trivial anyway."

"I can't ignore it."

"Matter of principle?"

"I've simply had enough."

"Well, I'm sorry. . . . Still, it's a good thing we fixed that equation."

"Yes, the equation is fine."

They went through the page of figures once again.

"You'll have to finish the article yourself," Krylov said.

"Not likely."

They were both silent for a time.

"What do you think about the whole business?" Krylov asked.

"Nothing," Pesetsky said crossly. "Nothing at all. I'm not going to get involved. The Old Man's running away from the truth, and you're running away from him, none of which has anything whatever to do with physics."

According to Pesetsky, they were all at fault; yet he found excuses for them all, even Agatov. It sounded logical but Krylov wasn't satisfied. However, he lacked the energy to argue with Pesetsky.

"The main thing is to keep the old subcortex busy," Pesetsky advised him when they parted. "You're just wasting your time now going around with your subcortex at a loose end."

Bochkaryov, of course, was horrified and wanted to rush off to Golitsyn and have the whole thing out, but Krylov said no. A reconciliation was possible only if Golitsyn apologised and revised his decision concerning Tulin. Bochkaryov called him a high-handed clot who didn't think of his friends. They quarrelled, and Krylov was able to feel thoroughly sorry for himself and completely contemptuous of this petty world in which nobleness of mind could be thus set at naught.

The sun crept over to the glass cube of the ink-well and sprang from it in a blaze of colour. Golitsyn closed his eyes. The ink-well had for long been a receptacle for paper-clips. Time and again the supply manager had suggested removing the massive bronze inkstand and its candlesticks, and refurnishing the room at the same time, but Golitsyn would have none of it. He wanted the room to remain just as it had been twenty-five years ago, when he had taken over after the death of the man who had been his teacher.

Not often in the course of those twenty-five years had he sat idle at this desk, breaking his customary routine. It was an hour and a half since he had written the order of dismissal on the letter in which Krylov had tendered his resignation.

He was expecting Krylov to come back. He was sure that he would. Say what you like, but the fellow was utterly devoted to science and there was nowhere else for him to go. He couldn't count on becoming head of the laboratory, not for another few months as least. He must be taught a lesson.

For some time, when Krylov first came to the laboratory, Golitsyn had felt disappointed. He could not see what Dankevich and Anikeyev, men whose opinion Golitsyn respected, had found in this ponderous, slow-witted creature. But gradually he had begun to perceive the underlying pattern in Krylov's actions. And as time went on the feeling became even stronger that here was an original though often erratic mind. Here was an urge to trace the connections in the chaos of facts, to integrate what seemed to be completely contradictory phenomena of atmospheric electricity.

At one time Golitsyn had been the same. Now the theory of thunderstorms that he had evolved was out of date; there were too many anomalies which it failed to explain. The theory was still referred to in textbooks; it was still quoted, but only because there was nothing else. If Krylov hadn't questioned it, someone else would have done. It would have been overthrown, reduced to the particular; no theories were eternal and one must have the courage in one's own lifetime to give way, if only to see what other theory would mount the throne in its stead. For a time he had hoped secretly that while Krylov worked on the basis of Dankevich's ideas, his, Golitsyn's, theory of thunderstorms would flow like a tributary into the common stream of Dankevich's overall conception. Apparently Dankevich had made a similar assumption. But Krylov was a cuckoo in the nest; he pushed out everything that restricted him and came to terms with no one. One after another he swallowed up the old thunderstorm theories until there could be no question of joining the common stream.

It was possible to work with Krylov, or so Golitsyn had at first assumed. But as time went on he had tried to put it off, avoided interfering. Finding all manner of new excuses for himself he had jealously watched the unexpected twists and turns Krylov was making in his quest. Discarding what seemed to be the most obvious moves, Krylov rashly thrust incompatible concepts together, impertinently encroached on the theory of probability and cast aside truths that Golitsyn would never have dared to question.

In recent years Golitsyn had become more and more painfully aware of the timidity of his own thinking. This was not due to old age. The changes that had come over the country since the Twentieth Party Congress had affected the institute as well; it was now possible to broaden the range of one's research, to recruit new forces, to have free access to any work that had a bearing on one's subject. But Golitsyn still couldn't straighten his back. It was strange that now, when there were no obstacles, he had begun to feel inhibited. The young men like Krylov, Pesetsky and Richard could not understand this feeling. They had never known his fears; none of them had worked in the days when one had to keep silent, when it was often impossible to speak one's thoughts, when the outcome of scientific discussion was decided in advance by directives from above, when he, Golitsyn, was afraid to answer letters from his colleagues abroad, when idealism could be detected even in a formula. To Krylov this all seemed ridiculous, but Golitsyn had felt the rub of it on his own skin. And it had left its mark. He was corroded by fear, it had soaked into his brain. He had become apprehensive of generalisations, of any unusual association of ideas. Men like Krylov were free of all this. Their minds ranged widely, without a backward glance, and he envied them, not because of their youth but because the present age had dawned too late for him.

Krylov did not return. Golitsyn felt secret relief and was ashamed of the feeling, and to salve his conscience he recalled how two years ago he had sought out a harassed, despairing young man named Krylov in Leningrad, taken him on his staff, pulled strings to get him a room, and given him complete freedom at work. He went over all the things he had done for Krylov. It was hard to get used to human ingratitude, but to complain of it was foolish, as foolish as boasting of one's good deeds. The thing that galled him was that he had been mistaken. It had always seemed to him that there must be a connection between a man's style of work as a scientist and his human qualities, and that if Krylov refused to manipulate the points on his graphs, if he was prepared to go back to first principles and not bow to authorities, he must be equally honest in his personal dealings, a man of integrity, incapable of hypocrisy. It was unforgivable for a person of Golitsyn's age to have been so wrong in his judgement.

Chapter Eight

The arrival of Agatov shattered Tulin's last hopes. Why did it have to be Agatov of all people who brought the report! There must be an unkind fate at work here somewhere.

As Yuzhin read out Golitsyn's verdict aloud, Agatov's pale face seemed to swell with an ill-restrained triumph. Every sentence rammed Tulin further down into his chair.

"*...Flights directly into thunderclouds*"—Yuzhin paused—"*are unsafe, premature and serve no purpose whatever.*"

Agatov had clasped his hands in an almost prayer-like attitude, displaying his manicured fingernails.

"Your grounds," he said to Tulin, "are insufficient. The great problems of science can't be solved like that."

Agatov and Yuzhin, the large desk with its telephones seemed to be drifting rapidly away from Tulin.

"How are they solved then?" he heard himself ask, as though from a great distance.

"Drop by drop," Agatov replied gently. "In the laboratory the size of droplets is measured year after year. And no one should be too proud to measure them. We all have to be content with the little we can achieve."

Yuzhin examined Golitsyn's signature thoughtfully.

"So the idea's a bit off schedule, is it?" He took no trouble to hide his regret. "Well, time's marching on. At this rate it looks as if I won't live long enough to get my own back. And I've got a good many scores to settle with Old Man Thunder."

"There's no other way, Comrade General." Agatov spread his arms sympathetically. "We are confronted with an enormous dissipation of energy and no regenerative process. . . ."

Tulin's face twisted.

"Absolute rubbish! You don't know what you're talking about. All they want, General, is to be left in peace and not take any risks. There is a certain type of scientist who'd rather die than set foot outside his laboratory."

The more furiously he attacked, the more complacently Agatov smiled. Soon he began to aim this smile separately at Yuzhin, as though they shared the same opinion.

"Hear that, General? The things one has to listen to when one tries to defend the national interest. Anyone else in Arkady Borisovich's position would have given an ambiguous answer and left it at that. But we believe in saying what we think. . . ."

Yuzhin's ruddy, weather-beaten face was inscrutable. He was staring hard at Agatov.

"Playing at novelty is a fashionable trick nowadays." Agatov raised a warning finger. "Remember this, General. Tulin doesn't have to worry, but if they have a crash it'll be you who has to answer."

The cynicism behind the phrase had little enough effect on Yuzhin. He was accustomed to joking at death and had used phrases that were cruder and harsher. The thing that irked him was something that no aircrew man has ever been able to stomach—a member of the ground staff presuming to judge the men who fight in the air.

He stood up and straightened his tunic.

"Very well, the picture is quite clear now. You may go." He turned to Tulin. "And so may you," he added a little more gently.

"I shall inform Arkady Borisovich that everything is settled," Agatov replied.

The door closed softly behind him. Tulin remained seated.

"Settled!" The general grunted. He looked at his watch expressively. "We shall inform your institute officially. There's nothing more I can do for you."

Tulin half rose, gripping the arms of his chair.

"I can't go back like this—empty-handed. It means starting all over again on something we know already. Don't you realise we know what's needed—"

"There's nothing more I can do for you."

Tulin rose to his full height, then suddenly sat down again, in quite a different attitude of comfortable repose.

"I'm not moving."

"What do you mean?"

"I shall sit here till I get permission."

"You've heard my answer. There's nothing more to discuss."

Tulin leaned his head back and examined the plaster moulding round the ceiling. Yuzhin came out from behind his desk and surveyed Tulin from all angles, as though measuring him up.

"Don't play the fool, man. It won't work with me." He waited a moment, then pressed a button. A young, rosy-faced adjutant shot into the room and came to attention in front of the general's desk, clicking his heels with all the pleasure of a boy playing at soldiers.

"Take Comrade Tulin downstairs, put him in a car and tell them to drive him home."

"Very good, Comrade General!" The adjutant looked at Tulin expectantly.

"As you were," Tulin said. "I'm staying."

The adjutant transferred his glance to the general.

"Obey the order," the general commanded. "What are you standing there for? Help him to get up. He's not feeling well. Can't you see how pale he is?"

The adjutant took one or two uncertain steps towards Tulin.

"I feel very well indeed." Tulin crossed one leg over the other. "So well that you'll have to bring in at least three men. And a stretcher. And it'll make a very funny picture, Comrade General. A scientist being tied up and carried out of the room—the latest method of putting an end to discussion."

The adjutant's face broke into a smile, but a sideways glance at the general brought him to his senses and he gave a terrible frown. It was too late, however.

"What's the joke? What are you grinning at? What do you think this is—a sit-round for the evening?"

But the fellow just sat lounging there, one leg over the other, not batting an eyelid. If an army man got an order, that was the end of it. Obedience, discipline. But these scientist fellows had no organisation, no generals, no senior or junior ranks. And they took advantage of it. You couldn't demote them. Look at the way he dangled his foot! So sure he would get his way. It might be sheer desperation, of course. He must be very disappointed. After all, he was not doing it for himself. Not asking for funds or a promotion. . . .

The two walls intersected with the ceiling, forming a three-dimensional angle. Yes, he'd had to solve a problem like that at an examination. Now, whatever happened, he must stick it out. If he left this room, it would be all up. Better not to think about that. While he was here, it seemed as if something was still being decided or might be decided. Yes, one never forgot the questions one was asked at exams. "Hooliganism!" That was the general speaking. Tulin stared at the corner of the ceiling. He buried his head in that three-dimensional angle. Now he must grip the arms of his chair and never let go. Curl his lip. Yes, the more arrogant the better. Narrow his eyes. It'd be a good thing to smoke, puff away coolly, just to keep a straight face. Never let go. . . . The only thing he had left was obstinacy, blind obstinacy, devoid of all hope. He just had to keep sitting here, in this chair.

The sudden silence made him look at Yuzhin. Something had changed. The adjutant had left the room. There was a gleam of something rather like sympathy in Yuzhin's eyes.

The general placed his hand on Tulin's shoulder.

"How old are you?"

Tulin tried to produce a sneering laugh but was afraid to part his lips. They might begin to tremble, they might say any damn fool thing and the voice that emerged might tremble. This great heavy hand resting on his shoulder had snapped something inside him and he was horrified to feel a suffocating tightness in his throat.

Yuzhin poured out a glass of water.

"Have a drink."

The water was warm. Tulin sipped it without raising his eyes. From the tone of Yuzhin's voice he realised how wretched he looked, and this was the hardest thing to bear.

He put down the glass and walked to the door.

"Wait a minute," Yuzhin said.

Tulin halted without turning round. Yuzhin came over to him. "Have a go at Golitsyn yourself," he said gruffly.

Tulin suddenly became calm. It was all over. He felt that final sense of release, when nothing else matters and there is only one pleasure left—to speak out.

"Well done, Comrade General! You've passed the buck. Now you can be kind and sensitive. Yes, you can offer advice. You're no longer in any danger. Every rule and regulation has been observed to the letter. No, I shan't go to Golitsyn. I don't need any favours from him. And why should they go out on a limb anyway? One day you will realise that I was right. At the moment we happen to be ahead of other countries but now they will have time to catch up. They'll get on to our method, and then you'll come to me, cap in hand. Please, Comrade Tulin! Here you are, Comrade Tulin, take all the aircraft you want. Hurry, make up for lost time, get ahead. You will become bold, terribly bold and generous. . . . No, I'm not trying to frighten you. For setting us back several years in our work you will receive no reprimands. No one will punish you for being overcautious. . . ."

Yuzhin was prepared to forgive these unreasonable reproaches. The man was obviously overwrought. Yuzhin knew, if anyone did, what enormous sums the state was spending on research into the physics of the atmosphere. Tulin's group was a tiny sector of a huge front of scientific inquiry conducted by various institutes all over the country. But the general had been impressed by something else. In Tulin's fiery outburst he had detected a passionate sense of conviction. What did it rest on? Why did it influence Tulin more than all these formulas, computations and reports? Perhaps it was not merely faith?

He searched Tulin's face, making the agonising effort that men must always make to reach the secret recesses in other men's hearts. Suppose what Tulin maintained was actually the truth? For a moment he thought he saw in Tulin's eyes not merely faith but truth itself.

"The whole thing's a bloody circus!. . ." And suddenly with a downward thrust of his clenched fist: "All right, go ahead and I'll take the consequences! I give my permission. Not for everything, of course. No flying into the thunderheads!"

Tulin drew a deep breath and closed his eyes. For some reason he felt nothing but a great drowsiness. At last Yuzhin stopped speaking. Tulin came to himself, seized Yuzhin's hand, then his shoulders, and kissed him first on one cheek, then on the other. Yuzhin was embarrassed but Tulin felt the spontaneous charm of his own reaction and recovered his former confidence in the inevitability of what had happened. From the outset he had known he would have his way, that it was bound to be so.

They sat down to consider the flight plans. Yuzhin marked out the zones uncompromisingly.

"There'll be no bypassing Golitsyn now," he warned. "You'll have to reach some sort of compromise. He will monitor your flights. Not himself, of course, some of his people. I'll talk it over with him."

Tulin shrugged that aside. He was too overjoyed to hesitate over such trifles, particularly with Sergei Krylov at the institute. Sergei would help him out.

He winked at Yuzhin. "Suppose we run into a thunderstorm? Suppose we just wander inside one and get lost there? What happens then?"

"I'll give you 'wander inside and get lost'!"

"But suppose we do?"

"If a pilot sees a thunderstorm ahead he flies round it. If he gets lost in it"—Yuzhin gave a short laugh—"it's not always possible to repair the plane afterwards."

Tulin laughed too. It seemed such a wonderful joke. He hastened to reassure Yuzhin; he was ready to promise anything, give any guarantees. If anything went wrong, he swore, he would make no more flights, request no more aircraft. Once again he was the victor and the victor could afford to be generous and make promise after promise.

He left the Board late in the evening. With the heads of various departments he had worked out the flight plans in detail; the prohibited zones were extensive, too extensive, but they had been given permission to fly closer to thunderheads than anyone had even contemplated.

This was the first stage, the break-through; the rest would be easier. The main thing was agreement in principle. The rest depended on radar. The sensitivity of the set could be adjusted. Yuzhin's stipulation would be formally satisfied. Nothing else mattered as long as the results were good. Victors were not judged; they judged others.

When he came out into the street the lamps were lit and the shop windows and neon signs were so bright that not a single star was visible in the evening sky.

He went into a food shop and bought a bottle of Armenian brandy, a large wedge of his favourite cheese and some ham.

He strolled down the street with his purchases, looking at the women. He thought them all beautiful—the slim, shapely ones in close-fitting slacks, the ones in light raincoats and short overcoats. Girls in anoraks, girls with bronze hair, girls with their hair combed up high, girls with fashionable slanting eyes and wide mouths; laughing, button-nosed, pert young things, the sweetly demure and the less comely hoydens in their wide rustling skirts, their bare arms all goose-flesh—chilly this evening but anything for fashion's sake. Where were they all from, these pretty young things? What had brought them out with the spring?

He had a sudden desire to speak to one of them. That long-legged one in the grey tight-fitting sweater, for instance, who was standing in front of a theatre bill-board. He asked her what she wanted to see. *The King Is Naked*, she said. Oh yes, just what he wanted to see. Why shouldn't they go together? She needn't be afraid, this was just his lucky evening. Why not take the chance while it was going, while he was in this generous mood? He knew it was no use putting the question timidly, being shy about it. He had to do the talking, make her laugh, tell her about himself. But he didn't have to make an effort, he simply shared the joy of his success. The girl's surprise and caution gave way to a condescending smile. So the man was just one of these harmless cranks, quite an amusing one, in fact. And after a few minutes she had decided he wasn't a crank, he was a nice, talkative boy. She agreed to walk with him to the theatre. There was no point in it, of course; there wouldn't be any tickets going for love or money. He said they would "see about that" and took her arm.

The theatre was only a few streets away. They pushed through a crowd pleading for spare tickets and reached the window of the manager's office. Tulin poked his head in and saw a harassed, perspiring fat man and said: "You've got asthma, you ought to be taking a cure. You ought to be in a quiet, easy job, not a madhouse like this. But what can you do about it if you're fond of this theatre and no one else has any organising ability? They'd be sunk without you. Only fools imagine that the manager does nothing but sit in his rabbit-hutch and hand out privilege tickets."

The impatient eyes stared blankly at him as if he were an idiot, then something clicked, and they smiled with a tolerant envy.

Two bright yellow tickets for the third row of the stalls turned him into a magician.

She had a wonderful figure and a pleasant low-pitched voice and she glowed with pleasure, but again that sudden drowsiness came over him.

"Here are the tickets and please forgive me," he said. "I've seen the play already and I'd forgotten I must go and see a friend."

It was not just an excuse. He had suddenly remembered Krylov and he wanted to stretch out on his sofa and tell him all about it, because only Krylov would really appreciate his achievement.

Chapter Nine

The key was in its usual place, on the right above the door.

The big, barely furnished room seemed uninviting, though nothing in it had changed. Tulin dropped on to the couch and stretched out his legs. The secret of rapid recovery was to relax completely and not think about anything.

The clock ticked. The refrigerator went on with a click and burbled frustratedly, as though trying to impart some hurried message.

He switched on the radio. A woman's voice was singing languorously in Italian: "Noble hearts will always love." Quite true. He jumped to his feet, picked up the bottle of brandy, broke the seal and knocked out the cork with the flat of his hand. Having found a glass in the cupboard, he filled it and, merely to cure his sleepiness, swallowed the contents, making a face as though it were medicine. It would have been an anticlimax to drop off to sleep on one's first evening in Moscow, specially after what he had just been through. The programme on the radio was a concert of some sort; he could hear the sighing and coughing of the audience.

Krylov's absence had upset his plans. He took out his notebook and looked for someone to ring up.

The telephone stood among the books on the desk. Tulin went over to it and saw a photograph under the glass top. It was of a girl in a tasselled skiing cap with snow-covered woods in the background. Her cap and curls were also powdered with snow. She had firm round cheeks and a shy smile.

Tulin looked round the room suspiciously. There was a pair of dumb-bells in the corner. The number of books had increased. Skis on the wardrobe—only one pair. He opened the wardrobe but it contained nothing to suggest the presence of a woman. The room still had the impersonally clean appearance, which Tulin himself knew so well, of being tidied by a stranger.

He felt relieved. It would have been sad if Krylov had got married. It would have been a loss.

He went through the names in his notebook. Old flames and chance acquaintances, half-forgotten faces that need not be recalled; there were some that it would have been pleasant to take to a restaurant, but even they would begin with reproaches. Why hadn't he written? Why hadn't he telephoned or visited them last time? He would have to make excuses, invent a story. Women could never simply enjoy meeting you, as men could. There was Zoya, of course, but Tulin thought of the tangled story of their relations and decided there was no point in making his life any more complicated. Sonya wouldn't let him get a word in all the evening. Galochka was purely for home consumption. He suddenly remembered Zhenya, the wide-eyed girl he had met that morning in the park. For some reason he felt sure she would be interested in his success; she would listen to him again, looking up at him with those shining brown eyes that reflected the lightning and the wet leaves. In a moment he had forgotten his intention of waiting for Krylov and spending the evening with him. He shaved rapidly and dabbed himself with what was left of Krylov's eau-de-Cologne. The notebook lay open at the letter "G". He was about to close it and thrust it into his pocket, when his eye fell upon the name of Golitsyn. He chuckled to himself.

"May I speak to Arkady Borisovich, please." While the line crackled voicelessly, he used his free hand to pour himself another glass of brandy. "Good evening, Arkady Borisovich! This is Tulin. I hope I'm not disturbing you. I read your opinion today. Thank you very much indeed for being so considerate about my health. You did everything you could. But even Caesar, as they say, is not above the grammarians. And the grammar of our life is that the new is bound to make a break-through. I'm not saying this merely to annoy you." He wouldn't let Golitsyn say a word. "I want you to keep fit, very fit, because I hope to see you in about a year from now, when I make my report on the results of our experiment. Perhaps you will even agree to attend the test flights? You might even agree to fly in a thunderstorm? After devoting so many years to them you must regret never having got inside one! Anyway, in deference to your intolerance, authority and great consideration for us, I shall try to be ready in a year at the most. Your very good health, Arkady Borisovich!"

He clinked his glass on the telephone receiver, while a furious burst of pips indicated that Golitsyn had rung off.

Krylov entered the room.

"Where've you been all this time? Get yourself dressed and come out for a meal."

"How are things with you?"

"We're going for a binge! Change your shirt. They're waiting for us. I'll tell you about it on the way."

Krylov shook his head wearily.

"I'm not in the mood. Go by yourself."

"No funny stuff!" Tulin burst out angrily. "I don't want to hear any excuses. Tonight it's my mood that matters. If you're not in the mood, I can't help it."

It was useless to argue with him. He harangued Krylov for having nothing to wear except a lot of expensive but tasteless shirts and rooted in the wardrobe till he found a brown one with an open neck.

Suddenly in the middle of his tirade he checked himself. "Have you got a girl?"

"I don't want any girls."

"What about her?" He nodded at the photograph.

"She doesn't live here."

"Where does she live?"

"A long way away."

Tulin examined the photograph again.

"Quite nice. All right, don't get het up. I suppose you're dead serious about it, as usual."

"How did you manage to cope with Agatov?"

Tulin grinned in anticipation of the pleasure to come.

"Everything in good time. Do you write to each other?"

"No."

"You're very secretive."

It was a social evening at the Scientists' Club. Tulin spent a long time choosing a table in the restaurant and considering the menu before ordering two shashlyks and salads. It made Krylov think what a boor he must be to have lived so long in the capital without even learning how to handle a waiter.

A man called Voznitsyn joined their party. He was assistant director of Tulin's institute, a small man who laughed uproariously on the slightest pretext. He had his wife with him, a pleasant, plumpish brunette, whom Tulin was within minutes calling "Simochka darling", though she was several years his senior.

Tulin had many friends at the club and he was constantly acknowledging their greetings, and leaving the table. He got to know that Ada was there—she had arrived in Moscow the day before on a business trip—and despite Krylov's protests, went out to fetch her. He brought her in, having rescued her from the company of aged professors who had been discussing the advantages of direct current.

The last time Krylov had seen Ada had been a year ago. She had scarcely changed. She was still as dazzlingly beautiful, still as proud;

the only difference seemed to be that she had taken to wearing very bright beads and a broad metal bracelet. They drank to the ladies, then to Yuzhin; when Krylov's turn came round, Ada asked in level tones what toast he would like for himself, as though proposing truce for the evening. Tulin clapped his hand to his forehead.

"Oh, my, I forgot. One of us here has had a big day today! He is now the head of the laboratory! Here am I bragging my head off while he, a true hero, remains modestly in the background as usual. In his person we salute. . . ."

Krylov hurriedly drained his glass and laughed at great length; the last thing he wanted to do was to spoil Tulin's evening for him.

The mere thought of the questions and condolences that would be showered upon him made him writhe. Ada would pipe up triumphantly with an "I told you so!" As it was, she said: "So you've made it. Well, it's still my opinion that your place is at the factory."

By the time he had thought of a reply no one was listening to him. Tulin was relating in detail the story of his interview with Yuzhin.

Voznitsyn cheered him on. "Good man! What a psychologist!" he cried, clapping his small hands. Tulin threw away restraint and invited them all to a grand banquet in a year's time.

The band struck up a lipsy. Tulin took the floor with Ada, and Simochka invited Krylov. Tulin and Ada were watched from every table; they were the finest-looking couple in the room.

"They make a perfect two-piece," Simochka said. "I'd give anything to be so photogenic."

Krylov made no reply. He didn't know what to say in such situations. Tulin couldn't stand Ada at any price. He called her a refrigerated pike and had probably invited her to dance only because her undeniable good looks attracted attention.

When the band stopped Tulin went over to the next table.

"Hullo there, Petrusha," he said loudly. "You ought to be congratulating me. But I hear you've had some of the wind taken out of your sails lately."

In the individual at the next table, who was as pink and round as a neatly peeled sausage, Krylov only just managed to recognise Petrusha Fominykh. Petrusha had been with Tulin and Krylov at college. Now he was presiding over a noisy group of overdressed young men.

Tulin casually borrowed someone's glass, filled it for himself and balanced it on his palm.

"You can't get by on cooked-up data these days. I give you a toast—to our progressive age!"

Before he could finish, Petrusha with a dexterity not to be expected in a man of his bulk snatched the glass from Tulin's palm, drank it and twirled it victoriously between his fingers. His dandified companions laughed. Tulin turned pale. The colour drained so rapidly from his face that even his eyes seemed to go white.

Ada squeezed Krylov's arm.

"Don't interfere, they'll sort it out themselves."

"They've been at one another's throats for a long time," Krylov told her. "First it was a girl. Then Petrusha gave him a tough time under Denisov. But Oleg can't afford to get mixed up in any rough stuff just now."

"Can you?"

"I'm a down-and-out anyway," he said, rising. "I don't count. . . ."

He walked over to Tulin and gripped his elbow.

"Oh, so you're here too," Petrusha jeered. "Take your pal away from here before I send him elsewhere."

"Aren't you fat!" Krylov replied. "You make me want to smear you all over with mustard."

He piloted Tulin away and made him dance with Voznitsyn's wife.

Ada was telling Voznitsyn about the troubles they had been having with direct current switches, but as soon as Krylov returned she asked him why he had said he was a down-and-out.

"Oh, just a phrase," Krylov replied. "What are they doing about those switches abroad?"

"That's just the point," said Ada.

Voznitsyn roared with laughter.

"Let the Yanks do the hurrying. We'll beat them to it just the same."

At that moment Petrusha came over to their table. He flicked up his trousers carefully at the knees and took a chair.

"I've no gripe against Oleg," he informed them. "There's no point in being offended with him because his mind's still in its juvenile state. He doesn't know anything about life. We all have to adjust nowadays." He straightened his spectacles. It was a very elegant pair, with gold ear-pieces. "Yes, Sergei, material life's a bastard, y'know. I consider it has to be attended to because so many things depend on it." He smiled at Ada.

"What are you doing now?" Krylov asked.

"Pushing automation techniques."

"But that's not your field," Krylov said in surprise.

"My field. . . ." Petrusha removed his spectacles and his eyes seemed sad for a moment.

Voznitsyn clapped his hands.

"What could be better! Automation makes work easier. Take the transmission and processing of information in meteorology, for instance. . . ."

Tulin returned to the table and, to Krylov's surprise, took a chair next to Petrusha and poured him a glass of wine.

"How can you know anything about automation?" Krylov persisted.

Petrusha sipped the wine and screwed up his eyes like a cat.

"Why should I know about it, you funny chap? All I have to do is push it. You can go on pushing a thing for years." He was looking at Krylov but Krylov felt that his words were aimed elsewhere. "A profession is merely a form of the existence of matter."

"You exist on indifference," Tulin said. "You're a new type of parasite. Do you enjoy your work?"

Petrusha grinned with pleasure.

"I have other things to enjoy. Not for me the birth pangs of scientific discovery—that's for the chosen few, for people like you. We're not even in the running. My interest is in material things. The principle of material incentives. Ever heard of it? Primatin, for short. Excellent stimulant. Do you take it?"

"I'm not that old yet," Tulin said. "But you're no good without it, eh?"

Petrusha tittered. Tulin's gibes seemed to bounce off him but he remembered them all and forgave nothing. He was goading Tulin on with his cynicism.

"Aren't you afraid of getting caught out one day?" Tulin inquired.

Petrusha eyed him as if he were a child.

"Only experimenters make mistakes. I never experiment. It doesn't pay."

"The perfect businessman," said Tulin.

Petrusha took a slice of lemon delicately between two fingers.

"You're out of touch with real life. That's bad. Money's a fact, it's the measure of what a man has done for our society." It was like someone talking to his dog or cat. Even the questions required no answer. "To each according to his work, and from each—how?"

"According to his ability," Simochka called out cheerfully.

"Quite right."

"You're turning everything upside down. Money, money! You think like they do in the West," Krylov said.

Petrusha looked at him seriously, and to Krylov it again seemed that behind those thick lenses a gleam of sadness showed itself for an instant only to dissolve in a mocking grin.

"Why in the West? If you've got money you can do just as well for yourself here as there. Consumer goods production is rising steadily."

"Yes, life is getting better and better," Voznitsyn chimed in happily. "There's no comparison. . . ."

"Happiness doesn't lie in money, it lies in the difficulties of struggle for a bright future," Petrusha said. "Take my difficulties and give me your salary."

"Come off it. Surely you haven't sunk that low," said Krylov.

"He was always that low," Tulin said. "He was always a fop. All he can do in life is feed his face, buy clothes and earn money on the side."

Petrusha sucked his lemon.

"How crude! Why have you got it in for me like this? Because I'm frank? Are you trying to get at me on ideological grounds? You were always so vigilant, Oleg. It was you who hauled me over the coals for being keen on jazz instead of devoting every minute of my time to science."

"Yes, of course, you used to play the trumpet!" Krylov exclaimed, remembering Petrusha at college.

"You, Oleg, as we all know, are an exceptional individual. You don't need money, all you need is fame. And when you're famous, the rest follows naturally. You don't need your own car, you'll be satisfied with the one the government supplies. But I no longer play the trumpet. You re-educated me. I've become like everybody else, just a rank-and-file toiler. Incidentally, how much do you earn? Three times as much as I do, I expect? That's why your life is three times as good as mine." He winked at Ada. "And four times as good as yours. That's why Oleg can afford higher ideals. His pangs of creation are not for us. We'll be quite content to knock up a few more rubles in our humdrum way."

"You great lump of puppy fat," Tulin said. "You're growing up! You've become a philosopher."

Krylov had been watching Petrusha for some time with a thought in the back of his mind. Suddenly it came out:

"I suppose you're sorry you gave up playing the trumpet. That was what you really were cut out for, wasn't it?"

Petrusha turned to him with a reply on his lips, but swallowed it and laughed maliciously.

"You're all so good and exemplary! It gives me the creeps. Particularly you, Sergei. You always used to be a fishy-eyed idealist and you still are. Not an inch of progress. I wonder how they put up with you at the institute. When they kick you out, come and see me. I'll give you a job."

Ada lighted a cigarette clumsily and stubbed it out at once.

"Now push off," said Tulin.

Petrusha put down the chewed rind of lemon.

"It wasn't a very satisfactory discussion. I apologise for my intrusion." He stood up. "If you want my advice, take Primatin.

Wonderful stuff, specially for family men." He thrust his hands
into his pockets and, chinking some coins, strolled back to his table.

Simochka was the first to giggle. The others followed suit. Krylov
also laughed without knowing why. They suddenly felt very young
and very hungry and fell upon their now cold shashlyks. "What a
specimen!" Voznitsyn kept repeating. He took a delight in everything.
It was a pleasure to watch him. Even his shashlyk was the best
imaginable. Tulin's subject held the finest prospects. Petrusha was an
outlandish phenomenon, completely untypical, recognised as such
and doomed to extinction.

"Sergei," said Ada. "What actually has happened to you?"

"To me? Nothing."

Tulin eyed him keenly.

"Wipe your nose. Your nose perspires when you're lying."

"Can't you give it a rest?" Krylov said. "If you must know, I
had a bit of a row with Golitsyn. What about it?"

"Ah, so you had a bit of a row!" said Tulin. "Your Golitsyn is
a skeleton strangling young talent. He's a backwoodsman, a legacy
of the personality cult."

"Worse still, he's unjust," Krylov added fiercely, and everyone
laughed as though he had said something foolish.

"That's right, pile it on, old chap. It's not enough for me to be
praised by my friends. I want you to curse my enemies. But"—
Tulin lifted the skewer of his shashlyk—"but you, Sergei, from now
on must be as nice as pie to Golitsyn, because he will be monitoring
our flights, and you must see to it that he passes that job on to you."

As Tulin expounded his subtle plans Krylov became even more
gloomy. Finally he had to speak.

"It can't be done. The point is that...." His mouth went dry
and he took a gulp of wine. "Well, I've left the institute."

"I felt there was something," said Ada.

They made him tell the whole story. He was cheered by their
attention. Why shouldn't he tell them? Why hang back? Nothing
terrible had happened. His conduct had been exemplary as far as
Tulin was concerned. He deserved praise, consolation, gratitude.
He had sacrificed himself in defence of a noble cause and was entitled
to all the honours of war.

Tulin ate his shashlyk in silence. When Krylov had finished his
story, he went on eating. He coated each piece of meat with mustard
and tore at it, as if it were living flesh. He was frightening to watch.
Ada and Simochka were quite subdued. Finally, Tulin wiped his
lips, tossed aside his napkin and began to examine Krylov's face.

He invited them all to admire this pink-cheeked idiot, floundering in ecstasies of self-pity. Like an exhibition guide, he drew their attention to the various interesting features of this extremely rare example of the human obtuseness.

"Look at him! He's waiting for us to fling ourselves on his neck, for the women to burst into tears and the men to wring his hand warmly. So that's why it was Agatov who came with the report. Who asked you to brandish your wretched principles?" he roared. "You ought to have brought it yourself instead of striking an attitude. What a bloody mess you've made of everything!" Tulin clutched his head in fury. "We'd have handled Yuzhin quite differently. I was hoping that you in your little hen-coop would be able to give me some protection. Now you've ruined everything. You obliging fool, you village idiot!" Only the presence of the women restrained him.

Ada attempted to intercede. If Krylov didn't share Golitsyn's views, it was obviously his duty to say so. Surely everyone had the right. . . .

She might have expressed what Krylov really felt, but Tulin didn't let her finish. With savage thrusts he tore her arguments to shreds.

"Utter twaddle! What principles has he got! Principles are judged by what is achieved, not by good intentions. Any cat can make a mess in a corner, but a man ought to be able to do better! This sleep-walker has always been the same. He always has to be more righteous than anyone else. You know that, Ada, better than we do. Oh, how noble of him to sacrifice everything for my sake! But I don't want it. I don't want your sacrifices or your services."

"I didn't do it for your sake," Krylov said.

The words brought Tulin up short against something hard and unyielding. It was not the first time something Krylov had said had done this to him and, as always, it ministered to his wrath.

"So you did it for yourself? You do everything for yourself. Life has taught you nothing. You left Dan in the same way, with your nose in the air." He was choosing the sorest spots he could find. "What's the use of your heroics? You only upset other people's affairs."

While he lambasted Krylov without mercy, Krylov heard Simochka's voice saying he shouldn't take it to heart. The unexpected tenderness made him raise his eyes and he saw that she was stroking Tulin's arm.

Ada said: "You wouldn't listen to me, would you? Now where will you go?"

Her mat white skin made her face look as cold as a marble statue in the Hermitage Museum. Where would he go now? What did it matter? Why should she be interested in something of so little importance? He realised with surprise that he wouldn't have to go to the institute tomorrow. Nor the next day either. And the flux-meters would stand there awaiting adjustment.

"Now listen to me. You've got to make it up with Golitsyn," Tulin said in a tone that brooked no refusal.

"For the sake of the cause," Voznitsyn chirped in support. "Why make things awkward for yourself?"

"No," Krylov said. "I can't do it."

"Disown me, tell Golitsyn you've changed your mind about me," Tulin went on. "Agatov is a swine and there's no sense in pulling our punches...."

"Golitsyn thinks the world of you," Voznitsyn took up the theme. "Conflicts are out of place in this day and age. We're all working for a common cause." It was good to see a man who solved every problem so easily.

Krylov tried to return his smile.

"I can't do it."

"Well, you're a swine!" Tulin said. "How can you call yourself my friend after that?"

Krylov smiled guiltily. He had not attempted to defend himself. He had humbly accepted Tulin's punishment, but after every blow he had popped up again like a Jumping Jack, with the same guilty smile, as though apologising because Tulin would have to knock him down again; and this made Tulin even more angry, though at bottom he acknowledged Krylov's tenacity. The others couldn't appreciate this dogged self-effacing courage. But Tulin knew there had been a hard core in his friend's character in the old days, and now he felt that its weight had increased.

"What will you get out of leaving?" he said. "You're simply being selfish. You're leaving the road open to dregs like Agatov. My God, how you've let me down!"

Krylov wondered whether he wasn't really being selfish, both towards Tulin and Bochkaryov, and to the others as well. Nothing would have been easier than to go back to Golitsyn. The old chap would be glad, they would agree they had both been hasty and every-one would be happy, Tulin included.

"No," he said. "I'm not being stubborn. How can I go back to Golitsyn if I don't agree with him, and if you, Oleg, don't agree with him either? Disown you? But I'm not looking at it just from your point of view. It would mean disowning myself. If I have convictions I ought to stand by them. And if I can't do that, it's better to get out than compromise. It won't be easy for me either; I was just beginning to make some progress with my own work...." He remembered Pesetsky, the equation, the spectroradiometer he had ordered. He thought of all the reasons why he had joined Golitsyn and the task he had set himself, the fact that he had reached the key stage in it after two years of persistent effort. "I've got to leave. There's no alternative. To mean something to others we've got to mean something to ourselves. . . ." He lost the thread of what he was trying to say, but it no longer seemed to matter.

There was a long and painful silence. He smiled awkwardly but no one smiled back.

The ice-cream was served.

Voznitsyn began to talk about a typhoon in the Caspian. Ada expressed indignation that such things were never reported in the newspapers, to which Voznitsyn replied that surely there was no point in alarming the public without reason.

Krylov obediently ate his ice-cream. He hated the stuff. Why was he here? What was it all for, this ice-cream, this chatter? He realised his gloom was weighing on the others. Yes, he always managed to be too serious, too long. It occurred to him that he had never been able to refuse Tulin anything. Now he had refused, although he had already done him a bad turn and there was no telling how it would all end. The thing he could not understand was why he felt no remorse; he merely felt ashamed to be upsetting people who were his friends.

The streets were bright with neon signs urging the population to eat ice-cream, to keep their money in the state savings bank and to call the fire brigade in the event of fire.

"Why don't you come back to our factory in Leningrad?" Ada asked him.

Why not, he asked himself. Why not accept Petrusha's offer? Why not go back to Anikeyev?

"Sergei," Ada said, and he prepared himself to listen to yet another of her plans for regulating his future. But instead, she said: "You did absolutely the right thing. Don't take any notice of what the others say."

It was exactly what he had so much wanted to hear, but now that she had said it, it seemed to fall flat.

"Thanks," he said.

"One day you'll realise that no one ever had the feeling for you that I have."

He knew that, but what did it add up to?

"I've taken a lot of risks because I've always told you the truth. There are others I needn't be so honest to. Or there will be. I'm not going to sit and wait for you like Solveig. You wouldn't want that anyway. But you still don't know what you do want."

She had a knack of always making him appear more noble than he actually was. She was probably glad this had happened to him. At least she could be sorry for him. Why not marry her? She was beautiful, she loved him, and she would never let him do anything rash or ill-considered. He could go back to the factory, go back to Golitsyn, go back to her.... So many sensible paths lay open to him.

"Thank you," he said, with all the gratitude he could muster.

That "thank you" was about the silliest thing he could have thought of. He felt sorry for Ada. Why did he have to disappoint the people who loved him? There were so few of them and he never brought them anything but trouble.

He kissed her carefully on the cheek, trying not to disarrange her hair or crumple her immaculate white collar.

"Would you like me to marry you?"

How easy and pleasant everything would be? She would make him do physical jerks in the morning. He had started that so many times and given it up. She would make him have cold rub-downs and take regular German lessons. They would both become exceedingly proficient in German.

"Would you like me to?"

"Why do you dislike me so much?" she said. "I know you're in trouble at the moment, but you shouldn't be like this. It's not fair."

At that moment he felt that if she had agreed he would have married her without a second thought. He was sorry for her and he would marry her and live with her. At least he would be making one person happy.

Tulin and Voznitsyn were waiting for them at the corner of the street.

"An idea!" Tulin shouted before they were anywhere near him. "I've got an idea! Down on your knees! I'm going to forgive you after all. I take you on! In my group! Just like that! Come on, you old fish. Since you've forced yourself on me, I accept you, damn it. Listen. you women! The two of us together will move heaven and earth!"

With sweeping strokes he drew a picture of their immediate future, and the work that would await them after that, when his group became the Institute of Atmospheric Electricity, and after that, when it became the Academy of Active Intervention.

He squeezed out the clouds, as though they were so much wet washing. The rain fell as and where he commanded. Plentiful, life-giving showers watered the deserts. He turned on clouds as he would the bathroom taps. Droughts and crop failures were effaced from human memory. He brandished sheaves of lightning. O lightning! O thunder! Mysterious concentration of energy that dwarfs the power of atomic plants. Why, a single thunderstorm dissipated as much energy as a hydrogen bomb. And how many thunderstorms rumbled around the globe every day, every hour, every minute! And had been doing so for millions of years! Why did humanity burrow so painfully into the nucleus when here it was, this untamed force, flashing and booming above their heads, only a mile or so away. We will pluck it from the skies, we will use it to blast mountains, to dissolve the rocks. . . . We . . . we . . . we. . . .

Why hadn't they got a tape-recorder with them. His speech should have been relayed round the globe, printed, carved on slabs of granite, learned by heart in the schools. It was delivered at midnight outside the baker's on the corner of Volkhonka Street.

Krylov echoed the applause, but instead of hugging Tulin and giving his assent, he muttered something inaudible and everyone decided that he was hopeless.

"You're a braggart, Oleg," Ada said. "A braggart and a dreamer. We can't even get proper air conditioning installed at the factory and you muddle Sergei's head with fairy-tales. He ought to go back to the factory. That's where he belongs, where he can do something of real use. Your schemes are really just pie in the sky."

They began to argue. Simochka defended Tulin—he could do anything if he tried. He could do everything he had told them about.

On the empty open-air stage in front of the old Manège Building a few couples were dancing to a transistor.

Krylov recognised Richard and Zhenya Kuzmenko, a final-year student, and walked over to them. The transistor was in Richard's pocket and as they circled round the stage the music swelled and died away.

"Tulin's here," Krylov called to him.

Richard nodded back and got out of step. Zhenya asked: "Who's Tulin?"

"The man of the age," Richard replied. "Come along and I'll introduce you."

"What, another genius? No more!" Zhenya refused to turn her head. "Aren't you going to dance?"

And they went spinning round again.

They turned off Gorky Street down side-lanes where among the great new cream-coloured blocks little wooden houses still survived, with their small fenced gardens where rows of lettuce sprouted and hammocks were slung between trees and in the daytime butterflies and bumble-bees winged to and fro.

"Yes, I can do anything," Tulin was saying. "Shall I tell you, my dear Ada, the secret of becoming all-powerful? It's quite simple really. You merely have to become stronger than yourself, overcome your own weaknesses. The man who is stronger than himself is stronger than other people, which means he is stronger than circumstances. You want to make Sergei weak. I want to do the opposite."

"You would like him as your shield-bearer, I'm sure."

They were all concerned about Krylov, they all wanted to help him. Now that they had forgiven him for what he had done they were indignant and annoyed that he seemed almost totally unmoved by their efforts on his behalf.

Krylov thought Tulin would come round for him in the morning but Tulin arrived shortly after he got home that night.

"Victim of my own virtue," he explained. "No one came to meet me and no one will see me off. Such is the fate of those who lead the way. They are always lone, misunderstood figures. They may be admired, but they're hard to love." And at last without flourishes he asked thoughtfully: "What is morality? The instinct of self-preservation? Education? Courage? What stops you from going back to Golitsyn? It must be that girl in the ski suit. Why did you choose her? We're a lot of fools; one can no more choose a wife than one can choose one's parents. Science has turned us into rationalists. Why didn't I sock Petrusha? Why am I wasting my time on you? If I could gain complete power over myself I should have power over everyone."

"What do you want it for?" Krylov asked.

"Believe me, I'd make this world a more rational place. For a start I'd make you come with me. No, I've got to be stronger and more ruthless. Let's start by having you sleep on the floor."

Tulin left Moscow two days later without obtaining any definite answer from Krylov.

There was something that Krylov had to make up his mind about once and for all. When he had collected his papers at the institute he walked to Teatralny Proyezd and stopped at the window of the railway booking office. The train he needed was due to leave at seven. He looked at his watch; he had forty minutes. He got into a taxi and, without going home to change, drove straight to the station.

Chapter Ten

All the houses were the same, block after block of smart new flats with brightly painted balconies. He had walked home with Natasha only once, on a winter evening. They were standing outside the front door when she quite unexpectedly asked him in for tea. She suggested it just like that—wouldn't he come in? She would introduce him to her husband, show him her son. Ignoring his protests, she tugged persistently at his sleeve.

"Do you mean what you're saying?" he asked her.

She looked up at him with round, innocent eyes. What was so unusual about it? Her husband was very fond of guests.

"Anything else your husband is fond of?"

Her pretence maddened him. How could she imagine that he would be able to join her at table with her husband, making conversation and looking him in the face? Even if such a thing did happen, it would mean the end of everything between them. Why should she want this? But if he had told her that, she would immediately have wanted to know what it would be the end of? And he would have had no answer.

As he walked home he suddenly realised what her reasons had been. She had wanted him to go in with her and make everything into just an ordinary friendship. It had been her only chance of resistance, her last stand.

It was summer now and the street was unrecognisable. The grass was long and thick in the squares. Plump pigeons were waddling about the sticky asphalt. Only the dusty packets of coffee in the shop windows had not changed.

It was strange how he sensed that this house, and no other, was hers. What was it that made him turn in with such certainty under this high archway? In the list of tenants his eyes picked out the name: "Romanov, A.V." At least his memory, his sole companion on this journey into the past, was doing its best.

He sat down on a bench that faced the front door. The window-panes were fluid and opaque in the dazzling sun. Some of the windows were open and the curtains were fluttering. One of those windows was hers. Any moment she might look out and see him. Or the front door might open and she would appear, blinking in the sunlight and leading her little son by the hand. She wouldn't notice him, of course, and he would follow her down the street. They would walk on like this, and he would be conscious only of her hair, the nape of her neck, her shoulders swaying before him, only a few paces away.

Some little boys were playing with a puppy. They had pulled a paper hat over its head. The puppy broke free and ran to Krylov's feet, barked and dashed on. The women on the next bench looked at Krylov and began to whisper. He pulled out his notebook. It contained all kinds of entries. Some of them made him wince—so many good intentions that had never been fulfilled, so many profound observations that would never be of any use.

"Plasma—ball lightning. *Electrical World* No. 14."

"Interesting to check effects of hypnosis if hypnotist is enclosed by strong electrical field."

"Read up on melting ice in Sanin."

How quickly a man accumulated unfulfilled ideas, only to drag them about with him all his life.

"Man has no electrical organs, he has muscles. Hence he tries to reduce everything to mechanics. The electric-ray fish would probably have a different approach."

He wondered how an electric ray would have acted in his place. Doubtful whether it would have sat here reading its notebook.

The sun beat down on the crown of his head. He leaned back and began examining the windows. Suddenly he realised it was Sunday. He had been aware of this before but only now did it occur to him that it was Sunday and she might be out of town for the day. Or perhaps she was on holiday in the country? He jumped up and entered the front door. Flat No. 11 turned out to be on the top floor. He rang the bell. There was a buzz somewhere in the depths of the flat. He longed to run away or go up to the attic landing and watch from there to see who opened the door. He glanced round. Two old ladies were taking their time mounting the stairs.

Muffled footsteps were approaching the door. He must ask for somebody of a different name. He tried frantically to think of a name, any name.

The door opened. Before him stood a tall dishevelled man in pyjamas and barefooted. His eyes were bleared and expressionless.

"You're too early, but it doesn't matter," he said.

"Excuse me, but is there a..." Krylov began but the man interrupted him.

"Yes, that's me. Alexei Romanov. Oh, come in!" Irritably he dragged Krylov inside and slammed the door. "And shut up, for God's sake. My head's splitting and I shan't hear you anyway. Have a look first, then tell me what you think."

He led Krylov down a corridor of closed doors into a large room with a wide bay window. The floor was littered with fag-ends. There was a pile of canvases and picture frames propped against the wall. The air was stale. There was a dirty bed-pillow on the couch. A plate of brownish pies stood on the paint-stained table among the crowded bottles.

"Sit down and keep your back to the light," Romanov ordered. "Want any liquor? No? To hell with you then."

He grabbed the nearest picture and put it on the easel.

Krylov listened attentively; there were no other sounds in the flat. What a situation, he thought. But why worry?

"Can you see properly?" Romanov asked. "Move your chair. Bit more. Now, look."

He waited a minute, then removed the picture and replaced it with another.

"Pull back the curtain! That's not enough. Oh, get a move on, man!" He shouted his instructions, scarcely glancing at Krylov. His gaze remained dull and indifferent and the movements with which he changed the pictures were mechanical.

Krylov obediently shifted his position, and moved his head, wondering all the time if Natasha was in the next room.

"Well?" Romanov asked.

"Very interesting," Krylov said loudly. "What kind of lathe is that?"

"Don't shout. What does the lathe matter? Let's call it a planing lathe. That do you? The point was to show a chunk of metal obedient to man, the contrast between cold steel and the human hand."

While he explained the picture with a frown of condescension, Krylov scanned the room for traces of Natasha, the faintest sign of her presence, some small thing connected with her.

"You like this one, do you?" Romanov asked impatiently. "I'll put it aside. Have you any notion of what painting is about?"

Krylov forced himself to attend, asked questions, nodded, gave the required answers.

An engine-driver, grimy-faced, white-toothed, standing by his locomotive. The locomotive was very well painted, just like a real one; the driver looked handsome and powerful to match.

Power Dam Builders. A gang of building workers striding across a dam, all of them stalwart and white-toothed—and as human as the reinforced concrete on which they walked.

The door was half open but no sound came from the corridor.

Steelmakers with the light falling just nicely for them. Again they were powerful, smiling figures, but not people, just feelingless robots. How many soulless pictures like these had Krylov seen in hotels, holiday homes and cinema lobbies.

"Amazing," he said. "Are these all your own ideas?"

"Well, there's what God sent me as well," Romanov replied. "This one was done from life. So was the dam." He yawned. "The thing is to achieve a correct balance between form and light. Here you've got an optimistic combination. . . ."

"Quite right," Krylov echoed. "There's the right form for every colour and the right colour for every form."

Something like a sneer animated Romanov's face for a moment. "Priceless! If other people's hogwash could make you any wiser I'd talk to you every day."

His pictures could not be described as coloured photographs. They were what are known in artistic circles as "faithfuls"—cold, uninteresting, yet executed with a skill and nicety of calculation that made them quite invulnerable.

Krylov waited. Why worry, when there was nothing to lose? But it was an odd situation, and not one that was easy to think a way out of. He must play for time. Surely she would have heard his voice.

Romanov placed on the easel a large canvas portraying part of a huge workshop. Several men were grouped round a marking table, examining some drawings. In the centre stood a dignified patriarchal figure, the refracted sunlight shimmering on the long grey hair that flowed from under his black skullcap. Grey masses of metal, a travelling crane, sheaves of sunlight dramatically slanting down through the smoky air. Each figure had its particular role. One was smiling, another was arguing, a third was deep in thought. Everything was correct. But who was this all addressed to? Why had so much time and paint been spent? It was one of those pictures that were praised for their subject but which evoked no emotion, pleasure or sense of discovery. Posters were better. At least their message was clear. Krylov remembered a photographer from the magazine *Smena* who had once come to the factory where he had worked. He had spent a long time arranging the various members of the team, thinking up a special pose for each of them, straightening their collars and so on, then he had said: "Now, please, talk as much as you like and look relaxed, but don't move."

The young men in this picture, too, had been ordered not to move. Krylov would have liked to tell Romanov exactly what he thought of it but time was short. He strained his ears and waited. At any moment now the door might open and Natasha might walk in. He longed for some sound denoting her presence.

"I'm sorry I'm not an expert," he said.

"I can see that. Still even a layman can be interesting. It won't do me any harm to listen. Do you realise who these people are?"

"Oh, yes," Krylov replied. "That must be the foreman. He's got a slide gauge sticking out of his pocket."

"Quite correct," Romanov encouraged him with a trace of mockery. Krylov looked at him with attention.

"That's a wonderful touch, a real discovery," he continued, watching Romanov. "And the man in the centre must be an Academician.

All Academicians wear skullcaps. But perhaps he's only a Corresponding Member. No, he has too much grey hair for a Corresponding Member."

"You've got it. A picture executed in silvery, optimistic tones. Can you remember that?" Romanov's face wore an expression of bored contempt and Krylov realised the artist must consider him an idiot.

"I've got a feeling I've seen it all before."

"What?"

"There's an impression that you're always adjusting yourself to the subject of the day."

"You can keep your impressions to yourself. Theme! Subject! That's not the right approach to painting. Incidentally, this particular subject—co-operation between Academy and factory—has never been put on a large canvas before. Any number of subjects have been painted. Think of all the pictures of Christ being taken from the cross, yet the great masters went on painting. The Virgin and child—hundreds of masterpieces. So what?" Romanov was not defending himself, he was merely handing out casual instruction. "The whole point, my dear chap, is *how* the job's done."

"Exactly! It's wrong to speculate on something like this."

Romanov's eyebrows rose slowly. He seemed to be waking up and the blue rims under his eyes looked almost like eye-shadow.

"What do you mean by that?"

"Can't you see what I mean?" Krylov said, blushing slightly.

He felt no triumph, only disappointment. Nothing irritated him more than work that was wasted.

He felt ashamed of Romanov, of all this useless hack work. He, Krylov, had left the institute but his research was being continued by Pesetsky. If Pesetsky didn't finish it, someone else would, because this was something that people needed. Mentally he thanked his dedication to his work. When he began an experiment he had never considered whether Golitsyn would like the results; he had been interested in the truth, not in opinion. Opinion was subordinate to the truth.

"But what exactly do you mean?" Romanov asked.

"Your pictures are just coloured patterns," Krylov said unwillingly. "They're robots."

"Oho, what daring! What spirit! So you actually have an opinion of your own? How brave of you!"

"Drop that stuff. I don't know who you take me for. . . ."

"For an ignoramus," Romanov calmly interrupted him. "What else? How can you judge painting? What do you know about chiaroscuro, about brushwork, about the rhythm of colours?" He scratched his leg. He was defending his pictures not because he considered them good but because no one but himself was qualified to judge them.

"Some people think they're very clever nowadays. But I'm well enough known. Look what *Red Banner* said about my *Co-operation*. See how Goloshchekin appreciates *Power Dam Builders*." He flung down in front of Krylov newspapers, magazines, albums of review clippings, and exhibition catalogues.

"Here are some reproductions, and here are some more! Doesn't that mean I was good? I suited everybody! But what has changed? Don't I paint as well now? What do you all expect of me?" His accumulated irritation broke through at last. "Now one thing's wrong, now another. No one can give you any proper instructions."

So you've got used to it, have you? You're used to being told what you may and may not do, Krylov thought to himself.

He wanted to tell Romanov so but amid the pile of papers he noticed several old sketches and water-colours. They looked like the work of a different artist. They had character of their own; they were daring, uninhibited. Campfires by the river, homeless urchins listening to a Cheka man. Budyonny's cavalry with sabres drawn. Red Army men patrolling the streets at night. Long-legged youngsters running towards an aeroplane.

"I was just playing about then, I was young." Romanov snatched the drawings away crossly, but there was a note of warmth in his voice.

So there had been a spark in him once, the ability to create. But he had begun to hurry, and on top of that, fame, money.... No, if he had been weak, it meant he had no talent. Talent was always strength. A talented man might go down under a rain of blows, but they wouldn't stop him. Even if he had to crawl forward on his hands and knees to accomplish what he had set out to do, he would do it.

Something showed for an instant in the crack of the half-open door.

"Is there somebody in the corridor?" Krylov said.

Romanov gave a start and they both listened for a moment.

"Nonsense," Romanov said. "There's nobody here. Only the cat."

"Oh, I see. I'm sorry, I must have been mistaken." Krylov rose to his feet. "Excuse me, but I must go."

"Oh no, we haven't finished our business yet. You mean you won't take anything? It may not matter a damn to me, but at least you've got to explain. I'm curious, you know." His dry lips twisted in a forced sneer. "So you think I'm a hack? Or a modernist? What am I supposed to understand by the term 'coloured patterns'? Mere abuse? Abuse is no argument. Spit and run, eh? That's not very civilised."

"You paint pictures of people you don't like," Krylov said. "You have no feeling for them, so I get no feeling for them either. You pretend to be sincere. But it's not so easy to disguise oneself these days. Anything false shows up as it never did before. For you these workers aren't people. They're just a fashionable subject. It's just calculation, arithmetic. . . ."

Romanov listened to him with half-closed eyes, turning his head away a little.

"Yes," there is calculation. I paint for the people, I do that deliberately," he replied. "And the people need something simple."

That particular phrase made Krylov furious.

"Who are the people? Do you consider me one of the people? Aren't I one of them? You look down on the people, don't you?"

"All right, don't shout," Romanov interrupted him impatiently. "Just go on and tell me what you expect of a painting."

"A painting is. . . . Well, it's. . . ." Krylov hesitated. "It's like a discovery, an invention. It can't be just repetition! To hell with your range of colours. You used to paint as if you were painting for yourself. . . . Can you paint like that now?" And he pointed to the sketches Romanov had put aside.

Romanov suddenly became wide awake. His face twisted with pain.

"But this is nonsense!" he shouted. "Paint for myself! That's ridiculous." He made a histrionic gesture. "Who wants to know what goes on inside me? What's that worth to anyone? What do you live on? You get a salary, don't you? That's why you sing this tune. But I've got a family. I mean. . . . Damn it all, that's not the point! Why the devil should I take risks? Paint for myself? No, I haven't time to play around. I work for the consumer."

Something inside him seemed to have broken loose. He gripped Krylov by the shoulders and talked and talked, breathing fumes of alcohol into his face. His bleared, moist eyes stared unseeingly. Suddenly he stepped back and, after a pause, asked uncertainly:

"So you think I've no ability left? All right, you can be frank. For once at least I've got to know. . . . Since I have such a lover of truth on my hands. You needn't be scared, I won't complain. To hell with your Palace of Culture."

"What Palace of Culture?" Krylov asked impatiently. The misunderstanding had already gone on much too long. "I'm not from any Palace of Culture."

"Well, it doesn't matter. Wait a minute. Let's have a drink first."

Romanov darted to the table and deftly poured out two glasses.

"Excellent brandy. Nothing to eat, I'm afraid, except yesterday's pies. I've been reduced to this wretched state by domestic conflict. I suppose you've heard about it?"

He was standing with his back to Krylov. His oval shoulder blades moved vigorously under the blue striped pyjamas. His broad back was all blue, round and shiny.

"What do you mean? No, I haven't heard."

Krylov waited tensely. Romanov turned round and held out a glass. Krylov gulped down the brandy eagerly, as if it were water. He could have drunk any amount just then.

"No, I haven't heard anything," he repeated. If only he had known how to be subtle and cautious.

Romanov held the brandy up to the light, examining it with half-closed eyes. He drank, wiped his mouth and began pacing about the room.

"What you said about me was pretty harsh. I don't often hear things like that. But, for your information, I can be even harsher myself. You see, I understand everything. That's the horror of it." He was speaking half to himself. "All my life I've been telling myself that one day. . . . There doesn't seem to be anyone to fight. Only now and then. . . ." Suddenly he put the question point-blank. "What do you think of me? Have I any ability or not?" The ironic smile that he tried to produce died on his face and he stared fixedly at Krylov.

"It's your own fault," Krylov said, with a sympathy that he had not expected to feel. "Sometimes a man is afraid before he's done anything. He feels beaten not because he took a risk but because he refused to do so. Why don't you try?"

Romanov's bare feet padded restlessly to and fro.

"Perhaps I've already tried. How would you know? No one knows anything. The closest of friends live on different planets. Shall I show it to you?"

"What?"

"Just something I did for my own amusement." Every trace of his indifference and aloofness had vanished. He went over to an easel in the corner which was draped with a grey sheet.

"It's here," he muttered, and with an imploring look at Krylov removed the sheet.

Krylov took a pace forward, then stepped back, groping for his chair. He failed to find it and remained in the middle of the room.

Looking at him from a crude blue background was Natasha. Her huge eyes surveyed Krylov in surprise, unable to comprehend why he was here. He could see she was thinking about him. The grey sweater he knew so well was blue, yet it looked grey just the same, and the dark lips.... One hand was resting firmly on the shoulder of a small boy standing by her knee. The arm was unnaturally long and the eyes impossibly large. Only now did he notice the lack of proportion.

Just as he was thinking this, Romanov's voice cut in worriedly: "What did you say?"

Krylov forced himself to turn round. And suddenly, for the first time, Natasha seemed to fit in with the big, handsome man to whom this flat belonged. They lived here together. It was she who washed these plates. Krylov noticed the bright striped pyjamas. The soft curly hair. The hair on his chest. The reddish fuzz round those weak lips. And if he could paint her like this, he must love her.

Krylov tried to avert his eyes but Romanov was looking straight into his face.

"Does it have such an effect? Well, what do you say now? Can I do it? I know I can. And you know it, too, don't you?" His feverish excitement kept him darting about the studio. Now he was boasting, now muttering incoherently and touching Krylov's hand ingratiatingly, almost with affection.

The whole situation was unpleasant and embarrassing. Krylov felt he ought to go, but he couldn't get away. He had no idea whether the picture was good or bad. Probably it was good, although it was unfinished and the lower half of the canvas was just a mess.

He felt Romanov tugging at his sleeve impatiently. He wanted to get rid of him and be left to himself, so that he could think. So this was their meeting! He should never have come. It had been a silly idea from beginning to end.

"Yes, it's her," Krylov said huskily, but firmly. "Now I understand...."

Romanov squeezed his hand gratefully.

"You're the first person I've shown it to. What about the background? Good, isn't it? Such an unyielding colour." Again he was muttering like a madman. "And that forehead? Did it with a single stroke. It's the combination that counts. And what an arm! I'll paint a little more red into her eyes. Doesn't that arm worry you? If only I could finish it. I've thought of something else, a lot of things...."

His slim dirty fingers scampered over the canvas, touching Natasha's belly and legs. Even while he explained how he would treat the rest of the picture he seized a brush and tube of paint.

"Don't touch it," Krylov said.

Romanov stared at him unhearingly. The brush dropped from his hand. He splayed his fingers and stared at them.

"My hands shake," he said quietly. "I haven't been able to work for a week. My hands shake and I can't do anything."

"You shouldn't drink."

Romanov shook his head.

"It's not that. I'm afraid. Suppose I'm criticised. All kinds of charges may be levelled at me. I'm worse than any critics myself. I know them. I've thought out everything they may say beforehand. They probably won't say it, but I'm safeguarding myself just the same. Because I'm afraid. Everything must be properly balanced, well turned out. And now I want to make this properly balanced too. But it won't work, I know. D'you think I can't see I'm beginning to spoil it? When she left me I was so cut up about it that I just flung myself into painting this portrait, not thinking about anything else, but then I realised what I was doing. And now all this time. . . ."

"She's left you? Why? How?"

"Yes, she's left me. And taken the boy with her. And all this time. . . ." Romanov stopped speaking and stared suspiciously at Krylov, as though someone had scraped the bleary film from his eyes. His cheeks slowly became hollow. Paint began to ooze from the tube he was holding. The pretty bright-yellow caterpillar that had crawled from the mouth of the tube dangled for a moment, growing longer and longer, then plopped to the floor.

"So it's you?"

Krylov nodded.

As though to defend himself, Romanov flung the tube of paint at Krylov. It missed and he grabbed a stool. Krylov didn't move. Romanov toyed with the stool for a moment, then closed his eyes and threw it. It struck Krylov painfully on the knee.

Romanov sat down on the couch, pressed his hands to his temples and rocked to and fro. It was all so cheap and theatrical. Krylov wondered how they would get themselves out of this sentimental orgy. What a situation! But why worry? All he wanted to know was where to find Natasha.

"Now we know each other," he said.

Romanov raised his head.

"I'm sorry. It's my nerves." He fingered the empty bottle. "I thought you were from the Palace of Culture. How ridiculous!"

"I told you I wasn't," Krylov said. "You weren't listening."

Romanov gave a nervous shiver.

"But this is even more interesting. So you're the man!" He surveyed Krylov disparagingly. "What on earth did she see in you,

I wonder. Face as plain as a pancake. No wonder I took you for a club manager.... What a situation!"

Romanov used the very phrase that had occurred to Krylov and Krylov almost laughed in surprise. The phrase provided a link between them.

"What did you come here for? To share out the family property?" Romanov was using all the sarcasm at his command.

"Where is she now?"

"Oh, you don't know? Wonderful!" Romanov lounged back on the couch and hooked one leg over the other. "Congratulations. So there's someone else besides us. A jilted husband is a pitiful sight, isn't he? I can't work because of her. Have you ever been jilted by a woman? Most unpleasant!" He tried the cynical pose, but it was no use. "I can't work, and unless I can work I'm finished. The bitch! She's knocked the last prop from under me." He began to moan, rocking from side to side. "What am I to do, Krylov? Give me your advice. I'm not ashamed to ask, you're so clever. This has broken up my family and you started it. It was you who put all these ideas into her head, all your scientific rubbish. You knew she was married and had a son. Had you no scruples? It was a low thing to do. You're a low scoundrel!"

Krylov asked himself what scruples he should have had. Was it unscrupulous to love? The flow of abuse made him feel wretched. Why should they hate each other? A moment ago they had been two men arguing about pictures and suddenly they had learned that they loved the same woman. Now they were enemies. They had to be. They forced themselves to be. As if enmity could help either of them.

"She'll come back, she'll come back," Romanov repeated wildly. "She won't stay with you. Did we have such a bad life? This is a new flat. Ah, help me! It's just a flash in the pan for you...."

A flash in the pan! How close he was to the truth. At the time it had seemed to be just that. There had seemed to be no reason why he shouldn't do a little flirting. The setting had been so conducive. At bottom he hadn't believed in his own feelings, or in hers either.

"All right, I agree. You love her," Romanov corrected himself. "But she's my whole life. I can't work without her. I don't want to go out of the house. I hate the sight of the sun. I hate everything." He buried his face in his hands and wept.

Krylov stepped away to the window.

I can't live without her and he can't live without her. What difference does it make whether he's a good artist or a bad one? It'll probably be worse for him because I've got my work.

His leg was hurting. He felt his knee and sat down on a chair. Romanov wiped his face hurriedly with his sleeve and ran up to him.

"Go and see her. Persuade her to come back. She'll listen to you. I accept any terms she likes to offer. Please help me, old chap. You're the only one who can."

Krylov turned away.

"Is it stupid of me to ask? I know it is. But I don't care. I'll agree to anything."

"All right," Krylov said. "Give me her address."

"Yes, just a minute." Romanov was dashing about the room again. "Do you promise? On your word of honour? You can have any picture you like. Just as a souvenir. I'll give it to you as a present."

He dragged on his socks, started looking for his shoes, suggested they should go and have a meal somewhere, take a look at the city. Then he paused.

"But I forgot," he exclaimed suddenly. "You don't like my pictures. And I was so frank! With you, of all people! What a bloody disgrace! Caught with my pants down! Well, now, at any rate, I can ask you whether I managed to express her character." He tried vainly to push his foot into his shoe without looking. "Perhaps it's a good thing you came after all. I'm sure now. The main thing is that I can. . . ."

"I haven't much time," Krylov said. "Give me her address and I'll go."

"Just as you like," Romanov agreed submissively. "As she isn't with you. . . . That's very strange, you know." He fiddled with the lace of his shoe and paused thoughtfully. "Women don't go away just like that, into nothing. A woman leaves one man for another. Of course, Natasha's different, she might have gone—" He stopped again and fixed his eyes on Krylov. "The way you look at her! Why, you must have come here. . . ." He flung the shoe away. "Oh, what a fool I am! You must have come here to take her away with you! And I, like an idiot, thought I could trust you. Oh, no!" He rubbed his hands triumphantly.

Krylov stepped out into the corridor. A pair of green cat's eyes gleamed in the half-light. He tried to open the door but couldn't find the hook. Romanov was behind him. Krylov could feel his breath on the back of his head.

On the landing Romanov suddenly gripped him by the jacket. His lips were twitching and his whole face was distorted.

"Want to buy the portrait? I'll let you have it cheap. For half a bottle and nothing else. It'll be a wedding present."

Krylov could never understand afterwards how he had found the strength; he was much the weaker of the two. But at that moment he squeezed Romanov's wrist with such force that the artist's fingers whitened and lost their grip.

Krylov's legs were trembling as he walked down the stairs, holding on to the banisters. He forced himself to walk out of the yard into the street. He stopped only when he reached the square and could lean against a news-stand.

Chapter Eleven

The buses to Ozernaya were packed.

Krylov got out at the circular road and stood on the corner for some time without moving. He was carrying a cardboard box with a cake in it for the Antonovs. There was a dent in the box and a coffee-coloured grease-spot had come through the cardboard.

The Antonovs' cottage was buried among acacia-bushes, and the tin weathercock on the roof was practically all that could be seen of it. Antonov had made that weathercock when he had come here as a young man, and it had been turning ever since, puffing out its rusty chest as if it commanded all the winds that blew.

As Krylov walked nearer, the garden shed came into sight. In winter the pinkish composition roof was crowned with a white pan-cake of snow. The March sun would eat into it and Krylov would stand at the window and watch it slowly disappearing. Just for the fun of it he had done a little research to find out to what extent the speed of melting depended on the discolouration of the snow. Not long ago he had been surprised to hear that some agrophysicists were interested in the paper he had written on the subject.

A little distance away the white screens of the meteorological station showed up brightly against the green meadow. He thought of the smile Antonov would give him concealing the loss of some of his front teeth with his hand, and how his wife would gasp and at once set about laying the table.

Krylov opened the gate quietly. A strange young woman was taking some washing off the line in the yard.

"The Antonovs?" she repeated in answer to his inquiry. "They moved long ago."

"How long?"

"About four months, I should think." That was a long time to her.

"Where did they move to?"

"Somewhere near Biisk. I think his wife has relatives there. They left their address. Are you one of the family?"

"I worked here in the winter. My name is Krylov." He looked at her with vague hopefulness.

"Mine's Valeria." She smiled coquettishly, revealing a metal denture. "I was sent here from Moscow. It's very provincial here, of course, after Moscow."

The window was wide open. Where the couch had once stood there was now an office desk and a typewriter with a cover over it. There was fresh blue paper on the walls. The yellow plush armchair that Natasha loved to sit in with her feet tucked under her was gone. So was the round mirror in its oak frame. From the kitchen came the sound of children's voices and laughter. No one knew about those who had spent a lifetime here. No one remembered them or had any time for them. The house retained no memories. With treacherous cordiality it was serving its new masters.

"Didn't the Antonovs leave anything behind besides their address?" he asked.

Valeria stared at him in perplexity.

He walked to the gate, then turned back and held out the cake-box. "Won't you take this? I expect you like sweet things?"

She clutched the washing in her bare arms and looked at him in confusion. Her nose was too large and her face in its frame of stiff black hair suddenly became painfully unattractive. She put out her hand and touched his quickly.

"But wouldn't you. . . . Wouldn't you like some tea?"

"No, thanks," Krylov said. "Don't bother. It's a chocolate cake. You'll like it."

There had once been a clearing between the birch-grove and the forest. They had made a snowman there and followed a ski trail down to the sledge road in the hollow.

With some difficulty he managed to find the clearing. Tall bushes of blossoming sweetbrier glowed scarlet on the edges. The shadows of birds flitted across the grass. The wind spilled light from the leaves. This world of sunlit green seemed to have banished that white stillness and that ski trail among the snow-drifts for ever.

What an ass he was to have thought that time existed only for himself. It existed for the Antonovs, for this forest, and for Natasha too. He had imagined he would find everything just as before, like the slumbering kindgom in the fairy-tale.

The birds were chirping and twittering to one another. Dry pine-needles rustled down. As Krylov listened he had a sudden panicky feeling that he could hear the stealthy retreating footsteps of Time itself.

No theories of relativity, no new systems or concepts of discrete time, none of the latest hypotheses of physics could help him. They were all powerless in the face of this simple fact of time, time that was measured by ordinary clocks, by the leaves of calendars and by the setting sun, time as relentless and primitive as it had been ever since the world began.

He came out on to the lake. The sandy beaches were in a roar, alive with human bodies. Beach balls were being thumped into the air. Varnished canoes plied to and fro and wet oars glistened in the sunshine where the figure of Natasha had once shown up darkly near a steaming hole in the ice. The Martian heads of skin-divers in their round face-masks kept popping up out of the water.

Krylov was seized by a cold, clear sense of desperation. At last he realised that he could never return to the winter that was gone. There was no time machine that could recall the past. He could go forward into the future; that was easy. But he didn't want the future; he was looking for the past.

"Comrade Krylov!" Valeria had just emerged from the water and was running towards him with the water sprinkling off her. "Comrade Krylov!" She halted in front of him. Her shoulders were glistening. Krylov said nothing. Valeria stepped closer to him. "What a good thing I saw you." She stared at him unsmilingly. "Are you alone? Won't you come and meet our party."

She tugged his sleeve. In the feeble shade of a striped awning Krylov sat down on the sand beside a fat man and a sunburnt blonde. They were playing cards.

Krylov took off his jacket and lay back on the hot sand. The blonde turned towards him, blocking his view of the lake.

"Want to play 'catch the fool'?" the fat man asked.

"What's the point, if you're an idiot already?" Krylov said.

"What are you implying?"

Krylov laughed. "Nothing, just a confession."

"Stop bragging," said the blonde. "Have you heard the story about the Jew at the seaside?"

Valeria looked at Krylov uneasily and began pulling on her clothes.

"Had the Antonovs gone before you arrived here?" Krylov asked.

"They were just packing up," Valeria replied.

"You don't know if somebody called Romanova came to see them?" He found it hard to pronounce the name.

"Natasha?" the blonde asked, displaying sudden interest.

"Yes."

"She's gone too."

"With them?"

"Of course not She was whisked away by a scientist who lived here in the winter. They had a terrific love-affair."

"Hooey!" said the fat man. "I bet she was chasing him herself."

"Nothing of the kind," the blonde said heatedly. "I was told the whole story. He came to fetch her in a car and lay in wait for her outside the house. When she took her child out for a walk, he just grabbed her and drove off. She didn't even call at her own home."

"Doesn't make sense," said the fat man. "She must have got her clearance papers at work. You can't get round the personnel department. It's paper, paper all the way."

"He was driving a black Volga," Valeria said.

"They were madly in love with each other," said the blonde. "He may have been a scientist but he acted like a real man."

"Why didn't he take her away with him when he had the chance, in winter?" the fat man asked suspiciously.

Why didn't I take her away when I had the chance, Krylov asked himself. I could easily have done that. And instead I just got into a train and went off by myself. What was I thinking about? Nothing. Nothing at all. About my wretched charts. About coming back to fetch her one day. No, not even that. How did I let it happen? How could I get onto a train and leave her behind?

"They were testing their love," said the blonde.

But he had written to her. Why hadn't she replied? Not a single reply. And his last letter had been returned unclaimed.

"Did you know her?" Valeria asked.

"I hadn't the faintest idea. . . . I mean, of course, I did."

"Was she so beautiful?"

"Very."

They were staring at him.

"Well, perhaps not very," he corrected himself. "I don't really know."

"Goodness, what a look you have on your face," said the blonde. She slapped Valeria on the back. "What about you? Your young man isn't going to carry you off, is he? She's got a Prince Charming now. He brought her a cake."

"Let's have some," the fat man said. "I'd like a nice bit of cake. They go off in the heat, y'know."

Valeria laughed, then looked imploringly at Krylov.

"I must go," he said. He stood up, brushed the sand off his trousers, and said good-bye.

Valeria ran after him and caught him up.

"I'm awfully sorry," she said.

Her head looked very small under her bedraggled hair. The fat man and the blonde were watching them from a distance.

Krylov took her hand and kissed it awkwardly.

The beach ended and he came to the deserted stretch of shore where the fishing village stood. Nets were hanging out to dry among upturned boats. The air smelled of tar and rotting fish. Out of habit Krylov took the path that led up past the smoking shed and the outhouses to the blue-painted refreshment room.

He knew it was the wrong place for him to go. At first he walked round it, then turned back, hesitated for a moment and pushed open the blue plywood door.

The table by the window was free. He sat down in his usual place, so that he could see the lake. "Well, shall we have something to eat?" he asked. Natasha didn't reply. He looked at the chair, trying to picture her sitting there in front of him, rubbing her cold cheeks. The chair was empty. She had let him down. He had come here specially to see her and she had let him down.

...They had just got back from making their rounds. Natasha pulled off her wet shoes, took a pair of slippers out of her suitcase and put out some tangerines on the table.

"What are they for?" he asked impatiently.

She blushed and gathered up the tangerines and he felt ashamed. They checked their entries and made them up into charts. It was the third day they had been working together and Krylov was amazed how quickly she grasped the significance of the measurements and acted accordingly, without asking questions.

"You're very capable," he told her.

She looked at him with unbelieving eyes, almost in fright. But the following day, when she had finished her calculations, she suddenly burst out laughing.

"It looks as if I can do it myself," she said in surprise.

When she arrived from town of a morning she always seemed tense and withdrawn and didn't thaw out till midday. It wasn't till they got out on skis in the woods that she became really relaxed. She had skied when she was a girl, but never after that.

"Why don't you ski with your husband?" Krylov had asked once.

She had looked confused and said that her husband was always too busy.

She had avoided talking about her husband and herself, but one day, when she had fallen through the ice and he had carried her back to the Antonovs and rubbed warmth into her frozen limbs and given her vodka to drink, she had asked him as she lay under the blankets half-asleep:

"What kind of a person do I seem to you?"

He had realised afterwards what the question really meant. She had been the eldest in the family and after a childhood spent nursing her younger brothers and sisters she had longed for freedom and independence. But she had married and had a child and again she never had any time to herself. At college she had been considered a bright student. Her husband was quite a famous artist and her hopes and ambitions seemed small and insignificant in comparison with his. She had tried to help and not get in the way. She had trained herself to keep in the background till she found herself quite unable to imagine how she looked to other people. She felt as if she had vanished, ceased to exist and someone else was walking and talking in her place.

She was a tall girl, slow, almost lazy in her movements, and her hair, too, was lazy and straight, but to Krylov she seemed quite small and he felt much older than her. It was a novel feeling and he liked it. He had to be careful with her, as one has to be with children. The slightest thing was enough to reduce her to frightened silence. She was like those frail March days with their timid sunshine.

Exactly at six she would gather up the charts, pull on her shoes and get ready to catch the bus.

"Can I leave these slippers behind, so that I won't have to carry them?"

"Certainly," Krylov had said.

Late that evening, when he went to bed, he had noticed those slippers—a little pair of gym shoes that had retained the shape of her feet. They looked so trusting. Perhaps it was then that he had started longing for morning to come, so that he would see her again.

Krylov ordered a beetroot salad, sausages and beer and took a quick glance at the waitress. She didn't seem to have recognised him. Her hair, which had been blonde, was now a dark auburn.

It was all make-believe. There was a legend about his kidnapping her and all the things he had built up in his own imagination were equally unreal. Nothing had really happened or, if something had, it was all over and done with. Never go back to a place where you've been happy.

He was not very good at dialectics, but he ought to have known that no one can ever enter the same stream twice.

He looked at the sandy shore, where the upturned hulks were lying. It aroused no feelings. He felt completely indifferent to it all. The salad was tasteless, the sausages cold. Why on earth had he been afraid to come into this place?

The old smoky-grey cat with a black mark on its forehead rubbed up against his leg politely. He took a salted cucumber from the plate.

"You used to eat cucumbers," he said. "But perhaps I dreamed that too."

The cat smelt the cucumber and took a delicate bite.

The waitress laughed.

"Have you come back here to work?" she asked.

"No, just a passing visit."

"Pashka recognised you, the old scoundrel. What a fuss he's making of you!"

She opened a bottle and put it on the table. The cat raised its tail and miaowed.

"It was Natasha who taught him to eat cucumbers," the waitress said.

Then perhaps it had happened after all, Krylov told himself. But why did she leave her husband?

"Well, how's life treating you?" said the waitress.

"Fine," Krylov replied. "I'm doing fine."

"Why didn't you bring her with you? Still, I don't suppose she would want to come here. She's too happy now to remember this place, I expect. She was so lonely here without you. Didn't she tell you?"

"No," Krylov said. "She didn't say anything about it."

"Didn't tell me much either. She would just come in and sit here, stroking the cat."

Somebody at the next table asked for sausage.

"Wait a minute," the waitress told him. "I can't be everywhere at once."

He sat listening to the popping of the bubbles in his beer glass.

The waitress returned.

"Will you be coming in again?"

"No," he said. "I'm leaving today."

"Give her my regards."

"I'm going on a long journey," he said suddenly, surprised to hear himself making the decision. "I'm joining an expedition."

"You seem to be a bit depressed about something."

"Not really. The beer's excellent. Nice to have seen you." He bent down and stroked the cat. "Well, so long, Pashka."

He drank up his beer and paid the bill.

"Thanks and good-bye."

"Come up together in the winter," the waitress said a little hesitantly.

"Maybe we shall."

He felt he needed another glass of beer. All the way there his mouth had been uncomfortably dry.

The feathery white trail of a jet had fanned out across the sky. Krylov stared up at the blurred sky-mark.

He went back by train. The white wave in the sky had melted away long ago but as he stood looking out of the window, Krylov felt he could still see it.

If she had taken this decision several months later it must mean that she loved him, had loved him right from the start. He remembered his letters and now he realised how awful they had been. Empty, cold, discussing everything yet saying nothing, because the one thing that really mattered was lacking—he had not asked her to be with him. Of course, he had thought he could come and fetch her any day. But when his last letter had come back unclaimed, it had set him thinking. Ever since then his mind had been full of thoughts and memories. The sight of a bus would make him think of her. If he drank water he thought of her. Yet he wasn't really thinking; he merely saw her lips and repeated her name.

The Moscow train left in the evening. It was the same train he had come up on and it left from the same platform. Krylov stepped into the carriage and stood at the window. People leaving and people seeing them off. Suitcases. Good-byes at every carriage door.

The train started with a slight jerk and no whistle. Whistles had gone out long ago. Now you felt nothing but that slight jerk. And suddenly it all came back to him—the moment when he had wanted to jump off the train and run back to her, letting everyone and everything else go hang. He had known he ought to jump, but he had gone on standing there.

The islands of light amid the dusk grew fewer and fewer. For some reason he thought of his childhood, of the summer camp and lining up for roll-call in the evening. Down came the flag. The last post. He could even feel the metallic taste of the bugle on his lips.

He went to his compartment, pulled a magazine out of his pocket and began reading a story. When he had read it, he started again from the beginning, muttering each word to himself as though he had only just learned to read.

PART TWO

Sergei Krylov had been sent down from the institute at the end of his third year. The reason given in the Dean's notice was, "systematic absence from lectures". An earlier, much harsher formula of "unworthy conduct" had been toned down thanks to Oleg Tulin.

At lectures on optics Krylov would examine the ceiling. He took no notes, he just stared up at the ceiling, which reflected the play of the sunlight on the leaves outside. On one occasion the lecturer, an Assistant Professor, stopped and asked if he was disturbing Krylov. Krylov stood up and reassured the Assistant Professor that he wasn't. Fifty other students laughed. The lectures were boring and they were glad of the diversion. If the Assistant Professor had been a little older he would have laughed with the rest, but he struck the rostrum with his fist, went red in the face and said that if Krylov knew the subject so well there was no need for him to attend lectures.

Krylov took the advice quite seriously. He considered the matter for a moment and said he really wasn't interested in the lectures because the whole subject was explained in exactly the same terms in the textbook and it would be much easier to read it up there before taking the examination.

The Assistant Professor's comment was that he could try.

Krylov stopped attending lectures on optics and attended a course on the theory of probability instead. He was given several warnings but his blue eyes merely grew round with surprise. Why shouldn't he? Wasn't it allowed? His innocence did not sound quite genuine and would have maddened anyone. A month later he was sent down.

Oleg Tulin, who had been secretary of the department's Komsomol organisation at the time, tried to persuade Krylov to go and see the Dean and promise to mend his ways. He was even prepared to go with him. Krylov refused. He was not worried about his expulsion, though he did feel he was letting Tulin down.

Now, after so many years had passed, it was hard to say how they had become friends. On Krylov's side there had been admiration for Tulin's gifts; for Tulin it had been a need to have someone under his wing, someone to help, and perhaps to feel himself admired. In addition, neither of them had any brothers.

In their second year they had done their laboratory work on electric discharges together.

"Let's set the electrodes at an angle," Tulin once suggested.

They were tired of doing exactly what was being done at the other benches and had been done by generation after generation of second-year men. They set the electrodes at an angle and soaked them in ink. The results were odd and contradicted the formula. The instructor said that presumably the formula was wrong for those particular conditions. He was not impressed, but Tulin and Krylov were staggered. It was the first time they had ever heard of a published formula proving to be inexact.

They stayed on in the laboratory in the evenings and Tulin thought up fantastic ways of achieving discharges of electricity. They packed the discharge apparatus in snow, then soaked it in milk, then enveloped it in steam, and finally there was an explosion that left a deep gash in Krylov's chin.

Henceforth they were barred from the laboratory and decided to devote their lives to science. They enjoyed debunking authorities. They had also discovered that science was in the embryonic stage of development. Elementary things like cybernetics had only just come into being; electricity had to be obtained by the primitive method of burning coal and no one knew how to decipher encephalograms properly.

Professor Chistyakov selected a group of students to do research for the department. Tulin was among the favoured ones, Krylov was not. He demanded an explanation and was rebuffed. He was told that he had shown very little ability from the start and was making no progress, and that was that. His "why" irritated even the most patient instructors. In the end he started thinking out his own answers and this gradually became a habit. He enjoyed creating his own theories, criticising recognised authorities, throwing doubt on everything within sight, destroying it and building anew, in his own way. His natural stubbornness and distrust of the opinion of his elders also played a part; in everyday life he remained a trusting simpleton but learning was becoming more and more difficult because even the most obvious truths had to be verified.

Few great men in their youth suspect what the future holds for them; yet great men and those around them usually manage to leave plenty of papers for the use of biographers. No papers concerning Krylov's life at college were preserved because it had been quite clear to everyone who knew him that he would never become great. Even Tulin's biographers would be handicapped by lack of material concerning this period.

Krylov and Tulin never corresponded, unless one counts as correspondence notes passed at lectures such as "Look at the funny sight on your left" or "Bag a place for me in the dinner queue". Nor did they keep diaries. They had no dealings with publishers, creditors or journalists. From the institute's records it may be established that Krylov received consistently mediocre ratings in all subjects during his first year. He seemed to have no particular interests. The minutes of a Komsomol meeting record that Tulin, an excellent student, was charged with the task of helping Krylov. Apparently it took Tulin a long time to get his protégé out of the rut because Krylov received no good marks at all until his third term.

Subsequently, when recalling their student years, Tulin and Krylov agreed that the historian's task was becoming extremely difficult. Modern life with its telephones and telegrams left few traces of man's inner life. Instead of objective evidence, scholars would be forced to rely on biased opinion. It is known, for instance, that Tulin called Krylov a crass idiot and swine when he refused to apologise to the lecturer in optics. "If you can't sacrifice personal interest for the sake of a greater aim you'll never get anywhere in life," Tulin had said. He had spent a total of thirty evenings trying to influence Krylov and had a right to feel hurt.

What annoyed him most of all was Krylov's unexpected obstinacy; Krylov had always been so easy-going and pliable.

Krylov's father arrived from somewhere near Novgorod and decided the case quickly and harshly. If Sergei didn't want to study, he could go to work and help keep his sisters while they took courses in Novgorod. And so it was decided. Tulin's elder sister was an engineer at a factory and she got Krylov a job as a technical inspector. He tried to thank Tulin but his friend turned away from him.

"I don't want to speak to you," he said hoarsely.

Krylov moved to the factory hostel. For the first few days his dormitory neighbour, Vitya Dolinin, a little crab-like fellow, pulled the bed-clothes off him and shouted: "Wakey, wakey, intelligentsia!" Eventually Krylov himself got used to rising punctually at 6.30 a.m. He made no attempt to win friends, and this was possibly the reason why he got on with the other lads quite well.

Physical work tired him out. He rarely had a chance to sit down in the course of an eight-hour day. He had to run from one end of the shop to the other, measuring bed-plates and surface areas; he had to carry instruments about and wrestle with massive gear-wheels. By the evening he was exhausted and his legs were aching. But his head was free. At last he could interest himself in what he chose. He would tackle several problems at once. What was the nature of the forces of gravitation? What was infinity? Was the law of the conservation of energy valid? In addition, he set about evolving a unified field theory, a problem which had baffled Einstein. He also intended revealing the contradictions in quantum mechanics. This was a period when his mind was exclusively concerned with the problems of the universe.

When he read about action potentials he decided that the potential of the human mind was infinite. If this was so, there was a case for achieving the power of autonomous thought, so that one could work while meditating on something quite different. He was given two reprimands and had to pay a fine, and on one occasion was almost crushed by a crane while attempting to combine measurements-taking with pondering the fundamental problems of the universe.

Time was short. He regretted the three years he had wasted at the institute on such useless subjects as chemistry. Thanks to the institute, however, he was aware of the need for some sort of system and realised his own weakness in mathematics. Most of the problems that humanity had been wrestling with for years he was able to solve quite easily; he had only to formulate his solutions in mathematical terms and give them a suitably scientific appearance.

He bought a four-volume course in higher mathematics and a six-volume course in physics. About six months later he discovered that there were flaws in some of his solutions, and after another few months certain ugly facts completely destroyed his splendid hypotheses.

At the factory they were nearing Quarter Day and the assembly men were hurrying to get their quotas finished and passed. Suddenly Krylov declared a whole batch of rods to be defective. He was absolutely sure of his judgement and nothing would shift him. The fitters were told they would have to work overnight, and it was also suggested to Krylov that he should stay on all night, checking and passing the rods as they were redone. He refused. The foreman told him what he thought of him in front of the fitters. The chief of the technical inspection department arrived and also heaped reproaches on him. What about the struggle to fulfil the plan? What about the heroic efforts of the collective, the honour of the factory, the Komsomol's fine record of achievement, and so on?

Krylov listened attentively, then asked him to explain why the contactors had to be handed in on the 30th of the month, when no one did anything but hang about on the 1st. What was the point in such formalism? How would it benefit the state to get the contactors a mere twenty hours earlier at the price of fagging everybody out and having to pay overtime, particularly as the men would afterwards be drawing pay for doing no work at all?

Vitya Dolinin backed him up and a first-class row developed. Krylov was summoned before the Komsomol Committee, but he asked them, too, to prove to him what profit the state would get out of rushing through the assignment.

A decision was taken that Krylov should be drawn into social activities and helped to get his ideas straight. He was entrusted with the job of giving talks on the honourable assignment the factory had received of making the electrical equipment for a certain type of excavator.

His talk was fascinating. Having conscientiously studied the excavator's specifications, Krylov proved to his listeners that the excavator's efficiency was practically nil. To move ten tons of earth it had to move twenty tons of its own weight. The assignment was in no sense an honour. The excavators were obsolete. They ought to be taken out of production and replaced by machines of the conveyor type.

At the Bureau meeting that discussed his conduct he simply looked surprised and said: "I think my calculations are correct."

Two members of the Bureau took his side and it is difficult to say how it would have all ended had not another incident occurred in the meantime.

The factory was having trouble with the operating mechanism for a new series of contactors for a semi-automatic press. The cast-iron contact-holders were breaking up during trials. The contact-holders had to move in a semicircle and the damage occurred when operating speed was achieved.

Walking through the shop one day Krylov ran into the chief designer Gatenyan, nearly stabbing him with a large pair of marking compasses. The chief designer let himself go. In the space of about two minutes he gave a very full description of Krylov and his parents and the shop foreman, who had tried to explain matters by telling him that Krylov was a sleep-walker and not quite sound in the head.

Gatenyan then took the compasses away from Krylov and he and his designers started measuring something in the operating mechanism. Krylov came to and saw the worried faces round the line with its broken contact-holder, and the new contactors lined up in the assembly section, awaiting their fate.

For a time he listened to what the designers had to say, then chimed in with a request that the next model should be tested. The foreman hissed at him to get out and stay out. Krylov turned and withdrew into non-Euclidean space.

But Gatenyan recalled him and asked what ideas this sleep-walker might have. Krylov was quite unable to give any sensible explanation. He just wanted to see on what sector of its path the contact-holder broke up.

The chief designer listened to this thoughtful reply with interest. Neither the years nor the post he held had taught him that a diploma was a substitute for a head. To the surprise of the engineers he ordered them to fit a new contact-holder and get ready to start the press. True, he did not forget to mention that each contact-holder cost a couple of hundred rubles.

Krylov then decided to refrain from having a new trial. "That'll make it even more interesting," he said and, having re-claimed his compasses, went off to measure rods.

When the shift was over he went up to the design office, where a conference was being held. When he put his head round the door the chief asked him in. He threaded his way to the table and asked about the path the contact-holder had to take. So it was circular. That was fine. Everything made sense. The contact-holder was bound to break up because there was a discontinuity in the derivative.

Gatenyan called the meeting to order and asked Krylov to repeat what he had said. The contact-holder suffered recurring impacts as it moved. . . .

The foremen and designers looked suspiciously at the scrap of paper without any drawings or figures, just a few scratched symbols. They were accustomed to dealing with coefficients, drawings, nomograms; they were not impressed by abstract equations.

He was asked what suggestion he had to make. Krylov shrugged. Up to now he had been interested only in the cause of the damage, not what ought to be done about it. He sat down at the table and meditated. The little internal switch that he used for cutting himself off from what was going around him operated smoothly. Then he switched himself into contact again, saw Gatenyan looking at him expectantly and replied that the semicircle should be replaced by a parabola.

Gatenyan gave him a job in the design office. He had to spend the first half of the day doing various calculations for the designers; in the afternoon he read physics. Like a connoisseur he chose all that he found most delicious, without pausing to think whether it was necessary. He read books on physics as if they were thrillers, enjoying every new twist of thought. An elderly designer who sat next to him would jump at the sudden rumble of his laughter. "Listen to this," Krylov would say in lieu of an apology, and, beaming with delight, would read: "The maximum value of the pulse does not depend on the place of ion formation, although the shape of the pulse curve does."

These were the best days of his life. The incident of the contact-holder had inspired him. When these abstract formulas were brought into contact with machines, with metal, they could strike a spark that would turn everything upside down. His physics, his mathematics virtually ruled the factory. For eighteen months the ultrasonic defecto-scope for detecting flaws in castings had been out of order. Krylov took up ultrasound and repaired the apparatus. Gatenyan gave him complete freedom of action. "Choose anything you're interested in. Just walk round and think," he said. "You can be our ideas man."

One day, when the director was taking an inspecting commission round the factory he found Krylov sitting on a desk in the office of the technical inspection department. Krylov was dipping a glass tube into a cup and assiduously blowing soap bubbles. The working day was at its peak. The rainbow-hued bubbles floated out into the shop and rose to the glass roof. The director was riled. But he became even more riled when Krylov stared at him and stated emphatically that it was extremely important to know how a bubble detached itself from a tube. And did the director know why bubbles burst anyway? The director must be given his due. He was far cleverer than the Assistant Professor at the institute. He knew that victory goes not to the man who answers the questions but to the man who asks them. So he asked Krylov whether he knew how Archimedes died?

There was quite a lot in the situation to remind one of the encounter between Archimedes and the Roman soldier. The members of the commission exchanged meaningful smiles, but Krylov asked the director to make an allocation for filming bursting bubbles in slow motion.

The next day the director had the chief designer up on the mat. Why do soap bubbles burst? It would have been hard to think of a nicer theme song for the malicious tongues at the Ministry. At every conference from now on they would be reminded of those bubbles.

Gatenyan tried to point out that nothing much had happened. Let the lad go around thinking and looking into things. No one could tell what might come out of it. So far he had paid his way for several years ahead. It would be a crime to tie him to a drawing-board. The factory had such a large staff there was no harm in having one ideas man on it. He was the type who didn't have to be forced to work. Such people stopped working only when they went to sleep. The main thing was not to interfere with them.

The speech the director made in reply was much shorter.

Gatenyan went back to his office in a black mood. He summoned Krylov and told him to collect his assignment for the day in the morning and go straight to the library. No drifting around the factory on any account. He must spend all his free time working for a university degree. Krylov's view of the exams was that they were a deadly bore. He gave in to the chief only because he wanted to be nice to him. But he managed to finish his study of soap bubbles and sent it in to the *Journal of Technical Physics*. It was published six months later and turned out to have a bearing on boundary layer theory.

Gatenyan brought the director a reprint of the article and said, "Great rivers cannot be measured with common yardsticks." The director took the reprint to the Board and placed it on the desk of the Head of the Board—"Even kings can be mistaken".

The Head of the Board skimmed through the reprint and sniffed superciliously, but at the next conference he recommended encouraging the scientific interests of the man at the bench. He presented the example of the soap bubble rather well. It sounded faintly self-critical and required absolutely no practical action.

Krylov began to be talked about at the factory. The chiefs of departments said good morning to him and shook hands. People liked the fact that he went on living in the hostel and receiving eighty rubles a month, thirty of which he sent to his sisters in Novgorod. He responded to the general attention vaguely, without much interest, and this evoked further curiosity. Things that had formerly passed unnoticed now leapt to the eye, and since people were feeling kindly towards Krylov they noted with appreciation his baggy cords and sweater and the raincoat he wore in icy weather, disdaining an overcoat even in winter. In this there was an element of unconscious bravado. It was as if he were saying, "I can be like this because I am interested in other things."

And this, too, was approved. At the hostel he was no longer considered a sleep-walker or simpleton; he was proudly christened the "Chief Theoretician".

The factory had many chiefs—the chief technologist, the chief mechanic, the chief power engineer, but these were official posts, confirmed by authority. There were chief technologists at all factories; only at the October Works was there a "Chief Theoretician". He became just as much the factory's showpiece as was Poroshin, a veteran of the Revolution, who had stormed the Winter Palace, or Glukhov, a mountain climber in the Master of Sport class. What other factory had a working chap who got articles published in the journals of the Academy of Sciences!

People loved him, as they love all happy-go-lucky dreamers who know nothing of the world. They loved him, they took care of him, and they exploited him mercilessly. From all over the factory people came to him asking for calculations, advice, solutions to problems.

Dolinin took him out to dances and on trips into the country. To the accompaniment of friendly laughter he would obediently plop into the water off the top board and do a dog-paddle, roaring with laughter at his own antics, and everyone knew he could allow himself to be a bad swimmer and a clumsy dancer because these things were not the real measure of his abilities.

And so it went on until Krylov was taken charge of by Ada.

In the course of two and a half years he had become utterly sick and tired of exams, of studying at night and of laboratory tasks, half of which he considered absolutely unnecessary. What bloody use was a degree anyway? Both his energy and his patience were exhausted and he might easily have chucked everything just before his finals had not Ada intervened. She offered irrefutable proofs that without a degree his future would be a wretched one, and that in any case he would be a sloppy-minded weakling if he gave in. What was he wasting his talent on—solving problems for people who were too lazy to do their own work! Weren't they ashamed to take advantage of his open-heartedness? With cool and polite efficiency she succeeded in getting rid of those who applied for Krylov's aid too frequently.

In the design office Ada was considered a capable engineer. Moreover she was quite definitely the best-looking girl at the factory. She was so beautiful that no one even tried to take her out. There wasn't a man in the factory who felt worthy to be seen at her side. In the design office they were all quite sure that Ada had a host of brilliant admirers with whom it would be hopeless to compete. Pride made her pretend that this was actually the case and she became even more aloof and unapproachable.

It had never entered Krylov's head that she might take a liking to him. He treated Ada as an elder sister, or an aunt, although she was his own age. With her strong will and incontestable powers of logic she knew how to wield power over others. Without becoming aware of it Krylov began reporting to her sheepishly on every step he took.

To start with, she convinced him that he had talent, but failed to appreciate his own worth and criminally squandered his abilities. Why on earth should he bother about insulation failure? There was no future in it.

From the day he put on his university badge, his life for the next five years—and to him it seemed the next hundred—was mapped out by Ada. He had only to move in accordance with the timetable from one station to another.

By this time Krylov and Tulin had made it up and Tulin unexpectedly gave Ada his support.

"What's insulation failure got to do with it?" he told Krylov. "Look at that figure! What hair! Helen of Troy in person. You're a lucky man!"

Later, Tulin changed his opinion, but at the time his enthusiasm flattered Krylov. It was pleasant to have such a beautiful woman on his arm and to feel the envious glances of other men, and to see that she had no eyes for anyone but himself. Secretly, he found Ada's guardianship a burden. In her presence he was constantly on the alert, tense in every nerve and muscle. She kept him on his toes. She was constantly "educating him", taking him to exhibitions, museums, concerts. They were most regular in attending political study groups, at which the role of the individual in history and the consequences of the personality cult were discussed. Afterwards, in the corridor they would stand arguing how it could all have come about. One by one people who had suffered unjustly began returning to the factory. What they had to tell was terrible and incomprehensible. More and more often the names of individuals Krylov had thought of since childhood as enemies of the people were spoken without a glance over the shoulder and with respect. Tulin suddenly told him that in 1937 his father had been expelled from the Party and sent into exile. Gatenyan's brother had been convicted of spying for four foreign powers; the wrongs, the tragedies suffered by many families and hitherto kept secret now came to light. Each of these discoveries was painful, yet at the same time the feeling of general catharsis increased. People were speculating about the future and assuring one another that the past was over and done with. They made plans, projected all kinds of reforms. Every new decree was greeted with enthusiasm. "I knew that's what they'd do. I was just thinking of it myself," Tulin would say; Krylov would mutter perplexedly: "There seem to be a lot of things we just never noticed." Some of the older people were inclined to play safe, but the young men laughed this off and insisted that this process was irreversible. They argued with Ada, who didn't see much point in this exposure of what had happened in the past. What was it for? Why cause so much disillusion? No one would gain anything by it and it would only make people bitter. Krylov was firm in his mind only about one thing: the truth could never do harm. And there was no substitute for truth.

The factory's seven-year plan was discussed. There were debates. The advantages of hydropower stations and thermal power stations were compared. Gatenyan reminded them of the discussion on linguistics, when millions of people at all the enterprises in the country had been compelled to study the problems of linguistics for months while the collective farms were in a shocking state and people were queueing up for bread. Krylov remembered with shame how he, who had surely been old enough at the time to have known better, had discovered some higher wisdom in that article of Stalin's.

The factory began to modernise its equipment.

Ada made Krylov get to work on an instrument for precision measurement. The instrument would bear his name. There must be articles in the press about it. The scientist at the bench—that was the value and significance of his work.

Krylov's conduct and appearance should be adjusted to fit in with this image.

The blank, heated to a suitable temperature by her ambitious plans, was put through the rolling mill and gradually assumed the required shape. Ada carefully scraped off the bits of scale, examined her creation with a critical eye, pronounced herself satisfied and Krylov went off to the trade union committee with an application for a room.

His dark-grey suit fitted him perfectly. His narrow tie was carefully knotted in the tiniest of knots. He made a list of all the jobs he had done for the factory and submitted it to the Inventions Bureau. He was awarded a prize and took out a season ticket to the swimming pool.

Something in him seemed to have broken free. The scales had fallen from his eyes and he had seen life in all its fascinating variety. Every evening curtains went up in twenty theatres. New films, foreign and home-produced, were appearing on the screens. Literary controversies were raging. Young artists were holding their own exhibition. The girls from the next hostel were asking him round to hear some Cuban records. Sunday, he suddenly realised, was a day-off. There was a yacht-club on the Islands, and there were the Islands themselves, in the white nights, the Strelka, the carnivals, and Ada looked marvellous in her black-and-yellow checked sundress.

"If you set your heart on it, you can become head of the technical department," she told him. "You can even be head of the central laboratory and assistant to the chief designer. Production's got to be put on a scientific basis, not just for the sake of your career but for the sake of greater efficiency."

She's as beautiful as a Greek statue, Krylov thought. But how can you take a statue in your arms?

They made a trip to Peterhof. When the boat got out into the gulf, the weather changed and it began to drizzle. Krylov put his jacket round Ada's shoulders. The slippery deck gave a lurch and Krylov locked his arm round Ada's waist.

"Let's go below," he suggested.

She shook her head.

The horizon rose and fell and the sea towered over them like a crumbling wall. They were alone on deck. Ada looked at Krylov. He guiltily withdrew his arm. Ada blushed slightly and he caved in completely. They were getting splashed.

Krylov couldn't understand why Ada was silent and it made him feel even more guilty.

"You must get down to control theory." There was a quiver in her voice. "It's the bed-rock of automation in industry. I want you to, Sergei. You will do it, won't you?"

She placed her wet hand on his.

"Of course, I will," he said joyfully.

"Have you...." She checked herself. "Have you read Wiener? He's amazing. Of course, he exaggerates the importance of cybernetics a little, but he's quite amazing."

O Lord, she knows everything, Krylov groaned to himself. And I'm just an ignorant clot.

"I suppose you haven't read Saint Exupéry either? What do you waste your time on?" And she plunged into a mocking tirade about his ignorance.

He was not particularly interested in the instrument she had got him to work on, but he realised the factory needed it. For a week he observed how the foremen, using various rules and tricks of the trade known only to themselves, determined the precision with which a certain part had been made. They had no idea that all their secrets were governed by Nichols' law. At night, when the shop was empty Krylov brought in his interferometer and used Nichols' law like a tin-opener to prise the lid off the foremen's secrets. The resulting apparatus was rather a crude affair. Krylov had adapted the instruments already in use in laboratories to industrial conditions, but it caused a stir at the factory. Krylov got his picture in the newspapers, and articles were written about him. "Innovator's initiative ... enthusiastic response...." He felt embarrassed until Ada proved to him that talented people never recognised the value of their work. False modesty was as unpleasant as conceit. He gave in to her as usual and wrote the application she dictated.

Gatenyan listened to his proposal in silence.

"So you want your name on it and promotion to senior designer?" he said finally and gave Krylov a kind of sad look. "In Armenia we say: if eggs could give you a good voice, a chicken's arse would sing like a nightingale."

That was all he said. He wrote out the promotion order and a few days later asked casually how things were going with insulation failure. One would have expected him to be glad that Krylov was solely concerned with factory affairs, but to Krylov the question seemed to contain a trace of anxiety and reproach.

Unbeknown to Ada, he resumed his study of insulation failure. He hardly knew himself why he had taken it up. In his heart of hearts he felt it was a vice. People had all kinds of secret passions. For some it was vodka or cards; his was insulation failure.

This was his first joy of discovery, pure and unclouded by any doubts. He had created his own theory of polarisation and arcing in certain media. Everything had come out beautifully, and he was the first man to understand all the intricacies of this complex mechanism. No one else knew the true picture. He alone was in possession of the truth, he and no one else in the whole world.

On the way home from the Public Library he felt as if he were treading on air. He might take off at any moment and go soaring over the Alexandrovsky Park.

What if he were to die at this moment? And this secret were buried with him? And nobody ever discovered it? The idea of death was absurd, but he liked it. He decided to go straight to see the chief designer at his home.

When the chief received him in his pyjamas, looking extremely worried, Krylov realised that the Public Library closed at half past eleven, and it must now be after midnight. But he quickly forgot it again because he had to share his discovery with someone.

The chief knew nothing about electrostatics but he had infinite faith in his protégé.

The next day Gatenyan got in touch through some friends with Dankevich himself and it was agreed that Krylov should be allowed to report on his work at a seminar at the Physics Institute of the Academy of Sciences.

The whole design office took part in the preparations. The girls drew superb graphs and diagrams for Krylov in Indian ink of various colours. The chief lent him his leather underarm case to put his papers in. Only Ada was cool. She failed to see the necessity for it. Nevertheless she made him recite his speech several times and change the title, dropping the "new theory" in favour of the more modest "A Contribution to. . . ." She, a professor's daughter, knew, if anyone did, how alerted a learned audience would be against any unknown discoverer of a new theory.

She saw Krylov as far as the door of the institute, straightened his tie, looked him over from head to foot and completed her inspection with a stern but permissive nod.

He did not return to the hostel that evening. Nor did he appear at the factory on the following day. No one knew what had happened to him. Ada rang up the institute and was told that Krylov had delivered his speech, it had been discussed and criticised, and that was all they knew.

He turned up two days later, unshaven, gaunt, his new suit stained and crumpled. He stumped silently to the chief's office, gave him his case and handed in a letter of resignation. In answer to questions he winced and said almost nothing. The factory decided that Krylov had been treated unfairly. How could those dry-as-dust Academicians appreciate the man in industry! Their Krylov would soon put paid to those bespectacled bookworms. Why should he let them upset him? They were just a lot of carping critics, guided by envy.

For some reason everyone came to the conclusion that the Academicians had offended Krylov beyond measure and it was because of them that he had decided to leave the factory. They nursed him like a sick man, trying not to aggravate his wounds. They talked to him about football. He replied with a forced smile but his eyes remained withdrawn.

The director signed his promotion to senior designer; in a month's time the factory's new block of flats would be completed and Krylov was promised a room there. Ada got him accommodation at a holiday resort, but he stuck to his guns. He was leaving. He was going to work for Dankevich, at the institute. But what as? As anything. Ada was certain that this was a sudden whim, a mere fad. Go and work for Dankevich, who had treated him so despicably? How did he know Dankevich wanted him anyhow? Personally, she despised these Academy of Sciences institutes, with their great men surrounded by a crowd of sycophantic scholastics, who could turn the simplest thing into a mumble of abstruse terminology. She had seen quite enough of their scribbling at home, at her father's. It had none of the joy of a real job. At the factory Krylov could within a year become the chief's right-hand man. After that, certainly, if he was still attracted by science, he could write a thesis. He must march into science as a conqueror, not knock at the door like a beggar, with nothing behind him.

Ada's words merely rebounded. Till then he had been clay in her hands; now the clay had suddenly turned into cement.

"I may make a complete mess of it," he insisted, "but I want to try."

The edifice she had erected with such pains, his career that had only just begun to take shape, his reputation at the factory, all the work she had planned for him, the whole thing was tumbling in ruins.

Even the happy-go-lucky Dolinin disapproved: "Why get above yourself? Better to be first lad in the village than last in the town." Everyone was as indignant over his decision as they had been warm in his defence. They called him ungrateful and accused him of getting above himself. In their way they were right; he owed the factory too much. Gatenyan refused to say good-bye to him.

If only he could have explained it all to them.

Ada presented him with an ultimatum—either he stayed at the factory or it was all over between them. He was perplexed. What was all over? Why couldn't they stay friends as they had always been?

"Friends?" She looked at him with hatred and suddenly burst into tears. It was so unlike her, he was so appalled to see the tears running down her pale, severe face, belying its marble immobility, that he felt he was a pig.

"All right, I'll stay," he said desperately. "But don't cry. Please."

It was unbelievable that this beautiful creature could be crying because of him. He couldn't understand what was happening. Ada dried her eyes. She wanted no sacrifices. He could go and good riddance. It didn't matter any more.

"I'm afraid you'll never make a real scientist," she said. "You're too unobservant."

Suspicion flickered in his mind and he looked hard at her. No, she was still Helen of Troy. Nothing else made sense.

The idea that he would never make a real scientist was what cut deepest. Tulin had told him the same thing. His two closest friends had both come to the same conclusion about him.

The trouble was he just couldn't explain to anyone how the talented young man, the "Chief Theoretician", had burst like a soap bubble.

Why did soap bubbles burst? He had some inkling of how that happened. Somebody's lips inflate a droplet. It swells and its shiny skin gleams with all the colours of the rainbow. It reflects the sky, the distorted shapes of houses and people. It begins to consider itself a planet. All that it reflects is real for it. These are its houses, its people. It carries them in itself. Who can make it understand that they are merely a reflection! It thinks just the opposite. The world and the people thereon are but an ugly reflection of its own beauty. It breaks away and floats in air, knowing nothing of winds or convection.

It floats on and on. Now it belongs to no one, it is its own master. It is the Universe. It has its own laws. No longer must it obey your Newtons, your gravity, your mechanics. It has everything of its own, even its own electrostatics. How splendid is this bubble! What a pity it was not blown a little higher! But why not try?

And suddenly—pop! It bursts. Nothing is left, just a trace of moisture in the air. Where has it disappeared, that beautiful iridescent world, with its own laws, its own sky, its own earth?

But before it bursts, it gives some people a lot of fun.

Krylov remembered with disgust how he had stepped up to the rostrum, puffing out his chest, how self-importantly he had opened his stylish leather case and drawn out his papers. For perhaps the first five minutes they had listened to him with curiosity. Then he was interrupted by a question. Before he had even expounded his argument they were asking him about the concluding formula, though he had not yet written it up on the board. How had they got to know about it? While he grappled with his astonishment, someone answered the question for him, then there were more questions to the person who had answered, and another answer was given while Krylov was still pondering his first answer and was unable to follow what was being said. They asked and answered their own questions and he lagged farther and farther behind them. As though suddenly remembering his presence, they asked him—more for amusement than anything else—to explain the mechanism of charge transfer. He recovered something of his wits and launched into an explanation, but someone at once politely drew his attention to an inaccuracy and showed that it must be corrected. Krylov was compelled to agree and tried to go on, but the first correction led to another and he became lost in a welter of side argument that prevented him from returning to his main theme. He realised he was going off at a tangent but could do nothing about it. The charges which repulsed one another began to attract, positive charges turned into negative ones, and, without perceiving how, he reached a completely absurd conclusion, proving the opposite of what he had set out to prove. He was a plaything in their hands. In the space of half an hour they dissected the theory it had taken him six months to evolve; they spotted things in it that still baffled him, and romped far ahead of him, while he could only stand and blink, unable even to take part in their argument. His ignorance was only half the trouble; the most humiliating thing was the leaden slowness with which his mind worked. His brain positively creaked, like so many rusty wheels.

For the first time in his life he realised what real talent was. He felt he was in the presence of giants, a council of the gods. In appearance they were no different from other men: crumpled shirts, sleeves rolled up, undergraduate expressions; some of them were no older than himself. Casual and derisive, they smoked the same Bulgarian cigarettes that he did and sat astride their chairs, but it would have taken Krylov hours of concentrated thought to cover the distance between the ideas they tossed about so lightly among themselves.

He had stumbled on Olympus. The immortal gods were laughing at him and he could take no offence. How could he be offended with the gods? In their presence he could feel only his own insignificance.

The Jupiter among them was Dankevich. The gods called him just Dan and he made no demur. Everything, no doubt, was possible among the gods.

And from that day on Krylov was theirs.

"Nonsense," said Dankevich. "Didn't we prove anything to you?"

"You did," Krylov replied.

"What exactly?"

It required an effort to look straight into Dankevich's incredibly black and brilliant eyes.

"That I'm a blockhead, an ignoramus and know absolutely nothing."

"Lack of knowledge and ignorance are different things. Lack of knowledge begins after science, ignorance precedes it. Your disease is more serious: your brain is infected with ignorant ideas."

"You're absolutely right," Krylov said.

"Science is not a game for amateurs."

"No, it isn't."

"We can't escape from all these young geniuses who consider themselves Einsteins and Rutherfords. They all have a new picture of the universe to offer. Physics has become an overfashionable science. At the present moment I have no room for any more scientists."

"I don't mind being a lab assistant."

"There is no vacancy for laboratory assistants either."

"But I've already resigned at the factory," Krylov said.

Dankevich's slim, flexible body flicked up, straight as a razor blade.

"That trick won't work with me. Go back to your factory. Your ideas can't do any harm there and you're making yourself useful."

"I won't go back."

A smile of contempt flickered across Dankevich's narrow, nervous face and vanished.

"Indeed! The most resolute beginnings mean nothing without endings. I suppose you think I've been waiting impatiently for you to come and see me. What are you going to do?"

"I'm going to work at your institute."

Dankevich eyed him curiously.

"In what capacity, I wonder."

One day, when he came to see Dankevich with his chief, Professor Chistyakov, Tulin happened to glance out of the window and noticed Krylov. He was helping a party of workmen to unload crates from a lorry in the yard. Tulin asked permission to leave the room and ran downstairs. Krylov greeted him with a smile. He had got a job as a mechanic in the institute's workshop. What happened after that, time would show. He heaved a crate on to his back and trudged off with it to the store. Tulin walked along beside him.

"Want me to have a word with Chistyakov about taking you on with us?"

"No, I'm going to work here," Krylov said.

"The persistence of born talent that no one will recognise. What a wonderful spectacle! All right! Put your back into it! You'll soon make the fifth grade and Dankevich will weep with delight."

Krylov dumped the crate on the ground.

"Stop goading me. I'm not asking you for anything. Leave me in peace. Why put me on the same plane as yourself? All I want is to work here, and if I give up and go it'll be the finish."

"So you think you'll move the stony hearts in this place? No one less than Dankevich is good enough for you? You think he'll turn you into a genius, do you?"

Krylov took his arm and led him into the room where the physicists held their Wednesday seminars. It was quite an ordinary room. It smelled of tobacco-smoke, and in it were the two rusty-looking blackboards and the little rostrum on which Krylov had endured his ordeal of shame.

"I've got to speak here," Krylov said.

"Wouldn't you prefer the conference hall of the Academy of Sciences?"

"No," Krylov replied quite seriously. "I'm going to speak here and they're going to listen to me."

"The dream of an idiot," Tulin said. "Is that the way to become a scientist?"

The next day Krylov happened to meet Dankevich in the corridor.

"Hey, you, what's your name?" Dankevich asked him crossly. "What do you hope to get out of this? Do you imagine you can wear me down? Don't flatter yourself."

Krylov felt his cheeks go cold.

"All right, I'm leaving. I see no other way of proving to you.... You can rejoice over the great victory you've won!" He suddenly felt the anger and rudeness in his words and realised that he was finished. He was in the presence of Jupiter, of Dankevich himself, but just because he deified this man he had to tell him everything. Every word struck cold into his body. When he returned to the workshop he was shivering violently.

He handed in his resignation. The same day it was returned to him with Dankevich's decision written across it: "To be appointed senior laboratory assistant in Anikeyev's laboratory."

Anikeyev's requirements were simple and unbelievable.

An experimenter must:

(1) Be sufficiently lazy not to waste time on superfluous details.

(2) Read very little. Those who read a lot lose the habit of independent thought.

(3) Be inconsistent. Without losing sight of the ultimate goal he must notice, and be interested in, side-effects.

In general, cut down on all flights of fancy and "great ideas".

The laboratory had two rooms and two research workers; the third was Anikeyev himself. Krylov was to work under him. The laboratory was investigating various electrical processes.

Only a few sentences were spoken all day. A measurement was taken, a calculation was made, another measurement was taken, another calculation was made. And so it went on, day after day, week after week, month after month. Yet how good it was! No one to stop you from thinking. Just the apparatus, the quivering screens of the oscilloscopes, the steady tap-tap of the vacuum pump. Deepen the vacuum, open the throttle. Discharge. Let's measure it. Put a detector in the circuit. Doesn't fit. Have to adjust it. Measure, compute, measure again. Sergei, trace that error, will you? Measure, compute, measure again. Got it? Right, start from the beginning. Measure, compute. Where does that jump come from? Do it again. Measure. That jump again. Strange. There must be some kind of induction somewhere. Check up on everything. Add some screening and try compensation. Again that jump. Where's it come from? Why is there a jump at just this intensity?

The work comes to a dead stop. Nothing left to measure, nothing to compute. Thank God there isn't for a while. What shall I do? Keep out of the way, go to hell, go and eat, go to the library. Go anywhere as long as you're not here.

Where could that jump come from? Anikeyev has nothing to say. Can even the gods be baffled sometimes? No light in the screen, all the needles flat at zero. Silence. Long days of depressing silence. At the next bench they're still measuring and computing. How good to be able to measure and compute. There might be interference from parasitic currents? But how could there be? What about the earth's field? Try it then. My God, he's right, it's the parasitic currents. Anikeyev's a genius. A real genius, a wizard, a sorcerer, a real, live wizard! Here they are, those eddies, the lovely little things. But how do we get rid of them?

"Sergei, let's hook in a coil about this size. Work it out."

Fine! We're computing again. In a moment we'll be able to switch on and that dead pile of apparatus will again buzz with life.

. . . .

"I'd like to know why the hell you've got a dip in that curve?"

"I extrapolated it according to Brakely."

"Who's Brakely?"

"But you said yourself. . . . Don't you remember his article last year?"

"So what?"

"Well, he writes that. . . ."

"People write all sorts of things! How much longer are you going to believe everything you see in print! What have you got on your shoulders—a head or a bookshelf?"

"But Brakely is a theorist, one of the classics!"

"And you, Krylov, are a classic idiot. Your Brakely doesn't know a voltmeter from a gramophone. I want measurements, not hot air out of that old windbag. You ought to have read your classics at the institute. There are no classics here. Here we have experiment, and nothing but experiment. And our own brains. Eat more fish."

. . . .

"If the curve doesn't dip, Brakely's calculations must be wrong?"

"Let 'em be wrong. Let the whole theory be wrong. Does that scare you? We'll have to go and show it to the theorists and let them work it out. Meanwhile let's get our electronics adjusted."

Every bloody instrument going crazy! Sheer mysticism. Never mind, electronics always was mysticism of a kind. No one knows why it won't work. And no one worries. That's how it should be. In a week's time the circuit will suddenly come to life, and no one will be surprised at that either. Electronics! The thing no one can understand now is how it could ever have stopped working. Now you can take any risks you like with it and it will still work. No one could stop it working. . . .

. . . .

"Polish a germanium plate. You don't know how? Well, learn then."

. . . .

"Trash. Paleozoic man could do it better."

. . . .

"Better, but still not good enough."

. . . .

"Krylov, if you're an experimenter you must be able to do everything that's needed and better than anyone else. Otherwise you'll never be able to do anything new."

"But then I'll never have time to become a real specialist. How about the big problems? I want to be able to see the interconnection of things."

"Leave that to the philosophers. A specialist! I don't know what that is. I know what a physicist is. The specialist tries to get to know more and more about less and less until he knows everything about nothing. And the philosopher finds out less and less about more and more until he knows nothing about everything."

. . . .

Eventually, after two weeks' work he polished the plate as well as a professional polisher.

"Passable," Anikeyev grunted.

They set up the plate in front of an emitter. The experiment lasted twenty minutes. The result was a five-figure table. Two days later it turned out that the hypothesis was wrong and the table and the germanium plate were consigned to the bottom drawer.

Anikeyev gave Krylov a wink: "Such is the life of the experimenter."

The man despised difficulty. He ignored minor failures, embarrassments, mistakes, time wasted. His respect and, consequently, disappointment were reserved for the real failures, the dead ends into which they were led in the course of their research.

Anikeyev was a born experimenter. You could tell that by watching his hands with their fingers, pliable as a child's, gently regulating an instrument or fitting a quartz fibre.

The tale was told that when he had been in France before the war he had taken on a bet with a representative of a firm of safe-makers that he could open any of the firm's safes in half an hour. He had won the bet and was immediately detained by the police and ordered to leave the country. When Anikeyev was asked whether this was true he would merely chuckle: "Everyone likes discovering other people's secrets but no one likes having his own discovered."

He never did talk much about himself, but the name of Anikeyev, one of the country's outstanding physicists, was surrounded by legends, which were the more numerous because no one knew much about him.

After the war Anikeyev had been appointed to a leading position in "Problem", that being the name for the atom bomb research project. He was in charge of a group of institutes and factories.

He was in direct contact with Ministers. Well aware of his own value, he did what he thought necessary, regardless of other people's instructions, even Beria's. Beria's unqualified, sometimes disastrous interference enraged him. Legend had it that after one of Beria's harangues Anikeyev lost patience and replied: "I haven't read any works of yours on physics. Nor have you read any of mine, but for a different reason." "I'll give you physics!" Beria had snarled back.

Anikeyev had followed this up by writing a letter to the Central Committee, demanding that "Problem" should be protected from

Beria's oafish interference. Such a challenge was suicidal in those days.

Anikeyev was saved from immediate vengeance by the fact that he was too well known and too much needed. However, on Beria's orders he was removed from "Problem" and transferred to a teacher training college in the North. His colleagues protested that Anikeyev was indispensable, particularly at that moment, when the project was nearing culmination. To no avail.

His friend Likhov, who had replaced him, told him bitterly: "I warned you. Now you've got your reward for your outspokenness. What have you gained by it? You've done only harm."

"No harm done," Anikeyev said. "I'm not leaving till the job's finished."

He was daring enough to stay on and direct the final stages of the work, though it meant practically living underground. This time he really was risking his life. The heads of the project pretended not to be aware of his presence. When the launching operation was completed, he left for the North.

At that time there was no research work being done in the area. With his own money Anikeyev got together a few bits of apparatus and did some research into the nature of smells. The experimental ampules he pushed up his nose were sometimes so savage in their effect that he lost consciousness.

He was one of that rare and fortunate type of scientist who makes a subject of research out of everything he deals with. He was asked to write textbooks and treatises. He refused. Instead he occasionally published small, two- or three-page articles in the magazines.

"The more carefully the work is done the less one has to write about it," he would say.

As soon as Beria was exposed Anikeyev was invited to Moscow. By that time Likhov had been elected a member of the Academy, received numerous awards and was in charge of a whole group of research centres. He offered Anikeyev the directorship of one of his institutes. Anikeyev refused. Likhov tried to talk him round. Wouldn't he consent even to become head of a department?

"I'm not interested," Anikeyev replied. "Give me a laboratory, preferably a small one, with a staff of about four."

This made Likhov think.

"Aren't you being too sure of yourself?" he asked.

Anikeyev shrugged.

"We shall see."

"I wouldn't risk taking on a laboratory at my time of life," Likhov said.

Anikeyev surveyed the huge, luxurious study.

"Can't part with this?"

"It isn't that. I'm afraid. In a laboratory there are no Academicians or lab assistants. There are just experimenters—good or bad."

"Yes, this place is on a different scale."

"Here I am an Academician."

When Anikeyev took his leave, Likhov said: "You're probably right. Sometimes even I have dreams about a galvanometer that I can't set at zero. It's the kind of dream the administrator physicist gets. When I wake up I spend a long time persuading myself that there has to be a scientist in this job too, and that I need this kind of scale. And then I set out for the office."

Anikeyev's laboratory had a special status because he had made it so.

He had organised a separate workshop for himself, acquired a couple of lathes, hired a mechanic and made himself completely independent. Hard-boiled supply agents handled his orders out of turn. Otherwise he would lash out at them at the next conference or complain to the Party Committee, the director, the Ministry or the wall newspaper. No obstacles existed for him. He ploughed ruthlessly through everything like a tank, rumbling and cursing. From his assistants he demanded absolute efficiency. "I've got more ideas than I know what to do with," he would warn them. "Quite enough for the lot of us. I need people who can do what I want done."

Krylov forgave him everything because at last his dream had come true. There was no prospect of any brilliant discoveries in the next few months. Anikeyev was not easy to please. Every day Krylov was found wanting in some field. He couldn't solder properly, couldn't type or couldn't get on with a glass-blower, there was always something he couldn't do. But five minutes after one of Anikeyev's routine outbursts the blissful grin would again spread over Krylov's face. He seemed almost to ooze happiness. Because it was Anikeyev who was cursing him. Because the mounting columns of figures in the tables were figures that he himself had arrived at. Because the beetroot salad in the institute's dining room was the best salad he had ever tasted.

He bought himself a corded felt hat. His grey suit with its heavily padded shoulders and wide trouser bottoms was now out of fashion, but that didn't seem to matter any more. The fact that he was working for Anikeyev elevated him even in Tulin's estimation. They began seeing each other again. Tulin introduced him to his friends.

They had nearly all by this time got Master's degrees, or were working on their theses. Krylov was the only lab assistant among them. They were a gay crowd.

On Saturdays they took their girls out to the Café Nord or to the Scientists' Club. They sported drainpipe trousers and gaudy shirts and enjoyed being taken for lay-abouts—let the squares grumble and sniff. The girls teased the sober ladies of the Scientists' Club with their tight skirts and scandalously long slits. To the music of the legalised foxtrots of the forties they jived with a vigour that made the oldsters blink.

From the Scientists' Club they would go on to somebody's house, usually to Tulin's, who lived with his mother and aunts in a large flat on the Fontanka, where they sipped wine, sang bawdy songs, and had furious arguments about the music of the future and the art of Picasso. They listened to tape recordings of ultramodern jazz, but by midnight they would inevitably find themselves discussing the relationship between micro- and macrocosm, radioastronomy, cybernetics, all the things that were of equal interest to amateur and expert.

For them Babel's stories and Koltsov's articles, only recently republished, were a discovery. Tsvetayeva's poetry was available once more. Documents that had been suppressed in Stalin's time were being published. Most of all they were concerned about the problems arising out of the cult of Stalin's personality, and they enthusiastically and confidently refashioned this imperfect world. In the company of Langmuir, Niels Bohr, Kurchatov and Kapitsa they wielded the most important science of the age. They believed that the future of humanity depended on them; they were its prophets, its benefactors and its liberators.

All of them had brilliant prospects, outstanding ability (two were gifted, three brilliant, the rest were geniuses); they were the bright young men, the "cream" of the young scientific world. They were an example to others and they threatened to cause an upheaval. They were preposterously young (each had approximately 0.25 of a wife and 0.16 of a child); on the other hand their tennis standard was high. In winter they skied; in summer they talked of their contempt for football. They could laugh off any accusation of ignorance but they were mortally offended if anyone doubted their skin-diving ability. They had all had articles published in the physics journals and earned extra fees by reviewing. The Academicians they worshipped they called "The Beard", "The Centaur" and "The Skeleton"; the rest they wrote off as sclerotics. They deliberately professed a liking for everything that was criticised or attacked. They were vehement in defending the expressionists, but none of them had any clear idea of what expressionism was. They sang the praises of concrete music but regularly attended concerts of the Philharmonic, queued up for tickets to hear visiting celebrities, and enthused over

Bach. But when a branch of the Academy of Sciences was founded at Novosibirsk they were the first to apply to go there. Tulin was in despair because his application was refused and for weeks he envied his friends who wrote him letters about a forest hut with an experimental chimney, and about their new idol Lavrentyev, who was shivering with them in their flimsy winter quarters while the future city of science was being built.

Krylov walked home through the nocturnal streets with his head spinning. It touched the clouds and he heard the crunch of other worlds as they collided and perished in the great abyss of outer space.

The galaxy was hurtling along through a curved space, a pulsating universe was contracting and expanding, but on the tiny planet known as Earth, which was for some reason divided up by frontiers, the inhabitants swarmed together in their hive-like dwellings, hearing and seeing nothing.

He felt like Gulliver.

When the working day was over, he walked out of the laboratory as though he were descending into the past, to a strange people that still travelled in tramcars and heated their stoves with wood.

He returned to them from the future, an envoy from distant worlds.

Hi there, people! Do you know what the future holds for you?

Well, I do. I've just come back from there! I've been helping to make the future for you.

Could he be seriously worried by the kitchen smells that penetrated the tiny room he rented from an eccentric old book-collector! It was merely a temporary sanctuary for his mortal frame. His spirit was in the laboratory. What were these domestic trifles to him!

But the moment he set foot in the marble entrance hall of the institute he himself became a Lilliputian. The theorists assembled in a large room, rather like a classroom, on the first floor. There was a cubby-hole next door where the catalogues were kept. Krylov would install himself there and, keeping the door ajar, listen to the theorists "nattering". They actually called their seminars "natters". The official title of "seminar" was quite unsuitable for these noisy gatherings, where every item of serious business came with a joke, and funny stories were related while formulas were written.

The problems that were discussed demanded such a mental effort that constant relaxation was needed.

From outside these theoretical discussions looked like the casual chit-chat of men at leisure. In fact, the theorists' whole working day

would have struck any outsider as odd. A robust young man would
turn up at the institute at ten, or perhaps even eleven, in the morning.
He would wander round the laboratories, drop into the library, look
through the magazines, exchange a few pleasantries with the girls in
the corridor. Very occasionally he might be observed seated at a
desk, writing something or merely staring at the ceiling. The rest
of his time would be taken up chatting to other indolent young men
like himself. And this was regarded as work!

But Krylov, who had known every kind of toil, was never more
exhausted than on the afternoons he spent in the cubby-hole listening
to the theorists "nattering".

He felt as though his head was splitting and his brain about to
burst.

"... If particles have structure they may have a quadrupole
moment. . . ."

"Thomas and Schwanger have shown that. . . ."

"To hell with Schwanger!"

"Let's have a look at this case of a particle with a zero quadrupole
moment."

There would be a scratching of chalk on the board. Blue wisps
of cigarette smoke would float through the half-open door.

"But Thomas and Schwanger say that for the magnetic moment. . . ."

"To hell with that! Ten to the eleventh power is impossible. It's
just a trick, a get-out."

"My dear chap, the best way of being tricked is to consider yourself cleverer than anyone else. So let's take ten to the eleventh. . . ."

It was a kitchen and he was listening to the truth being steamed
out of a hash of facts. From here it would travel a long road, clothed
in formulas that were at first clumsy and uncertain, that had to be
verified and checked in all kinds of chambers and traps and multi-
pliers; and for this they had to think up apparatus and work out
methods and build this expensive apparatus, and this was where
the funds, the supply agents, friends, telegrams, telephone calls, the
bank and affiliated enterprises came into it, and the whole band
of them grumbled and found fault, signed or refused to sign, and
meanwhile the mechanics were grinding and drilling, an odd structure
was taking shape and being adjusted in the middle of the laboratory,
corrections to instruments were being defined, until finally the experiments were carried out for the sake of getting a hundred or
perhaps several hundred metres of film and a few thousand recordings and photographs. Afterwards all this had to be processed,
computed, made up into tables and charts, analysed and passed on
to the electricians at the institute, who, of course, refused to be
bothered with a new formula and new ideas, and who had to be

talked into it until they finally took on the job and started approximating and simplifying, and pushing the thing about between the insulation experts and the vacuum experts, and from them to the designers, until the formula was gradually embodied in copper, glass and electrodes. And the result would be one very small valve or amplifier. But a few years later a valve of this type would be indispensable in a thousand new apparatuses committed to the power of technologists, craftsmen and the quick fingers of girl fitters, none of whom had any conception of the uncomfortable, uninteresting-looking room where this had all begun, and from which the springs of future rivers had bubbled forth, carrying new ideas and new laws of physics.

When the theorists dispersed, Krylov would step cautiously into the empty room, walk over to the rusty-looking board with equations scrawled all over it, and heave a sigh.

What was he? An experimenter or a theorist?

He told himself that experimental work was what really mattered. Apparatus was the tool with which man got his first glimpse of the secrets of nature. The important thing was to get at the facts. Ideas changed; facts were always facts. Facts were an eternal value.

He walked slowly down the stairs to the laboratory, leaving behind this inaccessible, higher world of pure thought, which was free of knife-switches, leads and the errors of the galvanometer.

Little by little he began to feel oppressed by Anikeyev's domineering intolerance. The man's intellect cramped him, tied him down. In his presence it was impossible to think. Even if you did think, he would make you think as he wanted you to. He hammered his own conceptions in by force; the power of his arguments excluded all other speculation.

Someone at the October Works got to know that Anikeyev was achieving promising results in his research on discharges. Gatenyan paid a visit to the institute and Krylov introduced him to Anikeyev. Gatenyan wanted to incorporate Anikeyev's work in the projected new equipment for transmission lines. Krylov was glad to be able to give his own people this modicum of help, but Anikeyev received the chief designer coldly.

"This is very odd," he said. "Have they turned the heat on you? Why don't you go on as you've been going on? We're still in a fog with what we're doing. I wonder who let the cat out of the bag." And he glanced suspiciously at Krylov.

"We'll shoulder all the risk," Gatenyan said. "We feel confident you'll bring it off."

Anikeyev bowed.

"Much obliged, I'm sure! But what do you get out of it? You're production workers, you ought to resist all innovation, yet here you are, grabbing at something before it's half-cooked. That's not the way of things. There's a catch somewhere."

The chief forced a smile.

"If your idea fails, we shall be in a hole. But we'll be in an even bigger hole if we go on producing the same equipment we produced in the forties." He showed Anikeyev the blueprints of the apparatus that was still being used on the experimental line.

Anikeyev frowned.

"Yes, that's a lot of old junk, of course. But give us a little while to polish our stuff up."

"That's impossible."

"If I give you my promise, you're quite prepared to start retooling?"

"We'll allot space for small circuit-breakers and get on with casting the pipes right away."

Anikeyev drove off with him to the factory, came back in a bad mood and pounced on Krylov.

"You dragged me into this! How can I refuse them? How, I ask you?"

They were taking a risk, of course. The result, which was technically quite feasible, had to be achieved by the scheduled date.

"It's like promising to pay a debt with the money in the purse you think you'll find lying on the doorstep next week," Anikeyev grumbled.

Krylov chuckled. He realised that in his heart of hearts Anikeyev admired Gatenyan and the lads from the design office.

Unfortunately, Krylov was foolish enough to draw Anikeyev's attention to a correction of scale that needed to be introduced. He suggested finding it not by experiment but by calculation. This would save time and effort.

Anikeyev listened with an inscrutable face to Krylov's arguments and, when Krylov had finished, he began humming to himself. With his eye pressed to an instrument he got through three melodies, *Toreador, In the Field a Birch-Tree Stood* and *Blue of the Night.*

Then he asked:

"Do you know, Krylov, what is more dangerous than a fool? Well, if you don't, I'll tell you. It's a fool with initiative."

One of the laboratory staff, Yuri Yuryevich, said to Krylov when Anikeyev had left the room: "Sergei, don't tell me you're offended. Anikeyev shoots off his mouth as naturally as a bird flies."

"He wants to turn me into a robot!"

"My dear fellow, Mayakovsky used to say we're all a little bit like robots. And that was way back."

"We'll see who does the roboting!"

He hated Anikeyev. Tyrant! Arakcheyev! Martinet! The word "fool" had stung him like a whip. He'd see who was the fool! Secretly he challenged Anikeyev to a duel, but at once got cold feet. Anikeyev's intuition was just a bit too accurate. But once the avalanche had started, it grew. While obediently carrying out all instructions, he argued mutely, ferreted out the weak spots, turned into a merciless enemy of his own work.

He stayed behind in the laboratory in the evenings, came at six in the morning and sat down at the computer. But there was something he didn't quite like about his calculations. In his haste he must have oversimplified the conditions. The solution lacked symmetry. He wanted to bowl Anikeyev over, pin him down.

Krylov turned off on to the embankment. His mind was in a fog after all those cigarettes and endless figures. To hell with it all, but at least he had arrived at the kind of proof he wanted. Beauty and symmetry were dubious qualities anyway.

On the edge of the Petrovsky Square a girl was squatting in front of a motorcycle.

"Hi!" she called out to him. "Could you help me, please?"

Krylov went over to her and helped her lever off one of the tyres.

"Don't go away," she said, "I shan't be able to get it on without you."

Krylov leaned on the embankment wall. The promenade was deserted, the small yellow moon anonymous amid the street lamps. The girl patched up the damaged inner tube. Her leather slacks and helmet brought out the boyish sturdiness of her figure.

"What are you wandering around for at this time of night?" she asked. "You a sleep-walker, or haven't you got a home to go to?"

"I'm a sleep-walker."

"That's fashionable, isn't it? Specially in March."

Krylov looked around unbelievingly. There was water everywhere. The whole city was wet. Roofs were dripping, drainpipes gurgling, manholes hissing; little moonlit puddles glistened on the pitted wall of the embankment. The ice on the Neva was a mere wafer.

It really was the end of March; women always know about such things.

The girl stood up and wiped her hands.

"I can give you a lift home."

They hurtled along the sleeping streets, splashing through the puddles. The motorcycle backfired deafeningly. Krylov clung to the pillion rest. When the girl lowered her head, the damp air hit him full in the face. Traffic lights were strung high all along the avenue. There was no traffic but the lights were still changing—yellow, green and red. The scanty darkness was floating out of the sky, taking the stars and the moon with it.

She skidded to a halt outside his house and Krylov lurched forward, striking his face against her shoulder.

"Fast work, eh? Were you scared?"

He mumbled something in reply.

"What are you thinking about all the time?"

The dawn was breaking. Above her apple-firm cheeks Krylov noticed a pair of wildly merry eyes that seemed to glisten like everything else.

"I was calculating how many people of this city we must have woken up."

"How many?"

"About seventy thousand."

"Fine! Who exactly are you anyway?"

"A physicist."

She eyed his shabby raincoat doubtfully.

"We'll assume that's so. And we woke up seventy thousand, did we?" She smiled as she got into the saddle again. "Well, physicist, I think you're nice because you didn't paw me. I can't bear men who start pawing me when I give them a lift."

His eyes slid automatically to the sharp breasts under her jacket, and he blushed.

"Thanks for your help!"

Her eyes were always smiling, but now she seemed to shoot out this irrestrainable smile with another, special smile that was just for him. Encouraged, Krylov pushed his hat to one side, and put his arm round the girl's shoulder in the best tradition of Tulin and company. "Mademoiselle, you're charming. What about Saturday? You will have a young scientist at your disposal for the whole evening. May I have your phone number?" Or words to that effect.

At first she stared at him in surprise, then she giggled, and he felt a complete idiot.

"Seriously tho'. Couldn't we meet sometime?" he tried again wretchedly.

"Off he goes! Always the same old story. Can't you do better than that, dear physicist?"

Her motorcycle backfired and she sped away into the misty stillness of the streets. All that was left of her were the black figures on her yellow number-plate. "52-67," he repeated gloomily to himself as he pulled off his muddy trousers and went to bed on his narrow couch.

He carefully revised his calculations, which showed that the correction Anikeyev had ignored altered the final measurement figure by 40 per cent. He drew a highly decorative frame round the figure 40, and under it, a coat of arms consisting of a defiant thumb protruding between two fingers against a background of apparatus pierced by a fountain-pen. There was an hour to go before work. With a reference book for a pillow he fell calmly asleep on Anikeyev's desk, enjoying the untroubled slumber of victory.

That morning for some unknown reason Anikeyev arrived at the laboratory before anyone else. Krylov was awakened by his booming laughter. Anikeyev was standing over him, holding the notebook in which he had done his calculations. Krylov stayed in his chair, showed no embarrassment, made no apology. Rubbing his eyes, he waited modestly in expectation of praise, general rejoicing and the confused acknowledgements that Anikeyev would feel obliged to make. Of course, he would be generous. Who hasn't made mistakes, he would say to Anikeyev. Let's forget the past. The mistakes of the great should be commensurate with their achievements. . . .

When he had finished reading the notebook, Anikeyev blew his nose loudly.

"You've proved it."

"Who hasn't made. . . ."

"Shut up. I don't need laboratory assistants that get above themselves. You can take yourself off."

"Where to?"

"Wherever you like."

He threw the notebook down on the desk and walked out.

"You'll have to accept my correction all the same!" Krylov shouted after him.

Like the other martyrs of science he was quite prepared to be burnt at the stake. As he emptied the drawers of his desk and put his papers together he thought out the wording of the last entry he would make in the laboratory diary. If Gogol had not already said it, he would have been satisfied with: "What are you laughing at? No one but yourselves!"

An hour later Anikeyev returned. Without looking at his assistant he said gruffly that on the director's instructions Krylov had been made a full-fledged member of the research staff and given a subject to investigate independently.

The astonished Krylov went off without a word to get the appointment registered, but turned back halfway.

"It must have been you who recommended me," he said to Anikeyev.

"Not likely!" Anikeyev replied. "Last thing that would occur to me!"

"Of course it was you. Thank you so much! You know...."

"For God's sake, Krylov, stop drooling and shut up."

"I'm afraid to take on an independent subject."

"In that case you'd better ask for a job as a book-keeper. But you might make the grade. Shall I tell you why? Because I haven't managed to teach you anything. If I can't teach a man anything, it means there's something to him."

To celebrate the event Krylov visited Tulin with a bottle of brandy. It lasted them for five toasts. For the sixth they went through the sideboard and used the last drops from sticky liqueur bottles, then set out with satisfied consciences for the nearest shashlyk restaurant.

Tulin ordered Kars shashlyks and winked with both eyes at Ostapych the waiter, whereupon Ostapych brought them shashlyks and two uncorked bottles of what appeared to be lemonade, and returned Tulin's wink. The "lemonade" was excellent. They swallowed it appreciatively and helped it down with mushrooms and onions, and gradually Krylov ceased to doubt his ability to do independent research.

"You're becoming almost human," Tulin said. "I've been teaching you for years you've got to stimulate the higher nervous activity. Now you're in orbit, you can get a move on. There's not a moment to lose.... Let's have another drink. And you've got to set yourself an aim. Have you got an aim? What do you really want?"

"I want ... I want what I want!"

"Exactly! That's the formula!"

"I'm my own master, I'm a grown-up person. The days of youth are over.... But tell me this, Oleg, why have I got this urge for theory? The theorists, you know, they're the chaps who do the steering."

"They're just windbags, that's what your theorists are! What can they say against an experiment? But perhaps you're a Niels Bohr? Or a Landau? You've either got to be an all-rounder or you can go and do administrative work. In an experiment, you know, you can sometimes bring off a real catch! There are too many theorists about. Sergei, old chap, if you'd only been at our place the other day. The chief and I—touch wood!—what a discovery we may make!

We're men of action. Give us something to get our teeth into, something we can feel and see. Leave the speculating to the academics."

"Yes, we'll leave that to them. We're the men who do the spade-work. We're the bed-rock."

"We'll measure that gradient. And then the theorists had better look out or all their theory will be upside down."

"Anikeyev's a genius. And Dan's a genius."

"What about Kapitsa? Don't you think he's a genius? Why, he's even more a genius than the others."

"You'll probably be a genius yourself one day, Oleg."

"Geniuses are out of date. A genius in science is like a sailing ship in the navy. Romance of the past! Nowadays scientists all get down to it together and solve any problem. Collective discovery—that's your genius for you! My chief is nearly a genius, but what is he without us—just number one. I may be a zero. In comparison with the chief I am a zero. But I'm a zero that makes number one into ten."

"I'm a zero too!"

"I'm coming round to the idea that quantum mechanics has reached a dead end. Why? See that red-nosed profiteer over there? Let him explain. . . . De Broglie's not a child, is he? What if he is a prince? Does that mean we needn't reckon with him? No, Sergei, he may be a prince but quantum mechanics is no good. . . ."

Krylov agreed and the two of them disposed of quantum mechanics without much difficulty. Then they set the elementary particles in order, but to complete the confusion and rout of the Niels Bohr school they had to order another bottle, which Ostapych brought them when they were well inside the atomic nucleus. They drank it in strict quantum portions and then they at last managed to split an electron. By that time Tulin was an Academician and a state prize-winner and Krylov was standing for his Doctor's degree. Tulin was his official opponent. Krylov gave a banquet and they invited all the girls they knew. They discussed Shostakovich's music, the lost secrets of fireworks, the radioactivity of crabs, the feminine charms of the Empress Catherine and cures for cancer.

When he heard Krylov's story of the girl on the motorcycle Tulin decided that they must go and find her at all costs and hauled Krylov off to the local militia station. When they were shown out of there they set off for the nearest Highway Inspection Department and Tulin gave the astonished inspectors an inspired description of how before his very eyes his friend had been run over by a girl on motor-cycle 52-67. She had not just run him over, she had ridden to and fro over his prostrate body and shouted that she didn't care a damn about highway inspectors. He declared on oath that this was all absolutely true, was ready to sign any statement about it, exhibited

Krylov as the meek and helpless victim and finally overwhelmed the inspectors by informing them that he and Krylov were on the threshold of the greatest discovery physics had ever known.

Had they been drinking? Yes, they had been obliged to have a drink to aid their recovery after the accident. With tears in his eyes he resumed his description of the attack by motorcycle 52-67, adding some even more harrowing details.

They were taken into the office and a report was made out, but when asked what his address was Tulin just couldn't remember the name of the street where he lived, so he rang up Professor Chistyakov to find out. Professor Chistyakov had a word with the inspector on duty, but this was not heeded, for Tulin and Krylov were by that time discussing whether Anikeyev wasn't a greater scientist than Chistyakov because Anikeyev wore braces.

They spent the next three hours in the company of three drunken drivers and a skilled pickpocket who had never read Freud. They had an excellent discussion with him about hypnosis and dreams, but some of their propositions remained unproven because in the middle of the argument they were taken back to the duty inspector's office to be introduced to the owner of motorcycle 52-67. Her name was Lena—Yelena Nikolayevna Belskaya. The matter was sorted out in five minutes. Citizen Krylov, gazing into Citizeness Belskaya's furious eyes, confessed with a sigh that he had received no bodily injury, and that all his evidence had been evoked by a desire to see Citizeness Belskaya again, against whom he had no claims whatever. Citizeness Belskaya at first wanted the case against Citizen Krylov to go before the court, and stated that three years' corrective labour would be just about the right penalty. She soon reduced the sentence to fifteen days, however. Citizen Tulin and the above-mentioned Krylov were both fined five rubles each. Furthermore, in view of his intoxicated condition and lack of money or identification papers, Citizen Krylov was detained in custody, pending confirmation of his identity.

In the morning Krylov walked out into the street with a headache that made him wince at every step. On a motorcycle standing at the kerb sat Citizeness Belskaya and she was smiling. She took him home and gave him strong tea to drink, and all this she did with such a smile that he flew off to the institute on a pair of snow-white wings that brushed the heads of common mortals as he passed.

He was asked to test the distribution of space charges. He was given a complete set of apparatus to work with. He was given his own desk and cupboard. He sat on a high stool surrounded by apparatus. He switched on and switched off, and made adjustments, he was his own master, fortune's darling. If that wasn't happiness, what was? Had the age of the individual scientist passed? Nothing of the kind! He worked alone without any feeling of loneliness. He discussed his problems with Langmuir and Stark and another score of old men who had some connection with his work. They made up an excellent team of debaters and advisers, though as the work proceeded they more and more often spread their arms in defeat.

After his first measurements it struck him that the distribution picture would be too approximate. He decided he needed more accuracy. He tried out several kinds of suspension fibres. He installed a supersensitive galvanometer. Then he had the idea of automatically stabilising the temperature of the instrument and taking into account the distortion caused by the transformer.

"Why don't you allow for the aurora borealis? And what about the charges in the doorkeeper's cat?" Anikeyev asked him. "You're ill. And your illness is called 'I can't stop myself'. You can't see the wood for the trees. You must learn to control yourself. When you've got an approximate quantity, just push on ahead. Looking for absolute truth is a waste of time. And does absolute truth exist anyway?"

But for Anikeyev he would have been hopelessly lost. The struggle he had with the compensator was a case in point. Krylov and the compensator didn't get on from the start. In defiance of all the laws the compensator produced any reading it felt inclined to. Krylov tilted it, changed the valves and poked his pencil furiously at the suspension until the compensator ran amok. They began to hate each other. The compensator deliberately reversed its readings. Krylov stripped it down to the last nut and bolt and assembled it again. Then the compensator played a foul trick; it pretended to be in perfect order but, just when he was in the middle of his measuring, it suddenly went haywire and upset all the other data.

Anikeyev came in and without a word smashed his heavy fist against the panel with such force that the compensator drew in its horns at once and began to work properly.

Anikeyev lent him a pulse generator. Anikeyev helped him to find one of the forty possible causes of error. Anikeyev poked his big pendulous nose round the dials as though trying to smell out something, and his face with its big ape-like jaw seemed to Krylov the epitome of kindness and brotherhood.

Krylov envied him and was painfully and shamefully aware of it. He lacked so many of the things that were needed to become even a half-good experimenter. He lacked the patience to struggle with instruments, the character to fight a war with a mechanism, the gumption to manage the departmental chiefs and to get round the glass-blower; he hadn't sufficient distrust of manuals, he lacked humour, imagination, pliability, firmness, daring and caution. Gradually he realised that he couldn't handle a vacuum, couldn't curse impressively enough, couldn't translate from Italian or make up a decent bibliography. The worst of it was that everyone in the institute seemed to be expecting something of him.

His tussle with Anikeyev and subsequent appointment had been taken as a sign of unusual character. His shyness was treated as modesty, his silence as an ability to concentrate, and even his lack of manual skill as freshness of approach.

He felt like an impostor, a charlatan, a trickster, who might at any moment be unmasked. He was particularly afraid of Dankevich. He tried to keep out of his way, and if Dankevich was speaking at a seminar he would go back to his old practice of eavesdropping from the cubby-hole.

Those who wanted to work for Dankevich had to pass a test. It was called the Dan test and consisted of a series of problems and questions devised by Dan himself. No official titles or diplomas were awarded for passing it, no marks were given, nothing went on record, yet every electrophysicist considered it an honour to take this voluntary examination.

It was of no importance to Dankevich whether he had before him a Doctor of Science or a young engineer; he made no allowances for anyone. Many of the well-established disliked this attitude but their objections cut no ice with Dankevich.

The young people worshipped him. He was pursued by a crowd of admirers, anxious to catch any remark he might make. At seminars he had the casting vote. This was not due to his seniority but to his superlative ability to simplify even the most involved problem. And since this simplified model or idea occurred to him sooner than to anyone else, everyone knew that there was no sense in going on if in the middle of a report he declared the whole thing "drivel".

What was the secret of Dankevich's talent? There had been mathematicians with more powerful intellects, physicists who had known more. . . . Anikeyev would answer the question with a smile: "It's quite simple. Dan sees everything just a little differently from us. That's the trick of it."

This city, like all big cities, was not equipped for love. There were people everywhere, and everywhere there was a chilly wind. The parks were closed. The sodden benches on the boulevards were occupied by old men and nannies. And every word that was spoken, every rustle of sound could be heard through the thin plywood that partitioned off Krylov's room.

Throughout the ages *he* and *she* had sought solitude and sanctuary and sought them in vain. They had to flee to the moon, to the farthest constellations or, when they managed to buy tickets, go to the cinema. There their refuge from the rest of the world was darkness. In that refuge there were no faces, no eyes, only their interlocking fingers.

Lena's flimsy squirrel coat gave her hardly any warmth. She looked sad and tired, not at all like the girl he had first met. She only just came up to his shoulder and he wanted to warm her, hold her in his arms.

They sat in the back row, munched chocolate wafers and talked all kinds of nonsense. But for that stupid arm-rest between them they would have been perfectly happy. There was no need to try to be clever; he said what came into his head and felt at ease, yet he couldn't bring himself to take her small rough hand in his and press it to his cheek, and this shyness made him feel good in a special kind of way. On the screen people suffered, fine words were spoken, breasts heaved with emotion. If Lena gave her quiet little laugh and said "bunk", the picture instantly turned into a parody. But sometimes Lena would cast him as the hero of the picture and put him at the wheel of the car in which they fled across mountain roads to the sea, escaping from some villainous landowner; or else they found themselves stranded in some remote hunting lodge, tucking into a huge ham in front of a roaring fire.

"I'm hungry," Lena would declare.

He would suggest going to a restaurant.

"Look here, physicist," she would say. "Don't show off. It doesn't suit you."

They bought hot pies and ate them there and then, at the counter, helping them down with tomato juice.

Krylov took her home. The sky was full of stars, and it gave him an idea. He presented it to Lena, as one might present a flower. He had never thought about such things before.

"Isn't it curious that we see the universe not as it now is but as it was when it was younger, a long, long time ago. The stars we can see may no longer exist. We are surrounded by images of the past; and only we ourselves are the present.... If there's anyone looking at us from some distant planet at this moment, they don't actually see us either. They may be able to see the October Revolution, or Pushkin riding out for his duel, or perhaps the morning the *streltsi* were executed, but not us."

Lena halted, stood on tiptoe, pulled his head down and kissed him. He glanced round at the passers-by but at once felt ashamed of having done so and kissed her salty lips, which still smelled of tomato juice.

"I'd ask you in," she said, matter-of-factly, "but you know what it is with a mother and sisters around—not the right atmosphere."

The swift warm spring did all it could for them. When it grew dark they climbed the fence of the Summer Garden and darted across the crunchy gravel of the shadowy paths, trying to keep out of sight of the watchman.

Green light dripped from the shoulders of marble goddesses. Their bare white arms seemed almost transparent. Lena stared up at them in delight, a gleam of moonlight on her teeth, and Krylov thought to himself that even the greatest art bore no comparison with the warmth of her small rough hand, that this girl with her button-nose and high cheekbones was much more of a miracle than any marble beauty.

Lena was an assistant cameraman at a film studio. She knew artists and composers, she had famous film stars at her beck and call. This was a mysterious, unknown world in which Krylov felt himself a boring and colourless oaf.

Strangely enough, she seemed not to be aware of her superiority and his questions bored her; but neither was she interested in his affairs. She liked wandering about the town or tearing across it on her motorcycle, getting involved in street incidents, being sad and having fun. She seemed to break out of confinement and fling herself into a noisy tireless game, extracting pleasure from everything.

"Today's the happiest day in my life," she would declare.

"You said the same thing the day before yesterday."

"The day before yesterday's over and done with. So's yesterday. We're living in today and we've got to make it the happiest of all days."

She made no demands on his time. Once when he was so carried away by an idea that he started drawing in his notebook, Lena quietly disappeared, without taking any offence. Later she merely warned him: "If you've got work to do, for goodness sake don't hold out on me. It's the dreaded end when a boy goes around with you because he thinks he ought to." He liked this attitude, but it worried him too. She might just as easily disappear altogether.

In a way she reminded him of Tulin. Was it her lightness of touch? Her love of life? He couldn't understand why Tulin made so little impression on her.

"We must be too much alike. That's always a bore," she said and screwed up her nose in disapproval at his new tie with its palm-tree pattern. "Why are you trying to look smooth? You ought to have bought yourself a pair of shoes."

He was disappointed but Lena put her arms round his neck.

"All right, you funny thing! I love you as you are, so you needn't sulk. You'll never outdo Tulin anyway. You're the hayseed type."

She kept things on a friendly basis and insisted on paying when he had no money. She despised conventions and could be brutally frank. At first this jarred on him.

"I had a boy trailing around after me once. Terrifically intellectual type. One day we'd been having a long walk and I could see he was in a tiz, so I asked him if he wanted to go to the lavatory. You should have seen how offended he was. Told me I ought to be ashamed of myself, then went on and on about the surrealists. In the end he began to get mixed up, so I let him go and he made a dive straight for the nearest backyard. That was a surrealist for you. I'm supposed to be crude and addicted to the lower instincts, while his trailing around with me for three hours dreaming of getting into a backyard—that's poetry, knightly conduct!"

There was a grain of seriousness in her gay challenging of conventions. She once confessed to him:

"Fine words set my teeth on edge. We spend all day rehearsing bits of dialogue. First the director has his say, then his assistant, then the sound producer, then the actors themselves. They all keep on repeating the same words over and over again to get them natural. I can't bear it! After a time it becomes a relief to swear. It kind of clears your throat. What they say is all so ideal and perfect, it must be like having sucked sweets put in your mouth. Yet I know those words had real meaning once and could stir real emotion."

That year spring came up from the South at a speed of about forty miles a day. Krylov was spurred on by the pace of it. His work suddenly began to flow fast and well. The packs of photographs he needed for his report began to pile up on his desk. The magazine *Technical Physics* published his article, and he presented Lena with an offprint.

When she tried to read it aloud she got stuck on every word. "Configuration space . . . fluctuation . . . relaxation." Horrors! Surely he didn't know what it all meant? She stared at him in admiration, as if she had only just noticed what he was really like. So he was a real physicist after all? She had to confess she had thought he might be shooting a line and was probably only a lab assistant or a mechanic.

She marched him off to a party at the Cinema Workers' Club and proudly introduced him to her friends as a physicist. While handsome, smooth-talking young men engaged her in conversation about sets, scripts and the editing of rushes and happily tore to pieces the work of a director they called the "reserve hatchet man", Krylov remained dumbly jealous and was quite sure that Lena must find every one of these young men more fascinating than himself. He couldn't understand why she bothered with him, or what use he could be to her.

As he stared about him, he happened to see above the heads of the crowd in the entrance hall a familiar unruly sheaf of greying hair.

"Look! It's Dankevich!" he whispered delightedly.

Someone turned round with a drawl of surprise.

A young director asked who the strange bird was.

"Haven't you heard of Dankevich?" Krylov exclaimed.

No one had. With an air of great knowledge the young director concocted a fantastic mixture out of Einstein, Fermi, Denisov, the atom bomb, anti-particles and the Tunguska meteorite.

Krylov was astonished. Anti-particles? Denisov? How could anyone know Denisov without knowing Dankevich! Why could no one see the shining halo round Dan's head? They ought to bow and make way for him. The man was a genius. He had given humanity far more than all these film-makers put together.

"So you think we ought to carry his picture during the May Day demonstration?" Lena asked.

"Perhaps. It'd make more sense than selling photographs of film stars on every news-stand."

"What exactly has he done?" the director asked.

"Done?" Krylov repeated eagerly. He mentioned several small articles of five or ten pages each.

"Is that all? Then he's not done much more than you," Lena commented.

Krylov flared up.

"He's only got two ears like me, too, but so what? He's a genius and I'm nothing." And he launched into a tirade about Dan that impressed them all.

As they walked together to their seats Lena whispered to him: "You were wonderful! But whatever you say, your Dan's got a neck like a plucked goose."

They nearly quarrelled. He told her that anyone could sneer at the great but it wouldn't make him any greater. On the other hand, said she, there were people who praised great men in the hope of enjoying a little reflected glory. And some other people, he began. . . .

What did people need other people for anyway, she interrupted. Since they didn't write scientific articles.... In ten minutes they got to the point of breaking off relations for ever, then just couldn't remember how it had all begun.

By the time the evening was over Lena said: "You know, I think your old goose has got something after all."

Krylov was happy. But that scraggy goose-neck! How was it he hadn't noticed that Dan had a long scraggy neck that was all goose-flesh?

For the past year Dan had been engaged in plasma research. The subject was controversial. Was there any connection with the earth's electrical field? Who cared if there was? It was all too abstract. The chances of success were small and the practical effect was dubious.

Dan himself was quite undisturbed by considerations of success or failure. At a seminar he said something that made a deep impression on Krylov.

"If a man does what he feels impelled to do, mistakes or failures mean nothing to him."

Dankevich lived on some eternal snowy peak that could not be reached by ordinary human doubts and passions. But Krylov must have been influenced by the intoxicating sense of lightness, by the belief in the impossible that emanated from Lena. Of course, his request was ridiculous and utterly foolish, but that was Krylov all over. Consider his actions beforehand? Impossible. He couldn't think quick enough for that.

He said to Dan: "I want to work with you."

For some unknown reason Dan agreed.

"Very well."

He said it quite calmly, as if they were merely going out for a walk, and quite suddenly Krylov's feet left the ground. Only later, in a conversation with Tulin, he felt surprised at his own audacity. In answer to Tulin's cool assessment of the situation (good-bye to youth, first results in ten years' time, if you're lucky), he merely replied: "Why don't you ever argue with Dan?"

Tulin burst out laughing.

"Even when I'm wrong I can still convince most people I'm right, but I might be right three times over with Dan and he'd still prove me wrong."

Anikeyev was disappointed by this betrayal of radioactive particles. Much though he respected Dan, Anikeyev was convinced, as usual, that his own subject was the only one that was really worth while, and that only a fool could leave his laboratory, particularly when the new apparatus was just about to be installed. Krylov waved him a careless farewell. He was flying high. Others could stay on the ground, with their common sense, their worries about results and other reasonable considerations.

He was flying into the land of his future, with its electrical storms and turbulence, its aurorae, its thunder and lightning, into the unknown chaos that surrounds the earth. All these years he had merely wandered among the galaxies and suddenly he had found his own road of stars. The choice seemed to him almost as inexplicable as love; out of a thousand possibilities he was enchanted by one, and it was an enchantment that might last for life.

He could accelerate ions, collect space charges, focus electrons into the finest of beams and make them follow any curve. These particles, of which he himself, Dan, everyone else, the whole universe were composed, actually obeyed him. He could measure their charges, mass and speed, he could do what he chose with them.

But these powers were of no use to him in his relations with Lena. Lena could disappear at any moment and he knew he had no way of stopping her. She lived in a different dimension, on another planet, where the usual ties had no effect. He could work with Dan, he could make any discovery, he could be elected an honorary member of the French Academy of Sciences, and Lena would merely say: "Terrific! Let's go to the Richter concert." His world was a stony desert where she could take no root.

Without telling Lena he tried reading the magazine *Cinema Art* and, armed with a battery of impressive-sounding terms, started holding forth. Things seemed to be going quite well, but Lena screwed up her nose:

"For goodness sake! Can't I be spared that jargon even with you? I'd rather you told me about your electric charges. By the way, I've learnt a smashing new song."

"Aren't you keen on your profession?"

"Yes and no." She paused thoughtfully. "Actually I am, but not very much depends on me. You see, you're always tied up with other people. I may pull my weight but good photography alone can't save a picture. Our decor artist, for instance, he's brilliant and he's made some wonderful sets. But what's the use? The picture's no good. Rotten script, rotten director. So all the artist's efforts are wasted. It all goes down the drain." She paused again. "You started telling me once about the universal law of the conservation of energy. If it's universal, why doesn't it operate with us? What happens to

all our work when the picture's a flop? Your law may work in test-
tubes but it's no good in life."

He had never seen her so serious and so sad.

"But when a picture's good, you get it all back again. People
laugh and cry, you make millions of them think. . . ."

"And where does that get us? When I was at school I thought
that if everyone had read *Don Quixote*, Chekhov and Tolstoi they'd
never be able to hurt one another any more."

She was so grieved by the failure of her picture that all mankind,
past and future, was condemned to eternal woe. He took her in his
arms and said firmly and quickly:

"I love you."

She nodded seriously.

"Lena, let's get married. Why don't you want us to be together?"

Even before he had finished speaking, he felt that something had
happened. She seemed to have slipped from his grasp. She was miles
away. He rambled on about getting a room, about moving and buying
things, while she watched him affectionately from another planet.

"But what's the hurry? Don't get yourself tied up, it'll only
hamper you. You're just starting on the hardest part of the journey.
You said yourself what a job it was to keep up with Dan. All that
can wait. Aren't we happy as it is?"

"No, I'm unhappy. I can't bear being without you."

"But we are together, Sergei. Consider I'm your wife. Does my
own darling like fruit salad? Because his sweetie Lenochka is going
to make her darling a nice little fruit salad." She giggled, jumped to
her feet and ran out into the kitchen. And again it was all a game.

Soon he was given a room of his own. Lena would come in, put
on an apron and wash and scrub, and spend hours rearranging his
two pieces of furniture, the couch and the bookcase. Sometimes she
would stay for several days, but never for good.

Krylov became more and more tormented by the uncertainty of
their relationship. Life with her was gay, unexpected and frighten-
ingly unstable. He could never be sure whether she would come back
tomorrow, next month or several years hence. Only her going was
a reality. She seemed quite confident that for him, too, it was all
just a game of kissing and wild motorcycle rides, a game that would
always remain a game, no matter how far it went.

He once made her so mad with his endless pleas for stability
that she jumped out of bed and left the house. It was 2 a.m. Krylov
got dressed, seized the vase of flowers she had given him as a birthday
present, threw it down the rubbish chute and went out for a walk.

By daybreak he had made up his mind that love was a weakness unworthy of a man, that the joy of work was the highest and purest of all emotions, that the earth received its electricity from non-terrestrial sources, that Lena had fat legs, that sex relations were purely physiological, that he was a nonentity, that no one could possibly find him interesting, that she was absolutely right, that he would go away and she would realise how much she had lost, and that women were only to be despised.

Everything had been child's play till now. Only now did he begin to understand what real work was, what exhausting, relentless effort lay behind the apparently aimless "nattering" of the theorists. The team had been working with Dan for several months and Krylov had to catch up, but he couldn't even follow the workings of Dan's mind, his impossibly concise statements. Dan moved ahead in colossal leaps and Krylov panted after him, trying to reconstruct his reasoning, miserably aware of Dan's impatience with stragglers.

From time to time the whole team would gather in Dan's office for a progress conference. Poltavsky, a young computer expert of a formalistic turn of mind and much given to displays of cynicism, complained furiously that Krylov had made him recalculate his results three times, when the discrepancy had actually been due to faulty screening.

"How was I to know?" Krylov retorted. "I don't trust your equations."

Poltavsky appealed to Dan.

"Look at this paranoiac. He doesn't recognise mathematics. It doesn't exist for him. Come to that, I can prove he himself doesn't exist."

"When you're through with this job, you had better calculate the heat balance of the new operating conditions," Dan replied calmly.

New operating conditions! That meant reassembling the whole plant. From this man's Olympic peak Krylov's efforts to fit a copper tube into the assembly without cooling the glass seemed petty indeed.

"How much longer are you going to muck about with this screening business?" Dan asked with genuine surprise. "Couldn't you have got it right from the start?"

The new screens were no use, and they had to install sparkless motors. After that they discovered they didn't know whether the scale was correct for simulating these particular phenomena. Dan calculated the conditions for which the model would be suitable, then the model had to be tested for operating stability. The amplifier, it turned out, was ineffective for low-power signals, so they ordered a special amplifier from the Radio Institute. The reply came back in the form of a request for detailed specifications, permission from the Ministry and the right to call in Dan for consultations at any time in the next ten years.

When everything had eventually been fitted, adjusted and measured, the results showed that the transfer of a single ion required an effort equal to that of about seventy-five electric locomotives, that an electron could not be accommodated in anything smaller than a two-storey house, and that every living creature on earth ought to feel like a person with his fingers on a live electric plug.

Once again they assembled in Dan's office to make bitter fun of the results of two months' unremitting work. The initial postulates were wrong. The formulas were absurd. The theory idiotic. The apparatus they had built and adjusted with such care was junk for the scrap-heap. Start all over again, from the beginning. But where was the beginning? The whole thing was just a blank. Law of the conservation of energy ... dead end ... lap of the gods. ... And what guarantee could anyone give?

Dan scanned the tables imperturbably and went on asking questions as though nothing special had happened. They left him and wandered off to lunch, disconsolately discussing why Mayakovsky had committed suicide.

In the dining room Krylov was told Dan wanted to see him.

"There's a call for you," Dan said when he reached the office. Krylov picked up the receiver.

"Sergei, are you ill?" It was Lena's voice.

"N-no."

"Why haven't you rung me for the past fortnight? Aren't you ashamed?"

Her indignation was perfectly innocent. Krylov remembered how she had left the flat, the crackle as she yanked on her stockings, the gleam of a bare shoulder at the window, and sighed.

"I thought. . . ."

"You think too much, and only of yourself. And all your talk is a lot of hot air."

"Well, just now, you see. . . ."

"I want to see you."

"I want to see *you*."

"Let's go to the Philharmonic this evening."

"All right."

"Where do we meet?"

He looked helplessly at Dan.

"At the door."

Dan sniffed absent-mindedly and walked out of the office.

"Are you mad?" Krylov bellowed into the phone. "D'you realise what number you got?"

"I was told you were with Dan. I explained everything to him. I think he understood."

Dan was standing in the corridor, biting his pencil. Krylov tried to slip past unobserved, but Dan stopped him.

"Congratulations!"

"I'm awfully sorry. . . ."

"Nothing of the kind, it's charming! It's just what we lack—a touch of the absurd! The most valuable thing in scientific inquiry is to find the absurd. And we've hit upon it. There's always something basically new to be found in the absurd."

Planting the damp tip of his pencil on Krylov's chest, he began a disquisition on how to "corner" truth. Amid the chaos of absurdities they had arrived at he insisted they must seek the one in a thousand, in a million questions that would be decisive and must be put to nature. It was a pleasure to trace his thoughts, but an exhausting one.

He would not be distracted or make any allowances for fatigue or failure. He seemed oblivious to human foibles. They evoked his surprise rather than sympathy.

How much Krylov would have given to be the same.

Yet secret disappointment had left a tiny speck of corrosion in his heart.

There was no doubt Dankevich was a genius and geniuses are permitted any amount of licence, even to the point of error, but it all ought to add up to something beautiful and striking, and it ought to happen much quicker than the prospects seemed to indicate.

Savushkin threatened to chuck the whole thing. He could not allow himself the luxury of two or three years' painful efforts for the sake of negative results. He had a thesis to defend. He had a wife and children. He needed a watertight subject to work on. Krylov made no demur.

There was no limit to Dan's demands. Now a more subtle experiment must be mounted. Then another, more subtle still. They must eliminate the influence of the magnetic field, the influence of the photo-effect, of X-ray irradiation. . . .

After two weeks' work it was clear that even to prepare elaboration of the methodology alone would take not one month but six, after which Dan would throw in a few additional conditions and the completion date would be shifted another hundred and fifty years forward. After this, having established the cause of the error, Dan would propose his next brilliant hypothesis.

Poltavsky stared despondently out of the window. The dusty city summer, with its ice-creams, soda fountains and the tap-tap of high heels, had invaded the streets. Some people were going away to live in the country, others were lying on the beaches, buying flowers. kissing, marrying, having children, and none of them gave a thought to these five men locked up in their laboratory who never saw the light of day.

"Ungrateful swine," Poltavsky appealed to the passers-by from his second-floor window. "Don't you care about the nature of the earth's electrical field? We're sweating blood for your sake and instead of waiting with bated breath for the results you go off to fish!"

At the end of July the newspapers carried an announcement about the work of Academician Denisov on destroying thunderstorms. There was a description of how thunderstorms had been brought under control by means of anti-aircraft fire.

Krylov read out the announcement enthusiastically.

"Denisov?" Poltavsky repeated. "Well, well!"

"What do you mean—well, well!"

"Just an interpolation."

Krylov felt a moment's anxiety for Tulin, who was also working on the problems of active intervention in thunderstorms, but dismissed the thought at once. Tulin was doing splendidly, as always. He had defended his thesis, and now that Professor Chistyakov was ill, he had practically a free hand in his department of the institute. Tulin was publishing articles (too frequently, in Dan's opinion); Tulin was a member of some commission or other. Tulin was liked, talked of, praised, and even Dan considered him one of the most promising young scientists.

In the middle of July Dan announced that instead of leave there would be a week of noble idleness, and the whole laboratory went off to the Riga coast. Krylov managed to persuade Lena to go with them. They lounged on the sand and bathed and talked of everything under the sun except physics. Dan turned out to be a fine wood-carver; he fashioned weird animals out of the old roots lying on the beach. He presented Lena with a fox climbing a branch. To their surprise they discovered that Dan had a great respect for the humanities and in no way shared their contempt for aesthetics, ethics and other futile subjects. On the contrary, he thought they were accorded too small a place in life. They suffered the same fate as the forests. Mankind was thoughtlessly chopping down the forests, causing soil erosion, creating barren deserts of rock and sand, and no one considered the disastrous consequences of the violence that

was being perpetrated on nature merely because the consequences
were not felt by the offenders but by their descendants.

"But I can be a scientist and a decent person without being a music
lover," Poltavsky argued.

"You can, but society can't," Dan replied. "What do you think
distinguishes man from the animals? Atomic energy? The telephone?
I, personally, think it's morality, imagination and ideals. Our studying the earth's electrical field won't make people better in heart.
After all, what's a cyclotron? What if somebody discovers another
elementary particle? Another ten of them? So what? The world
can't consist of figures. Don't confuse the useless with the unnecessary. Useless things are often what is needed most. Can't you hear
those birds singing?"

None of them were afraid to argue with him. He won the arguments
with his intellect and logic, not with his authority.

After they had been idling for two days one of the big papers
published an interview with Denisov. The Academician stated that
the problems of controlling thunderstorms had been theoretically
solved, that first experiments had been successful, and that now
it was only a matter of technical details.

"Another piece of bluff," was Dan's comment. He was noticeably
put out and decided to return to Leningrad the same day. The others,
except Krylov and Lena, went with him.

"I'm going to have my holiday," Krylov said. "To hell with Denisov. He's got nothing to do with us. What's all the fuss about?"

"Will you walk into my parlour. . .." Poltavsky replied mysteriously.

When they had seen off the others, Sergei and Lena took the night
bus into Estonia. At the first stop the next morning Lena suddenly
suggested that they should get off. They jumped out and found
themselves in a very clean, pretty little town nestling among towers
and ramparts overgrown with acacia. The town was still asleep and
the clock on the old town hall chimed the hours drowsily. Soon
women on bicycles began to appear, riding along the red-paved
streets to market.

Neither of them would ever forget the gentle warmth of that
morning with its market full of flowers, or the cool slippery yoghourt
which they drank straight from an earthenware jar, or the green
hill from which they looked down on the red-tiled roofs and the
distant stone farmhouses and the lake with its springboard, where
a girl was already flexing her sunburnt limbs.

The little town was packed with surprises for Lena. She was
always trying to guess what they would find round the next corner.
Suddenly they came out on to a square and were confronted with

the towering stalagmites of a huge Catholic church in scarlet brick. It was cold in the church. Light poured in through the high stained-glass windows and the thunder of the organ made their chests vibrate.

Late in the evening they suddenly realised they had nowhere to stay the night and made a dash for the hotel. It was full up, of course, so without more ado they walked into the park, pulled two benches together under the statue of some local botanist and lay with their heads on each other's arms. Lena looked up at the stars and said nothing could ever be any better than this, and even if it could, it didn't matter, because this was happiness and there was no point in putting it off till the future.

Krylov had heard Denisov's name mentioned often enough, in connection with many problems, but none of his questions as to what Denisov had actually achieved had ever yielded any very clear answer.

But this time he seemed to be making a sensation: "Power over Lightning", "Taming the Elements", "Scientist's Victory". Articles of all kinds, enthusiastic, practical, dramatic, kept appealing in the newspapers.

Denisov delivered a public lecture at the university. Krylov attended it. A stocky little man, who looked as if he might have been put together out of components taken from other people, mounted the rostrum. He had a bald yellowish skull, a fish's mouth and a plump pink chin. In spite of a rather strident voice and theatrical gestures, he quickly won over his audience with his cheerful self-assurance. Krylov enjoyed the lecture. The way Denisov put matters, it all seemed temptingly simple, cheap and quick, and Krylov thought regretfully of Dan's endless, unrelenting demands that held out no clear promises or hope of early success.

Denisov certainly had the power to sway his listeners. It was understandable that a well-known writer should have published a lengthy feature entitled: "The Friendly Sky". The writer expatiated enthusiastically on the power of the human mind that could penetrate into any field and give men control over thunder itself. He was not concerned with the details of the research done in this field, but he drew a masterly picture of the disasters involved—the roaring infernos in oil reservoirs ignited by lightning, the aeroplanes hurled from the sky by turbulence. He quoted the ancient songs of the Rig-Veda, in which Indra cleaves the clouds with a thunderbolt, releasing life-giving floods of rain upon the earth and allowing the sunlight to break forth.

"At long last that eternal source of religious obscurantism, humiliating fear, and hidebound superstition, that symbol of human helplessness, has been destroyed. Thunder the triumphant has been tamed. It will now be used as a harmless teaching aid for secondary schools. Thunderstorms will be demonstrated as and when the local education authorities require."

With a string of imagery he linked Denisov's work with the nations' longing for peace, for a clear and friendly sky above our planet.

Dan was indignant over the article.

"What makes it worse is that it's so persuasive."

He decided to speak on Denisov's work at the conference that the Board was to hold jointly with the Ministries.

On the day before the conference Tulin arrived at the institute. Krylov had never seen him so gloomy and upset. All he had to say about Denisov was a tight-lipped "lowest of the low".

After an hour with Dan in the privacy of his office Tulin emerged red-faced. He ran silently down the stairs and Krylov had difficulty in catching up with him. They dashed along the street, bumping into people, until Tulin came to a sudden halt between two tramlines.

"I was trying to help Dan and all he can do is reproach me. He's fighting the windmills! Or rather, he's trying to fight cannon with a wooden lance."

"What are you afraid of?" Krylov asked cautiously. "Let them argue. Truth is born of controversy."

"So you think you can teach me, too!" Tulin shouted furiously. "This is worse than a nursery! Can't you understand that Dan is just the kind of opponent Denisov needs to consolidate his position?"

They found themselves in a clanking red corridor between two passing trams. Tulin was saying something. Shadows flickered across his pale, angry face.

". . . they can all go and stuff themselves! Truth! If you want to know, truth is usually murdered in controversy!"

"Are you sure Denisov is wrong?"

"Your Denisov is an impostor! What else do you want to know?"

They stepped on to the pavement.

"Then why don't you speak out yourself?"

"A fly might as well argue with a steamroller. Who am I? Denisov's an Academician. Who am I?"

"If Denisov's got things wrong, someone ought to put him right."

"What is more, I'm working on the same subject. People will think this is a rat-race."

"One of you will turn out to be wrong, that's all."

"Even Golitsyn, Corresponding Member of the Academy, one of the patriarchs of Soviet science, and all the rest of it, isn't prepared to stick his neck out. He has also told Dan that this isn't a scientific controversy and it's simply undignified to waste one's energy on such nonsense. It's like trying to argue with a Mordvinian quack."

They stopped in front of the window of a shop that sold sporting equipment and surveyed in silence the row of sporting guns, the gleaming straps of game-bags, knives and waders.

"Of course, if I were in Dan's position, I would interfere," Tulin said.

"Huh!"

"But Dan shouldn't. Outside the realm of science he's no fighter. You've all got to talk him out of it. Denisov knows we're connected with Dan, and it's bound to recoil on our work."

"Let's go shooting. Anikeyev's been inviting me."

"I told Dan everything. He can consider I'm playing safe if he likes, he'll only thank me afterwards. Not that I need his gratitude."

"I don't understand you. You say Denisov's a humbug, but you don't want anyone to argue with him. Where are your principles? That means you're simply helping Denisov."

"Yes, I am. No one will unmask Denisov quicker than he'll do it himself. The worse, the better."

Tulin reeled out facts that showed Denisov was promising pie in the sky. For one successful experiment in dispersing thunderstorms there were four failures, about which nothing was said. It was a hit-and-miss operation and the effects could be quite the opposite of what was expected. Storms were sometimes precipitated instead of dispersed. The trouble was that Denisov's work had no scientific foundation. Without a qualm he had borrowed the successful work on combating hail that was being done in the Caucasus and applied it to thunderstorms in general. As for the processes taking place in actual thunderheads, the mechanism of storm development, with which Tulin was grappling, he simply ignored them.

"Why doesn't Chistyakov or someone have a go at him?"

"You haven't the faintest idea of what our people are like," Tulin said. "Who wants to fight Denisov! He's bound to win."

"But why?"

"My dear babe-in-arms, the cult is over, but those who ministered to it are still with us."

It was difficult, of course, to find one's way amid the conflicting and interwoven interests of the people of Tulin's circle, who had known one another for years, whose attitude to one another depended on rivalry, on concern for their pupils, concern for their own health, and many other considerations of co-operation and interdependence. But even Krylov realised that the young men at high-altitude stations in the mountains had neither the time nor the opportunity to tackle Denisov. It was quite clear that Denisov's project would interfere with years of serious work at laboratories and research stations scattered all over the country.

At the end of the day Dan called Krylov in and asked him to get together as much material as he could on active storm intervention for his speech at the conference.

Krylov hesitated. Tulin had almost convinced him, yet he understood Dan, and he was torn between the two.

Dan had a visitor, the grey-haired, dignified Golitsyn. Krylov had never seen him before. Golitsyn toyed with his ivory-topped stick and eyed Krylov with interest.

"What's worrying you?" Dan snapped irritably.

Krylov mentioned the tests that were due to take place the following day. Furthermore, he couldn't understand how his chief could get himself involved in Denisov's affairs at the expense of his own work. Dan's work was, of course, related to atmospheric electricity and the theory of thunderstorms, and Denisov's idea was impractical, but there was no direct connection.

Under Dan's penetrating stare he began to lose the thread of his ideas, but Golitsyn came to his rescue.

"There you are, you see," he said to Dan, evidently picking up an old argument. "Even the youngsters don't want to tackle Denisov. The man's as sly as a fox, and you've got your heart to think of, you know. What is he to you anyway? A rival? Don't sink to his level. It isn't the right atmosphere for scientific argument, it's not science at all. . . ."

Dan locked his thin fingers.

"Good heavens, man, can't you understand that this isn't a case by itself, it's like an infection. If we don't fight it, it'll spread all through the organism; it'll be too late when it reaches us. Denisov is creating illusions and it's our duty to tell the truth. What is there to be afraid of? We're still in the grip of our old fears. . . ."

He broke off and was silent for a moment. When he spoke again it was with an almost sorrowful anger in his voice. "You weaklings!" he said, giving them a look that Krylov was to remember long afterwards. It was as if Dan was looking past them, and far into their future.

Tulin's predictions proved dismally correct.

Dan spoke at the conference and without adjusting in any way to his listeners, using exactly the same strictly scientific terms that he used when arguing at the seminars, made an impartial analysis and pronounced his verdict. Apart from two or three experts who were present no one really understood what he was talking about. This was of no consequence to Dan. Truth didn't change merely because people were incapable of recognising it.

The audience, however, were irritated by the haughtiness of this aristocrat of science, who was trying to discredit Denisov and prove to them with his formulas that they were all a lot of fools and ignoramuses.

Few detected the irony in his "At last we have heard a report containing a clear summary of the scientific principles published in various textbooks over the past twenty years." His revelations ("If psi equals sixteen, anyone can see that the relaxation value of gamma is two orders of magnitude higher") and his conclusions ("Heavy ions will therefore behave like dipoles") escaped everyone.

Smiling complacently Denisov made his reply.

"I am very sorry to say, my dear colleague, that you have lost touch with life. These rank-and-file engineers here can appreciate the idea, but you can't. Why can't you? Because they are practical men, with practical minds. We'll sort out the dipoles later, but agriculture has got to be helped now. Think of the losses that are caused by hail! And what about thunderstorms? Have you ever thought of the oil workers? We mustn't forget the nation's needs. Immediate effectiveness—that's the decisive factor."

The chairman politely asked Dankevich what practical proposals he could offer to help the national economy.

"Nothing at the moment," Dankevich replied defiantly. "First, we must complete our inquiry into the methods of detecting storm centres. Possibly this will show, after verification...."

His "ifs" and "possibles" and "after verification" created an unfortunate impression.

"So there we are," the chairman said with a sigh of relief, as he summed up the debate. "There seems to be no end to it. But Academician Denisov promises us immediate results. How can we turn our backs on such an offer?"

The conference passed a clearly defined plan of work on the basis of Academician Denisov's researches, approved his initiative, and recommended concentrating all the funds available in this field in his hands.

As Tulin put it, the mechanics of what happened next were as straightforward as those of a falling stone.

With bitter satisfaction he showed Krylov an article about his chief that had appeared in a journal of which Denisov had recently become Editor-in-Chief. The article cast doubt on the correctness of the direction chosen by Chistyakov. Denisov was energetically clearing the key sectors of people who might prove a hindrance to him. His pupils and followers were appointed to faculties, research institutes and scientific boards. Assistant Professor Lagunov was sent to Dankevich as deputy director.

Tulin strode about the room, making bitter fun of the battered old book-stand and the Renoir reproduction. He took exception to everything he saw. He was irritated by the way Krylov sat, by the way he stood up, by the fact that there was no vodka, and that there was sausage; he was irritated by Krylov's silence and no less irritated by his questions. Krylov avoided meeting his glance as he would have avoided contact with a pair of high-voltage terminals.

Tulin halted in front of the looking-glass, pushed his fingers through his hair and looked himself straight in the eye. "Yes," he said, "the first shall be last and the last shall be first. They'll close down my subject very shortly."

"Who will?"

Tulin rubbed his cheek violently.

"Denisov?" Krylov asked.

"He's got plenty of willing helpers."

"What is to be done?"

Tulin swung round and thrust his hands into his pockets.

"What is to be done? Who is to blame? The Russian intelligentsia's beloved questions." He swept across the room, kicking over a chair as he went. "How's Dan's work getting on?"

Krylov told him. It was one failure after another. New difficulties had arisen, the initial suppositions had proved wrong. They had managed to get out a few models but the rest was a shambles. On the credit side there was some valuable data on the nature of atmospheric electricity and charges in thunderclouds, and if it weren't for Dan.... But he wouldn't let them branch out. He kept driving them on in a straight line.

Tulin sat down on the couch.

"So you can't expect any results in the near future?"

Krylov shrugged.

"Some hopes! Now we've got the inspectors after us. Dan never gets a minute's peace. And as luck would have it, I'm not getting anywhere either. I've got a hankering after atmospheric electricity. I wanted to ask your advice about it. You see, there's a chance of taking a different approach to the mechanism of thunderstorms. Instead of tackling it like you, I could tie it up with general theory. Energetics. . . ."

"Wait a minute! You say you've got the inspectors round. How perfectly logical! That's just the beginning. Denisov won't let him alone. He won't let him alone till he's crushed him."

"You're exaggerating," Krylov said. "After all, Dan's right. And even if he isn't. . . . No, that kind of thing can't happen these days. Perhaps we ought to go and tell somebody about it. I'll go."

"Other people have done that already. Bigger people than you. What did they get? The decision of the conference pushed under their noses. Doesn't it show that Dankevich was beaten in public debate? As for his being criticised, that's perfectly normal. Science needs criticism. So there you are—it's enough to send you up the wall!"

A shiver passed across his face and Krylov felt a sudden consternation. It was not so much what Tulin was saying but the fact that Tulin, his Tulin, should actually have been forced to eat humble pie.

"It's all Dan's bloody fault," Tulin said viciously. "He mucked up everything. Why did he have to tease the blighter? That's just what they want. They provoke him and he gallantly responds, ruining our chances and paving the way for them."

"How can you say that about Dan?"

"He's a fool. An utter fool," Tulin kept repeating with a kind of frenzied malice. "Pillar of science, my foot! If you ask me, he's a crystal lattice, not a human being, a veritable Olympian."

Krylov winced.

"That's going too far. How can you expect Dan to play the diplomat? His mind works on an entirely different plane. And does it work! Like lightning. I can forgive him anything."

"But what's the use of his lightning mind? You can't keep your arse warm with lightning. Everything's falling to bits while your Dan sits there gazing through his telescope."

"Don't you dare speak of him like that!" Krylov shouted. It was the first time he had ever shouted at Tulin, the first time he had rebelled. "How dare you! Dan's a saint, a genius!"

Tulin threw one leg over the other and smiled with cold self-assurance.

"Is he?"

Krylov hesitated.

"Of course, he is."

"My dear innocent little lamb. In this day and age people are recognised as geniuses *after* they are dead, but we've made a genius out of him in his own lifetime. It's gone to his head and he thinks he can do just what he pleases."

"Nothing of the kind. That's a lot of rubbish. Rubbish!" Krylov muttered.

"My advice to you is to leave him before it's too late. You've said yourself there's not a glimmer of success on the horizon. Dan has outreached himself. He's bitten off more than he can chew and you'll waste your best years because of him. And what's more, remember this. From now on, you won't be allowed normal conditions of work."

Krylov rubbed his temples in anguish.

"You're just trying to scare me. It's all a lot of rubbish."

"Why should I try to scare you? You know I'm right."

"If Dan would let me," Krylov said, "I'd ... I think that by using Dan's field theory I could examine the nature of thunderstorms. ..."

Tulin rejected the idea with a look of boredom. The whole thing was impractical, and far too vulnerable from the point of view of results.

"There'll still be time for that five years hence," he said. "You'd better keep your feet on the ground, old chap."

And the look with which he surveyed Krylov's round buttonnosed face was so expressive that Krylov blushed.

"All right, in five years then. I wouldn't expect anything sooner. Nothing may come of it but think how interesting it would be. Someone's got to make a start." Krylov paused. "It's all very well for you. ..."

"It's wonderful," Tulin replied. "My chief has already decided to throw himself on Denisov's mercy."

Krylov looked up. Tulin's eyes were glassy.

"And so shall I," Tulin went on. "We'll both flop down at his feet together. Take us, lord and master, we're yours. He needs deserters just now. It's the right moment."

"Stop clowning."

"Denisov, of course, will welcome us with open arms."

"But why should you?"

"We've got to save our work. Our work! My chief has the right attitude—sell your soul to the devil, as long as you get the job done. I suppose you think it's better to spend your time moaning and writing complaints? No, my friend, there's no need to be squeamish when you're dealing with types like Denisov. They've got to be fought with their own weapons, and no holds barred. Dissemble? Certainly! Tell lies? Of course! I'll do anything. There'll be time for me to wash my hands later."

"But where will all this get you?"

"I'll offer him terms. Dear ruler, I'll say, I won't give you any trouble. I'll beat my swords into ploughshares, but please don't interfere with my subject. Let me finish scratching my little burrow. Then he will state his terms too, of course. I'll accept them. I'll recant everything.... What are you sneering at?" He jumped up with his fists clenched. His eyes were glittering like bits of splintered glass. "You intellectual jelly-fish! All you pure souls, I'd like to.... You with your innocence! Your high-mindedness! But underneath there's just craven impotence!"

"Take it easy!" Krylov murmured. He was dazed by his friend's anger.

Tulin snatched his raincoat off the peg.

"And you, instead of backing me up.... D'you think I enjoy crawling in this shit? But I'm going to do it.... Of course, it'd look much finer to march to my execution! But that, my dear chap, wouldn't get you or me any farther with our work on thunderstorms. Denisov won't achieve anything. This is all just a racket for him. A way of boosting his own personality. Dan is right."

"But that's exactly what I say. I know Dan is a real scientist. He'll never go against his convictions. Like Galileo, he'll keep saying 'and yet it moves' whatever happens. No real scientist can do otherwise!"

They stood facing each other, belligerent and unrelenting, both of them hiding their doubts and confusion.

Tulin was the first to speak, his lips twitching.

"Oh, wise and learned man, don't you know that in spite of that famous phrase Galileo nevertheless recanted? And he did it so that he could go on with his work. He was a practical man. And as we know, history has vindicated him. History, mind you! And who are we? Perhaps history will erect a monument to me, and to you too. You needn't worry, if you leave Dan, you'll be all set for a posthumous memorial. I'll be mounted on a horse, and you"— he gave a wink—"will be riding a motorbike."

Once again he was the older of the two. No matter how they argued, no matter what Oleg did, he would always be the senior member of their partnership.

Krylov gripped Tulin's hand with a sudden boyish affection.

"Don't go over to Denisov. I can't believe you will."

Tulin asked gently: "What makes you so sure?"

"If you'd decided to do that, why should you tell me? You'd have done it and told me afterwards. But your conscience is troubling you." Encouraged by Tulin's silence, he said with conviction: "There are some things that have more power than science and logic."

Tulin merely smiled and said nothing. Krylov became confused.
"I'm also faced with a problem. You see, I'd like to. . . ."
Tulin looked at his watch.
"I wish I had your problems. I'd be a happy man."

Krylov went back into the room, plugged in the kettle, cut some
bread and sausage and had his tea. The one person in the world
he wanted to see now was Lena. He wanted her to come in and
sit on the window-sill and he wanted to have a good talk with her
and tell her everything.

Somehow he had always found himself in the position of listener.
Even when he needed advice he was invariably interrupted and
made to listen. What other people were saying was more important
than his own private worries. It never seemed to occur to other
people to ask him questions, and no one had time to listen to what
he had to say.

He sat at the table and his thoughts went out to Lena. You've
got to come, you've got to come, he told her. After all, there were
such things as remote effect, action potentials and telepathy, and
other mysterious phenomena. If he wanted her badly enough, Lena
would surely feel it. Surely there must be someone, someone in
the world who needed him.

The noise from the street flooded in through the open window
and a human form rose against the deep purple of the evening
sky. It was Lena gliding towards him over the steep waves of roofs.
It was like a picture with the window as its frame. Panting slightly,
Lena moved away the pots of cacti on the window-sill and seated
herself, smoothing out her skirt.

"I've got heaps of time," she said. "Don't let's go out anywhere.
There's nothing to be surprised at, you can just sit and talk as much
as you like. I'm dying to know what all this is about."

"A man must have someone in the world he can talk to, someone
who'll listen to him," he said. "People used to go to the confes-
sional and it gave them relief. Sometimes you've just got to have
someone to listen to you, just listen to you and nod occasionally.
A man has got to have someone to open his heart to."

"Come nearer the point."

"There you are, you see. . . ."

"All right, I won't say anything."

"I'd have special palaces built, with wise men on duty there,
just so that people could go to them and talk. They needn't have
any power. They must just be able to listen."

"District confessionals."

"Don't laugh, it's important. There are times when you don't feel like confiding in your family or even a friend. Oleg can't be bothered with me now because he's got troubles enough of his own. You see, I'm beginning to feel more and more of a blockhead and Dan gets furious. I don't know how to help him.... We've over-reached ourselves, by about ten years. But what's the use of arguing with him?"

"So you agree with Oleg?"

"Why not? Oleg's right. Oleg's always right. If he's got to retreat, why should I kick?"

"Not so much false modesty, if you please. You know you don't agree with some of his arguments."

"He knows what he's after and he's going to get there by hook or by crook. It's not for me to pass judgement on him."

"In other words, you've lost faith in Dan?"

"No! Can't you understand? Think of Einstein, who worked for more than twenty years trying to evolve a unified field theory and all for nothing. He died without achieving his aim. Now we know it was a hopeless, premature attempt Even Einstein could make such a mistake."

"Why are you eating your heart out like this? Give up the job. That's what Savushkin did."

"He simply ran away. At the first whiff of danger. Do you want people to think I'm a coward?"

"Savushkin's a coward because he is thinking only of his own safety. But your case is different. Why don't you have the whole thing out with Dan? He'll understand."

"I told him I want to study atmospheric electricity. He wouldn't even listen to me. That can wait, he said, it's too early for that yet. But why wait? We've been fiddling around for a year and a half and there's not been a gleam of hope yet."

"He knows best."

"He's treating me like an insect. What high passions can I have? I've no right to them. I'm supposed to live on his ideas. He won't hear of my having any of my own. But this problem's on my mind all the time. I know I've got to get down to it and think, make the calculations and ask his advice, and I just can't do it. He's got a grip on my brain and he's squeezing it dry. There's no time to think, to rest, he keeps driving me on. We've put our finger on something really amazing. Do you realise it takes a thousand times more electricity to restore the charge in a thunderhead than is expended in terms of lightning? The sparing estimates in the old theories are quite inadequate. What does it all mean? What goes on up there? I've got dozens of ideas about it. They flash through my mind, then they're gone. If only I had time to sort them out. . . . He drives me on, leaving all this behind. But I don't want to leave it behind. I can't part with it, any more than I can part with you. I've got to get down to the problem or I'll dry up altogether. Yes, I know I owe everything to Dan, even my own ideas and plans. I like him tremendously, he's been everything to me. But he doesn't need my love, he doesn't need anything except his work. What are we to him?"

"Geniuses are cruel."

"He may find it easier that way. Being human as well would mean forgiving, recognising human weaknesses. He can't allow himself that. I'm sure he's quite sincere in thinking I've got no right to branch out on my own. From the peak on which he stands all my problems are just a lot of ballyhoo."

"What are the others doing?"

"They're simply martyring themselves. They've sacrificed everything for Dan's sake. Or rather, for the sake of the work. But I've got my own idea, my own brainchild. It may not amount to much but I can't drop it now. Dan has no pity, he won't yield an inch. He's a fanatic. Perhaps it's the only way of achieving something great in science, but it's terrible. . . . Please don't go away, I've still got a lot to tell you. Even Frenckel, way back, had a very interesting hypothesis on the process of the formation of charges. . . ."

The sky was darkening rapidly and Lena faded into the darkness until only her face and sparkling eyes remained.

"I envy you," she said. "It may be hard for you but it's happiness."

"Happiness? Maybe everyone has his own kind of happiness. Remember what I told you about the conversation I had with Savushkin?"

"No."

"He said it was all bunk about the joy of creative work. What happiness or creative work could anyone enjoy in one room with a wife and child? Happiness, he said, is a three-roomed flat, or perhaps even a two-roomed one."

"Yes, I remember, you were upset about it. You thought he might be right in a way."

"Ah, so you did think about it afterwards?"

"No, I was hardly taking any notice. I'm sorry."

"I'm glad you're here now."

"I'll always be with you when you want me."

Her voice was growing fainter.

"So you're going after all," Krylov said. "I resent this. I don't want any dealings with ghosts."

"A sensible ghost is worth having. You needn't turn up your nose at ghosts. Don't I satisfy you?"

"I can't hold you in my arms."

He heard her laughter.

"Is that all?"

"I want you to be like this alive."

"Alive," she repeated thoughtfully. "That might be an illusion as well."

She put the cactus plants back on the window-sill and her form merged with the smoky blue of evening until it disappeared among the dim street lamps.

The next day after work he went to the studio and waited a long time for her at the gate.

A machine-gun cart came rattling out of the studio with a load of whiteguards and Red Army soldiers in Budyonny helmets lolling together in the back. Lena jumped off the cart while it was moving, ran over to Krylov and kissed him on both cheeks.

He squeezed her small rough hand and gazed into her eyes.

"What's up?" she said in surprise.

Her little apple face showed no signs of loneliness or even yesterday's readiness to listen.

"What were you doing yesterday evening?"

Her list began with washing and ended with practising yoga exercises. Did he want to see how it was done?

"Did you think about me?"

"Sergei, dearest, you're getting just like a girl."

"Do you need me at all? Tell me."

"Oh dear! He's at it again! What's this passion you have for turning us inside out!"

"Do you ever feel you miss me?"

"But we see each other so often. If we were apart for a long time, of course.... Oh, what a nagger you are! You don't realise you only love me because you need me. Come on, I'd rather go and see the Italians—they're a wonderful crowd."

They went to the hotel where a group of Italian film-makers were staying. Lena asked them all kinds of questions about neorealism and olives, told them collective farming was a good thing and recited Zabolotsky's poetry. Then they all went out for a walk and Lena whispered to Krylov: "Don't look now, but we're going to do a bunk. I'm tired of them."

They dived into a little shop together.

Embarrassed by the shop assistants' glances, Krylov bought some glass beads. Lena put them on at once and was delighted.

"You know, I really think the Red Indians were quite right in swapping their gold for beads like these!" she declared.

He reflected miserably how small her basic demands on life were. She needed hardly anything. From him or anyone else. She was quite content with that cotton frock, the beads, their evening walks and her sweet, laughing love game that had neither past nor future.

With an effort he stifled his pent-up reproaches. He was always promising himself that he would have it out with her one day and present her with an ultimatum, but he always put it off realising that it would lead nowhere. There was an invisible barrier between them that he just couldn't cross. Perhaps it was really only a matter of waiting, of patience, but he was tired of waiting.

The meeting of the learned council that discussed the work of Dankevich's group was attended by members of a commission of inquiry, a young journalist, representatives of various organisations and a few curious onlookers. The meeting was given all the trappings of democracy in spite of Dan's protests and demands for the removal of outsiders. The undue harshness of his "This isn't a circus!" had a jarring effect and antagonised even the neutrals.

He made no attempt to hide his discouraging results and took all the blame on himself. When asked for even an approximate estimate of how much time he needed, he at first refused to answer, then began to make malicious fun of his questioners. He might have the answer tomorrow, or it might take another ten years, perhaps a lifetime. Not that that worried him in the least, for he was confident that even the members of the commission would realise by that time that serving only the present and avoiding work that might take ten years was merely skimming the cream off the jug. Such an approach would yield no Tsiolkovskys. Soviet science was strong enough to go in for long-term planning.

Asked about the practical significance of his research, he stated that his subject had no practical application whatever. This was untrue. Dan's inquiry could have been linked up with radio engineering and navigation. Without sacrificing a fraction of his integrity, he could have shown the value of the theory to atmospheric electricity, to mention only one possibility. But Dan plunged ahead, oblivious of the pitfalls or, if he did notice them, refusing to stoop to participation in the struggle.

"But what's the use of your investigations?" the journalist asked, a beautiful white fountain-pen poised over his note-pad.

"We are trying to obtain scientific results."

"What will that give industry?"

"Nothing. Absolutely nothing," Dankevich replied. "You want us to increase iron production. That's not what we're here for. This is simply an interesting problem. Interesting, and nothing more."

He had grown even thinner of late. As Poltavsky was fond of saying, you could only see him in profile, and his heart was giving him trouble. He was angry not because of failure but because he was being held up in his work. Tossing his huge head with its greying mane of hair, he snorted with impatient contempt, like a stag trapped by hunters. He was strong but helpless, like a knight in armour in front of a machine-gun.

The journalist scribbled cheerfully on his large note-pad.

"So you deny the need for close contact between science and industry? You want pure, abstract science? What do you expect to get out of it?"

"I don't know," Dankevich replied. "If every scientist doing research had known exactly what he expected to get out of it, we should never have discovered anything."

At this point Krylov couldn't help shouting "Hear! hear!" and clapping loudly, for which he was nearly ejected from the hall.

The chairman was Lagunov. Now it was he who asked a question.

"So far you have received only negative results?"

"They have their value."

"Science cannot move forward on negative results alone."

Unfortunately, even Dankevich's friends were not satisfied with the course the work was taking. All kinds of results could be arrived at by calculation, but there was no experimental proof. And the apparatus itself, so defiantly simple, without any big condensers or other hardware, inspired no confidence. The contribution to the discussion made by theorists from an associated institute showed that they were unwilling to expose Dan's failure and play into Denisov's hands, yet integrity made them speak out. Very gently they tried to bring Dan round to the idea of achieving results incidental to his main theme, of having some specific task in mind. If only they could get him to take an interest in atmospheric electricity, Krylov found himself muttering, as if in prayer.

But this was the signal of attack (at last they had him at their mercy!) for those whom Dan had called mediocrities and impotents, who were never sure of their own ground, whose work he had ridiculed—the heads of departments and laboratories who had done nothing worth while for years, but who had never risked making mistakes. At one time Dan had attempted unsuccessfully to clear them out of the institute. "With our system of concern for the individual it's easier to reject a good man than sack a bad one," he had often said.

Mazin, "the grandfather of Russian post-graduates", who had been a post-graduate student for over four years, spoke of the after-effects of the personality cult and the harm caused by a man who surrounded himself with blindly worshipping admirers. He reminded the meeting how Krylov, for instance, had begged Danke-vich to take him on. Krylov had practically deified Dankevich, he was a typical victim of hero-worship.

Without raising any particular hopes of success for Dan's work, Anikeyev nevertheless defended him and made a furious attack on the abominable habit of blinkering oneself with the immediate problems of the day. He was infuriated at having to prove the elementary fact that the results of scientific inquiry could not be predicted in advance. Staring expressively at Lagunov, he said: "God himself never foresaw the consequences of creating man."

Dan looked down dispassionately on the disputants from his snowy peak. He seemed quite undisturbed by the course the discussion was taking.

"Scientific problems can't be decided by a vote," he said. "What's the use of a majority? The untalented are always in the majority. That's in the nature of things."

"You mean the majority of people in this institute have no talent?" Lagunov exclaimed, going red in the face.

"Yes, kindly explain that remark," the journalist called out.

"You can write what you like," Dan retorted.

Krylov bent forward to Anikeyev.

"We ought to do something. He's heading for trouble. They'll gobble him up."

"If they try, they'll choke," Anikeyev said. "Times are different now."

Over the next few days it really began to look as if Dankevich would come out of his job with a bump, but nothing happened.

Anikeyev knew what he was talking about. Denisov's efforts did not even lead to Dan's work being curtailed. Various auxiliary institutes and the Presidium of the Academy stepped in on his behalf. Either they were counting on a successful outcome of his research or they were generally opposed to a repressive policy. The Vice-President visited the institute and gave his full support to the principle of wide-ranging research on subjects of this kind.

On the other hand, however, Denisov was given a free hand with his projects for influencing thunderstorms by means of artillery fire. Dan's opposition to this had gone unheeded.

A strange state of equilibrium had been created. Poltavsky formulated it as "D minus D = zero". "It may be a good thing," he said. "Everyone ought to have the chance of proving whether he's right." But Krylov would have preferred it if their work had been closed down. The discussion by the learned council had confirmed his doubts. He didn't want to see Dan when he finally came to a dead end and was forced to admit complete failure. A short time later, however, Dan himself resigned his directorship on grounds of ill health. He was, in fact, being troubled by frequent heart attacks.

"He wants to concentrate on our work," Poltavsky maintained. "If he wasn't sure of his ground, he wouldn't have taken this step."

Krylov humphed. Savushkin suggested that Dan had been forced to resign but the idea was ridiculed and everyone realised with surprise that Denisov was not so powerful after all. The prophets of evil had disgraced themselves. Denisov could be criticised and was in no position to mete out punishment, as he might once have done. So D minus D equalled not zero but progress!

Tulin tried to temper their enthusiasm.

"Don't forget Dankevich is Jupiter. And what is permitted to Jupiter will not be permitted to junior research workers."

But even Tulin was confused by the discovery that his fears had proved unfounded.

At the end of the winter Dan had to take to his bed. The repercussions were rapid and unpleasant. The department's funds were immediately cut and it was allowed fewer hours on the computers. All workshop orders were to be dealt with strictly in turn.

Confined to his bed, Dan spent his time fuming and swearing over the smallest hitches. His immobility had made him extremely vulnerable. Tulin saw something rather old-fashioned in this lion at bay, but for Krylov he was a figure of the future. The scale of Dan's thinking now stood in tragic contrast to the capacity and funds of the laboratory, and the worst of it was that Dan would still make no allowances whatever.

On the spur of the moment Krylov went to see Lagunov, who was now acting director.

"You ought to be ashamed!" Krylov told him. "You must realise you can't do this to him."

Most of Lagunov's pink face was hidden behind thick horn-rimmed spectacles. For a time he surveyed Krylov from behind the massive lenses, as though he were examining some insect under the microscope.

Lagunov was feared by the staff of the institute and Krylov's impudence might have had serious consequences. But Lagunov unexpectedly said: "Well, I rather like being talked to in this down-to-earth fashion. In the real Russian manner. In fact, I've had a liking for you for some time, Krylov."

It turned out that he knew Krylov's work well, appreciated his talent and considered him worthy of complete scientific independence. Krylov blushed. It was the first time in his life that he had been praised so frankly to his face. What was more, it appeared that Lagunov had the greatest respect for Dankevich and also appreciated his work.

"Put yourself in my position," Lagunov said and made a sweeping gesture. "There's a whole mass of factors to be taken into account. Everything's terribly complicated. As for saving Dan from himself, you just try it. With Dan's bloody-mindedness thrown in on top." He lowered his voice. "Then there's Denisov to deal with. He's putting the screw on us. Anyhow, I trust you. Tell me, Sergei Ilyich, are you satisfied with what Dankevich is doing? Be frank."

Perhaps he should have evaded the issue or held his tongue, but he had to speak.

"It's no use counting on any results in the near future," he said.

Lagunov closed his eyes understandingly.

Encouraged by this attention, Krylov enlarged on his own views: "He's entitled to go on until he himself sees he's wrong. You know, I've often thought we have too many people who want to accomplish everything in their own lifetime. On the other hand, even Dan can't always see where he's going. There's never been a genius yet who hasn't wanted to do too much. He thinks pressure intensity depends on the altitude. . . ."

"I see you've no great affection for your teacher!" Lagunov said reproachfully.

Krylov gaped.

"You don't believe in him," said Lagunov. "But I do. You, young people, have no faith in anybody. Or anything. The poor chap needs a rest. Yes, a year's rest. By that time the heat of controversy will have cooled, he'll be able to sort out his ideas and everything will be fine."

"That sounds like an idea," Krylov said, surprised to find himself agreeing.

"Trust me!" Lagunov passed his hand over his soft wavy yellow hair. It was said he had it waved and tinted at the hairdresser's He was as clean and shiny as a varnished doll and the impression was pleasant until he smiled; his steel dentures lent rather a harsh glint to his smile.

"Yes, I think that's the best solution," he said significantly. "But you needn't waste a year of course. Scientists create until they're thirty. After that they develop what they've already achieved."

Lagunov was charmingly considerate and confiding. Krylov was surprised and delighted to find they had so much in common, and that Lagunov was no snake in the grass but just a plain, straight-forward chap holding down a tough job but ready to do everything he could for Dan. Showing the same practical concern for Krylov, he suggested he should spend the year on a voyage round the world with a geophysical expedition.

"You mean more to me than Dankevich," Lagunov stated bluntly. "The future is yours. There are others who will look after Danke-vich. Plenty of people are doing that already. If you take my advice, you'll think of yourself a bit more. It won't do you any harm."

Lena simply jumped for joy. A trip round the world—that was something! Jamaica! Jamaica rum! The Azores! Wasn't he lucky! He ought to jump at the chance. What was the point in living on this old globe if you didn't travel. Life went by like the Azores, Mayakovsky had said. So he might as well see them, or the Vasi-lyevsky Island would be all the romance he had ever known. They went out to buy souvenirs. She was so glad for his sake that he was untroubled by either reproach or suspicion.

Try as they might, the field between the two plates got distorted. It shouldn't have done, but it did. The spray jet should have pro-duced the expected charges, but it didn't. Krylov threw down the probe in desperation. Since his conversation with Lagunov he had lost all ability to understand Dan's ideas and the whole thing was a mess. He received no sympathy from Poltavsky, who had cast himself in the role of dumb executor of his master's wishes. "It's too late for me to back out now," he argued. "I've got to go through with it." He just obeyed orders blindly and refused to discuss what Dan was doing. Believing meant believing absolutely. Dan was an antenna receiving signals from the future. Dan thought in categories beyond the comprehension of ordinary mortals. In the same breath, however, he ridiculed both himself and Krylov, and expressed a cynical admiration for Denisov and his supporters. They were smooth operators who would go far. For two pins he would have changed sides but his conscience wouldn't let him, much though he would have liked to. No doubt Krylov had the same sinful desire.

"I'm fed up with taking things on trust," Krylov protested. "Why should I believe? What am I supposed to believe in?"

"In a bright future. We must always trust our elders and betters anyway."

"I've heard all that before and don't want to hear any more."

In his fury Krylov straightened out with his bare hands a core that only the day before had defeated the efforts of the entire laboratory.

In the corridor he ran into Lagunov, who asked him how the preparations for the trip were going. Mentally Krylov cursed all Lagunov's ancestors from ancient times down to the present day and finished up by saying aloud that, unfortunately, he could not leave Dankevich in the lurch and would have to give up the idea of joining the expedition.

Lagunov told him he was being hasty and advised him to reconsider his decision. There were a lot of people who wanted to go, but he would keep a place for Krylov for the time being.

The effect of illness on Dan was to make him feverishly impatient. Ignoring everything, including doctors' orders, he pressed on frantically, as though he had only a few months to live. In their haste they bungled things and failures became more and more frequent. Krylov lost the thread of the work and no one could keep pace with Dan's ideas. Miserably Krylov became convinced of the futility of their efforts. What was the use of it all? And what were they doing anyway? It was all for nothing, to no purpose.

The split occurred, as it always does, over a trifle. They discovered that the transformer was no use and they would have to rewind a new one for a higher voltage.

"Couldn't you have thought of this before? An elementary schoolboy could have done better," Dan commented acidly.

His sarcasm was unbearable. I haven't time to waste proving it, he seemed to be saying, but only a complete idiot like Krylov could have been satisfied with the present voltage.

"You think I don't know what I'm doing? Well, let me remind you that only recently you yourself accepted the standard voltage."

"You ought to have checked it. It won't do for the new operating conditions."

"I can't keep up with your chopping and changing. You have a new idea every day."

"I have no time to argue with you."

"This is impossible. How much more do you expect me to put up with?"

"Just as much as is necessary."

At that moment he decided to have it out with Dan once and for all, to bring him to his senses, persuade him to wait, to give up this mad rat-race, but instead he burst out:

"I can't do things I don't understand! I suppose you find me too slow. For your information, I have a mind of my own. I can't go on like this, getting nowhere. . . ."

If only Dan had uttered one word of comfort, of sympathy, but his huge black eyes remained as dispassionate as ever. They gazed down relentlessly from that icy peak which no cries for mercy could reach.

"I didn't know you were after quick success," he said. "If that's the case, you'll soon be a Doctor. You will write massive textbooks. You will deliver lectures. You may even become director of the institute."

"Yes, I prefer something tangible. I've suggested taking up atmospheric electricity. What we are doing is no good to anyone. There are some people, you know, who don't consider me a blockhead. You'll realise that one day. . . . You give us no consideration, but it won't get you anywhere."

The celestial being descended to earth and Krylov was blinded by the visage of outraged divinity.

"So you have no faith?"

"But you can't give any guarantee, you know it yourself . . ." Krylov cried, sick with his fear.

"If you have lost faith in our work there's nothing more to be said," Dan replied.

"No, there isn't, nothing at all!" Krylov pulled down the switches frantically, one after the other. "And I'm very glad there isn't."

Two days later Dan told him he had signed a testimonial recommending him as a member of the expedition. Krylov began to apologise, but Dan's huge black eyes were once again staring into the distance, and Krylov could have sworn that Dan didn't hear a word he said.

What with the kitting out, the briefings, the packing of apparatus, souvenirs, manuals and guide-books, all the hustle and bustle of leaving home, he had scarcely time to think before he was aboard ship. Tulin came up from Moscow and he and Lena stood on the quayside waving Krylov good-bye. Lena was crying and smiling at the same time. She waved to him with the tears running down her firm sunburnt cheeks, and, though he did feel a pang of remorse, Krylov was glad to see those tears. The day before, they had been for a last ride on the motorbike. Lena had swept along the wet leaf-strewn highway, overtaking lorries and cars. The trees at the side of the road had streamed past like an orange wind and, when Krylov had leaned forward and asked if she would miss him, the quivering of her shoulders had made him happy.

There had, of course, been bad moments when he had wanted to chuck the whole thing and stay at home. But he had known that in a few days it would be the same thing all over again and he would spend the long evenings alone, waiting for her.

And it was too late to refuse to go anyway.

Now he had no more memories and no more regrets. He stood holding the rail, flushed with a traveller's pride and a condescending sympathy for those he was leaving behind in the comfort and safety of the homeland.

The rattle of anchor chains, the hooting of tugs and the final words of command from the bridge brought to mind only the rustle of the hot sirocco, the cool freshness of the ocean and a vision of strange ports on the green and distant shores of Africa.

Tulin was stalking about the quay, shooting tigers and other big game and dancing with the natives. He was in high spirits. At the last minute events had swung in his favour. Denisov had forced no terms upon him and given him a cordial but rather indifferent reception: he was no longer interested in thunder.

Krylov was baffled. After so many resounding promises and with the date of fulfilment not far off, he had expected Denisov to press on with his plans. Relishing his perplexity, Tulin explained that Denisov would soon be making a fresh proposal concerning the long-term forecasting of thunderstorms. More sensational announcements, articles and meetings were in the offing. After the forecasting gimmick there would be another one, the utilisation of atmospheric electricity for industrial purposes, for instance. For each announcement there would be fresh promises of immediate advantages, practical science, fresh castigation of opponents, fresh appointments and fresh glory. It all sounded so absurd that Krylov refused to believe it. Why did people listen to Denisov? If he hadn't fulfilled one promise, there was no point in allowing him to make more. But Tulin had the facts at his fingertips and Krylov realised that Denisov's rise to fame rested almost entirely on promises that were not fulfilled. Previously Denisov had done well out of Michurin. He had proposed artificial climate, soil electrification for improving crop yields, and the use of vaporisers. It had all cost millions of rubles and the net result had been a stack of books and articles, and a fresh crop of sycophantic admirers and bewildered young enthusiasts.

"But how does he keep it up? What's he done? Why is everybody so blind?"

"Oh, Denisov's a great scientist!" Tulin replied triumphantly. "He has discovered a law that's worth all our work put together. It may be stated as follows: people love to be deceived with false

hopes. They believe the scientist who promises them immediate
benefits, in preference to the one who predicts prolonged difficulties. They try to forget past failures, they have poor memories for
anything that went wrong, and they prefer the future to the past.
Fresh promises count far more than old disappointments. And while
they try to remember the dates of old promises and get the record
straight, Denisov jumps ahead and tempts them on with fresh pie
in the sky."

Tulin talked and talked. He was delighted that he hadn't had
to compromise himself, and that Krylov had taken his advice,
broken with Dan and joined the expedition. He didn't even try to
conceal his envy, which was surprising indeed.

Before leaving the laboratory, Krylov had handed over his
apparatus and calculations to Poltavsky, given him his unfinished
article and explained various ideas. He grudged nothing; he was
anxious to atone for the guilt he felt towards Dan.

The only reason he felt guilty was that he had been unable to
persuade them to abandon a hopeless task. Poor Poltavsky stuck
his fingers in his ears to protect himself from Krylov's arguments,
and fought like a madman for his faith in Dan. Unable to defend
himself in any other way, he argued fanatically that if Dan couldn't
see his mistake, how could they? But eventually even he admitted
that he didn't understand Dan, and couldn't understand him, because Dan thought on a different plane, perhaps intuitively. After
all, weren't people only just beginning to comprehend Friedmann's
ideas? And so on and so forth. Krylov ridiculed the proposal. Blind
faith was for religion. As for justifying and working for something
you couldn't understand—that was not for him! Everyone knew
where that got you! Poltavsky asked whether scepticism gave one
the right to be disloyal. To which Krylov neatly replied that
fanatics regarded all freedom as disloyalty, but they were the slaves,
not the masters of thought.

Dan was standing by one of the test benches, sucking the tip of
his pencil, when Krylov came in to say good-bye. He stared at him
as if he were part of the furniture, and Krylov decided that he no
longer existed as far as Dan was concerned. If he tried to say good-
bye, Dan would be surprised at being accosted by a complete
stranger. It was beyond him how Dan could so easily have oblite-
rated him from his memory and forgotten all their work together.
Surely, after this they had no right to reproach him for leaving
Dan. But who were *they*?

His departure was a convenient, simple and courageous way out
of an impossible situation and he revelled in the sensation of being

free of Dan, of his hectoring demands and the obligation to do something in which he no longer believed.

Blue-sweatered and bareheaded, he stood with his feet firmly planted on the deck, his hands gripping the cold rail. The autumn breeze smelled of steamer smoke and the freshness of the swirling black water. Everything seemed to be fine, yet he knew something was missing.

He kept his eyes fixed on Lena and shouted to her about things that didn't matter at all, but still there was something wrong; he felt as though he had forgotten something absolutely essential and just couldn't remember what it was.

The ship heaved slowly away from the quay and soon the city with its spires and smoke-stacks was spread out along the distant skyline, but Krylov still kept his eyes fixed on the tiny dot on shore that he knew must be Lena.

He returned eight months later.

In his suitcase he had a thick folder full of measurements. He had managed to establish certain curious anomalies in the tension of the earth's electrical field. He had done so by recording all round the clock. During a storm in the Bay of Biscay he had even lashed himself to the mast to be able to work. Off Madagascar he had gone down with malaria and had such violent shivers that he couldn't write. He had lain on deck begging the oceanologists to leave their apparatus for a moment and help him to move his. Later, they had gone ashore for two days on the islands. There had been a temple with monkeys hopping round it. There had been drums beating in the nights and a bar with flashing neon signs and a naked Indian clerk sitting in the street tapping out applications on a typewriter.

Gaily painted feluccas with lamps dangling from their slender booms rocked gently on the phosphorescent waters of the bay. Krylov sat on the veranda of a harbour café with cool air hissing at him from an air conditioner and wondered how he was ever going to be able to remember all this and tell Lena about it.

On the Azores there were fantastic cacti sprouting along the roadside, just like the burdock that grew in Borovichi. The concrete runway of the airport ran straight down to the sea. There was a little shop where they sold hollow bracelets with enamel caravels on them. The air smelled of whale blubber and the beach was strewn with white, sun-bleached skeletons of whales that looked like the frames of strange new buildings.

They would gather round the ship's radio to listen to the news. The sowing campaign in the Kuban region had been successfully completed. A new section of the Leningrad underground was nearly finished. The Irkutsk Power Station had started operating.

At Le Havre on the way back they had met some French geophysicists. When the French heard that Krylov had been working for Dankevich they cheered and Professor Duras, speaking with some emotion, had proposed a toast to the country that possessed such a scientist as Dankevich.

From them Krylov heard that a month ago at an international congress Poltavsky had read out Dan's paper on the new theory of the electrical field. Recent sputnik flights had yielded considerable data confirming Dan's hypotheses, and his field theory was coming brilliantly into shape. It had an application in the designing of new apparatus for space navigation. New and unexpected possibilities of counteracting electrical interference had been opened up, and this would lead to new methods of computing in radioastronomy.

That night Krylov stood alone on the afterdeck. The smooth oily waves seemed to cling round the stern of the ship.

He had lost faith. Yes, he had lost faith and they had won through. A man who couldn't believe would never achieve anything. A man must learn how to believe. He must have the courage to believe.

What would become of him now? A Doctor of Science? Wouldn't that be just a preface? Who could have known how things would turn out? But should one tackle merely what one knew? No, one should tackle things one didn't know.

There were too many "shoulds" and "oughts" in this world.

One mistake was no safeguard against further errors.

But could he have guessed? He went over the whole thing in his mind, and even Dan's mistakes now seemed to him both wise and inevitable and supremely economical. Mistakes were the only really individual things in science; the truth was faceless and uniform for all.

The ship ran into a damp, stifling fog and began to give short plaintive blasts on its siren. Krylov felt wretched and frustrated. He felt as if he had been tricked, yet there was no one on whom he could place the blame. The deck seemed to merge with the sea. Everything was swathed in a thick, impenetrable greyness. He tried to take a deep breath, but couldn't.

The grey sky over Leningrad was shedding a few last flakes of wet snow. A fussy little tug took a long time edging them up to the wharf. While the ship was being moored Krylov scanned the waiting crowd in vain for Lena.

When he stepped ashore he stood for several minutes reading a "No Smoking" notice aloud and laughing because he was so glad and surprised to hear everyone speaking Russian and to see everything written in his own language.

He rang Lena straightaway, at the studio. While she was being called to the phone Krylov stood with his eyes closed, trying to guess the first word she would say when she heard his voice.

"Where are you ringing from?" Lena said.

"From the port."

"Oh!"

Her sudden silence started a chain reaction that he couldn't stop. They seemed to listen guardedly to one another, ear to ear.

"Are you all right, Sergei?" Lena asked at last and, without letting him reply, went on quickly: "I'm so glad. I've written you a letter. You'll find it when you get home. I'm going to be married. You don't know him. It all happened so suddenly. I can't really explain." And no longer embarrassed, she placed her joyful news trustingly in his hands: "Sergei, darling, I'm madly in love with him!"

Krylov rang off, picked up his suitcase and went to catch a bus. He was entitled to a fortnight's leave but he went nowhere. He would go out to buy yoghourt and a loaf in the morning and spend the rest of the day lying on his couch.

It was in this state that Tulin found him.

He had flown in from Moscow to attend Dan's funeral. Krylov knew nothing of Dan's death. Dan had died of heart failure three days before.

Tulin suddenly broke down. He stood in his fashionable steel-grey raglan coat and wept, rubbing the tears away furiously with his fists.

"There'll never be another Dan. That's justice for you, damn and blast it all," he said. "The cretins live on. The scum live on, crawling about on their bellies. Couldn't we at least have saved his brain? Transplanted it, preserved it somehow? At any price! I stood there watching them chucking earth on a brain like that. Just because of a heart! The world's going to be an empty place without him."

Krylov listened to the beating of his own heart. It was as steady as if nothing had happened. The valves opened and shut. Blood flowed from right ventricle to left auricle. Not a pause, not a tremor. Just a great big useless heart in an equally useless and healthy body. Tulin went on talking. Eventually Krylov saw him off. They had a drink at the station and Krylov kept rubbing his face, trying to soften the numbed muscles in his cheeks.

Tulin asked in passing how he was getting on and Krylov told him in an equally offhand manner about Lena.

"There's only one cure for women, and that's more women," Tulin commented drearily and started telling how for months Dan had worked sixteen hours a day to get his papers in order, as though he had known exactly when he would die. He had allowed nothing to distract him. He had simply ignored Lagunov's interference and press criticism. He was above all that.

"What criticism?" Krylov asked.

"Oh, of course, you don't know anything about it." Tulin shook his head.

The article entitled "In Isolation from Science" had appeared shortly after Krylov had sailed. With all the joy of a professional hatchet man, its author—the journalist he had seen at the meeting of the learned council, Krylov told himself calmly—drew a picture of Dankevich's laboratory counting seeds in cucumbers, wasting the state's money, preaching old-fashioned views about pure science and attacking Denisov, who was doing all he could for the country's economy. It was not surprising that even Dankevich's pupils were leaving him in disappointment. Savushkin, for instance, had left. Krylov, another young scientist, had been forced to go off on an expedition on the *Bogatyr* after criticising Dankevich.

"But you know it wasn't like that at all," Krylov said in horror.

Tulin made a vague gesture.

"I'm sure Dan didn't even read the article."

"What does it matter whether he read it or not!" Krylov shouted.

The next day he went to the library, looked up the file and read the whole article through carefully. From the library he went straight to the newspaper office, waited for the journalist to come in and asked him to publish a denial.

It was some time before he could make the journalist understand what he was talking about.

"But this was six months ago," he said at last, then he smiled and patted Krylov on the shoulder: "You've been having a good long sleep, haven't you? While you were about it, your professor has pegged out, you know."

"That's got nothing to do with it," Krylov told him. "I'm alive, aren't I? Did I ever repudiate him? My motives were quite different."

The journalist looked at his watch.

"Now don't come that on me, laddy. Didn't you tell Dankevich you disagreed with him? Didn't you have a row? And after that, didn't you walk out? And in any case, I wrote nothing against you at all. On the contrary, it was rather flattering. Why all the fuss?"

"Not on my own account! Your article slandered Dankevich. Are you aware that his work has been completely vindicated?"

He talked about the French scientists he had met and about the sputnik equipment. The journalist fingered his heavy horn-rimmed spectacles, and his flat, colourless little eyes gleamed impudently.

"Is that all?" he asked. "Well, all I can say is you're a queer fish. If his work was all that important, why did you walk out on him? You did walk out, didn't you? No, Comrade Krylov, if you want other people to be principled, you must be principled yourself. If you didn't know things were going to turn out like this, how was I to know? And anyhow, what good would a denial do anyone now?" He stared enviously at Krylov's tie. "Buy that in Paris?"

The worst of it is, Krylov told himself afterwards, that this dirty dog is right. There's no getting away from it. This is my punishment. Even this bastard has got me cornered.

At the institute no one tried to bring up the past. Poltavsky neither gloated nor asked questions. He seemed to have lost all interest in Krylov. Was this magnanimity? Condescension? Indifference? Or perhaps they despised him? That was quite likely, because he was a rat, a cur, and he had fallen flat on his face in his own dirt. He excoriated himself and avoided meeting his friends. He didn't want to talk to anyone. Sometimes he would not speak more than a couple of words to a waitress or someone from the planning department in the course of a whole day. He sat alone in the empty reading room, drawing up his report on the expedition. Punctually at six he would put his papers together and go down to the cloak-room with the library staff. He would spend the evening roaming the streets, have his supper in a youth café and try to get home as late as possible, so that he could just drop into bed. It was his first taste of real loneliness.

Ever since the death of Dankevich the institute had been in ferment. Anikeyev and Poltavsky were fiercely opposed to Lagunov, but Lagunov and his supporters made an idol of Dankevich and the result was that it looked as if they were defending him from Anikeyev.

Both sides seemed to have forgotten Krylov's existence.

One day, when he ran into Lagunov in the corridor Krylov tried to have the matter out with him. He got nowhere. Lagunov could remember nothing of their conversation or the advice he had offered. In a loud, reproachful voice he said: "I warned you that you didn't appreciate him sufficiently."

He was imprisoned in a pit of loneliness. At one stroke he had lost everything he possessed. He had no friends, no Lena, no proper work, and no future.

He had forbidden himself to think of Lena. That was all over and done with. He had never known the touch of her hands, the sound of her laughter. She had simply never existed. She had never come to this room, never lain on that couch.... But he ought to read Dan's last article. Dan had liked Lena. Everyone had liked her. He had better stand for his Doctorate, then perhaps she would regret chucking him. But the devil of it was that even if he became an Academician she wouldn't care a hoot. He had got to forget her, move out of this room, go to sleep.

The dream he had was quite a jolly one. He dreamt of the design office at the factory, of Vitya Dolinin and Ada. They were making a trip somewhere and Krylov was with them. He was wearing a little short jacket and a flower in his buttonhole, and somewhere nearby was the workshop with the red switch-boxes. Everyone was laughing and tossing Krylov in the air. Every time they tossed him he went higher and higher....

When he awoke, he lay thinking how good life had been when he worked in the design office. That was probably his real place in life.

He went to the factory the same day and asked the chief designer to take him on.

"You look awful," Gatenyan said.

The expression in his eyes told Krylov just what a state he must be in.

"Young man," Gatenyan went on. "No acorn can ever return to its branch, and you've got to be what you are. A man must be himself no matter what it costs him. Want me to go to the institute for you? Just tell me what you want. We'll give you all the help we can, but I won't have you back here."

Ada was sitting in the waiting room. She asked him what was the matter and why he was there.

"Oh, just business...."

"How are you getting on?"

"Fine."

They walked as far as the gate together and he talked to her about his trip.

Poltavsky believed in Dankevich, but you didn't. You believed only in yourself and you failed. So a man mustn't believe in himself? But if a man can't believe in himself, how can he be himself? No, wait a bit. Try and think. Why didn't you believe? Go over it all from the very beginning. It started when you had this idea about atmospheric electricity and Dan wouldn't let you go ahead with it. That was when you lost patience, when you began to imagine you were on the wrong track and were going to waste your best years. You were keen on your idea and everything else seemed to be in the way.

What about Poltavsky? Poltavsky is a soldier who's got to have a general. While I had no ideas of my own, I was a soldier too. Now I can believe only in my own idea. It may be wrong, but there's nothing else.

That makes you sound so good and honest, doesn't it? How cleverly you get out of things! So you never did anything wrong at all, eh? Well, if you want to know, you're a louse, and maybe worse than a louse. What was your idea worth compared with Dan's? It actually grew out of Dan's work. He blazed the path for you and you left him in the lurch. Who will ever trust you again? Dan's gone and it's all up with you. It was your own doing too.

He built up a logical pattern that led him to the conclusion that life had lost all meaning. He then began writing a letter explaining the reasons for his suicide. On the tenth page he realised that he was examining the nature of ball lightning and making preliminary calculations. It was foolish to have come into the world, but even more foolish to leave it without achieving anything.

At a meeting at the institute Poltavsky made a scathing attack on Krylov and cited him as an example of moral bankruptcy in science.

Speaking in reply, Lagunov unexpectedly came to Krylov's defence. The poor chap was being persecuted. That was unfair. If he was in trouble, he needed their help. Krylov was from the working class. Dankevich would never have allowed such treatment. Poltavsky was allowing himself to be led away by group interests. Lagunov went on and on in the same vein.

His speech was well received. After the meeting Savushkin caught up with Krylov as he was walking down the street and said: "Lagunov's a big man. You ought to stick with him. He'll make you into his winning pawn. This is one of those chances in a million when it's to his advantage to be decent. I suppose you despise me, you think I'm a trimmer? Well, I am. You see, if life was so arranged in my department that it was to my advantage to be decent, I'd be the most wonderful and high-principled person alive. But as circumstances are different, I have to be a dirty dog. It's tough, but there it is. I'd much rather be one of those decent chaps, but I've no choice. What about coming round to my place now?"

Savushkin had recently been given a flat. He had got his Master's degree and was now head of a laboratory.

When they had made an excellent cocktail and drunk it through straws, Krylov began to smile and to feel amused at Savushkin's blend of easy-going kindness and cheerful cynicism.

Savushkin was now earning twice his previous salary, but he did not find himself any better off. His wife nagged him incessantly. "I just can't do anything about it," he confessed. "I was born to live under somebody's thumb."

Krylov said: "And are you happy now?"

Savushkin's face darkened suddenly.

"Keep off that, will you! Happy? What else could I do?"

His answer took Krylov by surprise. What else could he do?

"You and I missed out on Dan's success," Savushkin explained. "We weren't quite bright enough. Let's face it. We're not going to set any rivers on fire and it's a silly occupation anyway. So don't let's stick our necks out. What I like about Lagunov is that we suit him as we are."

At the next meeting of the learned council Lagunov asked Krylov to sit beside him. When the institute's plan came up for discussion, he suggested to Krylov that he should write a thesis based on his work for the expedition.

On his return from Moscow he declared that he had proposed Krylov to represent the institute on an international committee. He then gave Krylov his annual holiday and advised him to spend it in the country. Krylov went to stay with his sister in Staraya Russa.

In the morning he would take out a boat and row upstream until his arms were tired. The timber rafts would drift past him, the raftsmen skipping over the slippery logs with their long poles. There were little plywood huts on the rafts and Krylov could smell the smoke from their fires and hear snatches of talk as he lolled wearily in the stern of his boat. Gnats swarmed over the water, humming as they rose and fell.

He chopped wood, mended his sister's fence and spent his evenings repairing the school's rheostats and voltmeters. His sister couldn't understand this way of spending a holiday. She felt ashamed in front of the neighbours to have a Leningrad scientist painting her fence in an apron.

A fresh-faced veterinary surgeon, her "young man", came round and over tea with cranberries in it they both asked Krylov about the Azores. "How lucky you are!" his sister kept saying. She was terribly proud of him and believed he was going to have a wonderful career. He would be attending all sorts of international congresses, he would have a flat in Moscow and she would come to visit him there. But why was he moping like this? What could be better than to be a scientist, engaged in such inspiring work!

To think that he had once fed himself on similar rubbish! But just try to prove to them that he had never been a real scientist, and that now science was just a job, a treadmill.

The cobbled streets led to a white cathedral. The little town went to bed early. Krylov wandered about in the warm twilight thinking that he'd like to stay here and become a schoolmaster. He walked down to the river, where the rafts were still floating by with their fires burning and the men calling out to one another. His own life and everyone else's now appeared to him as a river that men must sail together. They were tied by the age they lived in and there was no escaping it. For good or ill, he had to sail this river of life with the rest of his generation. And from upstream there would always be new rafts coming down upon the eternal current of time.

He had heard the neighbours' little boy ask his mother who Stalin was, and he had been astonished at the thought of how quickly everything passed. Could it be that one day people would find it hard to remember in what century all that had happened, just as people now got muddled over the dates of the Punic wars and Themistocles. Was it B.C. or A.D.?

Was anything in this life worth upsetting oneself about? Everything passes, and this, too, would pass.

No, he told himself. You won't get away with that, such excuses won't help you. For the tenth time he asked himself how he was to blame. He must be guilty of something because a man always got what he deserved. But surely the penalty was too harsh. Lena, Dan, and his work. He had nothing left. . . . Oh, no, he had Lagunov, his dear, kind Lagunov with his steel jaws. And in what way was he himself any better than Lagunov? What right had he to condemn him? He had got off more lightly than he deserved. But he could abandon any hopes of ever being a real scientist.

Night came down over the cathedral and the town. The trees withdrew from the boulevard and the gardens and merged with the darkness. Only the river with its fires drifting along in the mist remained.

At conferences they discussed all kinds of plans, took excellent decisions, struggled with the wording of them, made bold, hard-hitting speeches and cautious, tentative speeches. During the intervals they congratulated each other on these speeches and Krylov discovered that it was not what was actually done in the laboratories that mattered. It was the impression the institute made at these meetings, whether it figured in the minutes and in what light.

Lagunov towed him round from one conference to the next. They were all important and all of them were attended by worthy individuals, to whom he was introduced as a pupil of Dankevich. Krylov shook hands with them. They asked his advice and his opinion on various trends in science. He learned how to discourse pleasantly on the possible existence of an anti-world, to smoke unnoticed at meetings and make an ash-tray out of waste paper. He was rarely to be seen at the institute. Lagunov advised him to tell one of his laboratory assistants to write up his report for him.

"I shouldn't feel happy about that. It's my report, you know, for my thesis."

"You have more important affairs to attend to," said Lagunov and Krylov agreed.

Lagunov hated meeting foreigners. It was his firm conviction that this new fashion would never lead to any good. He pushed off all the work of receiving visitors on to Krylov, who spent his time showing them round the laboratories and taking them sightseeing in Leningrad.

By the end of the day he felt exhausted, although, when he looked back on it, he seemed to have done nothing at all. Sitting over his apparatus in the laboratory had never made him half so tired.

He seemed to be living in a kind of daze, with a vague sense of the unreality of what was going on around him. It was somebody else who was doing these things; he was merely looking on and awaiting the result.

Just before New Year Golitsyn came up from Moscow. The old man telephoned and invited him to the Astoria. He gave no reasons, and on the way to the hotel Krylov felt strangely excited.

They met in the restaurant. Golitsyn with his chiselled aristocratic features and big white hands resting on the old-fashioned stick between his knees was as majestic as ever. He spoke dispassionately but his eyes were suspicious.

"Dankevich telephoned me not long before he died. He told me you were interested in atmospheric electricity."

"I am," Krylov said.

"He asked me to invite you to our institute in Moscow."

Golitsyn talked about the work that was being done in his laboratory. It was like a generous Father Christmas handing out presents to a poor boy. Krylov wondered if he could bring back Lena.

"I'm sorry, but it's too late," he said. "I'm doing a thesis on a different subject."

Golitsyn drew a bulky packet out of his pocket. Krylov recognised Dankevich's scrawling hand and felt a fresh twinge of remorse. There was a letter from Dan, an outline of a plan of work, notes on the mechanism of thunderstorms, the nature of ball lightning and storm centres. Golitsyn read them out without paying the slightest attention to Krylov, as though he were merely performing his duty.

"Why did he send you this?" Krylov asked.

Golitsyn looked at him and his voice softened a little.

"I think he knew what would happen. He had had two bad attacks one after the other."

"What did he say about me?"

"That doesn't matter now," Golitsyn said. "Unfortunately, he was mistaken."

"Please, tell me. Our relations when we parted...."

"I know. I have read you what he wrote because he asked me to. He was sure you would never take up any other subject." Golitsyn's lips moved as if he were munching something. "That was an illusion," he added crossly. "However, I won't keep you any longer." And he tapped on the floor with his stick for the waiter.

The tall Christmas-tree was glittering with ornaments. Paper lanterns hung from the ceiling. Krylov stared at his untouched cup of coffee.

"I'm sorry if I have upset you," Golitsyn said. "Perhaps I should have come earlier, but I couldn't get away. I've been busy with one of the sputniks. And to be quite frank, I had no very great hopes either. Not many people nowadays are willing to commit themselves to years of.... Though he did assure me that you would be delighted."

Krylov nodded and, without trusting himself to reply, almost ran out of the restaurant.

There was a festive scent of pine branches in the air. Workmen were fixing up a large 1959 over the gates. Krylov thrust his cap into his pocket. His head felt as if it was on fire, but he was smiling. Suddenly he was himself again. He could feel his eyes, his smile, his tingling ears, the crisp, frozen hardness of the ground underfoot; people were walking home from work, hurrying to get to the shops; young men like himself were waiting at the bus-stop and he felt himself one of them, he fitted in like a cartridge in its clip. At moments there was a tightness in his throat and tears came into his eyes, but this, too, was happiness.

So Dan had remembered him. Dan had remembered him all the time, in spite of everything. Dan had been too big a man to nurse grudges. He had been thinking of the job. No, not just the job; he had thought of him. Dan was a man in the best sense of the word. And so was Gatenyan. They were both real people. Now he realised what it meant to be a real man, to be really human. . . .

It was a long time since there had been a meeting, but the old stench of tobacco-smoke was still there in the theorists' room. The brownish blackboards were bare and shiny. He sat down astride a chair facing the little rostrum and the chairman's table, at which Dan used to sit with his hands buried in his thick mane of hair.

Whenever he saw that rostrum Krylov remembered his first abysmal failure.

Suppose he didn't bring off anything with Golitsyn? Was he capable of tackling such a subject? But why bother about that? He thought far too much. He ought to be glad that at last he had been given the chance. But what about the thesis? It was such an easy, comfortable little thesis. And what about his career, and the place on the committee that had been promised him, and all those wonderful conferences? It would do him good to remember how he had begged Dan to take him on, even as a laboratory assistant. How bold he had been then! Why the hell should he be afraid now? Did he know all that he was capable of? Had he reached his ceiling? And what was his ceiling anyway? A man made his own ceiling. It was for him to decide, it was a matter of courage. To hell with Lagunov and his good offices! To hell with his own fears! The eye of the storm—that was what mattered. What was it? And what was a storm? And how did it all come about?

Lagunov and Savushkin decided that he was insane. Why on earth should he go over to Golitsyn? That was completely unknown territory. He would have to start right from scratch. Savushkin said that Lagunov would never forgive him. But Krylov merely grinned blissfully. "Do you know what a storm centre actually is?"

But it was a pity that he had never spoken from this rostrum after all. He stood up and ran his hand over its plywood front.

Youth was over. There was only his old desire to speak from this rostrum, and even that was not so keen now. Once before it had seemed to him that his days of youth were over, but now he knew that he was saying farewell to them for ever.

PART THREE

Chapter One

The windows of the plane were plastered with a thick grey paste. Tiny drops of moisture were crawling down the glass. From time to time a dim light penetrated the cabin only to be blotted out by even thicker layers of paste. Dark clumps of shadow swept past ominously in the gloom; the roar of the engines rose to a whine and Zhenya could feel the plane vibrating violently.

She remembered what the meteorologist at the aerodrome, a hook-nosed, grim-looking old man, had told her. "I wouldn't, if I were you, Zhenya lass. Take my advice and stay on the ground. You've got no business going up there."

The weather man had a soft spot for her. She would have liked to ask him more questions, but Agatov had taken him aside and Zhenya had been put off by their whispering together.

The plane shuddered. Zhenya glanced round at Agatov. He was sitting in the tail. In the ten days since they had left Moscow he was the only one of their group who had not caught the sun. His urban pallor seemed almost unnatural. He was watching Tulin out of the corner of his eye.

Pinkish light spurted into the cabin. Zhenya pressed her face to the window. The grey paste was thinning and breaking into smoke-like wisps that flashed past the windows. Then, all at once the ragged shroud had gone and the whole cabin was flooded with sunlight.

Zhenya gave a gasp of delight. She was looking down into a dazzling white valley full of towers and ramparts and strange monsters. She could see the shadow of the plane racing over hills and ridges made of the same gently heaving snow-white substance. It made her want to jump out of the cabin and stride across the shimmering buoyant surface of this undulating land.

When they took off, the earth had been wrapped in a grey drizzle and it had been hard to imagine that there was sun anywhere. Yet here it was, shining away wastefully in the stillness of this quiet valley, and now it was equally hard to believe that it could be dull and rainy on earth.

A ball of paper fell in her lap and she looked round. Katya, who was sitting on the other side of the gangway, was pointing to a flashing signal lamp on Zhenya's panel. Zhenya snatched up her pencil and jotted down the data. They were approaching a zone of high tension.

Had anyone noticed what was going on outside? No, they were all working, their heads bent over their instruments. Katya smiled vaguely at her and again bent over a small meter quivering on its rubber shock absorbers.

Through the open door of the pilot's cabin Zhenya could see Tulin pointing out something to the pilot. The sun picked out Tulin's sharp profile and the long lashes shading his eye.

Zhenya had fallen foul of him the day after their arrival, when he had refused to allow her and Katya to fly. In the middle of the argument he had suddenly smiled and said: "But we've met before, you know! Don't you remember a park in Moscow, a thunderstorm, a shelter?"

"What of it?" she had answered icily.

The snub had been effective. He hadn't known what to say. Since then he had kept emphatically aloof.

Tulin's fair hair flopped over his forehead and the sunlight flecked it with gold. Turning round suddenly he caught her glance and angrily shut the door. Zhenya gave a little smirk of satisfaction. She then fixed her eyes on Krylov's tousled head. It was at least a minute before Krylov stirred and began to look round. Their eyes met. Krylov stared at her, shrugged and turned back to his instruments.

Their dandified navigator Pozdyshev came swinging down the gangway, the brass fastenings of his smart flying suit sparkling in the sunshine. He gave Zhenya a wink, which she countered with a frigid stare. She enjoyed the awareness of men being so susceptible to her presence. It had been happening more and more often lately. In the underground, at lectures, in buses she noticed their eyes following her and even if they didn't look at her she told herself they were deliberately trying not to.

She levelled an imperious stare at Richard. He turned away from his instruments, began to fidget, caught her glance and blushed. She liked it when Richard blushed. His neck and face flared up together and made her want to stroke his burning cheeks.

The only person who appeared immune to her hypnosis was Agatov. No matter how much she stared at him, his white face remained busily concentrated over his instruments. If he turned his head, he did so only to look from his instruments to his notebook and back to his instruments again, like a smoothly functioning machine.

Zhenya began to feel bored. She switched off her meter and went over to Richard.

"I had a wish on whether you would come over or not," he said.

She felt piqued.

"What a marvellous hypnotist you are! All I want is a message form."

He obediently passed her a form, caught her hand in his and started telling her about atmospheric charges.

"I'll bet you anything Tulin is absolutely right."

"I'm fed up with your Tulin. I think he's just a bumptious dandy. Tulin, Tulin, Tulin—haven't you anything else to talk to me about?"

He squeezed her hand in embarrassment.

"There are some things robots needn't have and can't have. One of them is humour. Others are poetry, dreams, love. Robots can borrow things like memory, precision, logic from human beings, but the other things, the things people have invented to brighten their dull lives, are just so much rubbish for the robot. Well, how did you like that? I've got another speech about birds...."

"Phrase-spinner!"

"When I look at you I find myself talking all kinds of rot. I can't help it. But, in fact...."

"In fact, what?"

"Don't you know?"

"Not a clue."

She tried to pull her hand away.

"Let go."

"Stay another minute."

"Let go," she repeated crossly and he looked utterly crestfallen. His humility, which she usually found appealing, now got on her nerves.

"Would you like me to kiss you in front of everybody?" he whispered, attempting a smile, and there was such adoring shyness in his eyes that she wanted to kiss him herself. She burst out laughing.

"People do that without asking, you poor little hero!"

She walked away with a toss of her head and took one of the empty seats in the tail.

She had once allowed herself to stroke his cheek. He had almost choked with rapture and smothered her in kisses. That had been last winter. Since then, whenever she had let him kiss her he had been madly happy. She was surprised at the power she had over him. A mere frown from her was enough to upset him, and when she was in a bad mood he was utterly miserable.

In the spring they had visited an exhibition of Polish painting. Noisy arguments were going on round the abstracts. Richard, of course, had joined in, arguing that realism, particularly the Russian popular realist school of the last century, was out of date. The "loyalists" had, of course, jumped on him and challenged him to explain what all these blots and circles stood for, and he, of course, had replied that they didn't stand for anything; one had to grow up to an understanding of modern art. The meaning of music could not be conveyed in words. Just try to explain what colour was to a blind man. Abstract painting expressed the new physics. The atom made no distinction between a chair and a stool. The world was much bigger and more complex nowadays. "What about Repin?" they had shouted at him. To which he had retorted: "The Repin you're so proud of is just a primus stove."

When they left the museum, Zhenya had timidly confessed to being completely baffled by this abstract muddle of circles and washed-out lines.

"So am I," Richard had said. "It's crazy."

"Why did you defend it then?"

"I like their rebelliousness! Why do they try to keep them down? Let me sort things out for myself."

With a laugh of relief she said: "I like you."

The next moment she wished she hadn't said it. He ran up the steps of the Lenin Library, embraced a pillar and began to laugh like a madman. She couldn't get another word out of him. He just kept looking at her, smiling foolishly and holding her hand, as if it were a fragile piece of glassware.

Somewhere very deep inside her Zhenya had felt both frightened and overjoyed. Till now such attachments had passed off lightly enough with her. She had fallen in love with teachers and actors. In her first year she had fallen in love with a young professor and talked Katya into falling in love with him too, because it wasn't much fun alone. She had flirted with the senior students and on a farming trip to the virgin lands had nearly married a combine operator. But all the time she had known there was really nothing to it. She had enjoyed declaring with the other girls she knew: "There's no such thing as love. We children of the atomic age are free of such illusions." Her friends, however, had one after the other fallen head over heels in love, weeping and suffering despite the atomic age, and she had secretly envied them. And now there was Richard. She had felt how much it meant to him and the realisation had thrilled her—at last it was her turn, and perhaps her love would be even more exciting than the others'. He was touchingly gentle and terribly clever—reading for his thesis already, and Golitsyn considered him gifted. A formidable opponent in any argument, he lost confidence only in her presence. Such humility both flattered and frightened her. Sometimes she wished he would be less obedient and ignore what she had said about not liking pushers.

The others in the plane were still hard at it. Agatov and Lisitsky had got a piece of blotting paper in a tube and were measuring the charges of water drops as their programme required; Krylov was lost in thought. They were all busy, they all had some goal, some plan to work to. They all knew what they wanted. Richard was longing to become a great scientist. Katya wanted to pass her degree and get married. Pozdyshev's ambition was to be a lady-killer. Only she, Zhenya, didn't know what to aim for. She would get her degree and become somebody's wife, perhaps Richard's. She would go to work, bring up children and consider she was doing her job in life. Her mother thought it was happiness to be keeping up with other people. Perhaps she would also consider herself happy. But there would come a time when she would remember this day, this plane full of sunshine and the enchanted cloud land where she had longed to walk and climb among the white mountains.

As she sat there with her face pressed to the window, she saw in the distance a great billowing mushroom with a top that looked as though it were white-hot. Typical cumulus, she thought, remembering a lecture of Golitsyn's: "In ancient times our forefathers used to compare what we call cumulus cloud to the human brain. How superb was the imagination of ancient man, how infinitely daring and evocative! None of us bother to look up at the clouds nowadays. We just listen to the weather forecasts. . . ."

It suddenly became very dark again. The plane had plunged into heavy cloud. A tin box came crashing down the gangway. The floor heaved up at an angle. Zhenya gripped the arms of her seat. Tulin emerged from the pilot's cabin. Holding on to the door-frame, he ran his eyes over his busy research team. Zhenya jumped up in order to return to her proper seat, but at that moment the plane lurched downwards. She fell over and went slithering forward between the seats. She felt herself thrown up towards the ceiling and as her body again came in contact with the floor she made a wild grab at the cables that ran along by the seats. The tin box came crashing towards her head, then slid away again. She heard a frightened cry from Katya.

It occurred to her that she might be killed. What would people say about her? Died at twenty, before she had time to achieve anything. If only there were no pain. She had never thought how she would die. It would have been easier if she could cry out.

She bit her lip to stop herself from doing so. The plane was diving again, its engines screaming. Zhenya lay on the floor, clutching the cables, her legs in the air.

Someone picked her up by her belt and swung her into her seat. She saw Tulin bending over her. With one hand he was gripping the arm of her seat, the other was groping over her chest. "Fasten the seat belt!" he shouted. But at that moment she noticed that her skirt was nearly round her waist and, instead of feeling for her safety belt, she tried to pull her skirt down. Tulin's hand came down on her bare leg and pressed. She looked up at him indignantly as she felt the contact of his fingers and saw the flicker of impudent curiosity in his eyes as he, in his turn, became aware of her flesh. She hit out at his hand. He said something that she couldn't hear but there was humiliating condescension in the way his lips moved. Having strapped her in deftly, he bent down and, keeping his eyes fixed arrogantly on hers, planted a kiss on her cheek, then swung away down the gangway, gripping the arms of the seats to keep his balance because the aircraft was still lurching wildly from side to side.

Her first impulse was to look round. No one seemed to have noticed anything. Only Richard was looking at her. She pulled down her skirt and as he averted his eyes sheepishly she scolded him inwardly.

In the seat next to her Katya was lying back with eyes closed, uttering little moans.

Zhenya pressed her hands to her cheeks as she suddenly realised what Tulin had called her. Yes, she was sure of it, he had called her a silly little fool. Her fear and sickness vanished in a flash. Forgetting her bruises and scratched knees, she tried to pull herself up to run after Tulin and tell him what she thought of him. She felt even more indignant because she could still feel the touch of his hand, its imprint on her knee.

The fourth cloud was just what was needed. Its original "cauliflower" was developing fast into a massive storm-charged anvil. Such clouds were not so easy to find in just this state—young, promising, active, isolated from others and fully charged. They had to be caught at the right time because they lived only thirty or forty minutes before turning into the completely useless, unproductive kind of cloud that the sky was full of and that was merely a nuisance. Layer clouds were particularly annoying because they were so dead and immobile.

The meteorologist had been right. There was a fine selection of thunderclouds over Morozovskaya. But without Khobotnev's help Tulin would never have found this perfect fourth. The pilot had pointed it out to him well to the right of the course they were steering, and a quick exchange of winks had been enough to send them into a wide turn. They were now flying straight towards Cloud No. 4.

Yes, it was a perfect specimen. Its brilliant silver crest, frothing in the sunlight, rested on a massive grey pedestal that darkened towards its base. From a distance it looked the usual beautiful billow of whipped cream. But as they approached, the cloud loomed menacingly black above them and the aircraft seemed to grow smaller and smaller, until it was like a tiny insect winging its way towards a sheer wall of rock. Khobotnev's hands tightened on the control column. Tulin, standing behind him, gave the order to prepare for observation. He planted his feet wide apart, got a firm grip on a bracket with one hand and, holding the log-book tightly in the crook of his arm, craned forward expectantly. The plane also seemed to tense itself for the coming encounter. This was something it was impossible to get used to. You always had the same unreasoning fear that the grim grey wall in front of you was solid and the aircraft was about to cannon into it.

Khobotnev was steering so as to skim the very top edge of the cloud. This was strictly against their instructions, according to which they were permitted to fly over a cloud or circle round it but never to enter it. No one knew how much effort it had cost Tulin to bring Khobotnev round to his point of view. He had courted the pilot's goodwill in every possible way. He had plied him with cognac and helped him with his English lessons, but all in vain. One day, however, after the flight results had been analysed, Khobotnev had said:

"So it's no good, eh? You're not getting any results. We're just flying around for nothing?"

Tulin had sensed that what really got under Khobotnev's skin was this realisation that they were getting nowhere. The next day they approached a cloud in the usual way but, instead of flying over it or banking away, Khobotnev stabbed the edge of it. Tulin saw the wireless operator and the second pilot glance at Khobotnev, but no one said anything and the whole thing was treated as if a slight miscalculation had occurred. But Khobotnev then made a full turn and skimmed the edge of the cloud in the opposite direction. They went on exploring the edges of the cloud on all sides until it disintegrated, then they went on to another cloud. All the time the second pilot maintained a grim silence. Tulin realised that he was unwilling to get involved in this breach of instructions and bear the responsibility for it because the penalty might be discharge from flying duties. Later the crew grumbled at Khobotnev and asked him why the hell he was sticking his neck out. There would be no extra pay for it, it was a strain on the aircraft and, when all was said and done, what the hell—turbulence was turbulence. Luckily, however, they had sent in no complaints; they liked Khobotnev and didn't want to get him into trouble.

Today they had already explored three clouds. There had been a few bumps, but these were just big cumulus clouds. The fourth, which they were now approaching, promised something far more exciting. Khobotnev went in just a little deeper, and the effect was as if somebody had suddenly started pounding the plane with a huge sledge hammer. Tulin glanced at his stop watch: 1349 hrs 05 sec. All set? Begin! The task was to find the zone of maximum tension. Was everybody operating? What was Lisitsky doing? All he cared about was getting in the required amount of flying time. The pay system in this outfit was all wrong. "Kuzmenko, Zhenya"—now he was shouting into the intercom. "Readjust sensitivity!" He hadn't even time to look round. Aha, lightning! Fine! About two kilometres away. Lot of moisture streaming down the windows. How could there be moisture at this height, when the temperature outside was thirty below? Temperature effects.... What a bloody muddle the whole thing was! With vibration like this various side-effects might come into play. It didn't matter as long as the pre-amplifiers didn't break down. He was always expecting some sort of breakdown somewhere. It was a miracle when all the instruments actually worked at once. Each one of them had hundreds of parts that could go wrong at any moment. There were thousands of soldered joints that might come apart, contacts that might oxydise, insulation that might prove faulty. And when the whole intricate set-up actually worked in contradiction to all the laws of probability, Tulin experienced a secret, almost childish sense of wonder. He never ceased to marvel over this miracle. Droplets formed on rings mounted on the fuselage. The charges of electricity that they contained then passed through the pre-amplifiers, then through the amplifiers, then through the valves until at last they were expressed in a peak on an oscilloscope tape. That was a miracle too. By this time the plane was bucking as if it actually had to jump these peaks of maximum tension. Better note the differences in time when they came through on their return run. They would land in Rostov. Pozdyshev had said there would be Polish sandals on sale in the big department store there. It would take a week to process these measurements, then he could get down to his article. He must write it at once, keep his work in the public eye....

It was a good thing Tulin had warned them. Left to himself, Krylov would have missed that lightning. A fraction of a second, the lilac flash, the discharge—and the chaos of droplets acquired unity. Forgetting his instruments for a moment, he asked himself how lightning managed to collect all the separate charges contained in these billions of droplets. Lightning pierced a cloud as thought pierced the mind. It was like a stroke of inspiration, the instantaneous summing up of what had seemed the most absurd wishes and desires, their final vindication. In its blinding light everything fell into line, past and future acquired meaning. If only he could understand how it actually happened. Yes, it was like thought, but until thought was expressed in words, until it took shape, while it was still embryonic, a mere intimation....

The plane broke cloud at 1349 hrs 45 sec. Tulin stretched his cramped fingers. How much one could achieve, how much one could think and do in forty seconds! If only one could always live as fully, with all one's senses tuned, how enormous life would become! "Observation period over!" he shouted into the intercom, and burst out laughing. Khobotnev leaned back in his seat and responded with a restrained smile. Tulin nodded his gratitude and gave him a look that told Khobotnev he had piloted the plane magnificently, maintaining a perfect horizon, and that now he should turn round and fly back into the cloud from the other direction before it broke up.

Tulin pulled off his earphones and went into the main compartment. He was greeted by flushed faces looking up from control panels and apparatus with the same uncooled enthusiasm that he could feel in his own. Coloured bulbs were still flashing, needles were dropping, unwillingly it seemed, to zero, electric motors were moaning to a halt.

"Well, how did you like that? Nice bit of cauliflower, eh?" Tulin asked happily, as if he had made the cloud himself and presented it to them.

Something, of course, had gone wrong. The paper had got stuck in one of the recorders and a nought was missing. Alyosha was cursing his fluxmeter and couldn't understand why Tulin was so calm. Tulin felt almost hurt because people who hadn't nursed these instruments in their early stages could not see in them the miracle that he perceived. They took it for granted that everything ought to function normally. No one knew how much effort it had cost to make them.

He helped Vera Matveyevna to load a spool and tightened the index pin himself. It would have taken her half an hour to fix it. Amazing how people failed to notice the simplest details. He told Katya to use a pencil instead of a fountain-pen, which had, of course, dripped and blotted her log-book. He looked at Krylov's notes—the old dreamer had only caught half of what went on. The instruments had recorded three flashes of lightning in that wonderful cloud, not one. Never mind, they still had the return run to make.

The plane took several heavy bumps. Khobotnev must be turning pretty close to the cloud. Tulin hurried back to the pilot's cabin, but was delayed by having to help Zhenya Kuzmenko fasten her seat belt. The silly little fool probably thought he had ulterior motives for holding her down as he had. He smiled to himself as he entered the pilot's cabin but, on finding Agatov there, felt oddly confused.

Holding on with both hands, Agatov was staring at the screen of the locator. After a few moments he drew back, wiped his pale forehead and closed his eyes. The cloud was bulging ominously. Its slaty edges were reaching out round the plane, blotting out the sun. Tulin picked up the speaking tube, but at that moment Agatov tapped him on the shoulder. His bloodless lips moved. Tulin knew what he was saying. Agatov was forbidding them to enter the cloud.

"What's the matter, Yakov Ivanovich?" Tulin shouted. "Feeling a bit sick?" He did his best to appear considerate and sympathetic. "Take some tablets. There's no danger, I assure you."

He felt rather than saw that Khobotnev had turned round and was looking up at them worriedly. Placing himself between Agatov and the pilot, he edged Agatov back into the navigator's compartment.

He only needed about two minutes to prevent Agatov from noticing anything. If only Khobotnev had thought of throwing the plane about a bit so that Agatov lost his balance or started being sick. Pale and perspiring he could hardly stand as it was.

"Yakov Ivanovich, if we don't go on taking measurements, the ones we've just taken will be no use."

Agatov shook his head with an effort.

"No. It's not allowed."

Tulin felt the weight of his fists.

"Yakov Ivanovich, please. I take all the responsibility."

"No, I can't allow it," Agatov insisted. Great beads of sweat had broken out on his forehead. "For your own good!"

That damned Jesuitical formula—for your own good! Who knew best what was "good for them"! Agatov was so solicitous. He would make trouble for Khobotnev, he would get them all grounded. And, of course, it would all be for their own good.

Somewhere in the background he could feel Khobotnev's impatient glance. It would have been easy to push Agatov aside and shout the order. But Tulin again appealed to Agatov, smiling submissively.

"It's not allowed," Agatov repeated weakly, almost inaudibly.

In spite of his airsickness there was a faint gleam of triumph in his eyes as he looked up at Tulin. They would have to obey his orders because he was the man *in charge*. The power was in his hands and they, for all their freshness and strength, their immunity from airsickness, their talent, their brilliant programme of measurements, would have to obey.

Just as it was approaching the cloud, the plane went into a steep climb.

Tulin stepped out into the main compartment with a strained smile on his face.

"What's up? Why have we changed course?" The questions were impatient, worried, disappointed and he had to pretend that nothing had happened, that he was still leader of the group, still the man who knew everything and could do everything.

After they had landed he stayed behind in the plane. From the window he saw Agatov striding steadily across the airfield. Katya, Alyosha Mikulin and Vera Matveyevna were with him and they were all chatting amicably. Agatov politely offered to carry Vera Matveyevna's attache case.

When Tulin stepped out of the plane he ran into Zhenya Kuzmenko.

"What made you funk going into that cloud?" she said revengefully.

He looked at her wearily, pretending not to hear.

Chapter Two

The infinite variety of life delighted Richard and reduced him to despair. There were problems at every turn, each one more tempting than the last.

Wiener claimed that the future lay with cybernetics. Joffe claimed that it lay with semiconductors; on further inspection, it appeared to lie with action potentials, thermonuclear power and genetics.

For six months he had spent his evenings helping a friend to rig up an apparatus for achieving photosynthesis.

"Why didn't I take up photosynthesis?" he had complained to Zhenya. "It's terrific! All the problems of agriculture will one day be solved by photosynthesis."

To his architect friends he expounded his ideas on the blending of towns with the landscape.

He was confident that if he were to take up the subject of migrating birds, he would discover the secret of their powers of navigation, and this discovery would make it possible to equip aircraft with astonishing new navigational aids.

He envied journalists who travelled around the country ("Those fellows see life. What do we see?"), historians burrowing in archives ("History has got to be completely reassessed!"), and doctors ("We've got to find a cure for cancer!"). He believed himself capable of becoming an outstanding chess player, a brilliant aircraft designer or perhaps even a distinguished writer.

And what about radioastronomy? What a pity he hadn't become a radioastronomer?

"You know, they're actually preparing to send out signals to other worlds," he told Zhenya. "In ten or fifteen years we'll be getting an answer from outer space! We'll be in touch with intelligent beings on other planets. Humanity will cease to be alone in the universe. Can't you see that's absolutely vital!"

"What about cancer?"

He would wave that aside impatiently.

"Cancer! Why, once we get in contact with other planets it'll lead to break-throughs in all kinds of fields!"

If only he had time, he would take up biophysics. The cell, the chromosomes—that was the real, the basic problem of life.

As a boy he had been convinced that there was time enough for everything. Life had no limits. As yet there was nothing that could really be called the past, and the capacity of the future was infinite.

First he entered the geology faculty. Soon, however, he decided that geology was a purely descriptive science and transferred to electrical engineering. From there he moved to physics. His friends told him he was a rolling stone, but he was really seeking bed-rock.

Only when he became a post-graduate did he finally realise that he wouldn't have time to become a first-class basketball player and musician, that he wouldn't be able to prove Fermat's theorem, and that energy and time were, in fact, finite quantities.

The word "never" had a tragic ring. Never in this life? But there was no other. What was he to do with this world so full of things that were worthy of his zeal? Must he really choose only one and turn his back for ever on all the others?

Golitsyn consoled him by pointing out the general nature of this tragedy. Everyone wanted to do more than was in his power. Every year revealed further agonising problems. More and more time was needed to analyse the material that had already been collected. Research demanded ever more complex apparatus, and ever more time, while life remained as short as ever.

He was suddenly humbled. He would be "like everyone else". Science required soldiers no less than generals.

"Of course, I'm not the right kind of man for you," he told Zhenya meekly. "I'm just a humble worker. I shall never pluck any stars from the sky."

"Thank goodness for that," Zhenya had said. "If everybody started grabbing stars, what do you think would happen? I'd rather you got me a pair of sunglasses. But I suppose you are really a rather mediocre person."

"Why do you say that?"

"Because people with talent know their own worth. Can you get me a pair of sunglasses like that floozy's over there? You can't? Then keep quiet."

She was quite rough with him. It mattered nothing that he was a post-graduate and she had not yet taken her finals.

There wasn't really anything special about Zhenya. She was full of caprices, she was spoiled by having too much attention paid to her, she didn't do much work, and what she did lacked enthusiasm. But he could feel this was not all Zhenya. There was something in her that had not yet revealed itself, there was a promise of something in those slightly slanting, unbright eyes, which one could enter as one might a deep mountain gorge, to wander further and further amid its brown shadows.

Sometimes Richard had doubts as to whether a real scientist was entitled to spend his energies on love, particularly unhappy love. He was quite positive that it was unhappy, although everything was going swimmingly, and when he managed to fix things so that he and Zhenya went out together on field work under Tulin, he could scarcely have been happier.

He hoped that out here, flying with people like Tulin and Krylov, Zhenya would awaken to a real interest in her subject. Though he dared not contradict her on any other point and lived in mortal fear of a quarrel, he stoutly insisted that she had no right to live without some sense of vocation, without a passion for something. He stood firm against the tide of her wrath and on several occasions boldly broke the ban she had imposed on discussion of this subject.

She couldn't bear Tulin at any price and Richard was afraid to tell her about his thesis, which, after seeing some of Krylov's work, he had decided to devote to the possibilities of influencing thunderstorms by Tulin's method. This had to be done without Golitsyn's knowledge and it would mean a lot of rewriting. He doubted whether he would get it done in the time left, but he was prepared to take any risks. He had agreed with Krylov not to tell Tulin about it for the present, in order to avoid placing unnecessary responsibility on his shoulders.

Early the following Sunday Zhenya talked them all into taking a walk in the mountains. They climbed an abandoned rock-strewn road. The hot flints burned the soles of their feet. Below them they could hear the Ayanka rushing among the willow shrubs, and down on the plateau they could see the yellow-walled cottages of the settlement, the concrete runways of the airfield, the small shining crosses of the planes, and, beyond the box-like shape of the airport building, the long brick barn that housed Tulin's laboratory.

Richard said: "Now, kids, this is something for you to remember.

Photographs of this modest building will find a place in all future textbooks."

Katya snorted.

"Call that a laboratory! It's more like a stable!"

"Listen to me," Richard retorted. "All great discoveries have been made in hovels of this type. As soon as a laboratory gets good accommodation, it stops producing the goods. What makes Tulin a great man? First. . . ."

"Oh, how much more!" Zhenya burst out. "Your Tulin will turn our stomachs."

He couldn't understand her annoyance. Just to spite him, she started praising Bochkaryov, as though every real scientist ought to be a hunchback.

"We never give him any help," she declared.

"Why should we?" Alyosha Mikulin put in.

"Well, he's attached to our group. He's supposed to be responsible for our behaviour."

Richard supported her.

"He complained the other day that he had no idea what makes you tick. You might open up a little to him sometime."

"Why do teachers always want to know what makes us tick?" said Katya.

"So that they can eradicate your backward views."

"All oldies want to know in what way we're different from them," Zhenya suggested.

"Nothing of the kind," said Alyosha. "They want us to spend every minute of our lives studying. That's what it all boils down to."

"Even if we did, they'd still tell us that at our age their generation had higher ideals," Zhenya replied.

"Well, what views have I got?" Alyosha asked. "Don't ask me, because I haven't a clue."

"One day more means one day less—that's your view of life," Katya told him.

"Oh, sweetie-pie!"

"Keep your paws off me!"

"Well, don't oversimplify things then," Alyosha retorted. "I'm a bad boy. I don't want to be sent out into the provinces. I like bars and night life. I'm a cynic, and you've got to spend your time patiently reforming me."

And seizing Zhenya by her arms he swung her into a triumphant session of rock. As soon as he had arrived at the aerodrome he had acquired an air-force cap, put on a pair of homemade shorts and started playing the dashing air ace. He liked to be considered brilliant but lazy. He liked striking an attitude of cynicism or scepticism and was offended when people stopped taking him seriously.

They pulled off their clothes and slid, groaning and gasping, into the icy water, leapt out again and hugged the warm boulders.

Zhenya stretched out her arms above her head and gleaming trickles of water ran down her brown back. Richard caught himself staring at the dark triangle under her arm and turned away. He envied Alyosha for being able to slap Zhenya on the back and give him a wink—nice bit of stuff, eh? He would laugh foolishly but he couldn't bring himself to put his arm round her bare shoulders. Instead he would get angry, trying to tell them they ought to help Tulin or criticising Agatov. He longed to make clever, cutting, unusual remarks, but it all sounded rather flat.

None of the students had anything against Agatov. He suited them down to the ground. He let them copy other people's measurements, he never interfered and he had seen to it that they got paid for flying.

"And he's absolutely right to stop us flying in thunderclouds," Katya proclaimed. "Who wants to crash? The thought of that last bumping we got makes me heave."

Zhenya looked at Richard.

"You have less reason than anyone to criticise Agatov."

He maintained an embarrassed silence.

"We can't really judge," Alyosha said appeasingly. "Golitsyn knows better than us."

"But why don't you try and get at the root of things? You've got plenty of ability, if you'd only try!" Richard said.

Alyosha rolled over on his back and patted his stomach.

"Oh, damn my ability. It only causes trouble. You've got ability, you go to the root of things, and what happens? You have to fight. You have to take sides. You upset yourself. No, that's not for me."

He switched on Richard's transistor and picked up some music.

"What about a dance?"

Zhenya shook her head.

"Too hot."

She went down to the river, climbed on to an overhanging branch and lay face downwards, her arms dangling in the rushing water.

The fitful strains of jazz sounded odd among these hills with their red dog-rose thickets. The river maintained its pebbly roar and the blue-black mountains with their white draping of glaciers looked down thoughtfully on the scene.

Zhenya found the unaccustomed beauty of this region disturbing. The mountains were constantly changing colour. They were darkblue, light-blue or lilac, and sometimes they disappeared altogether. Now they were smooth and featureless, now they looked as old and seamed with wrinkles as elephant hide, with milky mist oozing from the deep cracks. It was as if another life were going on up there, wise and just and full of meaning.

The figures of Alyosha and Katya jerked and twisted to the relentless beat of the music and Zhenya began to feel embarrassed by their convulsions under the dispassionate gaze of the mountains.

"Pack it up!" she shouted. "Can't you find somewhere else to be decadent!"

Richard turned off the transistor. He always obeyed when she spoke in that voice.

"I see what you mean," Alyosha said. "The ambiance is too primitive. What we need is a mountain bar with a good supply of Bloody Mary."

Zhenya looked down into the water. The green swirls of the water tugged and tore at her reflection. A vague and faltering likeness stared up at her from the depths. Beneath it, among the shaggy rocks lay the fishes, perfectly still save for the occasional twitch of a fin.

"Would any of you agree to see how you will die?" she asked suddenly, without lifting her head.

"No fear!" Katya replied vehemently. "There wouldn't be any sense in going on living."

"There's no sense in living anyway," Alyosha remarked.

"There's certainly no sense in dying," Richard said. "There's nothing more foolish than death."

"I think that if people could see their own death," Zhenya said, "they would never be afraid any more. They would become better people. They would speak the truth."

Alyosha stretched himself on his boulder and yawned loudly.

"Who needs your truth? It only causes trouble."

"People ought to be able to tell the truth without that," Richard said.

Katya laughed.

"Just you try."

Alyosha laughed too.

"That's an idea, you know. Why don't you?"

"And you can start on Tulin," Zhenya went on. "Tell him he's a coward. He gave in to Agatov when we were in that thunderhead."

"Leave Tulin out of this," Richard said.

"There you are, you don't even want to listen to the truth! You're in love with Tulin. Look at him, he's even started doing his hair like Tulin!"

"That's right, Zheka, pin him down."

In spite of their friendship, they were ruthless with each other. They scorned affection and tenderness and other vestiges of distant childhood. It was their style, the done thing. Being angry was better than suffering, and ridicule was better than being angry.

In the lab Richard was the same, but with them he found himself involuntarily adopting a pose of seniority. He was irritated by their cheap cynicism, cheap because there was nothing easier than sneering. He could beat them at that any day, but he had realised that life was a far more complex process. At first, one's understanding was based on the laws of arithmetic, but later. . . .

They had jumped at the idea that truth meant nothing but trouble. But there was another system of measurement, and in this sphere truth was the supreme pleasure. It was a necessity. Too many lies had been told already. There would come a time when truth would no longer be a cause of dismay, but a necessity. How many times had he sworn to himself that from now on he would force himself to tell everyone and everybody the truth. No more evasion, no more silence. He would take every chance that was offered of telling the whole truth. People could take offence. It might mean trouble for him, but he was prepared for anything.

"Why are you always attitudinising?" he said to Alyosha. "It's an old game. Can't you think of anything more original?"

"Too lazy. My fat won't let me. My lovely, luscious fat!" Alyosha cooed blissfully.

"But what are you trying to achieve?"

"Not the faintest idea."

"You're just an alimentary tract! What positive programme have you got? What else besides cadging three rubles off your father on Saturdays, and queueing up at an ice-cream parlour? Girls. Clothes. Cribs. Volleyball. Cinema. Funny stories. Lipsy. . . . Anything I've forgotten?"

Alyosha spat.

"Why don't you write an article for *Youth*? Here's your headline: 'Is Alyosha Mikulin right? What do you think, dear friends?' And you'll get letters from twenty thousand old-age pensioners condemning me."

"He's unmasked you, Alyosha," Katya said. "But Zhenya is a bit too much for him."

Alyosha arched his body in a bridge to demonstrate his athlete's muscles.

"Unmasked me! But what can he offer instead? Yes, I like ice-cream parlours. And I don't care a damn for your thunder or your lightning, and the other riddles of nature. Look at your Tulin and Krylov. What have they got out of these great problems? They're still slogging away in this dismal hole. One day they'll prove to a handful of oldies that the charges are distributed in one way and not another. And that's the long and the short of it!"

Richard was entitled to feel pleased with himself. The hardest thing was to get them to argue, and he had achieved that. But his real concern was with Zhenya. He was really talking only for her, and she was silent. Most of what was being said at the moment was between them. Without looking at her, he could feel her lying there on that overhanging branch, her legs locked round its slippery base.

"We have a unique opportunity," he said. "The kind of thing that happens once in a hundred years. You can take part in a vital discovery. But you behave like a lot of lounging trippers! Agatov suits you very nicely. He's saved you from any dangerous flights we might have made. So what price your grand statements that life has no meaning—it's just an act! Fine beatniks you make! And you have the nerve to call Tulin a coward. Who is really the coward?" Now he had got into his stride and shaken off that wretched feeling of bondage.

"But Zhenya is a bit too much for you," Katya repeated.

And they laughed. He told himself to be careful.

"Have you nothing to say to this?" Zhenya asked.

He realised that this was a turning point in their relations, particularly for him, and that everything depended on whether he dared to go through with this discussion, which had, in fact, been started for her sake.

"You're putting on an act, too," he said. "You just pretend not to care about anything." He turned and faced her. "Sneer at Tulin, would you! What right have you got? What are you compared to him?" And throwing all caution to the winds, he asked: "What are you working for? You come out with your theories about death, but you're afraid even to glance at your own future. You have no sense of vocation. You're just an employee. Soon you'll be getting ready to leave half an hour before the bell goes. . . ."

He saw her wince and felt a pang of remorse, but he knew he must give no quarter. Instead of all this useless jawing he ought to have swung her up in his arms. She would have liked that. If only he'd had the nerve to do it.

All of a sudden she slid off the branch, snatched up her dress and shoes and started to cross the river, leaping from rock to rock.

In midstream she slipped and nearly fell into the foaming water. Katya gave a little cry of terror.

"Now look what you've done," she stormed at Richard.

"That's where your truth gets you," Alyosha teased him. "Sport is the only thing where there's any objective truth. They measure it in metres and seconds, and that's that."

On the far bank Zhenya pulled on her clothes and set off down-stream.

Tall reddish columns of larches marched high up the green slopes. The woods here were as neat and spacious as a park. The river rushed on, dislodging boulders, heedlessly, without aim or purpose. Zhenya had the feeling it had all happened before. Long ago, perhaps in childhood, she had known this river with its sunshine and burning rocks, and now she was horrified at the thought that childhood was so far away. Suddenly she wanted to be back in Moscow, with her mother, back in the days when her mother had called her Zhuzha, when there had never been any problems to solve and she could always ask why. It was not the first time Richard had set upon her with these beastly questions that upset her for the rest of the day. Richard, Krylov, Tulin, they all enjoyed their work so much, they had something to argue about, they got so excited about it, as if it was the be-all and end-all of life. They were so different, Richard and she. She felt older than him, she could make him do silly things, and yet there was something that set him above her and made him a more interesting person, and that something meant more to him than their friendship. Even if she broke with him now, he would still have his work. Or take Krylov. Katya had tried to start an affair with him, but it had come to nothing. He was young and manly but he was all wrapped up in his theories and formulas and was quite content to be so. People said he had once had a great love affair, but that wasn't the reason. There was meaning in his life. Yes, it was all right for them. But what about her? Soon she would have her degree, but where did she go from there?

Independence, womanhood—she had wanted them so much, yet now she wished to delay their coming. And the worst of it was that they were approaching unavertibly and nothing on earth could stop them. For some reason she remembered the huge old sideboard that had stretched all along one wall at home. It had been like a castle. When there was no one at home she used to rummage in the drawers and open all the little doors. All the shelves had had different smells. On one there were pots of jam, on another, little bags, on yet another, red teacups. "You fool," she told herself, "you utter fool." And she remembered Tulin's contemptuous glance and the words formed by his lips, and she felt even more bitter.

The sound of footsteps made her turn. Richard was running after her.

"Did I say anything to hurt you?" he asked.

"Of course not! I was simply bored."

He looked into her eyes so quickly that she had no time to hide what was there. But he seemed not to notice anything. He was full of repentance. Penitent and timid, he put his arms round her and kissed her, and she felt that she was regaining her power over him. She had only to smile and he would flush with pleasure. She felt his lips quivering and looked up thoughtfully at the cloudless blue sky. Whence this power? What was it for? And what should she do with it?

A big silvery fish leapt high out of the water. Zhenya gave a gasp of fright, then burst out laughing. The mountains were blue again, the birds were singing and there was a stupefying fragrance of thyme in the air.

They collected pine-cones, looked for bits of malachite and sang songs. Richard rejoiced obediently over the mountains and flowers, though he usually scorned all old-fashioned raptures over scenery. Zhenya was afraid to cross the river again by way of the rocks, so they walked on to the suspension bridge.

"Do you feel you need me?" she asked him.

"Very much."

The bridge swayed under them and the height made her head swim.

"You're good."

He looked at her thoughtful face and a barely audible sigh broke from his lips. She took his hand.

"I can't be ... I can't decide all at once, but I'll.... Only don't hurry me."

"I won't."

"That's fine."

In the settlement they ran into Tulin. Zhenya broke away from Richard with an unconscious alacrity that surprised her. She at once took his arm again and clung to him so tightly that he blushed. Tulin, who was carrying a box of instruments, noticed nothing. He was tired and harassed by the nets Agatov was casting round him. The head of the flight expedition had tightened up controls and the formalities and quibbles were endless. Even to fix a bracket they had to get permission from Moscow. He waved a telegram at his assistants.

"Let me send it for you," Richard offered.

He ran off, leaving them alone. Tulin dumped the box on the ground and wiped his face.

"I'd rather you used your charms on Agatov," he said. "Why don't you get him nicely entangled so that he can't bother us." He was looking not at her but in the direction of the post office as he spoke.

"Isn't it enough for Richard to be dancing attendance on you!" she burst out, thrilling at her own daring.

Tulin eyed her from head to foot, with frank male curiosity.
"No, I don't think you could subdue Agatov."
"I could subdue you, if I wanted to."
"Could you now?"
She aimed a contemptuous laugh at him and walked away, swing-
ing her hips boldly.

Chapter Three

Krylov would have made his home in the clouds had that been
possible. He would have set up his instruments there, taken his
measurements and made his observations, and tossed the tapes down
for processing on earth. Unfortunately, the flights were short and
all too soon he had to descend to earth, with its dining rooms, its
airport dormitories and its battery charging sheds.

Because of bad weather they landed at small outlying airfields
where there was nothing but old-fashioned biplanes and forest-patrol
aircraft. Krylov enjoyed this nomadic existence. One day they would
be in Odessa, the next in Gorky, with an overnight stop at a little
place called Ustriki. He liked the smoky, bustling control rooms,
where the smell of wet flying boots mingled with that of fresh apples. Somebody would be sending a bunch of tulips for Nadya, a
cash-taker in Magadan. Airmen would run into old friends for a
few minutes, only to be parted again until their timetable reunited
them a month or a year later somewhere in the Arctic or at Vnukovo.

After the flight they would mask the windows in their hotel
room, strip to the waist and develop films in the stuffy darkness
till midnight. At first light, they would be up again getting their
instruments ready, changing the batteries and examining the dry
reels of film. There would be fierce arguments about the flight programme because everyone had his particular sector and needed a
particular altitude and conditions, then up they would go again
in pursuit of clouds.

Tulin kept him busy making all kinds of additional calculations
and measurements. Krylov could work on his subject only at odd
moments, but he didn't complain because he saw that Tulin was not
sparing himself either. Tulin managed the enormous complexities
of the project with astonishing confidence. He spotted where the
data failed to tally, he knew who ought to adjust what instrument,
he could say why sensitivity had dropped; he even knew that they
had better land early at Krasnodar, otherwise there would be nothing
but porridge left in the dining room. Tulin had a knack of detecting

faults and suggesting improvements. Without his timely advice they would have wasted days, and he had such a jolly way of offering it that it was always palatable.

Sometimes they would get a free evening and turn up in a body at a dance, putting the local beauties in a flutter. Under Tulin's command they would saunter in casually in their leather flying jackets, romantic strangers from another world, and cast an eagle eye over the girls standing along the wall. Even Krylov would feel like a Don Juan.

But usually he would stay in his room, considering the data he had collected. And one day, in the middle of a flight he suddenly started measuring something quite different from what was pre-scribed in the programme. With his usual thoroughness he had got down to bed-rock and convinced himself that too much of Tulin's work was based on intuition and guesswork. Tulin was out for results; the problem was how to get them. He ignored the opportu-nities of investigating the actual nature and process of the build-up of storms. "You don't necessarily have to study the digestive system to be able to digest food," he argued, but Krylov refused to be put off. Their building had no proper framework, the structure was shaky. Tulin wanted to put on the roof, but Krylov insisted on strengthening the foundations.

What he wanted to find out was how the charges in a cloud were restored at each stage of its development, and what was the speed and mechanism of this process of restoration. He set about construct-ing a theoretical model of a cloud. He collected all the measurements, hundreds of them, and compared them in an attempt to establish a norm. His work demanded concentration and Tulin's odd jobs distracted him. The worst of it was that this made Tulin angry because he thought Krylov was checking up on him instead of help-ing—one of those voluntary inspectors!

Near Rostov they carried out a series of active experiments on big cumuli. Their wretched "Burun", a machine for pulverising dry ice, let them down several times. After a long search they would find the kind of cloud they wanted, switch on the "Burun" and in-stead of a shower of dry ice there would be nothing but noise and clatter. Down they went, switched on the "Burun" on the airfield and it worked perfectly, throwing out a steady stream of pulverised ice. Eventually Tulin realised that the machine must be affected by the cold at high altitudes, and ordered them to break up the ice by hand. They used anything they could grab hold of, bruising their fingers in the process, but by the time they had broken up enough and thrown it out of the aircraft the moment had passed. On the next run they started throwing the ice out too early and exhausted their supply. By the time they had obtained more ice, the cloud formation was wrong. They stayed on the ground for two days, cursing their luck, but eventually they found themselves flying over excellent clouds with a high-tension electrical field and well-developed cupolas, and the ice was ejected at just the right moment. Everyone rushed to the windows to watch and take photographs. Yes, it was a beautiful sight! The huge silvery billow of the cloud suddenly began to subside and shrink and the base began to drift apart. Before their eyes rifts appeared and through them they glimpsed the green earth. What had been a towering, formidable thunder-cloud had melted into shreds. They achieved the same result with a second cloud. Tulin was delighted. His suppositions had proved correct. They all cheered and hugged one another, all save Krylov, who had been watching closely from another window to see what was happening on the other side of the plane.

When they landed they lifted Tulin shoulder high, but Krylov stood aside, thoughtfully examining his camera. Finally he came up to the others and with all the shyness of someone presenting a valuable gift told them that unfortunately the experiment could not be regarded as conclusive. He had watched the clouds that had not been treated with dry ice and three of them had broken up in exactly the same way and at the same time. Everyone was annoyed and refused to believe him. Tulin tried to ridicule him and asked him for proof. But Krylov stuck to his guns. There was no proof that the clouds had broken up because of the dry ice; they might easily have broken up of their own accord.

"You've got to understand that a cloud isn't just a thing, it's a process. And before you can deal confidently with it you've got to know its laws. Now just imagine...." And he started drawing lines on the sandy airfield.

When he lifted his head, he was alone save for Agatov.

"I'm relieved to see that you appear to be coming round to Golitsyn's point of view," Agatov said.

"On the contrary," Krylov replied. "If we're going to refute Golitsyn we need far more exhaustive proofs."

The general high spirits were dashed. Vera Matveyevna and Alty-nov petted Tulin, as though he were a small boy whose ice-cream Krylov had tried to steal.

That evening Tulin and Krylov confronted each other in a stuffy hotel room with thick purple curtains on the windows and Tulin shouted that anyone could pick holes and he was going to throw Krylov out of the group. The group was desperately in need of suc-cess. They couldn't go on working without having anything to show. They would lose heart. Agatov was just waiting for something to go wrong. Pressure was being exerted by the institute and the project might be closed down. They had to have success as soon as possible. Couldn't Krylov put himself in his position? Krylov had no reply. He was sympathetic, he felt deeply for Tulin and would do anything for him, but he wouldn't give in, and Tulin realised that if the results were submitted for discussion Krylov would speak against them.

What irked him most was that Krylov had questioned his authority in front of Agatov and the students.

"You're playing into Agatov's hands. You're supplying him with evidence. I'm not going to stand for that. Can't you understand one simple thing? Yes, I'm hurrying, I'm skipping one or two stages, I'm taking risks, but that's the only way of achieving anything. No one judges the victors when the battle is won. We'll make up for what we've missed later on. In science correct tactics sometimes matter more than facts." Tulin smiled sourly. "Incidentally you're not taking any risks. That's my privilege, as head of the group. You'll be in the clear whatever happens. I'm the one who gets the kicks. I'm the one who's staking his reputation. I hope you'll agree that our losses won't be equal?"

Alyosha came in, sweating even in his shorts, to show them the wet prints of the photographs Krylov had taken. They perfectly illustrated the collapse of a cloud.

"Now look here," Tulin said, when they were alone again. "Do you want to wreck our work? You can do it quite easily. Take these photographs, take all your papers and go and see Golitsyn. Tell him how I'm faking the facts and your aim will be achieved. Our project will be closed down."

"I don't want that," Krylov said.

"But that's what'll happen!"

"I would like to take some control measurements. I want to exclude any possibility of doubt. And for that...." He started expounding his plans.

Altynov came in with some green tea. They drank it, mopping their faces with towels.

Krylov maintained that they ought to check the degree to which the aircraft's own electrical field influenced their results. He was not happy with the approximate coefficients that the group was using at present.

"Listen to this hippopotamus, Altynov," Tulin burst out. "He wants to catch us out. I think he's Agatov's agent. It was a bad day for me when I took him on."

Krylov looked wretched and suddenly Tulin burst out laughing, winked at Altynov and with all the generosity and largess that were part of his charm gave permission for the building of a special apparatus, and the use of funds and personnel, and ordered Altynov to get hold of a high-voltage mercury rectifier. In short, to make a proper job of everything.

Krylov was quite overcome. Once again Tulin had taught him a lesson in generosity and true friendship. After all, he was really indebted to Tulin for being able to do the research he had dreamed of doing and which now lay before him in all its complexity.

Meteorology struck Krylov as a heart-rending story of attempts to establish regularity in a field where it could not be established, where all was chaos. Winds, clouds, rain, fluctuations of temperature, all that came within the compass of meteorology emerged from innumerable coincidences, they were all interdependent, it was a tangle in which no one could detect a beginning or an end.

A mountaineer dislodging a pebble with his boot might cause a heavy storm of snow or hail.

Enormous courage and industry on the part of generations of meteorologists had built up a science out of what appeared to be a collection of random facts. Clouds had always been the biggest stumbling block among a long row of obstacles. Krylov realised that even to attempt to investigate the nature of clouds was a kind of heroism.

A great mystery was hidden in the formation of cloud. What unknown laws accounted for its sudden billowing and darkening? It was a mischievous elf that might play any trick. Having put on weight to the tune of several millions of tons, it could deluge the earth with rain. It could turn itself into a thundercloud and toss a heavy aircraft about like a grain of sand. From a height of several miles it could knock sparks out of aerials and send radio compasses waltzing. It could sprinkle the earth with a few thunderbolts or, given the whim, bombard it with hundreds. Or perhaps nothing of the kind would happen. It would just spread out into a docile ponderous rain cloud that would hover motionless for hours before it began to sprinkle its warm fine rain. Or it might melt away altogether in the course of a few minutes and vanish as mysteriously as it had appeared.

Everyone compared a thundercloud with the electric generator, that commonplace electrical machine that Krylov had studied in his second year at the institute. It sounded very plausible, but:—

It was a machine without terminals and no one knew where to plug into it;

No one knew what made it turn;

Or how it started turning;

Or why it stopped;

Or why all at once, for no apparent reason it ran amok and built up voltages that no one could foresee.

It was quite likely that there had never been two truly similar clouds. Even those of similar type differed in thickness, shape, age and behaviour. Each had a life of its own. Each was prone to the oddest changes that might take place in a few seconds or drag on for several hours.

And yet they must all have some features in common. There must be something that united them. But what was it? How and where did it operate?

Where were the heterogeneities that led to development?

More than once he had stumbled on the idea that in human society, too, development actually depended on heterogeneity. Where everything was uniform there could be no development. If there were no conflict of opinion, of scientific ideas, society would perish. It would become static, like stratus clouds, in which nothing happened for months, which shed exactly the same amount of drops as they had had when they first formed. Every discovery, every new idea was also a heterogeneity which would inevitably become clothed in reality, stir men's minds, struggle, grow and spread, like a cloud, until it finally demanded its fulfilment.

This was all very well, of course, but what was one to do about clouds?

Altynov compared Krylov with his project to the cranky photographer who tried to create a photograph of the "average" citizen of his town by taking pictures of scores of people, putting the negatives on top of one another and printing through them on to one piece of paper. This he repeated dozens of times, rephotographing the "average" portrait from each printing and printing the negatives together. And the final result was a general portrait, the face of someone unlike anyone in particular, yet possessing the features of all. The incidental features disappeared, the general were amplified. It was a portrait of everyone and of no one. A picture of everyone in which no one could recognise himself.

There was some truth in the comparison.

At first Krylov was confronted with the problem of how to collate his data. What was the principle to be? He harassed his assistants, trying various ways. They processed data from eighty-five clouds, drew up three hundred charts and finally reached the conclusion that the thing was impossible. For a few days Krylov went about shamed and humbled, obeying all Tulin's orders without a murmur. Tulin was pleased:

"The classics are right: man is ennobled by toil!"

And all of a sudden Krylov realised that a model of a cloud could not be a portrait, it must be a living organism, an internal process. That was where he should look for a law.

Richard was adjusting an oscilloscope. A nice, new oscilloscope. What a pity it was for Agatov's programme of measurements. "A Contribution to the Problem of Further Verification. . . ." Such measurements were no use for anything except padding a thesis. When Agatov's programme came up for discussion Tulin sang a little ditty about dripping raindrops.

As he peered into the dial of the wattmeter Richard saw the reflection of his own spectacles, his eyes, the bridge of his nose and his black sweeping eyebrows. Taken separately, they seemed to be all right but the total effect was deplorable. He had become concerned about his appearance of late. He wanted to be good-looking. What a face to be condemned to wear all his life! He would have made it dark and firm with blue impenetrable eyes, he would have added another three inches to his height, so that Zhenya would have to crane her neck to look up at him. Surely it was time people were given the chance of choosing their own appearance.

Agatov entered the workshop, had a word with Alyosha and Katya, then came over and stood behind Richard.

"How's it going?"

"I'm nearly through."

One could always detect Agatov's presence by the smell of his Lilies of the Valley Eau-de-Cologne. It was with him wherever he went.

"High time too. Has Tulin been distracting you again? I'm afraid you're much too fascinated by Tulin." Richard heard Agatov take a match out of its box. Agatov never smoked but always carried a box of matches, which he used for picking his teeth.

Richard snapped down the lid of the wattmeter and a dull spot of light slid over Agatov's big face. His face was ugly too.

"Man's a strange creature," Agatov said sadly. "Always far more ready to forgive ill-treatment than to appreciate what is done for him."

Richard reflected that to Agatov he must indeed appear ungrateful. It was only about six weeks since he had humbly begged Agatov to let him come on the expedition with the students. Richard had really only needed to go to an aerological station for material on his thesis and Agatov had failed to understand his insistence on joining the expedition. Richard had been compelled to hint at personal motives. Agatov had told him candidly that the duties Golitsyn had charged him with were complex enough as it was, and that if he took Richard with him it must be as a supporter, not an opponent. Richard had promised his support. He had been ready to promise anything. And he had to give Agatov credit for the trouble he had taken proving that he really needed Richard with him.

Richard recalled his own words: "Something personal, you know. . . . But what a question! Of course, I'll help you in every possible way." Agatov must also be recalling them. Richard was trapped by his sense of obligation.

Agatov shook his head understandingly.

"I've no claim on you. I'll manage. It's a hard furrow to plough, of course, with everyone against you like this. I'm supposed to be a tyrant, a conservative. But, you know, there are two sides to every-thing, Richard. It's that unity of opposites we used to be taught about. I'm responsible for seeing that this inquiry is conducted sen-sibly and safely. What it really amounts to is that I'm trying to keep Tulin alive, and to keep you alive. And for that I'm represented as a villain who intrigues against the whole project. That's what they say about me, isn't it?"

Richard nodded awkwardly.

"Quite. And why go far afield? You yourself think the same. Although I have done far more for you than your Tulin has. Do you imagine I don't know about your thesis, and about your chang-ing the approved subject without permission? It's my duty to inform Golitsyn at once and send you back to Moscow, so that he can deal with you as he sees fit. But I'm covering up for you, risking my own neck. Why should I?"

The frankness of his approach was disarming.

"But what else can I do, Yakov Ivanovich? Krylov let me read his work and it convinced me. Tulin may not have everything proved up to the hilt but I feel this is where the truth lies. I used to believe in Golitsyn's method, but it's really nothing more than a dogma nowadays. We have too many dogmas in science as it is."

"Where are these dogmas?"

"Everywhere. Just take Denisov. And you're wrong to attack Tulin. He's tackling a tremendous problem—active intervention in thun-derstorms! That really is something. And we ought to support him."

"There'll be nothing to stop you supporting him after you've done with your thesis, if you still feel so inclined. You'll have your hands free then. But you'd better be careful. You're ready to lean over backwards for Tulin, but what about him?"

"What do you mean?"

"I mean that he's not worth it. He's riding on your back. He's not in the least concerned for your future. Yet you reject me, though I am. I can't understand it."

Alyosha walked past, glancing at them curiously. The sight of him made Richard remember his vow to tell the truth without fear or favour.

"I really don't know, Richard, why I make such a fuss of you. But we could be friends. You would get more out of it than I should. You're just rushing into something with your eyes shut. They're simply deceiving you."

Agatov spat out a piece of match and placed his hand on Richard's shoulder. Richard recoiled.

"Yakov Ivanovich, you said I should take up Tulin's method after I've defended my thesis, didn't you? Well, what does that mean? It means you're not interested in whether the method is correct. The scientific side of it doesn't matter to you. But Tulin is ready to risk his life for the sake of science! He may be mistaken, but that kind of mistake is a hundred times better and finer than the cowardly caution of mediocrities."

He knew he was in the wrong. He hadn't kept his promise, he was deceiving Golitsyn, he would bear any blame, but he refused to turn against Tulin or renounce his allegiance to him.

"I'm afraid you'll regret this. And pay a heavy price for it," Agatov said sympathetically, and Richard felt a stirring of fear, a horrible creeping little fear that pinched his face into a smile. A thesis could be pretty difficult. Would he manage it?

He remembered what an effort it had cost him to make the grade for post-graduate work and all the plans and dreams it had seemed to offer.

"But I've changed the subject of my thesis because I believe in it. Krylov left Golitsyn because of his convictions, didn't he?"

"Yes, and where has it got him? The poor fellow has been regretting it ever since. Can't you see what a pitiful position he's in here? Tulin has no consideration for him at all."

"When people really act up to their principles they never regret it."

"That's just rhetoric. You must try to get rid of some of your rhetoric," Agatov said solicitously. He licked his dry lips. "How can you possibly hold up Tulin as model! If you want to know, the man's like a vampire. He doesn't care a damn about you or your ideals. He'll squeeze you dry and throw you aside when he's done with you. Do you think he'll care about your feelings? He doesn't care about them even now. And I don't mean the work either. I suppose you'll say I'm waxing lyrical, but he has no sense of morality. You poor bespectacled knight errant! You really are blind, like all lovers."

For a moment they stared deep into each other's eyes. Richard couldn't quite understand what had happened, but the whole situation had changed. Why did he have this feeling of impending disaster?

"You're quite wrong. You're making things up," he said quickly.

"Am I? Then surely it's odd that you should have had the same idea. I was merely saying how fond you are of Tulin." Agatov chuckled with amusement. "Now you're caught, aren't you? And you call me a backbiter...."

"I won't listen to you. I know you're only saying these things out of envy."

But he was merely stuttering helplessly. He was not even listening to himself. He was frightened. What had made him think of them? What had put this into his mind?

"You will come to realise that as far as Tulin's concerned you simply don't count. He'll walk over you without a moment's hesitation."

"You're envious of him."

"For what?"

Surely I'm not afraid? To believe such a thing would be treachery to Tulin.

"Because he's got talent."

Agatov's eyes suddenly darkened. Life seemed to withdraw from them and the shutters closed with a bang.

"I've tried to give you a friendly warning and this is how you twist it. It's most disappointing. Your attitude is quite unjustified, but I suppose it's no use trying to make you like me. You will have to go to Moscow. Let Golitsyn decide that matter. I have no wish to be held responsible for the games you're playing with your thesis." He took a deep breath and shook his head. "So Denisov is a harmful dogma, is he? So you don't like Russian scientists, Comrade Goldin?"

Richard turned pale. He suddenly found it hard to breathe. "Why, you...."

A smile spread slowly over Agatov's face.

"You had better hand in your report on the measurements you have taken."

He walked briskly to the door. His pale lips were twitching nervously. He was cut to the quick by human ingratitude.

Herds of crimson clouds were roaming across the sky. The sun was setting behind the mountains and the thick warm air was humming with gnats. Richard lay on the slowly cooling pebbles. He would never have believed it possible to lie like this, without a single thought in one's head, desiring nothing, conscious only of the passage of time and not regretting it.

Most evenings found him with a sense of dissatisfaction over the past day—so much time wasted on useless talk, time that he always promised himself he would somehow manage to recover.

Now nothing mattered. Time with its watches, its pot-bellied alarm clocks and their luminous dials, it could all go to the devil, along with the calendars and timetables, the sunrises, the plans and all the other rubbish. Perhaps it had been like that once, when nothing existed, not even time.

The light suspension bridge over the Ayanka gave a creak. Richard jumped to his feet and climbed the bluff. On the cliff face ahead of him he could see the curving shadow of the bridge with the figures of a man and a woman silhouetted in the middle of it. The man bent forward and took the woman's hand. She withdrew it. The bridge swayed slightly and creaked and the elongated shadows went shooting up the cliff. The man again put his hand on the woman's arm, higher this time, almost at the shoulder. He kept it there and she made no attempt to resist. Richard climbed the bluff slowly and walked toward the bridge. The sun was setting and shadows were lengthening over the crags.

Zhenya waved to him, showing no sign of surprise at his sudden appearance.

Tulin said: "Be careful, Richard. She may blow up on the slightest impact."

Richard hurriedly forced a laugh, painfully aware of Tulin's easy manner and the complete lack of embarrassment with which he took his leave and walked casually away.

"I've been looking for you all the afternoon," Richard said.

"I was helping Tulin to send up a sonde."

"Not so long ago you couldn't bear the sound of his name."

"You re-educated me yourself. But there seems to be no pleasing you."

They walked up the cliff path to the main road. Aircraft roared low overhead, their wings reflecting dazzling shafts of sunlight.

"What's the matter?" Zhenya asked.

He tried to tell her about his conversation with Agatov and realised that there was hardly anything to say; it trickled away like water between his fingers.

"You ought to have told Tulin about this." Her eyes were frank and open and Richard felt relieved.

"He's got troubles enough without that. . . . I can look after myself. And don't you dare start worrying him."

She laughed so heartily at his remonstrations that he finished by saying doubtfully: "I must be a complete idiot."

"You needn't be so doubtful about it. Sometimes I wonder what you ever saw in me."

"When you say things like that, Zhenya, you make me want to. . . . How would you like it if I produced a thesis that really gave them all a shock?"

"You needn't take any notice of Agatov. He's envious of Tulin and the way you look up to him."

"He can go to hell!"

"I shouldn't have gone out with Tulin, he has nothing to do with this. I've been acting rather foolishly myself."

They were approaching the cottage where the girls lived. Richard hesitantly slowed his pace.

"Let's go on walking for a bit," Zhenya said.

They strolled past the settlement and on towards the airfield. Richard put his arm round her.

A service bus went past and the airmen stuck their heads out of the window and whistled.

"If Tulin started getting fresh with me, would you hit him?" Zhenya asked suddenly.

"Yes, but not very hard, so that you wouldn't make too much fuss of him afterwards."

"When was the last time you had a fight? Not that it matters. You know, I expect there are some men who've never had a fight in their lives. Did Agatov say anything against Tulin? But perhaps Tulin *is* a bad lot? Can you see any faults in him?"

"In him? Never thought about it. I only think of your faults."

"How boring. I hate people thinking about me! I never think about myself. I tried once and it didn't work. I suppose I've got a consumer's interest in science, like Alyosha. Or Pozdyshev. I think handsome men are a pain in the neck. They get used to having all the hens, like Vera Matveyevna, cackling round them."

"Who, in particular?"

"Tulin, of course."

"You've got to make allowances for talent."

"Are you fishing? You're quite bright yourself, you know."

"Surely Agatov won't send me away?"

"I'll go with you if he does."

"Chuck it. If it comes to a pinch, Tulin will fix things. He wouldn't let that happen, he needs me too much."

Darkness flowed down from the mountains, flooding the valley. Gradually the settlement struggled out of the swirling gloom, switching on lights in houses, street lamps and the coloured signals on the airfield.

Katya was out. Zhenya kicked off her shoes, rubbed her feet and lay back on the bed with a sigh.

"Come over here."

Richard tiptoed across the dark room.

"Sit down."

He sat down and found her hands in the darkness. She felt all drawn up inside. It was a good thing he couldn't see her face.

"I'd like to be able to hand out truth to people like you do. But I can't be that ruthless."

"What cold hands you have," he said.

He leaned forward and kissed her and his spectacles scratched her cheek.

If it happens, there'll be no going back, she thought. Perhaps they would get married. Yes, they would get married. Then let it be soon and the other thing would be over and done with and life would be straight and clear at last. She lay without moving. He could do what he liked with her.

His hand touched her breast.

"Don't," she said.

She felt the effort it cost him to draw back.

"I'll go now," he said.

There was only darkness after he had gone. Zhenya felt utterly exhausted. She lay on the bed, smiling to herself and scolding him, thanking him, yet feeling sorry and despising him.

In the middle of the night she woke up Katya.

"There's not a word of truth in it."

"What's the matter?" Katya said.

"It can't be true that there is only one person in the world you can be happy with, and that he's the one you'll meet."

"Is that what you're worried about? Haven't you got enough men running after you?"

"But can't you see it's such absolute rubbish. You, for instance, love Alyosha. There were millions of possibilities, but you found him, the man destined for you by fate. And it just happens that this dream man of yours is at your institute, in your group. What a strange coincidence! But surely there are thousands of boys who can become your one and only? So what's the point in sighing and sobbing and making tragedies out of nothing."

"Who's making tragedies?" Katya asked indignantly. "Have you been having another quarrel with Richard?"

Richard again! As if no one could think of anyone but Richard. "Well, don't get so upset about it. You've had plenty of quarrels before. After all, he's mad about you. What more do you want?"

What more did she want? She would have Richard. Everyone was sure that was the right thing. There was no alternative, it was bound to happen.

She lay on the bed with her eyes tightly shut but the tears welled forth. She tried to tell herself she had quarrelled with Richard. It was all because of that and there was no other reason.

Chapter Four

Krylov had spent several days building an apparatus for measuring the intensity of the aircraft's electrical field.

Tulin was glad because it had kept him quiet for a time. It was hard work fighting on two fronts, Agatov on one side, Krylov on the other.

They needed a high-tension rectifier. From all quarters Altynov got the usual answer: "Why didn't you put in an application last year?" He and Krylov went off to try their luck in Moscow. At head office they spent a long time wandering from one desk to another until they found out that everything depended on a girl called Mashenka. She was only a minor official of some kind, but Altynov had for long been convinced that the most complex apparatus was to be had from the most humble sources. Mashenka was a gay little thing with a lot of freckles. She looked rather like a bedraggled sparrow.

"You see, we've only just had the idea of trying out a new system," Krylov told her. "So how could we have applied a year ago?"

"We live in a planned economy," she replied. "Industry can't wait for you to have your brain waves."

Mashenka was impregnable until Altynov whispered: "Invite her to come to a restaurant with us." To Krylov's surprise, she readily agreed and they had an excellent evening together. Krylov was in good form and told her a lot of stories about their flights and his trip round the world.

The next day Mashenka fixed them an emergency order and told them they would have the rectifier in a month's time. Altynov was pleased. He left Krylov to fill in the application form and went off with Mashenka to get various signatures witnessed. When they returned, Krylov was cheerfully drawing a diagram on the back of the form. He swept Mashenka up in his arms and announced that he had discovered a way of making a much simpler model without any kind of rectifier. It called for a little ingenuity, but that would only make it more interesting.

In vain Altynov tried to shut him up. To withdraw the order they had to go and see the Assistant Director. It was a most unusual case and the director himself came in to see what it was all about. A conference was held and Krylov stated indignantly that, if the truth were known, applications for equipment were granted too lavishly. Of course, it was easier to order a powerful machine than to think of a way of doing without it. Mashenka and her chiefs listened to him in delight, but one or two representatives of institutes who happened to be present looked as if they wanted to lynch him.

Krylov's apparatus was of the crudest kind and everyone laughed at it, but he took no notice. He was thinking of Dan and his ability to work on elementary circuits. Only now that he was really in the thick of things himself had he realised why Dan had avoided ordering large and complex apparatus. Dan considered that an overabundance of material resources discouraged thought. A simple machine revealed the essentials and forced one to think of the things that mattered. Krylov had been thinking a lot about Dan lately. It was the first time he had had to act without any supervision. He felt a need of criticism, he needed even Golitsyn, who was so adept at spotting mistakes and demanding fresh proofs.

A duralumin aircraft model was suspended on silk threads between two large plates covered with tin foil. With a little ball fixed on a bamboo cane one had to touch the aircraft in a certain spot, pick up the charge, transfer it to an electrometer, touch the electrometer, take the reading and note it down. There were about fifty points on the aircraft that had to be tested in this way. Then the potential difference between the plates had to be altered and the process repeated from the beginning. After that the position of the model between the plates had to be changed and the whole experiment repeated. Alyosha marvelled at Krylov's patience, but by the time Krylov had been at it for a fortnight his hands were so practised that he performed like a machine.

Alyosha tried to help him and in half an hour was complaining of arm-ache. Was this the thrilling, fascinating work that science was supposed to offer?

In the evening Alyosha was relieved by Richard. He knew, of course, that every research project had its dull moments, but surely such gimcrack arrangements in this day and age, with the kind of facilities that were now available. . . .

"I wouldn't have bothered either," Alyosha said, stretching himself. "I don't mind working under the right conditions. If the current's low I expect to have a bigger transformer installed."

Krylov listened to them grinning. He had taken off his shirt and the big shoulders and hairy chest under his green singlet made him look tougher than he usually did in his baggy suit.

"You don't agree then?" Alyosha asked.

"In Faraday's time," Krylov said, "there were not many brilliant ideas going. On the other hand, hardly any money was spent on scientific research. Now the funds are much more plentiful but brilliant ideas are just as hard to come by. And of course it's a lot easier to spend money than to rack your brains inventing things."

"So you think less money should be spent on science? If you go on like that you'll finish up in the backwoods!" Richard exclaimed.

"I'm not so sure, you know," Krylov replied imperturbably. "It might not be a bad idea if we were a bit stingier with our money. When science has unlimited resources, it runs to fat. Of course, there are limits. It can be a hell of a job to get hold of a twenty-kopek valve. But that's a matter of organisation."

For once Richard was stuck for an answer.

You never knew what Krylov would come out with next. He was quite likely to turn everything upside down and give it a twist of his own, and if there was a tussle it didn't matter whether you were a mere student or had your Master's degree, there was no subordination. And there was no need to be afraid of dropping a clanger. The main thing was that whatever you said it would be listened to.

They were full of reforming zeal. They abolished theses and brought them back again, but decided not to raise salaries on a degree basis because no man should make science his calling for the sake of gain. They inaugurated institutes of telepathy and laboratories of chiromancy. Anything was worth trying once and something new might come of it, otherwise there was no fun in life. Krylov was of the opinion that the scientist was the embodiment of the new man of communist society, for whom work would be both a need and a pleasure.

Alyosha nodded at Krylov.

"What a pleasure to spend every evening fishing around with a bit of bamboo!"

When Richard and Krylov were left to themselves, Richard heaved a sigh.

"Science is just one big forest. You can't even see what is close at hand. . . ."

Krylov looked up.

"So you have read *Faust*?"

"I have. I ought to read it again but there's no time. It makes me writhe to think how many good books have been written. Enough to last mankind a century. Not to mention all the films, plays and music! And that's masterpieces alone. We've got enough. Art could quite safely be closed down for about twenty years."

"Who's the backwoodsman now?"

"It's no use anyway. People like Agatov are immune to poetry."

"What makes you say that about him?"

"I hate mediocrities. They're the root of all evil. They've got to be crushed. They shouldn't be allowed anywhere near science. They ought to be pilloried, ridiculed."

"Has it ever occurred to you that to reproach a person for lack of talent is the same as laughing at a cripple?"

"Some cripple! Agatov would wring your neck for you if you gave him half a chance."

"Sometimes I feel sorry for him. He's a misfit. Of course, he's no physicist, but he might have made a good architect or a chairman of a collective farm. Who can tell? When a man knows he's in the place where he belongs, he's a better man."

"Are you trying to find excuses for him? Wherever he is, a man ought to stay human."

Krylov switched off the current and seated himself on the table.

"For a long time now I've been thinking that the vital thing is to help people find their true calling. Take our Zoika, for instance. She's a waitress in a canteen. Is that what she was born for? Take the principle, 'From each according to his ability. . . .' According to his ability, mind you! How many people there are who don't know what real ability they have! It's not enough just to say study and take your choice—everything lies before you. People have got to be helped to produce their maximum. . . ."

"That doesn't apply in Agatov's case." And unable to contain himself any longer, Richard blurted out his conversation with the project supervisor.

Krylov returned to the electrometer, rubbing his red eyelids.

"Don't worry. I'll have a word with Tulin about that."

"I'm sure Tulin won't let him send me away."

Krylov nodded and they both went on working.

He found Tulin in Altynov's room. Agatov was with them.

"Won't you sit down," Altynov invited.

They were drinking tea with honey. Altynov was fond of honey. He was fond of anything that was good for him, and when he provided tea it was usually with vitamin tablets and various other health-giving substances.

From what Tulin was saying Krylov realised that he had come in in the middle of a discussion about Richard and that Agatov had just stated his reasons for sending him to Moscow. Altynov was taking no part in the conversation. His mild, pudgy face remained impassive save for an occasional warning glance at Krylov. It was costing Tulin something to hide his annoyance but he had himself well under control. They were talking about honey and they all seemed to be good friends or, at least, something more than colleagues.

Agatov fixed his eyes on Tulin. "I wouldn't be surprised if they take him off post-graduate work altogether. With his opinions it would do him good to have a couple of years at a factory. Don't you agree?"

"So people say," Tulin replied. "I wouldn't know, I've never worked at a factory."

"But I have," Krylov said. "I don't think it's essential for Richard."

"Are you suggesting that mixing in with the workers is harmful, Sergei Ilyich?"

"Richard comes from a working-class family."

Tulin made a clatter with his spoon.

"I'm afraid you'll never do well as a lawyer, Sergei."

"He simply ignores Golitsyn," Agatov said. "Look at it this way. How can Golitsyn supervise the work of a post-graduate who is actually trying to refute his theories? He had better try and find himself another supervisor—if he can."

"What's so terrible about it?" Krylov said. "One can go against one's supervisor...."

Tulin gave him a look and turned to Agatov.

Altynov moved the honey-pot towards him.

"Help yourself, Yakov Ivanovich. Take as much as you like."

"He also says he wants to criticise Denisov. What do you think, Oleg Nikolayevich, is it worth his while to tackle a thing like that?"

"I understand what you mean," Tulin said gently. "That will complicate matters, of course. And things are complicated enough as it is."

"Exactly!"

Agatov laughed. Tulin forced a smile, but his eyes remained hard and unblinking.

"Lime-blossom honey contains about forty-five per cent grape sugar," Altynov informed them.

"Wonderful stuff." Agatov nodded appreciatively. "Do you like comb honey?"

These intellectuals, Krylov thought to himself, with their tea-party manners. Suppose I were to bash Agatov over the head with that kettle. He'd take me to court for assault and battery. But it is

Agatov sat down weakly on the ground, still clutching the rod.

"Yes, I'll do it for you," he repeated, his voice growing a little firmer. "It's such a shame the way they're treating you here." He looked up at Krylov's gloomy face. "I'm quite ready to do it for your sake. You don't believe me? You think I want to put something across you? I'll write the letter to Golitsyn in your presence, if you like. You can send it yourself. It's a pity I haven't any paper with me now."

Krylov took out his notebook. While Agatov was writing he reflected with surprise that force, plain physical force still had meaning for people like Agatov. It was the oldest and, sometimes, perhaps, the cleanest means of persuasion.

A bald individual of about forty, slightly tipsy, was sitting in the lobby of the hotel. His lips were moist and his chin was thrust forward. He looked rather like an ape. The receptionist, a stout, handsome woman, was saying smilingly: "If I got married I'd want a baby at once."

Krylov sank into a chair and lighted a cigarette.

"But I'm in no hurry," the receptionist went on. "I want someone out of the top drawer. A scientist, for instance. Somebody like that Lisitsky, who's living here. Or Tulin. I'd make a good wife for anyone. I was once offered the job of hotel manager."

It was hard to guess whether she was serious or merely teasing. The man breathed heavily, going purple in the face.

"That Tulin of yours makes too much of himself," he said. "These scientists are. all the same, sitting on the country's back, sucking all they can out of it. Turn up at work when they please. I'd like to see some of them down in the pits.... They've been fiddling about round here for two years now, and where's the results? If I had the power I'd give'em all.... They'd be up on the carpet before the Party organisation to start with."

"What have they been up to now?" Krylov asked, winking at the receptionist.

"Oh, you can always make out a case. They say Tulin got his pal Krylov a job here. That's one bit of evidence. And they both criticise the Academy of Sciences. I've heard 'em doing it myself. As for immoral behaviour, anybody can see that. I know about his goings on with one of the students. Altynov covers up for him. They're all in league. They get together in their rooms of an evening and whisper away. And it's the same while they're at work. You see one of these lay-abouts strolling up and down with his hands in his pockets and he's supposed to be thinking! I could think like that for the salary they get paid. Ah, if I had the power I'd make 'em sit up, I'd make 'em hop, that I would. I'd disband the lot. All these research institutes of theirs. Let 'em find out what it's like to dig coal, and their professors with 'em. Sputniks, sputniks, what's the use of these sputniks? The air's full of 'em, but there's no fish in the rivers. It's downright corruption the number of students they've saddled us with. Let 'em work seven hours a day in the factories. And I'd soon find something to keep Tulin busy. Stir up trouble, would you? You'd better cool down a bit, young fella'm'lad. . . . Yes, we've let'em get out of hand, there's no fear any more. . . ."

"Tulin's being kept busy enough as it is," Krylov remarked.

"Anyone can give orders. D'you think I couldn't? I'm as good at that as the next man. It's all a matter of chance. I just didn't have the luck these pushers have. What a jacket he's got, that Tulin! A checked one with a slit at the back. D'you think I don't deserve a jacket like that? You seem to be one of their gang, you're singing the same tune."

"You'd better go to bye-byes," the receptionist said. "When you had trouble with your kidneys, you went running to see a professor soon enough. You're all like that."

Krylov sat and talked to her for some time. He told her about the forest fires caused by lightning, the damage done to vineyards by hail, about the young scientists who spent the whole winter on Elbrus, studying the clouds. In the past year he had seen more of his country than he had ever done before. Dam builders, cotton-pickers, tractor-drivers and collective farmers, they all looked up at the sky. He felt they were looking at him, because he lived there, fighting the clouds for their sake.

The receptionist clapped her plump white hands and gasped.

"Don't you take any notice of him," she said. "He's only jealous. He's a message clerk, and he wants me to marry him."

Krylov was feeling jolly. After his encounter with Agatov he was in a mood to be a strong and gentle Gulliver. Why should he be angry? He was sorry for this message clerk who had cheated himself out of life. He would have liked to open that bald head of his and see what was inside, what the man was really cut out for. After all, he couldn't have been born to become a message clerk. He had been born for happiness.

He went upstairs and found Richard in the developing room. Zhenya, Lisitsky and someone else were at work there; Krylov could see their hands moving in the light of the red lamp. He waited for his chance, then whispered to Richard: "It's all right."

"I knew it would be. Tulin's a wizard."

Richard found Krylov's hand in the darkness and squeezed it and a few minutes later he and Lisitsky were arguing with Krylov that there was no need to make repeated measurements, and that Krylov's demands were purely academic. They both echoed what Tulin had said about the importance of intuition.

"If we go about this job the way you suggest it'll be at least a year or two years before we get any results."

Krylov shrugged. "Depends what you mean by results. I don't know if that's what really counts."

While they were getting into bed the two younger men discussed this absurd remark of Krylov's. In a way it brought you up short, of course. But Krylov's example was too hard to follow and it offered no reliable guarantee.

Chapter Five

An hour before take-off Tulin had to answer a trunk call. When he returned to the aircraft he told Krylov that he was leaving at once to meet Bogdanovsky in town. Tulin had been trying to get in touch with Bogdanovsky for some time, ever since the geologist had started taking an interest in his work and shown signs of being prepared to offer help. Bogdanovsky was one of those prominent scientists who were extremely difficult to catch in Moscow. Now that he was almost on the spot it would have been foolish to miss the chance. He had immense resources and far-reaching authority. Archeologists Tulin knew had spoken enthusiastically of his generosity in lending transport and personnel from his prospecting parties. Once they were assured of his support they could ignore Agatov. Bogdanovsky must have some practical interest in the work, and in the present situation he would certainly be a trump card.

"You'll have to take charge of this flight," Tulin told Krylov. He unbuttoned his flying suit and sat down on the grass to pull it off. "While I'm in town I'll pick up anything they have for us at base. I'd better take someone with me. . . ."

Krylov toyed gloomily with a screwdriver. The prospect of commanding the flight alarmed him. He would be sure to miss something or make a muddle of things. It also meant he would have no time to spend on collecting data for himself.

"You self-centred old thing!" Tulin told him, reading his thoughts. "Never mind, you'd better get used to it. Have a taste of power." He stood up and folded his flying suit. In his bright sports shirt, slacks and sandals he looked very young. "Suppose I take Zhenya with me," he said casually. "There isn't much for her to do here and while I'm with Bogdanovsky she can fill up the forms at base."

It was unusual for him to explain his actions and supply excuses. Krylov tried to catch his glance but failed. Tulin's eyes were scanning the airfield, the plane and the figures perched on its wings and fuselage. Their black pupils were narrow and expressionless in the sunlight.

The usual bustle of flight preparations was going on round the plane. Instruments were being put aboard and fixed. The morning mists were lifting and melting away in the sun.

"Wouldn't it be better to take Katya?" Krylov said.

He felt Tulin look at him but was again unable to catch his glance.

"Katya will do," Tulin replied, as if it were all the same to him. "Here's your programme for today's tests. Just take it steady, old chap, and everything will be all right. They all know what they've got to do anyway. I don't think Katya is quite the person I need. I want someone a little more alert."

He strode towards the plane and Krylov followed him.

"Oleg," he said suddenly, "leave Zhenya alone."

Tulin swung round.

"I think you'd better mind your own business!" He was now looking Krylov full in the eyes. "You take too much upon yourself."

Zhenya was mounting the ramp. The wind lifted her skirt and she reached down to hold it with one hand, clasping a brightly polished instrument case to her chest with the other. Her hair fell over her face and she shook it back, but it fell into her eyes again. She had scarcely spoken to Tulin lately but he felt there was some invisible contact between them. It was like radio. Inwardly they were aware of each other's presence; outwardly there was only the stark coldness of the aerials.

"I can't really explain this to you yet, Sergei," Tulin said as he watched her mount the ramp. "This might be something far more serious than you think." He was about to wink, but the look Krylov gave him made him say with feeling: "Do you think I'm incapable of any real big emotion? I helped you when you needed it, didn't I? Remember Lena? At least you needn't get in my way. Pity is quite useless in this kind of thing, you know."

Krylov watched him run up the ramp, overtake Zhenya at the door into the aircraft and speak to her in a casual, business-like way.

From a distance Agatov noticed Tulin and Zhenya standing together at the top of the ramp. Zhenya disappeared into the plane and Tulin walked down the ramp to meet Agatov. They exchanged exaggeratedly polite smiles. In the cabin Richard was kneeling before a control panel, talking to Vera Matveyevna and Alyosha. Agatov came up to them, pretending to examine his meters. Richard was arguing that certain changes ought to be made in the circuit layout. At the same time he was solving an equation for Vera Matveyevna. He loved displaying his abilities, particularly by solving problems in his head while doing something else.

"I'll change them over," Alyosha said.

They changed the leads very quickly without switching off the current.

"That's it," said Richard. "And the first root of that equation will be log K minus log H."

"Thanks," said Vera Matveyevna, making a note of the solution. "You're a genius. You ought to be in a circus."

Richard dusted the knees of his trousers. At the sight of Zhenya at the other end of the cabin he called out to her. She waved back to him.

"Just a minute!"

Richard walked towards the door, turning his head away as he noticed Agatov.

"Just a moment," Agatov said.

Richard stopped. Agatov smiled and waited. It was a favourite trick of his.

"Well, Richard, I'm not a vindictive person. I've decided not to send you back to Moscow. You can stay here and get on with your work." He spoke quite softly, but he knew he could be heard in spite of the noise caused by the whole crew working, by the knocking and shifting of crates. He had a special voice, which he used for that purpose.

"No, I don't bear grudges," he went on. "You're wrong of course, but that often happens. Anything can happen when you're young. One day you'll realise.... But for the moment we'll consider the matter closed."

"Thank you," Richard said and then, feeling that even this was a concession to Agatov, added: "I don't really know what I'm thanking you for...."

Agatov nodded understandingly.

"...I probably ought to be thanking Tulin."

"Tulin?" Agatov repeated. "What a joke! You mean you really think he stood by you?" He broke into a laugh. "Not on your life! It was I who didn't follow Tulin's lead. You see, I thought I'd ask his advice. When I was still angry, you know. You'd have got pretty short shrift from him, I can tell you...." He frowned and dismissed the matter with a wave of his hand. "It's not really worth bringing that up now." He looked out of the window and shook his head. "When will they bring that oscilloscope?" He turned away from Richard and left the plane. He was indignant. It was so unjust, so unfair that everything should be put down to Tulin's credit.

Presently he heard Richard's panting voice behind him:

"Yakov Ivanovich, I didn't quite understand what you said about Tulin."

Agatov took his time explaining to a laboratory assistant where to put the oscilloscope, then glanced round at Richard.

"Does it really matter? I don't want to upset you." He patted him sympathetically on the shoulder, as much as to say: "They're making an awful fool of you."

"If you don't mind I'd rather know. It does matter a lot to me."

Agatov scratched his neck frowning.

"I think you'd better ask him yourself. Or you can ask Altynov, who was present at the time." He paused, then cleared his throat. "Oh, there's no point in hiding things really. For your information, Tulin agreed that you'd better be sent back to Moscow. He didn't raise a single word of objection. Personally, I had the impression that he couldn't have cared less. In fact, he seemed rather glad to take advantage of my hastiness." Agatov raised a warning finger. "Of course, that last remark of mine is purely subjective. You must treat it as an aside, because I believe in keeping strictly to the facts. That's a principle of mine. If you don't trust my opinion, you can get the details off the others who were present."

Krylov was hurrying across the airfield towards them. Behind him was Altynov.

Agatov waited with an air of righteousness. There was a glimmer of hope in Richard's eyes as he looked at Krylov, or rather, at Altynov. He could not bring himself to address Krylov. Altynov returned Richard's glance with a look of pity, as if he had remembered something concerning Richard that called for sympathy. Krylov asked Agatov to postpone the taking of certain measurements.

"Certainly not. May I ask how long it is since you have been in charge here?"

Krylov explained that Tulin was going away on business and had left him to supervise the programme. Richard quietly withdrew. None of them had any time for him. He leaned against the undercarriage. Katya, who was passing, stopped to ask him what was the matter.

"Have you seen Zhenya anywhere?"

"She's at control."

Richard walked towards the airport building. After a few paces he broke into a run. The control room was full of people. Zhenya was leaning on the counter, writing something. Richard wiped his damp forehead.

"We'll be back by six," Zhenya was saying.

"You'd better put that down on paper," said the controller.

Richard took Zhenya's arm. She turned round, nodded, and handed a slip to the controller. They went out into the corridor together.

"There's something I've got to tell you," Richard began.

Zhenya glanced at her watch.

"Is it urgent? I'm terribly pressed for time. I haven't changed yet."

"You mean you're not flying?"

"No, I'm going into town."

"With him?"

"But this is on business. How can I refuse!" She looked angrily at Richard and made an effort to master her temper. "We've been over all this before."

He clenched his fists. "But you mustn't! Don't you dare go with him! Don't you dare!"

Zhenya froze at once. Raising her eyebrows, she said very distinctly: "Will you, please, not shout! I refuse to listen to you."

"Don't you dare!" he repeated wildly.

"You must be mad! How can you speak like that?"

"Zhenya, please!"

"Good-bye. I hope you'll cool down by this evening."

Her heels clicked sharply on the white and brown floor-tiles and every step vibrated in Richard's head like a hammer stroke. Feeling as if his skull was splitting, he ran after her.

"I meant to tell you.... I want to talk to you...." His voice sank to a whisper.

"We'll talk when I get back," she replied without looking round.

Richard went into the men's room, wetted his handkerchief under the tap and wiped his face. It was twenty to ten. On the airfield he saw Tulin striding quickly towards the road. Afraid of catching his eye, Richard looked the other way and walked on with his head stiffly averted.

At the aircraft he was swept up in the noisy bustle of the last few minutes before take-off. Pozdyshev was indulging in some picturesque abuse of all scientists, the Academy of Sciences and meteorology in general. He had just discovered a new data unit fixed to the right wing, which meant that two new holes had been drilled.

"You're turning this plane into a colander!"

He started complaining to Khobotnev. According to instructions the flight ought to be postponed until the holes had been "certified" by the aircraft's designer. Both Khobotnev and Pozdyshev knew that no one would "certify" the holes and the flight would take place as scheduled but everyone listened to Pozdyshev, pretending there was a crisis, and he was satisfied. Not knowing what further appeasement to offer, the health-minded Altynov produced a huge Chinese thermos flask and offered Pozdyshev and Khobotnev hot coffee.

Difficulties descended on Krylov from all sides. With his slow smile he bravely tackled one misunderstanding after another but there seemed to be no end to them and he became painfully aware of his inability to organise. Apparently they had forgotten to check the signalling system. Lisitsky said he had left the job to Vera Matveyevna, she said she had left it to Katya, and Katya told him it was Alyosha's job. Despairing of finding the culprit, Krylov went and checked up on the control circuits himself. But the next minute Vera Matveyevna was after him, demanding complete revision of the flight plan. For the whole past week Tulin had been promising her a flight for taking special samples at four different altitudes and she had brought the necessary apparatus and drawn up the tables. Katya backed her up and, staring at Krylov with huge, beseeching eyes, began to talk about her graduation work. Meanwhile Lisitsky remembered that he urgently needed some streptomycin, which was not available at the local chemist's, so could they land at Adler, where he knew someone who was a doctor?

A laboratory assistant, crawling about among the seats in search of his fountain-pen, refused to leave the plane until he found it.

Alyosha appeared with the news that a piece of tubing had come unstuck and could only be fixed with a special glue.

Krylov began to feel that far from leaving at the appointed hour they would not get off the ground till the following day, or perhaps even the following month. All kinds of things had cropped up when Tulin had been around, but they must have been a lot simpler, judging by the speed with which Tulin disposed of them. Krylov took every demand absolutely seriously. He couldn't understand how Altynov could be so unconcerned. Instead of doing something he told funny stories and the whole group laughed as if nothing else in the world mattered.

Ten minutes before take-off Krylov decided in despair to postpone the flight. Altynov stared at him in astonishment.

"Why? What's up?"

When he had heard what Krylov had to say, Altynov remained as unperturbed as ever.

"Things'll work themselves out. You take everything at its face value."

By some miracle everything did work itself out by take-off time. Krylov realised that it was quite impossible to get to the bottom of the process—why Katya wasn't flying, what Vera Matveyevna had agreed to, whether Alyosha had got the glue. Moreover, if he had tried to do so, he would immediately have been faced with dozens of new questions and misunderstandings.

Only when the aircraft was in the air and the mountains had turned into soft green mounds did Krylov realise the wisdom in Altynov's remark: "The less you do the less you have to do."

Gradually his brain cleared. When he saw Pozdyshev checking the parachute packs he remembered the meteorologist assuring Khobotnev that there was thunder in the air because his rheumatism had told him so.

The forecast had promised fair weather, which was probably why the meteorologist had fallen back on his own personal indicator. He would have been perfectly happy if he had been allowed to draw up his forecasts on the basis of rheumatism. Pozdyshev and the younger men had laughed at the meteorologist but Khobotnev had looked thoughtful.

Life in the aircraft was following its usual routine. People were going through their log-books; Vera Matveyevna had lost a nought, as usual; only Richard was staring listlessly in front of him. Krylov noticed that because it was so unusual for Richard to be inactive.

Krylov wondered whether Richard had any suspicions and, at the thought of his clash with Tulin, suddenly felt depressed. There was nothing he could say that would console Richard. It was all so complicated. Tulin had acted badly and Krylov felt partly to blame. He asked Richard to check the circuit of the storm-detector and take over his readings.

Richard nodded indifferently. Krylov remembered the failure of his own hopes of curing himself by work when he had lost Lena. He had sprawled on his sofa in despair, deaf to the world, never dreaming that he would soon be working for Golitsyn, and the work would go well and he would write a successful thesis and meet Natasha. For Krylov, as he was then, the future didn't exist and it couldn't help him. Even if he had known the shape of things to come it would have changed nothing because it was a different Krylov to whom all this was to happen. One had to go through these things. Richard couldn't care less about the storm-detector at the moment. One always tried to console other people with something that had failed in one's own case.

The melancholy he knew so well began to spread over his mind. but he knew how to check it, and with a touch of regret he reflected that the trick was becoming easier with practice. He compared his longing for Natasha with what Richard was going through, and experienced an elder brother's tenderness towards Richard. I shouldn't have taken him on this flight, he thought. It's the wrong thing for a man in his condition.

. . . Later he was to remember distinctly noticing Richard's parachute lying in one of the seats. It had occurred to him then that this was against instructions, but the look on Richard's face had prevented him from making any comment.

Just let him try, Richard had been thinking at that moment. I'll let him have it! I'll tell him just what I think of them! What a pity Krylov had turned away like that without saying anything. It would have been good to tell him just what he thought of Tulin and enjoy the expression on his face, to tear the mask off this friend of his and show him up for what he was. Tulin, the wonder-boy, the man of talent! The man to whom everything was permitted, even the lowest trick. It had to be, because he was so talented!

No, it wasn't jealousy. It would have been absurd to condemn anyone for falling in love with Zhenya. In fact, he was proud when other men showed an interest in her. He didn't mind Zhenya kissing Alyosha, or flirting with Pozdyshev. At the institute the captain of the basketball team had trailed around after her and Richard had caught her out more than once, when she had told him she had work to do and spent the evening with that lanky creature instead. None of these things mattered. He was more jealous of the actor Medvedev, whom she was so enthusiastic about, or of Mayakovsky or Joliot-Curie, men whom there was no competing with. The only person he had never suspected was Tulin, the man whose merits he had praised, whom he had gone out of his way to build up in her imagination.

Tulin had been his ideal. Tulin had been what Richard himself wanted to be. He couldn't be suspicious of himself, of his own image.

Even on the bridge that evening he had regarded it as Zhenya's fault. Tulin had been blameless. He had been quite happy about Tulin because he knew that he could always tackle him about it. "What's going on between you and Zhenya?" he would have said and Tulin would have replied: "Smashing girl, but I value your friendship more. I know you need her more than I do, so don't worry."

The thing that really frightened him now was that Zhenya would start making comparisons. He would seem such a helpless puppy. Tulin was a bit old, of course, but he was good-looking, he had a score of scientific papers to his credit, he knew lots of amusing stories and, anyhow, girls liked older men. No one could stand comparison with Tulin.

Till now he had thought Tulin was indifferent. But if Tulin had agreed to send him back to Moscow it meant that Tulin knew about him and Zhenya and had decided to get rid of him. He had weighed up the odds, completely discounting the fact that Richard was writing a thesis about his method and had quarrelled with Agatov on his account. Basically, the quarrel had been over Tulin. But suppose Tulin knew nothing about his feelings for Zhenya? He would have given anything to be sure of that. Perhaps Agatov was deliberately leading him on?

As he mechanically took down his readings he tried to find excuses for Tulin, thinking of all kinds of coincidences that might have prevented Tulin from knowing.

His slate-pencil broke and he looked round at the seat where Zhenya usually sat. Immediately he remembered the other flight, when it had been bumpy, the figure of Tulin bending over Zhenya and the kiss he had given her. He had scarcely seen that kiss then and certainly paid no attention to it.

So the rest had been mere pretence. Both Tulin and Zhenya were acting together, they both wanted to get rid of him. These two people, whom he loved, had both betrayed him. He saw her brown eyes, her moist lips, then Tulin's eyes and lips.

He looked out of the window. Through a rift in the clouds he could see the earth. But the eyes and lips were there too. Smiling, laughing lips. They were laughing at him. And he had followed Tulin around like a dog, repeating his remarks, winking as he did, trying to imitate the slow, harsh voice that he sometimes adopted.

No, there was no such thing as friendship. Principles were mere words. Truth didn't exist. What use was it to him? Once he had believed in its power but it had no power over lies. Truth was useless.

Agatov's face was quite near his own. He could smell the eau-de-Cologne. That smooth, taut skin....

"...batteries haven't been changed...plug in to your power supply?"

That face was like a cinema screen. It bore no more relation to its owner than the screen did to the projectionist. It would show any picture. Agatov knew what he wanted. Only scoundrels could enjoy life. They had no illusions, no disappointments. They believed everyone else to be as unscrupulous as themselves and they were usually right.

"I don't care," he said. "Take the batteries, do what you like."

Yes, scoundrels like Tulin. He and Zhenya were together now, she had changed specially into that striped jumper. . . .

". . . have to do his job for him," said Agatov's voice and the face smiled.

But what else was there to believe in? Perhaps they thought they could go on deceiving him.

Agatov had asked why the batteries hadn't been changed. His instruments were dead.

Getting no response from Richard, he went over to the batteries himself, disconnected the lead to the storm-detector that had been fitted to the pilot's dashboard and plugged in his own instrument instead. When Krylov needed the detector it could be plugged in again, but Agatov knew that it wouldn't be needed because they had no right to enter thunderheads and, besides, he hadn't much belief in this storm-detector, just as he hadn't much faith in Tulin's work in general. He despised the whole risky, outlandish undertaking and the seriousness and fervour that Tulin and his admirers attached to every detail of it. Half a dozen or a dozen profitable and safe research projects could have been completed with the same expenditure of time and effort that had been wasted here. The results could have been published. Several people could have got Doctor's degrees.

With Alyosha's assistance he began measuring droplets. When he gave the signal, Alyosha inserted a blotting-paper cartridge and took it out again and they noted the size of the spot on the blotting paper and the readings on the instruments.

Richard went to get a pencil from Alyosha. Krylov was sitting on the arm of one of the seats, blocking the gangway.

"Feeling rotten?" he asked Richard.

"You needn't worry. I'm quite all right."

"You seem to have changed lately."

"I'm changing at this moment. I love changing. I keep changing all the time." Richard reflected bitterly that he had once believed in Krylov.

"What's the matter?"

"Nothing. Nothing at all. I just happen to have heard how Tulin stood by me."

Conscious that he was blushing, Krylov lost his temper.

"Stop acting the fool. You're carrying on like a kid. There are some things you don't seem to understand. It's about time you realised that, whatever the man's like, his job is our job."

Richard laughed in Krylov's face.

"I'm not a kid any more. I'm quite as grown-up as you and Tulin. You understand everything, you can always make the proper distinctions. In fact, you know so much between you that you don't even have to believe in anything."

He took the pencil and went back to his seat, fixed a table to the board and began filling it in. Trying to offer him consolation. Ashamed of his friend. Just keep on working for Tulin. Krylov could argue with Tulin as much as he liked, but others were expected to submit. They had to submit for the sake of the idea, they had to pretend that nothing had happened. Yes, Sergei Ilyich, you give in to your friend Tulin as well. But I can't go on like this. What's the alternative? The man and his job?

He remembered why Krylov had left Golitsyn. Tulin would never have done that. And Krylov had been foolish to do so. He had left the field open for Agatov. The work had suffered and the laboratory had suffered. But Krylov had resigned. Tulin wouldn't have done that. Krylov's contradictory, sometimes apparently absurd conduct now acquired a meaning that was not yet quite clear but was in some way connected with the problem that was torturing Richard.

What had Krylov meant? Was it possible that he had long since lost faith in Tulin but went on working with him because he believed in the work, because it meant more to him than Tulin, more even than friendship?

Why not take revenge on Tulin? Seek out the weak spots in his work—those that Krylov had pointed out would do—and expose them, put them on show? Agatov would be delighted and Krylov wouldn't have a leg to stand on because he himself had maintained that field dissipation took place in different thunderheads in different ways and no definite regularity had emerged. Move over to Agatov? It was only a matter of a few yards and he had every right to do so. But he knew he was incapable of doing a thing like that. What was more, he realised he would still go on with Krylov helping Tulin. That was what he wanted. He couldn't help himself. It was a part of him.

But suppose all these arguments were mere weakness? No, he was not conscious of weakness. Rather, on the contrary, he felt he was now motivated by that higher feeling of dedication to truth that inspired Krylov.

A patchwork of fields spreading out from the mountains came into view. They were threaded with roads and dotted with settlements. From above there appeared to be perfect order on earth, everything appeared to be in its place. Only the big things, the things that really mattered, could be seen. It was as if he had climbed to a point from which he could look down upon his own life.

People came into the world and left it. What remained but the grave-mound, too insignificant to be noticed from above? Towns, empires, even entire cultures, all disappeared; books became outdated, machines obsolete, sciences were replaced by others. Only one thing remained—the search for truth. It was passed on from generation to generation, regardless of disillusion and disaster. He had once loved to ponder on the meaning of life. He had attended debates, written notes to lecturers. There had been so many arguments. So many quotations, references. The conclusion he had now arrived at might not be a discovery. But for him it was a revelation and a support. Where else was he to find strength? When he saw Zhenya and Tulin this evening, what would he say to them? What would they say?

Chapter Six

The road weaved between high cliffs, now plunging the lorry into cool shade, now exposing it to the burning heat of bare rocks. All the time a river babbled below. On gentle slopes the driver switched off his engine and the sound of running water could be heard above the crunch of gravel under the tyres. The rivers took over from one another in relentless pursuit of the road. Each new river had its own particular colour and sound.

The Ayanka turned aside and the chase was taken up by another river Zhenya had never heard of; it was deep-green, like pine-needles, and it flowed unevenly, sometimes flooding out in wide steady reaches, sometimes breaking into foaming rapids.

Huge yellowish-white pillars of rock towered above the road and flocks of sheep, motionless as cirrus cloud, dotted green valleys.

As they rounded the bends Zhenya was thrown against Tulin and she felt his shoulder against hers. Once he put his arm round her waist and held her tight. When Zhenya tried to move his arm away he squeezed her fingers and said: "We'll soon be coming to the oak-woods."

He took his hand away of his own accord and Zhenya clutched the seat. They were riding in the back of an open lorry and they tried not to look at one another. Each kept his eyes fixed on his own side of the road.

Tulin felt Zhenya's tense expectancy. It excited him because he knew that this expectancy would grow until caution gave way to impatience. He knew every move in this ancient game to perfection. If he tried to kiss Zhenya at this moment she would push him away indignantly, tell him not to get fresh and go into a long sulk. Yet even so, she wouldn't be really offended because it would not be an insult but a tribute of admiration and women could feel that at once.

How nice it was to be able to think about these things in a relaxed way. It would be a long time before he forgot the wretched state Krylov had got himself into over Lena. And that other woman, whose photograph he kept on his desk, was another mix-up. Poor old Sergei, he was always getting himself into a tangle. He took everything so seriously, as if love was something to be pondered over. A healthy dose of cynicism was the best safeguard against unnecessary emotional tension. Emotion was something he could do very well without at present. Love-resistance was a good thing when you were working at high pressure and the best way to acquire it was by submitting to reason. Too rationalistic? Well, there was nothing to be ashamed of in rationalism. This was an age of rationalism. Feeling of any kind confused the reason, and emotional excitements, particularly those connected with love, were distracting. Yet how enjoyable it was to observe Zhenya's excitement! Should he let her fall in love with him? Better not. Not fair. But if she could stop loving Richard and fall in love with him, it must mean she didn't really love Richard. So why make her secure in false feelings? Natural development was the best kind of development and the only right kind.

Green avalanches of forest rolled down the mountain slopes, growing thicker and greener as they descended. The road plunged through light-speckled woodlands, through noisy villages and again into the deep, luxuriant green of maple groves and blue-eyed plum orchards. Suddenly they rounded a corner and emerged into a blaze of light. It had seemed as if this sunny day with its breath of early heat could not possibly be any lighter than it was. But this soft, rippling light sprang from below, as if sent up by the earth itself to meet the dazzling shafts of sunlight streaming through the leaves. The shadows became lighter and were tinged with blue. The air itself became bluer and acquired motion.

"It's the sea," Tulin said.

Zhenya jumped to her feet and the huge silvery expanse spread out below seemed to strike her in the face. With every turn in the road it revealed new depths. It shimmered on her cheeks and she felt it in every pore of her skin. Her eyes opened wide to take in the hugeness of the sea and the smart white city below with its long harbour wall, the toy-like ships lying at their moorings and the spreading wake of a departing steamer. A fresh breeze fanned her cheeks.

"How glorious!" she exclaimed.

Tulin's hands closed on her head and turned it towards him and she saw his eyes very close and they, too, were brimming with this silvery light. She tried to pull herself away but instantly felt how strong his arms were, and the thought flashed through her mind that Richard would never have dared to handle her like this. She closed her lips tight and shut her eyes.

The second that followed consisted of several quite separate incidents. Orange spirals span round very quickly on her closed lids, then slowed down, stopped and waited expectantly. Then something changed on the outside. She opened her eyes. Tulin was still looking at her. But now he was holding her at arm's length and smiling. Zhenya tried to pull his hands apart. He didn't move. He just stood there looking at her and smiling thoughtfully.

"Let me go at once!" she shouted angrily.

He seemed not to hear. She was sure he couldn't even see her. His eyes were focussed on some point far in the distance.

With a sigh he relaxed his grip. She drew back fuming at the humiliation she had experienced and realised that he had released her not because she had told him to but merely because he had felt so inclined.

"It cost me quite an effort not to kiss you," he said.

Anger helped her to control herself.

"Why don't you make a few more efforts. Perhaps you'll become more human."

"I waste so much energy contending with my feelings," he continued thoughtfully. "We're so busy we just can't afford the luxury of distraction. One has to save both energy and time. On the other hand, the amount of energy one spends on restraining one's feelings increases. There comes a point where restraint becomes a liability."

"You'd better draw a graph," she said. "And find out where the curves intersect."

"I've found that already." Tulin gave her a frank glance. "I'm no worse than Richard at doing problems in my head. My maths are quite good."

"Oh, I felt so good. Why did you have to spoil it all?" She turned to look at the sea. "What's that over there on the mountain?"

"The ruins of a monastery. Fourteenth century, I believe. Like a sweet?"

"Thanks."

"Your eyebrows are curved like the wings of a swallow."

"And what's that over there?"

"A grain elevator. To the right of it there's a theatre, and on the headland there's a stadium. After that come the sanatoriums and you can read the rest in the guide-book. I'll present you with one. You know, it's the first time I've seen eyes that change as much as yours. I want to tell you just how you appear to me."

He knew intuitively the right tone and the right words to use. One false note, one exaggerated phrase, and the whole edifice would have collapsed. But he cemented it firmly with the cool indifference of objectivity, the rough-and-ready frankness of a man unable to pay compliments, and the kind of irony that conceals admiration.

Gradually her scornful smile disappeared and she stopped trying to interrupt. He lowered his voice so that some of his words were drowned by the noise of the engine and she leaned forward to catch them. He felt sure that no one had ever described her eyes, her hands, her gestures, her walk so frankly. Her excitement made him slightly envious. He, too, would have liked not to know what was to come, but he knew already.

Now he could quite easily have taken her hand, but he refrained. When the lorry rounded a corner and he was thrown against her he felt her breast and drew back calmly. There was always pleasure in lingering and taking things slowly.

The lorry drove up to the stores. Tulin and Zhenya agreed to meet in an hour and a half's time at one of the beach cafés.

What he had heard about Bogdanovsky, the chief of a large project, did not fit in at all with this sun-blackened individual, who looked more like the foreman of a tractor depot. His big boots with concertina tops, bright checked shirt, skullcap, fingers like steel springs, suggested both the worker and the peasant.

The office in which Bogdanovsky received him, with its white curtains, small deal table and red plastic inkstand, was not the office of a prominent scientist but rather of some local government official.

Tulin was disappointed. But perhaps this was camouflage? He couldn't imagine Bogdanovsky in a dark suit and tie, padding the carpeted expanses of a Moscow office.

With the condescension and deliberate politeness of a scientist paying a visit to the man at the bench Tulin asked Bogdanovsky what he could do for him.

Afterwards, when he told Zhenya the details of their conversation he was quite unable to explain how Bogdanovsky had somehow avoided answering him and in the course of the next few minutes completely turned the tables, so that it was Tulin who had to answer questions, find arguments and excuses and make the requests. Injecting his brief questions and interpolations with the skill of a conjuror, Bogdanovsky sliced away superfluities and left only the stark essentials that were often to Tulin's disadvantage. He seemed to be able to grasp in an instant what had appeared to be purely scientific subtleties.

In the focus of those small gimlet eyes Tulin for the first time in his life had the feeling of being confronted by someone who could think faster and better than himself.

In a mere twenty minutes Tulin had, quite against his own will, described the actual state of research done by his group, the basic organisational difficulties that faced them and their prospects for the future. It would have taken him at least two hours at any conference.

As soon as he mentioned financial difficulties Bogdanovsky wanted to know the reason for the cut in his allocations. The project was in danger of being relegated to the reserve programme of work. Why? It was considered unreliable, no one knew how it would turn out. On what grounds? There were no grounds and the results had been good up to now, it was simply too problematic, and also rather dangerous. But why had no one been worried at first? Something must have changed. Perhaps there had been unfavourable comments? Whose?

"One or two of Denisov's pupils may have spoken against it," Tulin confessed reluctantly.

"Golitsyn is against you, too, isn't he?" Bogdanovsky gave him a quick, penetrating glance.

Tulin was about to parry with a "You seem to know everything already?" but foresaw the type of dialogue this would lead to.

Bogdanovsky: Naturally I have made inquiries.

Tulin: What are we wasting time for, then?

Bogdanovsky: I'm not wasting time. It's you I'm investigating, not the general situation.

Nothing would be gained by such an exchange, so he said aloud in a slow, thoughtful manner: "Oh, Golitsyn's attitude is rather a different story. I was just going to tell you about that."

"Don't bother. It's clear already."

Bogdanovsky then proceeded to give a somewhat abstract statement of the reasons for his own interest in Tulin's work. Suppose there were certain mineral deposits in the mountains and he had a party prospecting them at the moment. The area was subject to frequent thunderstorms and regular supplies and transport could not be maintained by air. Extracting operations were due to begin quite soon. The question was whether it would be possible to ensure a regular and safe air service to this area.

The details of the set-up were something like an algebraic problem, which Bogdanovsky had evidently tried out on more than one occasion.

Tulin realised at once what tremendous scope this new proposal offered his group. It would be possible to test the new method in the most effective way. It would give them independence, a definite purpose and timetable, a field of operations and valuable support. Hiding his joy, Tulin said as reluctantly as he could: "We could try."

Bogdanovsky gave a comprehending little laugh.

"How long will you need? We'll give you everything you want."

"Things don't happen like that." Tulin chuckled as he thought over his reply.

"Ten years won't suit me. But if you say a month, I won't believe you."

Tulin felt that every word he said was being carefully weighed behind that high sheer forehead. It was an examination and only full marks would be good enough.

He said: "Have you ever had to do any research?"

"Have you ever been given the task of finding a certain deposit—cadmium, say—in one year?"

They looked at each other and laughed.

"Do you want me to give you a time limit?" Bogdanovsky asked.

Tulin nodded.

"Six months. Is that realistic?"

"A year," Tulin said.

"But you can already distinguish the field of a heavy shower from that of a thunderstorm, can't you?"

"I say! You're very well informed."

Bogdanovsky paused expectantly.

"Who gave you the information?"

Bogdanovsky frowned.

"Let's get this straight," Tulin said. "The scientific side is our worry."

"Very well. Self-confidence is always a good thing. Then we shall want a guarantee."

"What do you mean?" Tulin was finding it difficult to keep up.

"You're offering us a pig in a poke," Bogdanovsky explained impatiently. "You don't want to show us your goods. That's up to you. But you'll want a lot of money. That money belongs to the state, not to me. So give me some guarantee."

Tulin spread his arms.

"Shall I write a receipt?"

"Humph! I see your point. . . ." Bogdanovsky eyed him closely. "Pride is worth something but not enough. How much money and equipment will you want?"

While they were busy with calculations a young woman entered the room. She had firm round cheeks and big grey eyes. Tulin had a feeling he had seen her somewhere before. She returned his inquiring glance with a look that revealed nothing but surprise. It was the first time she had seen him, yet he felt he knew her. How could he? He had an excellent visual memory and his present lack of recall annoyed him.

Bogdanovsky addressed her as Natalia Alexeyevna. She withdrew with the paper he had signed.

"The snag is that I have no right to make a mistake," Bogdanovsky said, examining the notes he had made. "You scientific people make mistakes that work out on the credit side. In any case they're inevitable. . . . We can't permit ourselves anything like that. It costs millions to build a road through the mountains. And think of the time, and what that costs. What value do you put on a month of your own life?"

Tulin smiled.

"You're right."

"For this country two years can be invaluable. If a thousand road workers work for two years, it adds up to two thousand man-years. The results are solid, but they take too long."

"Now I remember!" Tulin suddenly exclaimed.

Even Bogdanovsky was taken aback.

"I'm sorry," Tulin apologised. "Please go on."

The risk was too big for Bogdanovsky to be able to take an immediate decision. There was a lot to be said both for and against the project and one of the most important factors was the man sitting in front of him. When all was said and done, a lot depended on the ability of one man to solve a particular problem quickly. If only one could set a hundred scientists on the job! But the trouble was that numbers were not always decisive in science. It was often a matter of inspiration, brilliant guesswork on the part of one man. He peered at Tulin, trying to fathom out what was going on in his head. Every plan of action, unfortunately, led eventually to some individual. There was always an individual at one end and another individual at the other. In this case the man at the other end was Bogdanovsky himself. Between them lay the ore deposits, the mines of the future, factories that needed the ore, aircraft, prospecting parties, road builders, the fate of thousands of people. In one way or another everything that had to be done would be done, irrespective of either Tulin or Bogdanovsky, but *one way or another*— that was the essence of it. It could be done in one way, it could be done in another. It always boiled down eventually to "yes" or "no". He had been choosing between those two words for many years. It was basically the same work as that of a computer. He tried to be as accurate and fast as a computer. Some people reproached him for this and said he had no soul. They used the word "computer" with contempt. But why? Was not this machine a child of the human mind? It embodied the best that human intelligence had yet produced. Why should one learn from books, yet be ashamed to learn from a machine?

Bogdanovsky never gave way to moods, and this enabled him to assess the moods of those around him. He took their weaknesses into account. But to do so he had to be devoid of weakness himself. He had got used to sending people out into the taiga, into the mountains, to shouldering the responsibility for decisions that would change the face of the country. He knew himself and he was inwardly serene. But now he actually had to transfer the responsibility to someone else. What was this handsome young man with the merry eyes really like? He was a little cunning, a little dandyish, a little impudent, but what else was he?

Bogdanovsky would have liked to trust him, yet something put him on his guard. A bit too emotional, he thought.

"So we'll consider your road as good as built?" Tulin said.

Bogdanovsky gave a grunt and smiled enigmatically.

"You won't regret it," Tulin promised. "Your name will go down in the history of science. I am sure the effect will exceed your expectations."

I'd like to know what you're really sure of, Bogdanovsky was thinking. Is it just yourself or the work you are doing?

Tulin found Natalya Alexeyevna in one of the adjoining rooms and asked her to come out into the corridor.

"Are you Natasha?" he asked.

She nodded guardedly.

"I recognised you. . . ."

She waited calmly.

". . . by your photograph. Guess where I saw it?"

She looked amused.

"What's this? Your special way of introducing yourself?"

"In that photograph you were wearing a striped jumper."

And now she was wearing a blue overall coat with the sleeves rolled up. She was tall and sunburnt. He felt slightly disappointed. For some reason he had always imagined a sad, languorous little creature. Before him stood a calm, self-assured young woman. Only in her eyes, which were soft and gentle, was there a trace of the Natasha he thought he knew.

Tulin had always found it easier to talk to women than to men, but here he was up against something special. In spite of his enigmatic introduction, he seemed to have produced no real impression, not even curiosity. Only her gentleness and tact, it appeared, prevented her from going away and leaving him.

He offered her his hand.

"Tulin, Oleg Nikolayevich."

"Where does that get us?"

"So you don't know anything about me? Disgraceful! Well, I know something about you. Frosty woods. Skis. Knitted cap sprinkled with snow. I spent two hours with that photograph until its owner turned up."

"My photograph...." She stiffened. "So you're Tulin! But, of course...." Her eyes lit up with interest but she asked no questions.

"Well, if even that is of no interest, I'm sorry to have bothered you. Apparently I was right."

"What about?"

"When I told Sergei it wasn't worth taking such things seriously."

"Where is he? How is he? When did you last see him?"

He glanced at his watch.

"Unfortunately, I'm in rather a hurry."

He really ought to have played her up, but he saw it meant too much to her. He felt a stirring of something rather like envy.

"All right, remember me in your prayers. Krylov's in my group. No, he's not here, about a hundred kilometres away. Do you want his address? Our melancholy friend will go right off his rocker when I tell him I've met you."

"Don't tell him. I'd rather do it myself."

His instinct told him something but he was not quite sure what it was.

"You don't want to see him?"

She had superb self-control. With a simple trustfulness she said gently:

"I think it's too late. Better leave things as they are."

She was not the kind who could be questioned or talked round. But she was a woman and Tulin knew what women were like.

"Here's the address."

Poor old Sergei, he thought. He's going to find her quite a handful.

Chapter Seven

They were in luck at last. They had found big high-tension cumulus clouds. At Krylov's request Khobotnev maintained a steady altitude and they were able to measure the intensity distribution, the charge of the aircraft, and the charges of the drops and their spectrum. The instruments were like knives dissecting the interior of the cloud.

Hundreds of flights had been made in cloud. Taking the world as a whole, the number would run into thousands. Yet these flights and the miles of film taken during them had revealed only the infinite complexity of the processes at work in those bubbling cauldrons of weather. They were chaos itself. So dissimilar, so unique in appearance and structure, in the interaction of their charges were they that at times they seemed to the despairing Krylov the inspired improvisation of God. Gradually certain regularities had emerged, but the intrinsic meaning of what went on in this grey fog remained a mystery, an inexplicable whim of nature. For some reason the charges in the droplets would suddenly change. At a certain point the plane would pass from a positive field into a negative field. The droplets became denser and bigger and it began to pour with rain. Why? How?

At this moment water was streaming down the windows. Krylov gave the signal, a light went on and everyone began taking measurements. No one noticed the bumps and the air pockets. Khobotnev looked round and watched the tense faces scanning the instruments. Their excitement, their impatience were driving him on.

Krylov was standing beside him, sketching the cloud on a portable drawing-board. He was wearing his usual checked jacket. His sleeves were far too short for his long arms, his trousers were bulging at the knees and Khobotnev felt that for Krylov the sky was nothing more than a laboratory bench with specially prepared clouds arranged upon it. He liked working with Krylov. Tulin's methods were often erratic and incomprehensible. He revised and worked things out as he went along, in response to various intricate considerations of his own. Krylov's approach was much simpler and clearer. They explored the cloud methodically, flying back and forth in a way that Khobotnev could understand. He helped Krylov because he felt that he was unused to giving orders.

When they broke cloud at ten minutes past twelve Khobotnev noticed that a change had occurred. He could not yet say quite what it was. It was merely a vague sense of alarm evoked by the change of colours and the piling up of still more clouds. It was as if the previous confusion had given way to a sudden menacing purpose.

The forecast had predicted a thunderstorm about a hundred kilometres from the area in which they were now flying. Khobotnev glanced at the storm-warning indicator. The needle was rising rapidly. But the sun was still shining and the soft golden clouds looked innocently reassuring. He told Pozdyshev to ask for a weather report. Krylov came in from the main compartment looking delighted.

"Wonderful data!" he shouted. "We seem to have caught the actual moment of formation. Amazing jumps in intensity."

Khobotnev looked at his cheerful button-nosed face and banked the plane steeply before making his next run.

As he came out of the turn and the sun's rays hit him full in the face, he felt rather than saw a pale flash somewhere on his left. At the same moment he heard Pozdyshev's voice in the earphones: "Storm approaching from the west. Front widening rapidly." But Khobotnev had already realised that there were thunderheads on both sides and that he had to get through the corridor between them, if it still existed. He forced the control column back and went into a vertical climb right in front of the cloud. He had not quite finished his turn and the plane skimmed the edge of the towering cumulus. They plunged into shadow and the next moment a blue flash of lightning tore across their front. Khobotnev was dazzled and the plane lurched off course. Everything was rimmed with sparks. The pilot's dash was a dark blur glowing with lilac and green fire. He knew his sight would return in a few seconds but those seconds and the distance the plane covered during them were decisive.

Khobotnev was an excellent pilot. It was an old maxim for him that in the air quick decisions were usually the best. The storm had walled up in front of them and there was no exit. They were caught in a narrow wedge and to turn round and fly away from the storm they would have to fly into it. Everything would depend on how deep they had to penetrate and how he made the turn, whether he could reduce speed to the proper minimum and maintain the correct angle of bank. Yet he also knew that all his calculations and intentions might count for nothing when they actually entered the thunderhead.

The stinging pain went out of his eyes and he wiped away the tears. The needle of the storm-warning indicator had risen to twelve. The compass and locator were out of action. The cabin was hazy with smoke. For the last time he caught a glimpse of the sun and the innocent pearly opal of the clouds, then everything darkened and the aircraft plunged into the gathering gloom.

The second pilot was staring in awe at the violet electric discharge crackling over the glass roof of the cabin. Catching Khobotnev's glance he tore his glance away.

"Terrific!" he shouted, but his voice was hoarse and exaggeratedly cheerful.

Just a kid, Khobotnev thought. He knows only what he's been told about storms, so he's both afraid and not afraid of them.

He felt that Krylov had returned to the cabin and was standing behind him, calmly taking notes. Did he realise what was happening or was he, too, blissfully ignorant? He saw Krylov bend down and point to the dial of Tulin's storm-detector that had been fitted to one side of the dash. The needle was flat at zero. Khobotnev nodded. "They'd better put on their parachutes in any case," he told Pozdyshev through the intercom.

After that he had no eyes for Krylov or anything else that was happening in the main compartment, where everyone was struggling into parachutes and helping each other adjust the harness. He saw only the dial of his air-speed indicator, the racing needle of the altimeter, the dancing hell-fire beyond the thin barrier of the perspex hood, and the lightning-slashed darkness into which the aircraft was plunging.

There was tremendous impact as the rising air currents seized the wings. The whole plane groaned and shuddered and the suffering of metal and stays transmitted itself to Khobotnev. He felt the straining of levers, the tautening of control lines, as though his own limbs and sinews were being racked to the limit.

The bucking of the plane and a cry from Agatov startled Richard out of his torpor. The sight was awe-inspiring. Electrical discharges flared like blazing magnesium round the windows, flooding the whole aircraft with light. Empty seats. Glittering instruments. Pale faces. Then they were in darkness again and only a quivering pink halo showed round the edges of the wings. Richard had never seen a halo so bright and distinct. He switched his recorder full on to measure the charge on the aircraft. Then he switched on the discharge counter and the storm-detector recorder. Switching his instruments on and off, he noted the readings in feverish haste. He mustn't make a mistake! Whether they had got into the storm by chance or design, this was a unique and wonderful opportunity of picking up and measuring precious data. Just outside, within arm's reach was the zone where lightning was formed; they were near to the eye of the storm itself, the holy of holies, the secret of all secrets.

The fury of the storm swept the bitterness out of his mind. At last they had penetrated right to its heart, to its very vitals. This was where they could finally test Tulin's calculations, his detector, his method. What had happened between them, what they thought of each other no longer mattered. That was trivial and unimportant. His idea was good and right and Richard would serve it, work for it. After all man was usually less than his idea. What did their quarrels matter to science? The main thing was to get at the truth. They were on the brink of discovery. Chance was helping them. At last they had penetrated to the heart. . . .

Alyosha was helping Vera Matveyevna to strap on her parachute. Agatov reached out and clutched his arm.

"Go to Khobotnev!" he shouted. "Tell him I order him to turn back!" His face was green and twitching. He tried to unfasten his seat strap but fear got the better of him and he clutched the arms of his seat.

Alyosha made his way towards the cabin. As he passed Lisitsky he noticed him sipping hastily from a flask.

"Want some?"

"Later!"

Pozdyshev was scowling at the radio. Communication had broken down. At first he had tried to get a weather report and find out the altitude of the thunderhead. Now he simply wanted to report that the radio compass and piloting instruments were out of action and they had lost all sense of direction. The storm was probably carrying them towards the mountains. They had lost their way in this swirling gloom. Ground might be able to hear them but they could hear no reply. And what could the people on the ground do for them anyway? But Pozdyshev would have liked to hear some response, just a word, even a curse, anything to be rid of this feeling of complete isolation. But there was nothing. Only the hiss and crash of static in the earphones.

If they had known there were no mountains below they could have tried to bring the plane down, even if it meant pancaking.

It seemed years, centuries since Khobotnev had flown into the storm, hoping only to skim its edge. Now there was no edge, no left or right. The magnetic compass was spinning wildly, the plane was being tossed about like a chip of wood. At times he didn't even know sky from earth, earth with its instructions and regulations:

"Maintain horizontal position. Acceleration may cause dangerous overloading." The reality was nothing like it. They needed to climb and climb, so that at least he could keep the plane under control. Even now they needed four hands to hold it, but another, stronger hand was wrenching the control column from their grasp and trying to hurl the plane earthwards. The engines were whining shrilly. He could feel the terrible strain on the wings. If only they could get away from the storm centre. That was the real danger spot. But where was it? What direction should he take to escape? The detector was lifeless. That famous detector on which so much praise had been lavished was the only thing that could have helped them to get their bearings, their only chance.

He saw Krylov squeeze his way towards the detector and tap the dial. His face was so thoughtful and remote from what was going on that Khobotnev swore.

Krylov watched the moisture streaming down the windows and the short sclerotic threads of the discharges. He was comparing the suppositions he had made over the past year with the actual workings of the storm. His brain was acting smoothly and methodically and he was immune to anxiety or fear. Right up to the last moment Krylov hoped that they were hovering somewhere near the fringe of the storm. It took him time to realise that the storm-detector was out of action. Bumping his head on levers and partitions he felt for the connections. They seemed to be all right. He went back to the main compartment, where everything was rocking and swaying. Pozdyshev was struggling with the emergency hatch. Vera Matveyevna was sinking helplessly to the floor, her eyes closed. He caught her by the elbow and she suddenly began to vomit.

Agatov appeared in front of him. Krylov told him the detector had gone phut. "Ask Richard about it," he said.

Agatov shouted something back and disappeared. Alyosha appeared in his place, grabbed Vera Matveyevna and helped her away. Krylov tried to get at the recording apparatus of the detector at which Richard was sitting.

"Is it working?" he shouted to Richard.

Richard said something that Krylov couldn't hear. He stepped forward over the cases and cylinders that were sliding about round his feet and suddenly the plane gave a lurch and the floor slipped from under him. He was flung across the seats into a corner and his knee hit the wall with a crack. It seemed so loud to Krylov that he thought the plane was breaking up. He tried to kick himself away from the wall and failed. His leg was useless and the sound he had heard must have been the cracking of the bone. As he realised this, a flood of pain swept over him and for a few seconds he lost consciousness.

On any normal flight, if Krylov had found the lead from the storm-detector installed in the pilot's cabin disconnected, Agatov would have made no bones about admitting that it was he who had disconnected it and plugged his own instrument into the power supply instead. It didn't matter much. Or rather, it wouldn't have mattered much if they hadn't got into this thunderhead. But who could have known that they would fly into a storm? They were not allowed to fly into thunderheads, it was against all rules and regulations. He was not to blame for what had happened. How could he be? The detector wouldn't have helped anyway. Golitsyn didn't believe in it. Neither did he, Agatov. He had never had any faith in this idea of Tulin's.

When Krylov had shouted to him that the detector was out of action, Agatov had been about to own up, go over to Richard's seat and reconnect the lead. At that moment he almost believed that the wretched apparatus might help them to find their bearings. Perhaps if the detector had been working from the start, they wouldn't have got into this mess. But this thought paralysed him. For an instant he saw quite clearly what would happen on the ground. All the blame would be placed on him. He would be trapped, beaten. They would say it was all his fault. He would be put on trial, his career would be finished.... He was gripped by fear, fear was stronger and more palpable than his sense of danger. A few moments longer, perhaps, and the threat of destruction would have forced him to forget everything else, but he was given no time to think. The plane lurched, a box hit his leg, he saw Krylov's body flying through the air. He himself was pitched across the compartment. He gave a cry and grabbed at a bracket fixed in the wall.

He found himself near Richard. There was a draught whistling through the compartment. Pozdyshev had opened the hatch and bits of paper and other odds and ends were being sucked out into the slipstream. The lead he had disconnected was hanging loose from the wall behind Richard's seat. It was a miracle that in the midst of this nightmare of confusion Agatov should have seen the lead he himself had disconnected. He fancied he could hear it tapping against the metal coping. He saw Richard standing over him and felt Richard grip him under the shoulders and lift him. Suddenly he came to his senses and made a dash for the hatch....

Krylov opened his eyes when Alyosha began dragging him towards the hatch. He saw Agatov's distorted, fear-stricken face and behind it the hazy shape of Richard.

"The drums! Don't forget the drums!" Krylov shouted.

"I'll get them!" It was Richard's voice that answered.

"Help him! Take the detector drums!" Krylov shouted to Alyosha.

"To hell with them," Alyosha shouted back. "A fine time to think about them!"

Pozdyshev pushed Agatov aside to make way for Alyosha and Krylov.

"Where are the others?" Krylov clung to the edge of the hatch but Alyosha deftly knocked his hand away and they both tumbled out of the plane together.

Before him Agatov saw Pozdyshev's back with the straps of the parachute harness crossing over his blue jacket. Like a massive partition it hid from him the swirling grey under the open hatch. With all the strength he could muster Agatov drove his shoulder into Pozdyshev's back. The push was well timed. Krylov and Alyosha had just jumped and Pozdyshev was about to turn round to make way for Agatov and Richard, but Agatov's push toppled him over the edge of the hatch. The slipstream did the rest and the heels of his carefully polished shoes disappeared into the clouds. Agatov lost his balance and was tossed along the gangway between the seats.

Richard was struggling with a drum. As usual at such moments it had got stuck and he had to wrench it free. The pen of the recorder calmly went on tracing out data, and the perfect self-denial of the instrument induced something like calm in Richard himself. "Is it working?" He remembered Krylov's question about the recorder of the storm-detector and suddenly realised what had happened. In the pilot's cabin the detector was not working. His eyes flashed to the lead Agatov had been looking at and he saw the end of it dangling loose. Richard reached out towards it but his head struck something hard. Once and then again. He felt blood trickling down his face and stared in horror at Agatov crawling toward the hatch. He reached out and grabbed the strap of his parachute harness.

"The detector's power supply was cut off!" he shouted.

Agatov turned round and, as their eyes met, Richard read all that was written there.

"So it was you!"

"Let me go!"

Agatov kicked out and fell to the floor himself, grazing his forehead on a protruding piece of metal. He felt Richard's grip on his harness relax. With a last effort he dragged himself to the edge of the hatch and toppled out.

If the ground below had been flat Khobotnev would have tried to make a forced landing, but beneath them were mountains. The sixth sense that he had acquired from a year's flying in this region told him that for sure. None of his instruments were functioning except the artificial horizon, which he used to keep the plane on a more or less even keel. His only aim now was to give the rest of the group time to bale out. Sometimes he managed to prevent the plane losing height for ten seconds or so. How it happened he didn't know, but the storm would lose track of him for a few moments in this whirligig, then find him again and start throwing him about. Anything might happen in these damn thunderclouds. There was nothing worse than this battering they were getting. It caused more injuries than anything else. Gradually the storm was taking possession of the plane and turning it into a strange, wild creature. Khobotnev seized his chance, switched on the automatic pilot and ran to the hatch. He could see no one in the compartment. He was sure that Pozdyshev and the second pilot hadn't let him down. They would have done all that was humanly possible. He could feel the slipstream dragging at him. He didn't want to jump. There was trouble in store for him on the ground. Clumsily he slithered out of the hatch and the plane vanished at once in the swirling grey. For an instant he thought he could see a dim shadow plunging earthwards.

Richard's limp body was flung several more times against the wall until a fresh stab of pain made him open his eyes. There was no one left in the plane. He felt that at once. A clinging weakness seemed to swaddle him and he was unable to move. He felt the plane spinning as it hurtled towards the ground. He was half lying on the floor between the seats, his body clamped by gravity to the cool metal. As a child he had hated roundabouts because they always made his head spin. There had been a roundabout by the old guns near the church. And there had been a stall where they sold long sweets. . . . Zhenya had asked him if he would agree to see his own death. What answer had he given? But what did that matter? He had other things to think about. He must jump. Somehow he must get out of this plane. But he couldn't move. He couldn't even feel his body. The pain seemed to come from somewhere else and his mind, too, was detached and separate.

No one will ever know about that lead Agatov disconnected. The plane will crash but I won't be killed. I'll get hurt, I may be knocked unconscious, but I won't be killed. I'll recover, I'm sure I will. I'll come to sooner or later. Whatever happens I'll stay alive. I can't die just like that.

I haven't had time to do anything yet. Oh, Mother! Maybe we'll come down in the trees. Why did they leave me here? This damned drum! It's all because of that drum. I ought to have checked the power supply. Krylov warned me. How damn silly! If it hadn't been for Tulin.... The plane might pancake on a slope and just slither down it. It's been known to happen.

He felt the drum in his hand. He mustn't lose it. Krylov had asked him to take care of it. Not death, not complete and final! He would close his eyes and lie there and think. And listen. What a swine Agatov was! Not death, not that! If they could get at the eye of the storm they could destroy it. A shaft of clear sky would slice through the cloud and they would fly out along a blue, sunlit path.

In his mind's eye he saw a fantastic and wonderful spectacle. Towering black clouds packed with thunder and lightning, and an aircraft flying calmly through them, leaving a wide strip of clear sky in its wake, and the clouds shrinking, cut off at their source, destroyed in the womb of their development.

He had time to think again of Zhenya, to see her smile and to see his mother's face beside her.

They would come to visit him in hospital. The bones would mend quickly and he would begin an entirely new and different life. He had better work out all the designs and circuits he had thought of and get them down in the rough at least. Anything might happen to him. He must crawl away from the plane as soon as possible after the crash. That day the boys had let off a hand grenade in the yard he had got off with a mere scratch. His mother had said he was born lucky.

It only took a few seconds to think of all kinds of things. You could understand such a lot, see such a lot. But you couldn't do much, that was the trouble. It was too late to put anything right.

But suppose he began again, right from the beginning?

"Richard, take the drum!"

Why did you dash back to your instrument as soon as you heard Krylov's voice? You ought to have run to the hatch and jumped. But you grabbed the drum and grabbed Agatov and he saw in your eyes that *you knew*.

Perhaps you shouldn't have spent so much time before that thinking of Tulin and Zhenya? Perhaps you shouldn't have joined this group at all? But that wouldn't have been you. That would have been someone else. If it had been someone else, you would never have existed. That would have been worse than death.

The parachute opened and everything seemed to stop. For a few moments Krylov felt as if he wasn't falling at all, just swaying to and fro, suspended in mid air, then the weight of his damaged leg began to drag him down faster and faster. Alyosha had been carried away into the impenetrable mist and Krylov could see no one. There was no earth and no sky. He was falling through a grey heaving substance that seemed to have no end. Here they were at last, the thunderclouds he had sought. He could reach out and touch them with his hands, feel their damp, cold flesh.

The storm had not passed. Thunder was still rolling and lightning flashes lit up the canopy of his parachute. He hoped desperately that they would all come out of this alive. Now he hated thunderstorms with all the hate that was in him. Once again that hostile, senseless force had evaded them, given them the slip. Its triumph was sickening. He felt as if he would choke in this suffocating darkness. From somewhere beneath him came the heavy, muffled roar of an explosion and he winced.

The cloud below seemed to grow darker and suddenly the earth came into view. A huge black-green expanse, it was rushing up towards him at terrifying speed.

Already he could make out the crowns of the larches. He fought the impulse to close his eyes and forced himself to manipulate the shrouds of his parachute, trying to guide it towards a clearing.

He fell on his side, trying to save his injured leg, but rolled over and hit the trunk of a larch and for a time lost consciousness. Luckily the parachute had caught in the branches of the tree and broken his fall.

His face was buried in the wet grass. He could hear rain dripping off the trees, then his nostrils caught the pungent scent of rain-washed leaves. He opened his eyes. There was no sun yet but the rain had stopped. Everything was dripping. Big heavy drops were plopping down off the trees. They were like voices talking in the forest.

The fresh green foliage was stirring slightly. Not far away Krylov could see a herd of horses, all bunched together. The dark bronze of their cruppers merged with the bronze of the tree-trunks. The horses were standing with their heads on one another's backs, scarcely moving. A big stallion with white pasterns levelled its black eyes at Krylov and snorted.

The rain-flattened grass was slowly righting itself. A bird began to sing, then another. The forest was coming to life again. The storm was forgotten. It had passed, clearing the air and freshening the leafage. Krylov lay on the ground, wondering at the stillness and tranquility all around.

With a fresh ability to appreciate his surroundings he observed the colours of this mountain forest and the beauty of the horses with their long tails and glistening manes.

The stallion continued to stare at him, as much as to say: "What do you want here?"

The warm, rain-soaked earth yielded gently under Krylov's fingers and he felt that there was nothing more beautiful. He was back on earth again and he needed nothing else except the earth. Wasn't it enough to be able to live, to breathe in this fragrance, to feel this beauty? He thought with revulsion of the stormy, treacherous sky and relived the pain he had felt when he heard the plane explode.

If only they had all got down safely. Nothing else mattered really. He saw Pozdyshev pushing Vera Matveyevna towards the hatch, his forced smile of encouragement and her pitiful screaming mouth. He felt he had in some way done them wrong. Why should they suffer and risk their lives?

As he lay here under the larches, it all seemed so futile. All his work, these flights, the danger they had exposed themselves to. Why study the charges of raindrops? What difference would it make to this forest? It wouldn't be any more beautiful just because someone knew how charges of electricity were distributed in the clouds. It was all foolishness. Wisdom lay in these columns of larches, in the patter of raindrops and the stately beauty of the horses.

There could be nothing better than this. Yet instead of delighting in the forest and admiring the sky, people had to fiddle with instruments and probe for electricity. The word "field" had long since lost its real meaning for him. He had forgotten that besides electrical fields and magnetic fields there were also ordinary green fields of grass, with flowers and bees.

He watched the horses roam apart and begin to graze, uttering little snorts as they reached down to the succulent grass.

He didn't feel like moving. If it hadn't been for the pain in his leg he would have gone on lying there, staring up at the idly stirring branches. He doubted whether people would be any happier just because they had learned to command the thunder. They would be spared certain misfortunes, but fewer misfortunes did not necessarily mean more happiness.

Chapter Eight

Before going down to the beach they had lunch in the floating restaurant. The peppery *chebureki* left a fiery heat in their mouths. Tulin ordered a bottle of Tsinandali. The light dry wine was cool and made them want to laugh. The air was pungent with spicy

smells from the kitchen. Their table was on the edge of the veranda.
The green water lapped beneath them and shoals of big-headed
mullet scurried in the luminous depths. Zhenya tossed them bits of
bread.

The beach was quite near. Zhenya went off to change and came
back in a kingfisher swimsuit that looked marvellous. The water
was warm and surfy. They swam out a long way and clung to the
red buoys.

Tulin swam fast, displaying his skill in the crawl, then turned
over on his back and floated with his head cupped in his hands.

They came out at the other end of the beach and walked along
the pebbly shore, inspecting the seaside belles in their sunglasses
and gaudy swimsuits recumbent under Chinese parasols, and
enjoying the colourful spectacle of the crowded, noisy beach rimmed
with the glittering surf. Tulin was hailed by Moscow friends, but
he merely waved back. He suddenly realised, almost with surprise,
that he didn't want to be with anyone else but Zhenya. They
splashed through the shallows hand in hand, chatting and laughing.
He watched her dark-brown eyes and lithe, confident movements and
admired her. It was good to feel for once that something special
was happening to him, something quite unlike any of his previous
affairs. Those other women had not been to blame. They had liked
him, fallen in love with him and suffered when he left them, but he
himself had hardly ever taken their feelings, or his own, seriously.

The fact was that, like Zhenya, he had merely allowed others to
fall in love with him. He had enjoyed being loved and tried to evoke
love, but that was all. When women accused him of being calculating, he had assured them offendedly that he was not the same
with all women. He had also maintained that a scientist must have
one domineering passion, that everything else was a hindrance. In
those days he had been at peace with himself and content with his
freedom.

But now, with Zhenya, he found himself dreading the day when
he would have to think up explanations and excuses, tell himself
he was too busy, too deeply involved in his work, dreading the
day when his life would once again resume its normal course.

He squeezed her bare arm. She looked at him in surprise. Then
he took her by the shoulders and in full view of the whole beach
he kissed her on the lips. A laugh went up and someone whistled.
For a moment her eyes darkened with anger but, when she drew
away, there was laughter in them. She splashed some water
over him and ran away. Her kingfisher bathing dress darted
among the sunburnt bodies, sunshades and tents. Tulin caught up
with her and took her gently by the arm. He was fascinated and

delighted by this switching from one mood to another, from serious-ness to that friendly state when nothing has yet happened, or one can pretend that nothing has yet happened, this initial wavering, this beginning.

They lay down on the pebbles. Zhenya put a paper parcel under her head.

He asked her what it was.

She lay looking up at the sun with half-closed eyes, then said with unexpected defiance in her voice: "A present for Richard. He's been longing to have a sports shirt like yours. So I've bought him one. Like to see it?"

"No."

"Why not? It's a very nice shirt."

"Zhenya!"

She closed her eyes.

"This is all wrong somehow," she said.

Her brown shoulder, all encrusted with sand and salt, was very near Tulin. He could feel the sunny warmth of it on his cheek. He decided to take the plunge.

"What has Richard got to do with it? Priority? Priority counts when it's a matter of scientific discoveries. You're not Richard's discovery."

She sat up and said as firmly as she could:

"You must remember, I love Richard."

There was a kind of pleading anxiety in her voice that made Tulin want to drop the subject.

"Let's go for a walk."

"Why don't you answer?" she said impatiently.

"If you loved Richard, you wouldn't have come here with me. But you did come. And you brought your bathing things with you. You knew exactly what would happen. You knew we should lie on the beach and what I should say to you."

Zhenya bowed her head.

"But. . . ." She looked despairingly into his eyes.

Words meant nothing now. It was eyes that decided everything, and something else, even more mysteriously accurate. Tulin submit-ted to her glance, joyfully aware of his own sincerity and frankness.

"Why be ashamed, even if you do feel that way? Your feelings are more honest than you are. I think it's immoral not to let your-self feel what you really feel, not to be with the person you want."

"Shall we go into the park?" she asked, after a pause.

"I don't mind."

"Let's then."

Huge oaks with interlacing branches. Cool shade. Sturdy groves of boxwood. Light, salty air.

"Zhenya, suppose this is the real thing?"

"What then?"

He burst out laughing.

"We shall go forward from strength to strength, shan't we?" He wanted to be really frank. "If it was, I could let myself be weak and wretched in front of you. I never allow myself that now. I may let up sometimes, when I'm with Krylov, if it gets too much for me, but that's not the same thing. With you I want to be myself—not afraid of revealing my true feelings, not wondering whether you'll like what you see."

Zhenya reflected that it had been just the opposite with Richard. He had always said that with her he would be strong and capable of achieving great things.

"... You see, up to now I've always tried to appear better than I really am. I thought people would like me more if I was gay and successful, with a brilliant future before me. I always liked to preen my finest feathers. But I don't want to do that with you."

"You've nothing to fear. I know everything already. You can let yourself be what you like. But I.... What am I compared to you? A mere undergraduate."

"You're Zhenya."

"Isn't it funny to think of you, the famous Tulin, lined up with a person like me? It makes me feel so small and insignificant. I'm such a fool. You told me that yourself. And you still treat me like a little girl."

"That's because I'm selfish. I'm always thinking of my work. Even now, d'you know what I'm thinking? Not of you, not of us, but of how falling in love will affect my poor work."

She and Richard had always avoided the word "love". They had considered it cheap. But Tulin used it freely and loudly and it sounded wonderful. And there were no other words that could replace it.

"... I suppose it's a good thing I don't know why. Up to now, I've always known why I've liked a person—beautiful figure, fun being together, and so on. But someone always turned up who it was more fun to be with."

He let her walk on ahead a little and watched her, now in shade, now all agleam in the sunlight. She was wearing a striped jumper with a long slit down the back.

Her damp brown hair hung limply over her shoulders. Her skirt rustled with every stride. The gravel crunched under her white summer shoes. Every little thing about her fascinated him.

"I can't understand why I didn't notice you were so beautiful before."

"Because I was a witch. No witch can be beautiful. I hated you."

"You must have been a beautiful witch, but I can't really remember now. When I saw you in that park shelter in Moscow you were a pretty nice-looking one."

"I was only a student then, and you were. . . ." She broke off in confusion.

"Well, what was I?"

"A swank."

"So you remember everything. Well, who was right? Didn't I promise you would be controlling thunderstorms with your own hands?"

"Yes, you did. How strange it all seems."

"It's fate," he said with conviction.

"I wonder what fate has in store for us now."

For some reason she remembered Richard. What had he wanted to say to her before she left?

There was a rumble in the distance. Thunderclouds were creeping over the mountains and the sun lit up smudges of slanting rain among the hills. Zhenya listened worriedly.

"Let's go back."

They had at least another hour to spare and there was no point in driving back through the rain, when they could wait till it passed over. But Zhenya had the bit between her teeth, and the more he tried to dissuade her the more firmly she insisted on leaving.

They found their driver at the depot and climbed into the back of the lorry. The rain caught them when they were about halfway back. Tulin suggested Zhenya should get into the driver's cabin, but she refused. He took off his jacket and put it over her head. When the warm rain began trickling down his back he laughed, as if he were being tickled. Nothing could damp his spirits. He revelled in the rain, caught drops of it in his mouth, sang at the top of his voice and fooled about.

"Our first day of creation began with a thunderstorm, too. If that isn't fate, I don't know what is!"

Zhenya stared up at the violet-black sky that was quivering with distant flashes of lightning. For an instant the mountains, the wet, glistening trees, the rocks and the road were bathed in light, then they were enclosed in darkness, even gloomier and more intense than before.

"What imagination had ancient man!" Tulin crowed, imitating Golitsyn.

"Oh, do stop!" she burst out.

"What's the matter?"

"Suppose they're. . . . Suppose they're up there."

He laughed, to keep away anxiety.

"If they are, they're damn lucky. We're all being specially favoured by fortune today." He poked his laughing face under the jacket covering her head. "It's terribly hard, you know, to be both happy and modest."

Again he broke into song. He had a pleasant voice, but sometimes sang out of tune. With a bitterness she herself could not understand Zhenya asked:

"What are you going to do about Richard now?"

"Of course, it's a pity it had to be him," Tulin replied unabashed. "I'd much rather it had been Agatov." He rubbed his wet cheek on her hand.

He liked Richard and he would do everything he could to keep his friendship. No one died of such things. It was something every man had to go through, a kind of baptism of fire. Next time Richard wouldn't let another man take his girl away from him.

He was in such bubbling high spirits that Zhenya couldn't help smiling.

The rain beat down on the sodden jacket, the lorry rushed on and on, and Zhenya wished the road would never end, or that it would take them to some other town where they would be complete strangers to everyone.

Chapter Nine

They carried the coffin on their shoulders all the way to the cemetery, and through the cemetery to the grave. Someone offered to relieve Tulin but he walked on heedlessly, gripping the handle of the coffin and wondering why it was so light. It seemed to be empty.

Perhaps nothing had happened. Perhaps this was all a dream. He would wake up in a moment, splash some water over his face and go to the dining room, where he would meet Richard. All he had to do was wake up.

He turned his head and saw the small tears streaming steadily down the cheeks of Richard's mother. She was being led along by Alyosha Mikulin and Agatov. She had arrived by air that morning. A large fawn handbag was dangling from her elbow.

Alyosha spoke, then Altynov. The last to speak was Agatov. His rich, powerful voice could be heard by everyone. He read his speech in clear, solemn tones, like someone reading out an order. "The tragic death of a young and gifted man.... A hero of Soviet science.... Such a promising career cut short by a pointless accident.... Our hearts will always cherish the memory of our dear comrade.... This example of dedication to our common cause...."

It was very hot. Agatov omitted a few paragraphs for fear of getting sunstroke.

"We have been forced to pay too great a price for the unsubstantiated theories of those who desire quick success." He shook his head sadly and many people glanced at Tulin.

The coffin was lowered clumsily into the grave. Someone said: "Pull out the ropes." Richard's mother bent down and picked up a lump of earth, but her fingers clenched and she was unable to drop it on the lid of the coffin. Embarrassed at feeling herself the centre of attention, she made a pitiful attempt to smile.

That smile set all the women crying. Then came the minute of silent grief, the most poignant at all funerals. Suddenly there was a stir among the crowd, voices were raised and the ring of people around the grave parted to admit the pale, wild-eyed figure of Krylov.

"Let me speak!" he cried in a quite inappropriately loud voice.

Agatov gave a start and drew back, stumbling in the loose earth and muttering as if he had seen a ghost.

"No, Yakov Ivanovich, friends, that's not how it was," Krylov began wildly. "Richard didn't die for nothing. That's not the way to look at it. I can explain everything...."

He gulped for breath and suddenly became lost in thought, as though he had completely forgotten the people around him. In the oppressive silence that followed someone whispered: "He wants to justify himself."

Krylov gave a start and looked up. Some of the mourners were staring at him with indignation and disgust, others were too ashamed and embarrassed to look at him.

"I have no excuses to make. On the contrary, I take full responsibility. But what we've got to do now is to prove that there is a point, a purpose in what we do." He shook his fist in angry frustration.

Vera Matveyevna put her hand on his shoulder. "Calm yourself, Sergei Ilyich."

By this time Agatov had recovered his wits. Holding on to the little plywood obelisk that was to mark the grave, he knocked the earth off his shoes and looked round to see whether anyone had noticed his terror.

In a firm voice he said to Krylov: "This isn't a public meeting."

Krylov made a helpless gesture and limped away, leaning heavily on his stick. Noticing Richard's mother, he bowed to her.

"I want you to know," he began, but his voice broke. "Your son wanted to become a real scientist. He died like a real scientist. His name will live in scientific. . . ."

Richard's mother recoiled in fright.

"What's going on?" "This is scandalous!" Loud whispers rose from the back of the crowd, adding to the general unpleasantness of the situation.

Agatov wiped his face and respectfully offered his arm to Richard's mother.

"You must forgive our comrade," he said. "Richard's death has been a very great shock to us all. It is a terrible lesson. Over his grave we swear that nothing of the kind shall ever happen again. May the memory of Richard's death drive all petty vanity from our minds." It suddenly occurred to him that the outcome might have been much worse because he himself might have been killed. His voice faltered. "Of course, Richard didn't die in vain. It may well be that we all owe him our lives. From now on these criminal attempts will be banned." There were tears in his eyes as he took Richard's mother by the arm. "We shall always be at your side."

He did all he could to restore the atmosphere of solemnity which he considered essential to such proceedings, and which it would be wrong and insulting to the dead man to violate, as though death could in any way be insulted.

But at that moment another indignant and desperate shout was heard from Krylov:

"Why the hell can't someone say that wasn't what he died for!"

The little obelisk was placed in position, and wreaths were piled around it. Richard's mother stood before it in silence for a time, then walked away towards the gate with the students and other members of the group accompanying her.

Again Krylov barred her path.

"Excuse me, but I can't leave it like this. I meant to say that Richard believed in our work and we shall prove he was right. You'll see for yourself. . . ."

She looked at Krylov with hatred in her red, tear-swollen eyes.

"What difference does it make to me? You're all alive, aren't you?"

She turned away and Agatov helped her along, holding her arm considerately and telling her about the insurance she would receive.

Agatov was haunted by the thought that he himself might have been killed. This funeral might have been his own. The proceedings would have been just the same, there would have been similar speeches. Krylov, no doubt, would not have made all this fuss, and Tulin would certainly not have been so upset. None of them would have remained standing over his grave. Worriedly he rehearsed the names of his relatives and friends in his mind. Which of them would have shed any real tears? The funeral, perhaps, would have been more impressive, more wreaths would have been sent, there would have been an announcement in the press, but everyone would have left the cemetery at once and on the way home they would have discussed who was to be appointed in his place. Yes, if he hadn't managed to shake Richard off, they would both have been killed. At least, fate had treated him fairly at that moment. Why should he have been killed for the sake of Tulin's madcap idea? He, who had protested from the very beginning?

But this was his moment of triumph. It was he who had warned that the whole thing might end in disaster, he who had demanded suspension of the flights. He had been right. And they, they were to blame for everything.

At the cemetery gate he stopped and turned round. Krylov, Zhenya, Tulin, Alyosha and Katya were all standing by the grave, at a little distance from one another.

"Do you know why they are still standing there?" he said to Richard's mother. "They feel they are to blame."

There were always simple motives for everything. Krylov's strange behaviour had been caused by his fear of responsibility for what had occurred. He had been in charge of the programme, he had commanded the flight. Fine words were always used to conceal self-interest. It was only a matter of detecting it.

What had Richard wanted to tell her before the flight? It must have been something important, otherwise he wouldn't have run after her, begging her to stay behind, insisting that she should. Every word he had spoken, every gesture had now acquired a special significance. Zhenya reconstructed them in her mind, trying to solve the mystery that was now buried in the earth with Richard. "There's something I've got to tell you. . . ." He had been panting for breath, there had been anger in his dark eyes, he had waved his thin hands in the air. The final shy touch of his fingers had been so desperate.

Why had she failed to understand how much he needed to tell her that "something"? What could he have wanted to say? Why just at that moment?

She had questioned Alyosha, who said Richard had not spoken to anyone. He had sat in the plane looking sort of stunned. He hadn't come to life till the storm hit them, but then there had been no time for discussion. And now she would never know. Never! It was that "never" that brought home to her the fact of death.

What had he been thinking about in those last few minutes? While she had listened to Tulin making fun of him.... She could feel the reproach in people's glances. Richard had asked her not to go, begged her not to. If she had yielded, everything might have been different. This might never have happened.

Zhenya hesitated to place her flowers on the grave. She dared not weep. She waited till the crowd had left, then stepped towards the mound with its pile of wreaths and halted.

Was this all that was left of Richard? Why this grave, these flowers, this coffin buried in the earth, and the lifeless thing that was in that coffin? What had they to do with Richard? Where was Richard himself?

Something prevented her from bowing down to the grave. The sound of cautious footsteps behind her froze her to the spot. Someone touched her arm timidly, just as Richard had once touched it. She shook the hand off.

"Go away," she said to Tulin. "Leave me alone."

"Zhenya, I can't bear to be alone now.... I feel so rotten. You must help me. The commission will be here soon. I've got to be able to cope somehow."

Always thinking of himself and no one else. Everything had to be for him and him alone. It wasn't Richard's death that worried him but his own troubles.

She tore her arm away and suddenly something seemed to break loose inside her. It was all because of him! He had made her go with him, made her quarrel with Richard. It was his fault Richard had been killed.

She swung her arm and struck him on the cheek so hard that his head jerked and he staggered back. Almost exultantly she felt the pain and weight of the blow on her palm.

Krylov, Alyosha and Katya were standing by the grave. Only now did they become aware of one another's presence. They stared at Tulin. His lips were tightly compressed, and a red mark was slowly spreading over his cheek. Had he moved an inch, or said a word, she would have flown at him in frenzy. At such moments murder is done.

But he said nothing. He just looked at her and his eyes became very large, until they seemed to fill his face.

This golden boy, this general favourite, so resourceful, so secure from all disaster, he stood before her now, at a loss for a reply.

It was for him to bear everything that she or any of the others meted out to him.

A spasm of grief seized her throat and she ran out of the cemetery, stumbling over graves and through hedges, seeing nothing but him standing there with that purple mark on his cheek.

With typical energy and determination Agatov helped Richard's mother to make out the forms entitling her to compensation and a pension. There were all kinds of formalities to be gone through, but he made short work of them.

The next day he was on the airfield to meet the commission that had been sent down to investigate the accident. It consisted of Lagunov, Yuzhin, Golitsyn, Chirkayev, the aircraft designer's representative, and various representatives from the meteorological service and the institute. Agatov helped to get them accommodation at the hotel and stayed up late preparing the documents. He slept badly, dreaming of the grave and the silent figures standing round it. In his dream he knew that they had been standing there for months and would go on standing there for years; there was something menacing about it.

He woke up feeling utterly depressed and heard his watch ticking loudly under the pillow.

That morning he ran into Zhenya Kuzmenko in the street. She flushed and lowered her head. At first he couldn't understand what was the matter, then he realised that they, she and Tulin, felt guilty in the eyes of other members of the group. Where had they been? What had they been doing when the plane had been caught in the storm?

Lisitsky came up and shook his hand sympathetically. How right you were!

It was so sincere, so grateful that the anxieties of the night seemed absurd. So everyone realised that he was in the right. In the long run he had turned out to be wiser and more far-sighted than either Tulin or Krylov. If he had only had more power, this would never have happened. For the first time he felt not merely relieved but overjoyed at his own escape. He was still alive, alive today. What did it matter who stayed behind after his funeral or whether anyone wept for him? He was alive. That was better than any tears.

He had lunch with Golitsyn and Lagunov in the hotel restaurant. He ordered a jellied sturgeon and black caviar, and drank two cups of black coffee.

Chapter Ten

Golitsyn did not visit the scene of the crash and did not attend the first sittings of the commission. He was busy checking the results achieved by Tulin's group. He went through the materials trying to find out the main thing—whether the crash had been merely an accident or the result of faulty methods of research. Agatov could not understand why on earth Golitsyn spent days on end tiring himself out in such stifling heat. "Our point of view, or rather yours, has been fully vindicated," he said. "You were right all along the line. There's absolutely nothing to worry about. Our task now is to punish these adventurers. You can be quite satisfied." Golitsyn shouted at him: "Satisfied over what? That Richard has been killed?" He fumed at the idea that everyone else must be thinking he was gloating. Krylov certainly must. None of them realised how dispassionately Golitsyn weighed the evidence, making a careful note of anything that spoke in favour of their ideas, even though he derived a secret satisfaction in discovering the failures that he had predicted, the departures from strictly scientific methods, and the premature conclusions.

The deviations obtained here were only a tenth of what should be allowed for lightning. It was still not clear how the regeneration of charges took place. The most convincing measurements had been taken by Krylov, but even these were inadequate. The rest was flimsy, vulnerable stuff. No explanation was offered of cases outside the general pattern. . . .

Before he had left Moscow he had received a telephone call from Anikeyev, who was worried about Krylov. Golitsyn had grunted jealously: "Just what he deserved!" But he had looked forward to meeting Krylov with some excitement.

It had been rather an anticlimax. Krylov had shaken hands with him as impersonally as with the other members of the commission. Golitsyn had been sure that Krylov would call on him in his room that evening. He had ordered wine, a melon, grapes. Krylov did not appear that evening, or the next. Golitsyn told himself he must be afraid of appearing to court the favour of a member of the commission. Yet it would have been only right for him to come and confess honestly that in their last argument he had been at fault. Golitsyn had proved that. The crash had proved it.

Yuzhin paid him a visit. He came in puffing and blowing, unbuttoned his tunic and cursed Lagunov, the heat, the weather men, his own confounded job, thunderstorms in general and all their charges and discharges. He maintained that Krylov had behaved stupidly when he appeared before the commission by taking all the blame on himself. He had insisted that the storm-detector ought to have worked. He had argued with Lagunov. He had gone on and on, repeating his own ideas. Instead of showing some sign of repentance he had stubbornly stuck to his own point of view. Apparently he felt no pangs of conscience whatever and, unlike Tulin, was not in the least sobered by the crash. Whereas Tulin, who bore no direct responsibility for the flight, was badly shaken and obviously very upset.

"What about Krylov?" Golitsyn asked.

"Krylov doesn't give a damn!" Yuzhin exclaimed indignantly. "Though he was the one in charge of the flight programme. He even hopes to be allowed to go on with the project. In fact, he demands it! That young man had better think himself lucky if we don't put him in court. He ought to take his cue from Tulin. Tulin knows a thing or two. The lad's a bit depressed at the moment, but I hope. . . ."

"But what about Krylov?" Golitsyn interrupted him again.

"You seem to have a thing about this Krylov fellow! I could understand if it were Tulin. I'm sorry for him, that boy's got talent. But this other fellow—I shouldn't waste any tears on him!"

Golitsyn lost his temper.

"Talent! Talent's not the whole answer by any means! What does talent consist of?"

Over the past few days he had often found himself thinking about that rare combination of qualities that go to make up the real scientist—will-power, an ability to keep oneself within limits, a capacity for joy, for surprise, for knowing how to fall, how to endure devastating criticism, the strength to begin all over again. And so many other things besides, things that could not be combined mechanically but only as a chemical compound, in the very strictest proportions, for a deficiency in any one of these qualities rendered the others valueless.

Richard's mother had given him her son's unfinished thesis to read, and Golitsyn now knew that Richard had turned against him and sided with Tulin. The thesis contained a few bold propositions and interesting calculations concerning the electrical charges in clouds. None of it was strictly scientific, but Golitsyn had no wish to contest these opinions. Richard's death had given them a special significance. And after all, why should he contest them? Richard had not only left this life, he had left Golitsyn. By the time of his death he had become an opponent. Krylov, too, was Golitsyn's opponent. All his best pupils were leaving him. At the age of sixty-five he was alone. There had been many people who had stood for degrees under his supervision and were considered his pupils. But he could claim no one who had followed in his footsteps, as Ani keyev and Dan could. At bottom, Krylov had always remained a pupil of Dan's. That was why he had left Golitsyn.

But he would have to come back There was nowhere else for him to go now. Golitsyn picked up his pen. He was sorry for Krylov. Krylov would have trouble enough without this, but Golitsyn simply couldn't resist the temptation. His final conclusion was scathing: "According to these measurements it may be deduced that lightning does not, in fact, exist. Thunderstorms, therefore, are also non-existent. May we then consider the problem of combating thunderstorms solved?"

His arguments were devastating on many points. It was unlikely that Krylov would succeed in disproving them. Lagunov would be delighted with the magnificent tomb he had constructed for consigning all gambles of this kind to oblivion. Faultless logic, strict analysis without hairsplitting or pedantry.... Yet why was there no satisfaction? Where was the feeling of a job well done? There must be something wrong somewhere....

Just before the morning sitting Krylov was called to the telephone to answer a trunk call. He waited in the booth for some time, with the receiver pressed to his ear. At last the operator told him he was through.

"Hullo, Krylov speaking...."

"Sergei...." The voice broke off.

"Who's speaking?" he asked.

Silence again, nothing but an occasional crackle on the wire, the sound of breathing, and the throbbing in his own temples.

"Are you all right? I've only just heard what happened. They said someone had been killed."

"Natasha? Where are you? Where're you ringing from?"

"Are you quite all right?"

"Yes, I'm fine. How did you find out where I was? Natasha!"

"Are you in trouble?"

"Oh, nothing much. Can you come and see me? I'm supposed to appear before the commission, but to hell with them! I'll come and see you myself."

There was another long silence and when she replied her voice had changed.

"No, don't do that. I only wanted to be sure nothing had happened to you."

"But surely.... Hold on.... Hullo! Hullo!"

"Why do you keep us waiting?" Lagunov asked testily.

Krylov sighed and looked at him as if he and his commission were creatures from some prehistoric age.

What was the implication of this phone call? All that year Krylov had lived in hope of meeting Natasha again. Now she didn't want to see him. Yet she had rung him herself. All kinds of things might have happened in a year. She might have fallen in love, got married, had a baby. By this time he knew what a difference one year could make to one's life. Lena had taught him that. So had Natasha. Then why had she phoned?

"Why do you think Goldin failed to use his parachute?"

He would have liked to go and lie down, shut himself off from everyone. He would have liked to prop up his injured leg and perhaps take some sleeping tablets. Or better still, he would have liked to go drinking with the mechanics, and get so drunk that he could forget the whole bloody lot of them, the commission and Natasha included, and not have to think of what might happen tomorrow.

The sound of his own firm voice helped him to regain his composure. There was no point in losing one's temper. They were only doing their job. They had to find out the actual circumstances of Richard's death. Come what may, everyone must carry out his duties. Some must ask questions, others must answer them.

When Lagunov arrived he had said: "I warned you that this would turn out badly." It was a fact. Lagunov had warned him when he accepted Golitsyn's offer. Savushkin had also warned him not to make an enemy of Lagunov. And Golitsyn, too, had warned him. What far-sighted people they all were! It was amazing how they had all known what was going to happen to him. But why didn't he know a damn thing, either about himself or other people?

He remembered Richard's face as he had last seen it, during the flight. Yes, he had failed to find the right answer, the words that would have supported him, held him up like a parachute. Perhaps he ought to have told him the whole truth about Tulin. There had been no need for those white lies, the pretence that Tulin had stood up for Richard against Agatov.

He glanced at Tulin in his white shirt with the sleeves rolled up, his dark, tight-fitting slacks and pointed moccasins. They hadn't had a chance to have a word with each other and Krylov felt that Tulin was avoiding him. He answered the commission's questions with brief yeses and noes. Today he was taking no part in the proceedings, and just sat there silently, chain-smoking. He could give no information concerning Richard's death.

Voznitsyn asked about the drums. Had there been time for Richard to remove them from the recorder? Chirkayev, the aircraft designer's representative, asked whether there had been any need under the circumstances to worry about the drums. It was obvious that Chirkayev was motivated by a sincere desire to understand Krylov's conduct and Krylov answered willingly, though he realised what he meant was: were the drums so valuable that it was worth risking a man's life to save them?

The question had not even occurred to him while he was in the air. Now it seemed all-important.

"The drums contained a record of the work of the storm-detector," he said. "If we had them here now, we might be able to state definitely that the detector was doing its job."

"But it wasn't working," Chirkayev insisted.

"The dial on the pilot's dash must have been out of order, but its recording apparatus might have been working."

"How could that be?"

"I don't know," Krylov said. "There must have been a fault in the circuit. All kinds of things could have gone wrong."

"Why didn't you take steps to repair the fault?" Lagunov asked.

Krylov shrugged.

"Have you ever tried to repair apparatus in the air? I can't do it."

He realised the tactlessness of his reply too late. Lagunov had never flown and it was a good many years since he had had anything to do with any kind of apparatus.

"Comrade Agatov considers that your apparatus is unsound because your whole method is unsound. What do you say to that?" Voznitsyn cut in before Lagunov could react. For the members of the commission Agatov was an expert, the head of a laboratory, Golitsyn's assistant.

Krylov looked at Tulin again. So did many of the others. He was sitting with one leg over the other, still smoking.

"Now let's get it clear just what happened when you started baling out," Yuzhin suggested.

With Pozdyshev's help he started reconstructing the sequence of events. Yuzhin asked for Alyosha Mikulin to be called in.

"I'm not the only one who considers the method of research unsound," Agatov put in suddenly. "I merely share the opinion held by Arkady Borisovich."

Golitsyn gave a grunt. He had his glasses on and was looking through his report.

"We'll come back to that later," Lagunov said.

Yuzhin was looking thoughtfully at Agatov.

"By the way, Yakov Ivanovich," he said. "You were the last man to bale out. What was Goldin doing at the time?"

Agatov rubbed his forehead, as though trying to remember. His fingers touched the piece of plaster covering the scratch on his forehead. Again he felt himself crawling, kicking Richard away, bumping his head.... He gave a start and looked at Yuzhin. It was quite natural that Yuzhin should be looking at the scratch, but Agatov felt something freeze up in the pit of his stomach.

"I bumped my head," he said lamely, conscious that his lips had twisted into a pleading smile.

Yuzhin kept his eyes fixed on the scratch and Agatov began to panic.

"Yes, yes, I saw him. Richard was fiddling with the drum. It must have got stuck. Drums often get stuck, you know. It happened to get stuck just at the wrong moment...." His eyes seemed to be riveted to Yuzhin's, he couldn't tear them away. With an effort he forced himself to look at Lagunov. But perhaps Yuzhin would realise that he was deliberately avoiding his glance? He shouldn't have said anything. It would have been better to say he hadn't seen Richard at all. That would have been much safer.

"...Krylov asked Richard to do it and he stayed behind and the drum got stuck. Or rather, I suppose it did, because I don't know exactly. Krylov has been doing his best to prove that we got into the storm by accident. He says that because he must have an excuse, and that's the only excuse he's got. The detector wasn't working. It's quite certain that the detector wasn't working...."

"Do you think Richard could have baled out?"

"Yes, of course."

"Then why should Krylov have bothered about the drums?" Yuzhin asked. "The drums must also have shown that the detector wasn't working."

Agatov was shaken, but he managed to recover. As though it was all coming back to him, he went on: "Krylov and Tulin had been arguing about this for some time. Everyone knows that. Do you think Krylov doesn't realise that Tulin's theory is built on sand? Of course, he does. Ask him. I dare say he wanted to prove it to Tulin with the data in the drums. In fact, I'm sure of it. Now, of course, they're trying to cover up for each other. If I had known, I would have countermanded Krylov's order. But I didn't quite hear...."

He simply couldn't check himself, although he was aware that Yuzhin and the others must have noticed his strange volubility.

"You were near Goldin at the time," Yuzhin said. "You say you saw him trying to remove the drum? But it's a long way, you know, from that apparatus to the emergency hatch."

"I do believe you're trying to catch me out?" Agatov had meant to say it sarcastically, but his voice trembled. "I've told you I didn't go away from the hatch! I saw what Richard was doing from a distance. Do you think a person can't see anything from a distance? You're trying to put me off. I know you've got to defend Tulin, because I warned you, in writing, that this might happen!"

"Yes, indeed, and how right you were! You're a good chap, but you've had a nasty shaking. Your first crash, eh?" And Yuzhin chuckled amiably to relieve the tension. "I'm only trying to get things straight for your sake. I don't want people to come picking holes in what you've said later on."

Agatov drank some water and relaxed a little. The discussion shifted to the question of radio communication and the weather forecasts. Quite casually Yuzhin showed Agatov a map with the crash area and the spots where the parachutes had been found marked upon it.

"This is where Pozdyshev landed, and this is where you did." Yuzhin's pudgy face was a picture of benevolence. "I can't understand why the distance is so great."

"What difference does it make?" Lagunov asked.

"Of course, it makes a difference. Yakov Ivanovich states that he was thrown forward, pushed Pozdyshev out and fell out himself. But the distance goes against that."

Khobotnev gave Yuzhin a curious glance and decided not to intervene. If Yuzhin said it was so, he must have a reason for saying it.

Agatov lifted his hands feebly from the table. He tried to open his mouth, but it wouldn't open. He closed his eyes and felt himself falling. Then he heard Golitsyn's voice:

"The most extraordinary things may happen in an electrical storm. There was a case in 1955 when a parachutist was wafted about by air currents for twenty minutes." And Golitsyn launched into a description of the mechanics of air currents.

Agatov drew a deep breath, opened his eyes and said firmly: "Now you understand, I hope?"

Yuzhin nodded amiably.

He didn't understand a damn thing. His intuition told him unmistakably that there was something wrong and he tried carefully to pull the thread out of its tangled skein. The thread had broken and there would be no finding it again. How he would have liked to lock up the learned Golitsyn in a cupboard for the rest of the sitting. Confound the man and his erudition!

It was the first time Alyosha Mikulin had had to give evidence before the full commission of inquiry, with Golitsyn and all the other representatives present. Krylov, Tulin and Altynov were there, too.

There was a stenographer taking down every word he said, and all these important, serious people were listening to him with interest and paying tribute to his courage. He tried to answer casually, as if he had been in enough air accidents to have become rather bored with them, as if he were a veteran with scores of parachute jumps to his credit. What was so remarkable about his dragging Krylov out of the plane, perhaps even saving his life? Anyone would have done the same. The country at large was rather inclined to make a fuss about quite ordinary achievements.

Nevertheless he was delighted when asked to give the full details. As he listened to the sound of his own voice, Alyosha marvelled at the good sense he had shown in this emergency.

"Could you, for instance, have removed the drums under similar circumstances?" Lagunov asked.

"Of course," Alyosha replied. "Nothing to it really."

"Is it a fact that Krylov asked you to help Richard with the drums?"

"It is," Alyosha affirmed complacently and grinned at Krylov. "But I couldn't very well leave Sergei Ilyich to fend for himself just for that. And in any case...." He had been about to say that he had thought Krylov's concern over the drums unreasonable, and still thought so, but checked himself, realising that this might harm Krylov.

"In any case—what?" Lagunov insisted.

Alyosha didn't want to let Krylov down. He remembered the weight of that big, solid body, the damp air sucking them through the hatch, and then the horizontal flash of lightning. "Sheet lightning," he had noted mechanically and remembered Richard saying that sheet lightning was something diffused over distances of a hundred miles. If Alyosha had been the last man in the plane, he would have been all right because he had confidence in himself, but Richard was the wrong man to leave behind....

"Actually I couldn't care less about the drums," he said.

"What do you mean—you couldn't care less?" Lagunov asked acidly. "Try to be more explicit." But to the other members of the commission he said complacently: "It would appear that even this student, who held no position of responsibility, thought that the drums were not worth risking his own life, or Krylov's. But you, Sergei Ilyich, were not deterred by such considerations."

"Just a minute," Chirkayev interrupted, and turned to Alyosha. "How would you have acted in Krylov's place?"

Something in the eyes of the young engineer with the Chekhovian beard warned Alyosha of danger. He realised that there was more in these proceedings than he had thought, and that his evidence might make a lot of difference to Krylov, Tulin and the rest of the group. He had got to stick to something, but he didn't quite know what. Richard, he knew, would not have hesitated. . . .

"I. . . ." He hesitated. "I would not have given Richard that order. Because"—he sighed at the thought of the heroic image of Alyosha Mikulin that he was about to destroy—"because Krylov and I are different kinds of people."

Golitsyn, who was still poring over his papers, said abruptly: "Had I been in Krylov's place, I would have tried to save the drums. It would be the natural thing for any scientist to do. He was quite right not to give the order to Mikulin. That would have been a mistake. There are such young men about—with no ideals or inspiration."

Golitsyn's words suddenly showed everything in a different light. Till that moment Alyosha had been sure that Richard ought not to have stayed behind for the sake of the drums, but now it occurred to him that it was Richard and Krylov who had shown real heroism, though it hadn't achieved anything. He suddenly wanted to argue the thing out with Richard, but because Richard was no longer there to argue with, Richard was right. Up to now he had thought of Richard as if he were alive. Death was something so unusual, so out of place in the world he lived in. And it was only now, several days after the crash, that he was beginning to feel that Richard was gone, that he couldn't talk to him any more, and no matter what he, Alyosha, might do or become, this would remain so for ever. For Richard he would always be a young good-for-nothing queueing up outside an ice-cream parlour.

Lagunov marshalled the facts against Tulin with relentless skill. This was not the first time flights had been made into thunderheads. In spite of Agatov's protests, Tulin had persuaded Khobotnev and the crew into breaking regulations. This systematic infringement was bound to lead to an accident sooner or later. Instruments had been mounted on the wings and under the fuselage without permission from the designers. And on top of all this was Tulin's trip with one of the girl students. Lagunov spoke disparagingly of Tulin's relations with Kuzmenko. His remarks developed into quite a speech about the moral example that should be set by persons in authority. Contrary to Yuzhin's expectations Tulin made no attempt to defend himself. He seemed to have nothing to say. Krylov's clumsy attempts to cover up for him and deny the charges enabled Lagunov to turn the sittings of the commission into interrogations, to call in witnesses one by one and create a general atmosphere of suspicion.

Yuzhin saw that Lagunov was hoping to earn himself the reputation of a man who had exposed a fallacious scientific trend, an indomitable defender of the nation's interests. Enchanted with himself in this role, he was trying to build up a case for criminal proceedings. Yuzhin knew from years of experience that any accident inquiry was lost as soon as it became a search for scapegoats. He tried to intervene, to caution Lagunov, but Lagunov merely smiled politely and gave him to understand that he had better support the chairman of the commission and not put obstacles in his way. It was Yuzhin who had given the permission to fly in thunderstorms, so when he defended Tulin he was merely trying to defend himself. It was Yuzhin who had been informed by Agatov of infringements of the regulations and failed to take any appropriate steps.

No one on the commission knew that Yuzhin had for this very reason refused to preside but, since it would have been cowardice to refuse to work on the commission at all, he had consented to go as an ordinary member. He had been fully prepared for Golitsyn's malicious reproaches ("I warned you, but you wouldn't listen, you tried to talk me round") and the sermonising of those who had given no warnings at all ("Now do you realise what comes of trusting people like this?"), but faced with the complex reality of the situation he regretted being so scrupulous.

He sensed that certain old scores were being settled between Agatov, Tulin, Krylov, Lagunov and even Golitsyn. In spite of the ambiguous position he was in, he tried to do what he could. He managed to prove that the aircraft had got into the storm by accident. His instinct told him that Khobotnev was not to blame. The lightning had put his instruments out of action and it had been a miraculous piece of flying to have enabled the group to bale out under such conditions. Lisitsky and Pozdyshev had escaped with bruises, Vera Matveyevna had broken her arm, Krylov had injured his leg, but it might have been far worse. There might have been other fatal casualties besides Richard.

Khobotnev was badly cut up about the whole thing, and his face showed it. How could he have abandoned his plane with Richard still aboard? How had he failed to notice him?... Yuzhin could imagine the chaos of those last few minutes. Richard must have been thrown down somewhere between the seats. But Khobotnev would make no allowances for himself.

Lagunov demanded that criminal proceedings should be instituted against Krylov.

"What for?" Yuzhin asked.

"What for?! For negligence, for failure to take precautions, for the crash—everything!"

But Yuzhin succeeded in drawing a subtle distinction. Either Krylov was to be tried for negligence, in which case there was no need to close down the project, or, if the project was closed down, there was no justification for taking Krylov to court.

Lagunov was genuinely disappointed. "Can't we do both? What a pity!"

It would have been much easier for Yuzhin if Tulin had given him even a little help. But Tulin had lost heart, given the whole thing up as a bad job. As Chirkayev remarked, he was completely demoralised. Yuzhin had once believed in Tulin and was loth to admit his mistake. Was he really so blind about people? Was Tulin just a philanderer? Had this weakling led him up the garden, bamboozled him with his fairy-tales? And was this Agatov fellow the man with real foresight? Krylov's stonewalling was equally irritating. An attitude that would have suited Tulin was all wrong for this simpleton, who made one blunder after another and merely antagonised both Lagunov and Golitsyn.

Tulin read the pity in Yuzhin's eyes. With repressing clarity he recalled in every detail that magical day in Moscow when by sheer high spirits and force of personality he had made Yuzhin believe in his ability to win through. He remembered that huge red morocco armchair that he had clamped himself into until he got what he wanted.

Suddenly he found himself involuntarily trying to adopt the same pose. In an agony of shame he jumped to his feet, but a cool stare from Lagunov made him sit down again. He wondered miserably what would happen to him. The sun was making his eyes ache. Everything was unbearably vivid, like a film setting. The expression on every face, Lagunov's huge spectacles, the large room with its out-of-date posters on the walls. He felt he would remember these things to the end of his days.

"The atmosphere in the group was abnormal," Agatov was saying. "You kept hurrying us on. You wanted results 'at any price'— wasn't that your expression, Oleg Nikolayevich? It was a race for publicity."

"Couldn't it have been enthusiasm?" Tulin retorted. "Our people were working like Trojans, and they knew what they were working for."

But his words lacked conviction and they failed to impress. It was no use trying to defend oneself. It was all a foregone conclusion. He had realised that the moment he saw Golitsyn and Lagunov stepping out of the plane. They would be gloating. True, Yuzhin was there, too, but why should Yuzhin stand up for him after such a failure? He had let Yuzhin down and Yuzhin would not forgive that.

Lagunov asked him about the difference of opinion between him and Krylov.

Whenever they had a chance they used Krylov as a stick to beat him with. He could easily have supplied an answer. Basically, it was all Krylov's fault. If Tulin himself had been in command of the flight, nothing would have happened. He would have been able to cope with any situation.

Vera Matveyevna had stated as much before the commission: "If Tulin had been with us, he would have found a way out." With a woman's disregard of proofs she insisted that Tulin was born lucky.

No, he was not going to throw the blame on Krylov. Let everyone see how unjust it was. Let them say his luck had failed, let them be sorry for him. It was no use trying to save anything now. The project would be closed down and Krylov's attempts to salvage something from the wreckage were absurd. Tulin had no wish to appear absurd. No man who appeared absurd could be considered either important or dangerous.

This was the first time Golitsyn had attended a sitting. Tulin recalled his gleeful, boyish prank on the telephone, when he had rung Golitsyn from Krylov's flat. It looked as if Golitsyn had not forgotten it either.

With an expression of distaste Golitsyn listened to the story of Tulin's trip with Zhenya and to Lagunov moralising about it, waxing indignant, and revelling in the piquancy of the situation.

Never in his life had Tulin experienced such humiliation. His past, his future, everything he had achieved, the project that had begun so brilliantly, were collapsing in ruins. He imagined how the news would go round, embroidered with gossip: "What a hole Tulin's got himself into!" A year, ten years would pass and the label would still stick: "Ah, yes, the fellow who made such a bungle of things!"

What did it matter to Krylov, to Altynov—they had nothing to lose. The sooner the whole shameful affair was over the better. He would have been glad of an earthquake, an explosion, war, anything, as long as it meant he would be forgotten.

The heat blazed in through the windows. Somewhere a trumpeter was learning the Marseillaise and there was no escape from the naked piercing wail of his instrument.

During the interval the members of the commission kept away from him. He seemed to be surrounded by a zone of estrangement that could not be crossed. It was quite impossible for him to go up to them and offer them apples, as Agatov was doing, impossible even to tackle them in argument. His old self was gone.

Someone nudged him. Voznitsyn was walking beside him. Pasha Voznitsyn, his friend, the deputy director of the institute, now, as a member of the commission, to be addressed as Pavel Konstantinovich.

"Tell Krylov to stop being so obstinate," Voznitsyn murmured. "They're going to shut down the project anyway. There's no point in goading Lagunov. You must realise that under these circumstances no commission would take on such a responsibility. Continuing the project means continuing the flights. Why should Lagunov take the risk? Who would? It'd be madness. Lagunov's best bet is to crack down and put a stop to the whole thing. It'll give him a reputation for toughness and keeping his scientific standards high. Your aim now must be to cut your losses. There's no point in covering up for Krylov. If you survive, you'll be able to help him later."

"I've no intention of selling Krylov down the river."

"You won't be," Voznitsyn replied. "When there's a fire people try to save what's worth saving, but you've got the family sofa on your back. Your tactics are all wrong. You've lost your head."

"True enough," Tulin admitted. "But can't you see how things have piled up against me? Like a conspiracy. And on top of it all. . . ." He flushed. For a moment he had imagined that the imprint of Zhenya's hand could still be seen on his cheek. "My God, you've been showing yourselves up lately! Even you! Advising me under your breath. You haven't got the guts to back me up in front of the commission, have you? What they say goes. You want to keep on good terms with your masters. You'd vote the same as Lagunov on any issue."

Voznitsyn's plump cheeks caved in and baggy wrinkles appeared under his eyes.

"I'm defending the interests of the institute. It'd be different if I had only myself to think about. One has to rise above personal considerations. As it is, the whole institute will have enough unpleasantness to put up with for the rest of the year. And what can I do in any case? Who am I? Just a manager. You're an M. Sc. You've got a name. You can always get a job somewhere. But if they kick me out, what do I do? Sell tickets for the circus? Anyone else in my position would come down on you like a ton of bricks. You've no ability to appreciate what's done for you, that's your trouble!"

"So you're worried about your comfortable perch, you scared chicken. You're all scared."

"I'm certainly no fighter. Who is? Show me someone. Do you expect me to take on Lagunov? No, thank you. Give me a receipt first stating that nothing can happen to me. Even then I'd think twice."

"You're not the worst, I must say," Tulin said with a sneer. "You're quite prepared to be decent when circumstances allow."

"Why should I go out on a limb? I know what you mean and I don't like it myself. I'm being quite frank with you, but you don't appreciate it. You haven't been scared yet. You've lived in a protected area. This is your first taste of buckshot, but I. . . ."

Tulin said nothing.

"Sometimes I dream," Voznitsyn went on quietly, "that I'm standing up at one of the conferences at the institute and telling them all exactly what I think about everything. It's glorious!" He sighed dreamily and his face became plump and kindly again.

"Look here, Pasha," Tulin burst out hopefully, but Voznitsyn resumed his strained business-like expression.

"You are very lucky. The commission is being extremely lenient," he said hurriedly. "Even Lagunov is keeping within bounds. Don't goad him on and everything will be all right."

At dinner Tulin found himself at the same table with Agatov. They had both ordered meat soup and a chop. The chops were tough, and they both ate without appetite. Agatov put out a cautious feeler about Yuzhin. Why was Yuzhin so anxious to find fault, so suspicious?

Tulin's stubborn silence stated plainly that he was not to be drawn out by these crude tactics.

Agatov said: "He's trying to protect you."

"Why should he?"

"Yes, I know you think you're in the clear," Agatov went on bitterly. "I saw you sitting there, when they started grilling me, as if you were not concerned."

At least in Agatov's presence he managed to recover something of his former poise.

He narrowed his eyes. "Concerned about you? Not one little bit."

It was unwise, even reckless, but he couldn't play safe any more. He put into the words all the accumulated contempt he felt for this grasping mediocrity, who had caused him so much trouble. He was glad to see the shaft sink in.

Agatov leaned forward over the table. "You won't succeed in shoving the blame on me." He spoke in a rapid whisper, his eyes pale with hate. "You had better know that Richard asked me whether it was true that you had agreed to send him away."

"And what did you tell him?" Tulin strove to preserve his disdain.

"The truth, exactly what happened."

Tulin sawed through his chop and smeared it with mustard.

"He realised the rest himself. Visually." Agatov laughed but his face remained tense.

Tulin lowered the piece of mustard-smeared meat that he had taken on his fork. It would have been better not to ask, but the temptation was too strong.

"What did he realise?"

"D'you remember that visit you paid us at the institute? Drip, drip, drip. ... You're very good at knocking the stuffing out of people, you know. Luckily, I'm not so sensitive as Richard."

Tulin gripped the top of the table.

"Rubbish!"

"Yuzhin wants to know just how it all happened. Personally I think that was what was at the bottom of it. Richard realised everything. Everything! You know how morbidly young people react to that kind of thing!"

"So you were behind it, you told him all this stuff?"

Agatov laughed again and Tulin realised that he had been waiting for this question.

"Your friend Krylov also had a chat with Richard, you know."

"You'd better leave Krylov out of this," Tulin snapped. "That trick won't work."

He placed a one-ruble note on the table and walked out.

Krylov had only one aim—to save the project. He no longer hoped for support from Tulin. There was a burnt-out look in Tulin's eyes as he sat hunched in his chair, taking no part in the proceedings.

"Soviet science is exploring outer space," Krylov said. "We have reached outer space, we are sending rockets to the moon, yet the layer of air about twenty kilometres thick that surrounds our own planet has for some reason been declared the preserve of cowardice."

He climbed to the heights of pathos, he brandished the condemnation of succeeding generations, and the successes of the West. He brought up quotations, made clumsy appeals to the commission's better nature, to their sense of honour. If only he had known how to manoeuvre, to flatter, to play to the gallery. He gave a hopeful, enthusiastic account of what the group had already achieved. They were approaching the decisive stage in their inquiry, although, naturally enough, much was still open to argument.

"But I assure you that we are on the right track," he concluded.

Lagunov gave a disdainful sniff and winked expressively at Golitsyn. Krylov also looked at Golitsyn. The old man's tussore jacket hung loosely from his bony shoulders. Golitsyn had withered. He was all silvery and light, almost transparent. It would soon be a year since they had parted company. No one here knew how matters really stood between them.

Golitsyn said nothing. Lagunov, with Voznitsyn's support, then began trying to persuade Krylov that the project ought to be closed down. Voznitsyn hinted that if he gave his consent all would be well.

This solution would have suited everyone. It would be a case of a method turning out to be unsound. That was something quite natural to science, it had happened to lots of people. But what about the project? If that was abandoned, it would never be taken up again. Tulin would be left high and dry.

"Are you suggesting that this work should be continued?" Chirkayev asked. "You mean you want to go on flying? In spite of everything?"

His aggrieved astonishment brought Krylov up with a start, but he stuck stubbornly to his point.

"Yes, I do."

"But how can you? One man has been killed already and you expect us to turn a blind eye to that—never mind, chaps, what's one fatality, after all!" Chirkayev had gone red in the face and Krylov noticed the scars on his neck and cheeks that the beard could not altogether hide. "We didn't send a man into space until we were absolutely confident of his safe return."

Suddenly he saw himself in Chirkayev's eyes. Inhuman, doltish obstinacy, completely unwarranted, maintained blindly in the face of facts. Why should he, Krylov, be right and everyone else wrong?

He nudged Tulin. Couldn't he offer any help at all? After all, it was his work that was at stake.

"Stop kicking," Tulin muttered. "You won't get anywhere."

Later, when Golitsyn began to speak, he whispered to Krylov: "I know what I'm doing. You're only spoiling your chances."

If Tulin himself had nothing to say, why should the commission believe him? Who was Krylov in the eyes of people like Chirkayev or Yuzhin? He had a vision of Richard's face and heard him say: "Grown-up people understand so much they don't even have to believe in anything."

"You have my sympathy," Yuzhin said. "It's very difficult to admit mistakes, but there's no other way. Everything has to be paid for."

"But how?" Krylov asked. "I know we've got to pay. But the whole question is what with."

Yuzhin frowned.

"Suppose you have another crash? More deaths? Can you give us any proof, any guarantee that it can't happen?"

"No, we can't. I mean, there's bound to be a risk.... But it's quite a normal risk. Injuries occur in any factory." He scanned the faces of the commission, encountering nothing but hostile, disapproving glances. Only Golitsyn's face was pensive, almost melancholy. Krylov stepped towards him. He suddenly remembered all the good things that linked him with Golitsyn, and, through him, with Dan, and further back, with Anikeyev, and further still, with those unsuspecting years of youth, when everything had begun so well.

"Can't you see, there's no other way? We're taking a risk, but we're prepared to do it. You talk about Gagarin. Didn't Gagarin take a risk?"

Golitsyn rose slowly to his feet. Leaning on the table, he shuffled round it into the middle of the room.

"Sergei Ilyich, I have no doubt that you are prepared to offer yourself as a sacrifice, so to speak."

He glanced at the stenographer and she put her pencil aside.

"And you, of course, regard this as heroism! But I have grown tired of such sacrifices. There have been too many of them—cruel, unwarranted sacrifices. I have had enough. You hurl your reproaches at us, but in this case you speak with the voice of the past. Yes, in the old days they would have made you go on with the work regardless of sacrifice. Ten men, a hundred men might die, but that was of no consequence...."

"Yes, Krylov, you have adopted a Stalinist posture," Lagunov chimed in.

Golitsyn paused deliberately, then went on: "It would be quite easy for me, without any offence to my conscience, to join with those who demand that somebody should be punished for what has happened. But I refuse to oblige. I know that you were neither ill-intentioned nor negligent. Your distress at this moment is greater than ours. And when all is said and done, we are all, in some way, responsible for Richard's death. One man may be killed, but the responsibility lies upon many. So let us admit that we have sacrificed Richard. What have we gained by it? The need for more sacrifices? As if fresh risks and fresh graves could rehabilitate an idea. You, Oleg Nikolayevich, insisted on testing your detector under thunderstorm conditions. Now you have tested it. Your idea was a promising one, but through unnecessary haste you have compromised it for many years to come."

"Quite right," Lagunov interjected.

Golitsyn looked round at him in annoyance and his long thin arm flicked out from behind his back, like a rapier.

"I am afraid our commission attaches too much importance to the purely formal aspects. I am convinced that Krylov and"—his voice faltered, but he went on firmly—"and Tulin, too, have even in this inquiry proved themselves to be competent scientists. They must not be harassed for nothing." He gave Lagunov an icy stare. "This is not Denisov's kind of handiwork. It's on quite a different level. In those days we were accused of scepticism, pedantry, and it was Dankevich who had to bear the brunt of that battle. I am too old not to remember these things."

"Dankevich was a remarkable scientist," Lagunov affirmed cheerfully. "Your remarks, Arkady Borisovich, have touched us all." Lagunov was sitting at the head of the table. His large spectacles gleamed like headlights. "But perhaps you should have made them earlier, when Krylov was working for you and Goldin was one of your post-graduates. Your pupils. . . ."

"Heroism and sacrifice have nothing to do with this!" Krylov shouted, interrupting Lagunov. "It was simply an accident, and nothing more. Why don't you stick to the point? Discuss our project!" Perspiring and excited, regardless of the pain in his leg, he limped back and forth before the table, brandishing his stick absurdly and shouting challenges at Golitsyn. He was confident his opponent had no argument except authority. His nose, which had begun to peel, gleamed impudently. These bureaucrats! These officials! How dare they!

Golitsyn held back the flood of his own irritation with difficulty. Krylov appeared to have no interest in the moral side of the question. He was the only person present on whom Golitsyn's speech had made no impression. He was equally unaffected by Golitsyn's attitude, his chivalrous generosity. The last straw was Krylov's reference to the fact that Lomonosov, undaunted by the death of Richmann, had appealed for continuation of research into atmospheric electricity.

"We are no Lomonosovs, of course," Golitsyn retorted. "Nevertheless, if you insist, I am prepared to discuss essentials. . . ."

Dispassionately as an examiner conducting an examination, he asked question after question. No, quite wrong. . . . Where is the proof?. . . Could the detector have worked under such-and-such conditions? If not, what conditions could it work under? There were no grounds for that statement. . . . His logic, as usual, was impeccable. He drove Krylov into a corner because these were the very questions that Krylov himself had put to Tulin. How could Krylov explain the peaks on the graphs, when he himself had told Tulin that they weren't reliable?

Golitsyn opened his manuscript and read out his summing up. Where was the proof? How was one to understand. . . . Ambiguous terms of reference. . . .

Krylov twisted and turned, making stumbling efforts to defend himself, but these were death-throes. Golitsyn read on and on, suggesting hypotheses that it would have taken decades to disprove.

For Krylov the subject of this examination was his work; for Golitsyn and everyone else present it was a corpse, and Golitsyn was conducting an autopsy to test the accuracy of his findings.

Krylov went over to Tulin—now they were the sole survivors, hemmed in by enemies—and shook him by the shoulder. Tulin made no response. His shoulder was flabbily pliable. Krylov was standing behind his chair. From behind, Tulin looked just the same—fair hair growing down the back of his neck, immaculate white collar. But his face had changed. Had he merely changed or aged? Perhaps it was the same thing? Change is always in the direction of old age.

"We need time to go into this," Krylov said. "We shall prepare a written reply. I am sure that we. . . ."

"Who is 'we'?" Lagunov asked.

"Tulin, myself, and the rest of our group."

"How can you speak for them all? The group has a leader. What have you to say, Oleg Nikolayevich?"

Tulin crushed his cigarette into an ash-tray.

"Arkady Borisovich has presented us with formidable objections. Some of them are arguable, but the essential truth remains. One must have the courage to admit it." He spoke in an easy, almost casual tone, as if it were a matter of secondary importance that had long since been established beyond all doubt.

"But that's nonsense!" Krylov burst out. "What are we to admit? On the contrary, we must go on seeking. These aren't mere mistakes!" He stumped up to Golitsyn. "They're contradictions. We've got to find explanations for them. They hold the key to the whole process. I am sure. . . ."

"Sergei!" Tulin spoke patiently, like a father apologising for an obstreperous child. "We have no right to insist. Neither moral nor scientific. People who conceal their mistakes merely lay themselves open to new ones. I don't want to do that."

"That is both honest and reasonable," Lagunov said, almost joyfully. He was pursuing his goal with serene confidence that what he was doing was far more important than anything that Krylov, Tulin or the others had been engaged upon.

Krylov stared furiously at that large mouth with its stainless steel dentures. Yes, he had only himself to blame. He had failed to uphold his point of view, to stop Oleg chasing after results at any cost. He ought to have insisted on what he thought was essential. Yes, he was to blame for everything. Difficulties could be overcome, but there was no escaping responsibility for one's mistakes.

Now he was completely isolated. Just as Richard had been, left behind in the doomed aircraft. Had Richard been alive, they would have made a last stand together. But Richard was gone and there was no one to take his place.

"I'm afraid you have an exaggerated idea of your own part in this," Lagunov said urbanely. "We can't very well ignore Oleg Nikolayevich's opinion."

At such moments Lagunov waxed almost lyrical. He felt benevolent, he was so satisfied with life that he was prepared to console and sympathise and say all kinds of nice things.

Tulin had probably taken the wisest course. Under the circumstances it was pointless to resist any longer. Krylov realised this. He had no facts, no arguments, nothing with which to answer Golitsyn. By refusing to yield he was creating an impression of obstinacy and merely courting disapproval. He realised that he had lost any support he might have had from the way people were trying not to look at him. Voznitsyn and Lagunov seemed to have hidden their eyes somewhere. He was surrounded by eyeless faces. How often had Tulin told him to be flexible, to manoeuvre and play for advantage. All in vain. Krylov could make concessions but he had no idea how to retreat. He was like a car that would not go into reverse.

Golitsyn was sick at heart. He knew only too well where this zealotry would lead. Any idea, even the falsest, had its fanatics. He could picture Krylov's future from many similar cases. Endless sitting in waiting rooms, letters, reports written in the absurd hope of convincing and gaining support. A losing battle that made a man more and more embittered as fortune turned from bad to worse. He had seen more than enough of these luckless inventors, with their useless gadgets and false theories. They wasted years trying to refute and substantiate, making themselves the slaves of their own misconceptions, coming to see nothing but ignorance and intrigue all round them, making files of their correspondence, keeping copies of every letter.

If only he had known how to warn, to check this young mule!

Golitsyn was so taken up with these thoughts that he failed to notice that Krylov had suddenly adopted a different tone. There was something new and fresh in his voice, his face had cleared. He was calm, almost genial, and embarrassingly self-possessed.

Nor could any of the others understand what had come over Krylov. Only a moment ago he had been an absurd, embittered figure, driven into a corner, peering desperately through Golitsyn's notes, and everyone had known that there was no escape and he must surrender. But without relief Yuzhin had reflected that for a long time to come he would be spared any fresh responsibility for these young fanatics. And all of a sudden everything had changed. It was as if Krylov had discovered something that outweighed the significance of any decision that might be taken here.

"You can close down the project, if you like. No courage is required to take such a step. But I warn you that the time will come when you will feel ashamed of your decision." He glanced quickly at Tulin, as though to gain some assurance, then went on even more calmly: "We have made a lot of blunders, but we are working on the right lines. You have found certain mistakes, Arkady Borisovich, and you believe that this destroys the significance of our work. But I believe you have set us questions that we must answer. Someone will have to answer them eventually."

He was tolerant and kindly. He seemed to be addressing them from some future age, when the outcome of all that was taking place now would be known. He no longer felt alone. On the contrary, he was essential, and all the rest was mere accident. He felt himself free, free of Tulin, free of the fear of saying the wrong thing, of hindering or spoiling his work.

Through the window he could see the sky, white and shimmering in the heat. The young poplars on the boulevard were wilting and the parched earth boomed like a drum under the feet of the passers-by. Yet back in Staraya Russa, so his sister wrote, the fields were waterlogged and the potato crop was rotting because of incessant rains.

He was alone, but at least he could do what he really wanted to do.

Golitsyn requested that Krylov be given a few days to examine the commission's findings. When he had made a closer study of them he might be more prepared to yield.

"It is our duty to give Krylov this opportunity," he said, gallantly generous to the last.

His proposal was supported by Chirkayev. After hearing the opinion of all members of the commission, Lagunov said he was quite prepared to reopen the matter if any further facts in favour of the project emerged, but at the present stage, as chairman of the commission, he saw no alternative, in view of the majority's opinion, to closing down the project and all work on this line of research.

PART FOUR

Chapter One

His body was lying on the bed. The pain in his leg was as long and heavy as a railway track.

Yet neither the pain nor his body were a part of him. He seemed to be floating further and further away from them, floating away from Tulin, from the confusion of his own feelings, from the shambles left by the commission.

Why hadn't the detector worked? He reconstructed the circuit piece by piece, stage by stage in his mind until he could feel it as a man feels his own muscles. What exactly had each component been doing at the moment of the crash? He turned himself into a detector. He plunged into the cool dampness of the clouds. Lightning crackled round him. Charges built up on the plates and went through filtres. Valves picked up signals. Hundreds of resistances, condensers and coils filtered, rectified and amplified them, and it all ended in the movement of a needle. The whole complex mechanism existed and functioned solely for the sake of that slim little needle. So it was with the human organism—it lived solely in order to produce an idea, an action. Yet few people managed to live so purposefully, without fuss and distractions, needless talk and emotional strain. No, he mustn't think about Natasha. It was a good thing the consciousness could not split in two. While he was thinking about Golitsyn's questions, everything else ceased to exist. An ammeter is concerned only with the strength of the current; it reacts to nothing else.

All things considered, the detector ought to have worked.

Golitsyn's objections were serious and well argumented; they arranged everything into the neat categories of the correct and incorrect. The old man treated it all as a mere collection of facts, the bones of a skeleton. . . .

The door creaked.

"You asleep?"

Krylov closed his eyes. The light went on. Tulin stood for a moment in the doorway, then switched the light off again. Krylov heard him making his way across the room, bumping into chairs, pushing open the window.

"Well, the show went off with quite a bang, didn't it! Now they're all so nice and kind. Golitsyn is offering me a job at the institute. He'll take you on, too, if you ask him. They'll make quite a song about it. The return of the prodigal and all that. Even Lagunov is displaying his generosity. Yes, they're all great humanists. What kindness! What noble gestures!"

"Oleg, can you remember how the detector was earthed?"

Tulin burst out laughing.

"And so he worked on heroically, an example of perfect dedication to the cause! Here he stands before us, the ordinary Soviet man, backbone of the country!"

Krylov snapped his fingers.

"Suppose it was a double short circuit? What about that? Then there would be—just a minute—no, it doesn't work out." He opened his eyes disappointedly.

Tulin was sitting on the sofa with his fists pressed to his eyes. "Power failure—that's the only thing it could have been," Krylov said.

"It won't help us now."

"But it couldn't be anything else. I can prove it!"

"What for?"

The hollowness of that voice was unnerving.

"Well, then they'll have to reconsider. . . ."

"What for?" Tulin asked again in the same tone. "It'll make no difference, it won't change anything. The dead can't be resurrected. You and I are chained to a dead man for ever. No matter what you prove, they'll always point to Richard's grave." He swore despondently, without real anger. There was a bitter thought at the back of his mind and it kept nagging him. "Just suppose the detector had worked? At this moment you and I would be sitting in a luxury suite in Moscow writing up a report. Everything would be just the other way round. Tomorrow we'd be holding a conference, there'd be stenographers, reporters taking down every word we said. Agatov and Lagunov would be eating out of our hands, congratulating us. Yuzhin would be strutting around like a turkey-cock. Yes, I did the right thing when I decided to put my faith in you, Oleg Niko-layevich. Then the banquet, the bonuses, the trips abroad. . . . What a game of chance it all is! The whole rotten gang of them would be looking up to me as an authority, the man who was right from start to finish. What rotten bad luck! What did I do to deserve it? Just one absurd accident and the whole project ruined! Written off just like that. And what a project! For three years I worked like a slave. . . ."

"Oh, well, we've got to get over it somehow."

"We can always find the strength to get over other people's troubles!" Tulin leaned back and pulled a sweet out of his pocket. "Want one? When I cried as a little boy, my mother used to pop sweets in my mouth. Now I have to pop 'em in myself."

"Did you agree to work for Golitsyn?"

Tulin tossed him a sweet. Krylov didn't want it but for some reason felt unable to refuse. The warm, squashed sweet was sickening.

"If you work for him, you'll be doing the very things you made fun of," Krylov said. "That's no good."

"Can you tell me what is 'good'? And what is 'bad'?"

"You simply have no right to act like that."

"For God's sake, stop bawling at me. How people love bawling!" He kicked off his shoes and began peeling off his shirt.

"You think only of yourself," Krylov said quietly.

A lazy chuckle came from under the shirt.

"Maybe I was thinking only of you."

"How do you mean?"

The shirt went flying on to a chair. Tulin drew off his slacks and stretched himself till his bones cracked.

"Did you think they were just having fun and games with you? They might have got you on a damn serious charge for a crash like that. And you'd have stood trial all by yourself. But I had my own little axe to grind. As soon as I thought of myself having to take you parcels all the time you were in gaol, I said to myself, 'No, gentlemen, Krylov is my friend, and as there's not much sign of the truth anywhere, you had better shut up our little shop for us.'" He was clowning. His body gleamed greenishly in the faint light of the moon. "Yes, it was all for your sake."

Krylov swung his feet to the ground and sat up.

"You needn't make me an excuse. Stay here and work if you want to, I'm quite ready to stand trial. They can charge me with negligence if they like, but there's nothing wrong with the project."

Something had happened. Their eyes were invisible in the gloom but both men were looking where the other's eyes should have been. Tulin suddenly felt he was making a fool of himself but, shaking off the feeling, he went on sarcastically:

"Aren't you a dear little angel!"

"All right, I know you're going through the mill just now. You'll feel better when you've had a rest," Krylov said.

Tulin got into bed and pulled up the bed-clothes.

"You know, it's all perfectly logical," he said thoughtfully. "While I was doing well, you were friendly and respected me, as everyone respects people who do well. Add to that the fact that you needed me and I always did everything I could for you. But now? As soon as a man falls from the saddle, he's worse than the dirt. When a man's down he gets kicked, and the people who kick him hardest are those who worshipped him most before."

"I've got a bad leg," Krylov said. "Otherwise I'd push your face in."

Tulin placed his hands behind his head.

"I've had some of that already. On the cheek. You can add some more, if you like. It's so easy hitting a man when he's down."

"Oh, drop it," Krylov said with an effort. "I know you've got more to put up with than I have." It suddenly occurred to him that this might really be the case. "It's all a lot of rot anyway. Let them do what they like. Anything rather than see you in this state."

Tulin laughed sarcastically.

"You don't really suppose I couldn't have found a way out if I had really wanted to?"

"Well, why didn't you?"

"I don't want to!"

"What's wrong, Oleg?"

Tulin was silent for a while, then asked with genuine curiosity: "Look here, what's all this to you anyway?"

"I don't see what you mean."

"Well, what are you making all this fuss for? Why should you?"

"Because it's all so unjust and besides—there's a job to be done. I want to know the answers."

"Ah, so it's unjust, is it?" Tulin snapped. "What a lover of truth and justice! Well, I'm fed up. I've had enough. We sweat our guts out, we struggle with all kinds of moral problems, and who reaps the benefit? The Agatovs. See what a good thing he's made for himself out of our crash. And Lagunov. We have lofty ideals, we give ourselves hell, we want to benefit humanity, and they just make their career by coming here to pronounce judgement on us. The Lagunovs will always be on top whether we achieve our aim or not. They'll live happy and contented. They won't feel any pricks of conscience because of their selfishness, their lack of principle, or what have you."

"But I'm not really concerned about them." Krylov sighed despondently. "That's not what I was talking to you about. They can go to blazes for all I care."

"Look here, you young nature-lover, I'm tired of listening to you. I want to go to sleep."

The mattress creaked and in the silence that followed the buzzing of cicadas could be heard from the window.

"We'll see how you explain all this to the others," Krylov said.

"So it's come to this! You're threatening me! If you want to know, I'll just refer them to what the commission said. Our dear, darling commission has banned the whole show. And in any case our people all realise we've got to knuckle under."

"I'm not knuckling under."

"Oh, aren't you?" Tulin whistled and sat up in bed. Krylov saw the white blur of his face. "And who are you? But, of course—you're the great prophet! You foretold all this, you exposed me. Golitsyn himself has confirmed your criticism. So you, too, have the right to preach at me. You're prepared to go on with the work without me, are you? You'd even like to step into my shoes? You think you're entitled to? Well, listen to me. I've spared you up to now, but I can open your eyes for you. You're a failure. Why the hell I ever had anything to do with you, I don't know. Failure is infectious. . . .

If it hadn't been for you, the flight would have gone off perfectly. Everyone knows that. It was your fault that Agatov was sent here. Remember what I told you in Moscow? I knew it would happen. So you needn't preach at me! He hasn't knuckled under! How brave! You've simply got nothing to lose, that's all your bravery amounts to." Tulin lowered his voice unexpectedly to a whisper. "And who prevented Richard from being sent away? You did! I agreed to pack him off but you kept him here. It's been your fault all along. Not mine but yours. If you hadn't interfered, he'd be alive today."

The moon peeped in. The whitewashed walls acquired a greenish tint and the floor seemed to quiver with uncertain shadows. There was a suitcase on the top of the wardrobe and its nickel fastenings gleamed. So did a hairy cactus on the window-sill and the white linen tablecloth. It was all very beautiful, like a scene in the theatre.

Krylov went out into the corridor, which smelt of the lavatory. He stood for a while on the steps of the porch. They were cold and he realised he was wearing only his socks. He went back to his room and got into bed.

Had the detector been properly earthed? It didn't matter now. It might have been or it might not.

That sweet had been sickly and, when he spoke, his own voice seemed equally so.

"All right, enough said. We'll have to think about Golitsyn's objections. I'm afraid I won't manage it alone—not enough phosphorus." He took a deep breath, hating himself for playing up to Tulin. "He's got to be answered, after all. Why get het up with me about it? I'm only doing my best."

He coaxed him regardless of pride. He refused to think about himself, about what Tulin had said, but he was no longer sorry for Tulin. Now Tulin was merely somebody to be made use of, just a brain to pick.

For a moment he thought he had succeeded. They began to discuss possible reasons why none of their recordings had shown any actual storm centres.

"No, I can't go on," Tulin said suddenly. "I can't have anything more to do with it. I keep imagining how the whole thing will be bandied round Moscow."

Krylov went on reasoning aloud, but Tulin was not listening.

"No, I've got to take up something quite different. If only I could check the whole thing. Tell me, why should anyone want to destroy thunderclouds? Why try to invent things? Why make this detector?"

Krylov suddenly smiled.

"Now what?" Tulin asked, sensing the invisible quizzical smile in Krylov's silence. "But I don't need your explanations anyway. No one can explain anything, nothing has any meaning at all. Let's have a smoke."

"All right."

They stood by the window. Tulin struck a match and held it for Krylov, peering closely into his eyes. He had never seen Krylov's eyes so steady and impenetrable; they were the eyes of a complete stranger. A tiny flame seemed to burn and leap in the blackness of his pupils.

"No, there's no meaning in anything," Tulin repeated challengingly. "And one ought to live a meaningless existence. All right, I'll work for Golitsyn if I have to. What's the difference! I'll live like other people, I don't want to have any more ideas. Suppose I did build another detector? Suppose I found out that storm centres occur purely by chance? What difference would it make?"

"Who to?"

"To Richard's mother, for one. No, I don't want any more risks or sacrifices. Golitsyn was right. None of us live twice. I've got to find something quick and effective. I've got to make up for lost time. And don't flatter yourself that you're an exception. When all this hullabaloo has died down, we'll see what can be done."

"No, I can't leave it like this," Krylov said. "I must try to get to the bottom of it."

"By yourself?"

"Yes."

"You think you'll manage it?" There was amusement in Tulin's voice.

"I don't know. But I am going to try."

"Well, go ahead. It's only to my advantage."

"But what about your dream of breaking up thunderclouds, controlling storms, flying in turbulence, using the power of lightning?"

"You're the virtuous one, you'd better carry on with your good deeds. But I can tell you in advance, with a set of morals like yours you'll never get anywhere. What's the sense in being good, if good people get it in the neck? They always come off worst. You, for instance, stick to your lofty standards, and what's the result? What have you achieved? You merely make it easier for the scoundrels to get on top."

"But at least I don't compromise."

"Our whole life is a compromise," Tulin insisted. "We can never be completely honest or do what we like."

"I don't know what sense there is in being good. But isn't there some sense in being a man? If you've got to live, you might as well live like a man and not like a caterpillar. I don't know whether that's being good for yourself or for other people. I don't refuse to fight, and I'm going to fight honestly. If I myself use dirty methods, I shan't be fighting scoundrels, I'll just be fighting for a place among them."

... There was no end to the things he had done for Krylov. It had started when they were students. After that he had helped him to get a job at the factory, then at the laboratory. He had helped him to smooth over his tiffs with Lena, made him write a thesis, lent him money. He had kept him amused, encouraged him when he was down, got him a job on this project after he had quarrelled with Golitsyn. In their friendship the giving had been all on one side. And now, when he, Tulin, had run into trouble for the first time, he was full of accusations. Tulin had defended him before the commission, and he.... What a terrible thing ingratitude was, the unkindest cut of all. Surely after this he would learn to turn his back on everyone else and think only of himself?

How quickly everything had collapsed! One blow had been enough. Only a little while ago he had been a promising young physicist, head of an important project. He had had friends, admirers, Zhenya. He had enjoyed prestige, authority. And now it had all vanished. He had no work, no friends, no future. Now people could see only his mistakes. Defeat had laid them bare. Yet had there been victory, all Krylov's doubts and demands would have dissolved in its radiance.

Defeat had engulfed everything. No one wanted to salvage from the ruins that brilliant little circuit he had thought up for a data unit, the instruments he had so cleverly assembled. And what of the nights spent in poring over calculations, his fingers, yellow and cracked with acid?

He passed his hand cautiously over his cheek and the skin at once began to tingle. Strange to think that this was the first time he had really let himself go for years, and yet she had been able to reject him with such ease. But why should anyone love him now? Sergei had been his last refuge, his last stronghold, all that he had left from the past.

Talent was to blame for it all. Talented people always came off badly. If you were a dullard, no one envied you, no one expected anything of you. Zhenya would have been sorry for him, Sergei would not have been disillusioned. The trouble was that he had not lived up to their expectations. But let them wait. Everything might still take a turn for the better.

... And this was the man Krylov had followed without a moment's hesitation. For Tulin's sake he had broken with Golitsyn, given up the laboratory, left his work unfinished. He had pardoned his weaknesses, stood up for him against all comers. Yes, he would have sacrificed a lot for Tulin. He had been proud of him—Tulin, his friend, Oleg Tulin.

If Tulin had been just a windbag it would have been understandable, but he had talent. Why, then, was he so keen on success, recognition, fame, and all the other trash that the Agatovs longed for, and that the Lagunovs clung to? Why should a man like him let himself slide? But he hadn't. He was just tired, hurt, he needed a rest.... So again he was seeking excuses for him. Tulin could do that for himself, he had plenty of fine-sounding excuses.

Such things always came as a surprise. Even Lagunov had once been a competent electrical engineer. He had written several quite sound articles. But after that he had been made head of a department, chairman of a committee. He had learned to make speeches, to fulminate against this and that, and so it had gone on. The works of post-graduates appeared over his signature, then it was nothing but pamphlets and interviews: "My Impressions of the Congress in Britain", "A Reply to Mr. Weinberg", and so on. Moves were afoot to get him elected a Corresponding Member of the Academy.

But that was Lagunov, not Oleg, his Oleg. The old flat on the Fontanka, those all-night arguments, the sailing trip along the Vuoksa, the way he had wept after Dan's funeral, his keenness to go to Novosibirsk. What had happened? When had they drifted apart?

Suddenly he realised that this was the parting of their ways. They had quarrelled before, many times before, but it had been quite different. Even now they could have burst out laughing, slapped each other on the back, and had a drink to take the taste away. There was still a bottle of Riesling in the wardrobe. But where would that get them? The trouble would crop up again and they would always come back to the same crossroads. And there, eventually, they would have to part.

Krylov told himself he was to blame. There should be no submission in friendship. He had been ready to compromise in order to preserve their friendship. So how could he reproach Tulin for compromising? He was losing his last friend, the best thing left to him of youth. This could never be put right, never be retracted. They would part, there was nothing for it. But this is Oleg, he told himself. Think of the things that bind us together. He'll be all right, but I'll be lost without him.

"Sergei!" That cheeky voice seemed to reach him from the depths of the past, as though nothing had occurred. "Sergei, I completely forgot. I saw your Natasha the other day."

"Where?"

But when he heard the answer, he replied quite calmly:

"I know. She rang me up."

Chapter Two

At the turns the beam from the headlights leapt the black depths of the gorge and flashed on the green bluffs of the opposite bank. The road swooped away into the darkness till the headlights caught it again, snaking between the yellow spurs of sandstone. Krylov stood in the back of the lorry, trying to spot the kilometre posts as they flashed by. His eyes were streaming in the wind. He was thinking of nothing, imagining nothing, building no plans. He felt nothing but feverish impatience. It had been easier to bear a year's separation than to wait till the end of this hour's journey. They rumbled lurching over bridges. The engine roared as they climbed through the clinging warmth of woods into the blustering winds at the top of the passes. Then a swift silent descent, scattered lights in the valley, and beyond them the faint glimmer of the sea, the white resort buildings, and the shimmering haze of light over the town. And soon there were street lamps, the barking of dogs, a noisy drive through the deserted streets, a hotel door, much knocking, a porter's sleepy face pressed to the glass. Krylov went on ringing and knocking until he opened the door.

"What's all the row about?" the porter said. "There's no room. Not even a bed."

He was in his vest and trousers, with his braces dangling—a little domesticated old man. Only his voice was stern.

"I want to see Romanova."

"No one of that name here."

"She's my wife."

"Is that so? Did you know it's three o'clock in the morning?" the porter asked argumentatively.

"Please help me."

The porter yawned.

"You'll get ten days for disturbing the peace."

Krylov pulled out of his pocket an invitation card to a French exhibition and said in English:

"I think you will like me better then."

"Ah, why didn't you say so before? *Bitte.* We have an Intourist room. I'll wake the manager. *Bitte.*"

The drowsy manager passed him on bewilderedly to a maid, who led him down a long, dark corridor. There was more knocking, then whispering and rustling. Krylov read and reread the hotel rules pasted up on the wall.

When he saw Natasha he could not even smile. His lips stiffened and not a single muscle in his face would obey him. Natasha stood clutching the collar of her dressing gown in fright. The light made her screw up her eyes, and when she opened them, Krylov caught the gleam, which died a second later.

"What's happened? What's wrong with your leg?" She asked and looked round at the maid.

For some reason he nodded.

"So you know him," the maid said. "He understands Russian but he can't say anything."

"Just a minute, I'll put my clothes on," Natasha said.

In the orchards behind the low sandstone walls apples were falling. The muffled tapping came from all sides, like invisible drummers beating an alert in the darkness, as they climbed the steep crooked street to the square.

Krylov told her about the journey and how he had argued with the porter, then he told her about the crash and his quarrel with Tulin, then he started again about the journey, about the hotel in Rostov and about Richard's death. He couldn't stop talking. But it was better while he talked because, when he did pause for a moment, the silence was unnerving.

This sturdy, business-like woman was nothing like the Natasha of his dreams. She didn't even speak the same. The same weather-cock on the roof, the same house, but there were different people living there. That strange checked windcheater, the cloth sandals, the dress; even her lips were oddly big and dark. Only her hair, straight and heavy, was like it had been. He reflected miserably that he might not have recognised her in a crowd.

Up to now he had thought all would be well as soon as they met; the rest would sort itself out. He had been sure he would find her, but she had known nothing of this and had lived in the belief that it was all over between them.

He had been prepared to defend himself but she had no reproaches to make. It was just the way things had turned out. They had both been a bit silly. People often were.

In the square stood a seamen's memorial—the bows of a ship mounted on bronze waves. They sat on a bench facing the sea, and watching the greenish darkness growing lighter. On one side rose the black hump of headland. Occasionally it was lighted by faint, glimmering flashes, as though an electric welder were at work somewhere below the horizon.

It was all very simple. A year had passed and the old feelings were buried under it. Krylov had no part in her present life. He had become the same for her as Ozernaya Village and Alexei—a sad, perhaps even annoying memory.

"I did everything I could to forget you, and I forgot you," she said.

What did it matter whether she was now in love with somebody else. It would have been pointless to ask. But why had she telephoned?

"Just an impulse. I expect I still love you in a way." Her voice was calm and amiable. "Sparks from an extinct volcano."

There was no bitterness in her joke. She was no more affected than if they had been discussing friends. He wondered why he was listening to her so calmly, why he didn't shout and weep, why the world didn't collapse, why it was so quiet all round, with only the apples falling in the orchards.

Quite calmly she told him how she had left her husband. After Krylov had gone, she realised that she didn't love Alexei any more, but she had kept up a pretence in order to save the family. Eventually it had become too much for her and she had told Alexei the truth. Then he had begun pretending too, in order to save the family. For their son's sake. In the presence of strangers or of Kolya they smiled and talked to each other. But one evening when she was putting Kolya to bed, he had asked her: "Why don't you love Daddy?" She had denied it and assured him that they both loved each other very much. Kolya had turned away and pretended to fall asleep. She had realised that her own child saw through them. In a year or two he would learn to pretend for the sake of the family. They would all three be trying to preserve a family that no longer existed. It was then that she had decided to go away because what they were doing for the child was really against him, because a life of lies and deceit would harm him far more than not having a father.

Her story was restrained but he could imagine those days and nights in the big silent flat, and the evenings, when guests arrived, the noisy conversation, the tea, the pretence of a happy, well-regulated family. He remembered that before he left he, too, had discoursed to her about thinking of her family. He had lied both to her and himself. Now it had turned out to be all one big lie. Lies could pile up one on top of the other until they engulfed you.

"And so you drove off in a black Volga."

"What Volga?"

She drew back and looked at him as though she hadn't quite heard what he had said. Her eyes were big with surprise, like two billowing grey clouds.

"Why, you're just like that portrait of you!"

"So you did come back?"

She paused, laughed quietly to herself and again lapsed into a long silence.

"Did you go to the refreshment room?" she asked.

"Yes. I fed Pashka on cucumbers. . . ."

She sighed. They lingered affectionately over their past.

"What now?" he asked.

She turned away and was a long time powdering her face.

"What now?" he repeated.

She shrugged.

The striped beacon on the tip of the headland flashed red for the last time and went out. The breeze dropped. The houses with their open windows emerged peacefully from the darkness.

Krylov bent forward and buried his face in his hands.

"Never mind," Natasha said. "You lived a whole year without me." She stroked his hand to console him. It would have been better if she hadn't.

The knot of tension inside him that had grown so tight over the last few days was drawn tighter by her touch. Everything he had closed his mind to—Richard, Oleg, the commission, Golitsyn—now took ruthless possession of him. He had a sudden vision of the year he had spent without her, of the towns where he had patiently scanned the faces of the passers-by, hoping to meet her. He had grown used to seeking her because he had been sure they would one day run into each other in the street, that he would spot her from a distance and run towards her, and that there would be no need for explanations because she would know everything already. But perhaps he had simply made himself believe in this beautiful dream? After Natasha's phone call he had sensed that things were not quite as he had pictured them. Now he knew they had become complete strangers. It was something that could not be put right and she was in no way to blame. He felt only pain and shame for having accepted it so easily. He wished she would go away.

"Don't take it like that, Sergei, dear," he heard her voice. "It'll pass. It may all be for the best. Such things can't be mended." She talked to him as if he were a child who knew nothing of real pain and real trouble.

They walked down the crooked street to the hotel. His stick scraped in the sand. They stared at the patch of sea between the houses. Something there was fading and something else was growing brighter as though someone kept scraping off the colours and applying others. And suddenly the colours came right and a crimson eye peeped out over the horizon between the headland and a bank of cloud. It seemed to look round to reassure itself, then began to climb the sky, sweeping away the rest of the shadows with broad scarlet blades of light.

"So that's that," Krylov said. "I thought you would understand everything. There must be somebody somewhere who understands."

"It's a pity it's happened just now, when you have trouble enough already," Natasha said. It was light now and he could see the tiredness in her face.

They reached the hotel. He gripped her hand.

"Listen," he said. "Perhaps we're being silly. I won't let you go. Come back with me now."

She shook her head slowly and smiled in a way that made him want to strike her.

"You're too late," she said. "Much too late."

Krylov released her hand.

"I've been making mistakes all my life. Oleg told me it was my fault Richard was killed. They think the whole thing was my fault. I was wrong about Dan. Now I've ruined everything there was between us. Oleg is giving me up. Why do I keep making mistakes? I feel one thing and do something different."

He told himself he was talking rubbish, he must be in a very bad state.

He had got to act like a man. He couldn't strike her or break down and start crying. He had got to be a man. That was the only thing left for him to be.

"It's strange," Natasha said. "But I remember only the good things now."

She yawned, covering her mouth with her hand. They stood for a time at the door and talked in quite a different vein of various things, of her work, his work. He said he would convince Golitsyn, prove it to him, and, sooner or later, the flights would be resumed. Natasha asked whether it was dangerous. He thought for a moment and said there was, of course, a certain degree of risk.

The street was light and empty. At such an early hour, until the people and cars appear streets seem very wide. He walked to a bus-stop. He must hurry. He must work. The commission would soon be leaving. He must work, find a solution, answer Golitsyn's questions, then go on working. It was his job to work, and work hard, to measure and calculate. There was nothing else he was any good at.

Chapter Three

The general sympathy for Tulin increased when it became known that Krylov had turned against him. Krylov, the chief culprit! His round sunburnt face showed no signs of a stricken conscience. "But just look at Tulin!" Vera Matveyevna exclaimed. "How haggard he looks!" How terrible for Tulin to have lost everything, and for no reason at all. Tulin, who was least of all to blame, had lost most. Yet he had been taking it so well, with such courage, and now here was Krylov leaving him in the lurch. That was friendship for you!

To Zhenya it seemed that the same reproaches were being levelled at her. Was it not she who had wronged Richard more than anyone else? And now she dared to treat Tulin like this. She could find no excuse for herself. She must apologise to him. She was ready to do anything to gain his forgiveness. But even that would not be enough, she must try to help him.

They were walking along the river.

Fish were leaping in the rapids. A long silvery shape would flick out of the foaming green like a knife, then return to its sheath.

"Are they trout?" Zhenya asked.

"Probably."

"Can you catch them with a spinner? Have you ever done any spinning?"

"No, I haven't even fished with an ordinary hook and line," Tulin said. "I've never had time to go fishing or hunting, or to play skittles."

She listened miserably while he mocked himself; he was so defenceless, tired, lost.

"You need a rest."

"It would also do me good to start collecting stamps, matchbox-tops and badges. Or perhaps I ought to take up embroidery, eh?"

Zhenya felt utterly helpless and foolish.

"What's all this in aid of?" Tulin said.

"Oh, look—a blackthorn! Do you like sloe berries? They're nice. I wonder if this is what they used to make the crown of thorns out of?"

"What's all this in aid of?"

"I can't bear to see you like this."

He looked down at her.

"You don't look as if it were doing you any harm."

She flushed hotly.

"You can't be harsher with me than I've been to myself."

"Of course, people like me aren't worth getting angry with."

"Let's sit down," Zhenya said. "I've got out of the habit of walking in high heels."

They sat down on the soft, crumbling trunk of a fallen elm. Zhenya kicked off her shoes.

Tulin watched her small bare feet sink timidly into the grass. Her firm sunburnt calves were scratched like a boy's.

"By the way...." He smiled bitterly at his own way of bringing up the subject. "There's something you ought to remember, my dear. Before the commission I stated that I had no feelings for you whatever, and you had none for me, and there had never been anything between us."

He stared hard at her and she tried to smile.

"So what?"

"We shall have to live up to my statement. Wisdom always lies in recanting at the right moment."

"I don't care a damn for them," she said. "I'm my own mistress."

"What about public opinion? The principle of the thing? What will they say about you?"

"Is there anyone in the world who isn't gossiped about?"

Tulin bent down, plucked a blade of grass that had been touching her feet, and bit the end of it.

"Let's give up pretending," he said. "You're quite entitled to call me a scoundrel because I richly deserve it. And anyhow, there's no point in your getting involved with me now."

"Aren't you ashamed of yourself!" Her voice was trembling. "Oh, you shouldn't! You mustn't run yourself down like this!"

The blade of grass was bitter and its bitterness filled his mouth. He frowned and spat it out, then took Zhenya in his arms. Her lips parted and the whiteness of her teeth lit up her face.

He gave her a long, searching look.

"You're glorious." He kissed her carefully on the cheek, then on the lips. "All right, I'm sorry. Please, forgive."

The brown depths of her eyes grew lighter and lighter, but they were focussed on something far away. There was a look of pity in them he found unpleasantly familiar. Suddenly he remembered that he had seen exactly the same expression in her eyes when they had lain together on the beach, talking of Richard.

He released her.

"What are you thinking about at this moment?"

She looked at him thoughtfully, as if returning to his presence. "Don't ask."

"No, I will ask," he said harshly. "You were thinking of him. We are both thinking of him. The moment you look at me you remember him." He stood up, clenching his fists.

She gripped his sleeve and made him sit down.

"Now listen. Get all that out of your head. Once and for all. I am more to blame than you are. More to blame than anyone. You had nothing to do with it. So don't interfere."

He eyed her suspiciously.

"Do you really believe I had nothing to do with it?"

"Absolutely," she said. "It's just your nerves."

She rose and walked through the grass, lifting her feet high. "If only we could always go about barefoot...."

"Yes," he said. "We must get away from here as soon as possible. I'll meet you in Moscow."

"... and live in the mountains." She stood, her face uplifted to the sun, her eyes closed, paying no attention to what he was saying. "These rocks look as if they'd been here ever since the world began. It's like seeing the planet in its natural state. In a place like this you could start life all over again. Aren't you sorry to be leaving?" She came up and squatted in front of him. "Oleshka"—it was the first time she had addressed him so tenderly—"we mustn't run away from here. Specially you. It would be a retreat. If you just drop everything...." She hesitated, then went on firmly: "Then you really will have killed Richard."

"Him again!"

"You must help Krylov."

"Your Krylov is just an idiot. Even Golitsyn managed to prove that." With a kind of gloating pleasure he began expounding Golitsyn's calculations to her.

At a loss for a reply, she said: "But can't you think up something?"

"I don't want to think up anything." He couldn't understand why he was so furious. "What can I think up? Why should I? What difference will it make? Why should it be my duty to think things up?" He seized her hands and crushed them painfully in his own. "So you really think it's all my fault! But do you want to know who is to blame? Do you really want to know?" he shouted. "You yourself! You and Krylov! Yes, you're to blame as well. It was because of you that I wasn't on that flight."

She tore herself free and stood up, picking up her shoes.

"All right, let it be because of me," she said, straightening her dress. "Does that suit you? I can take it."

The grass rose slowly in her wake. Her pink frock gleamed among the tall red larches.

"Hi!" he cried. "Off side! That was against the rules!"

He caught up with her.

"That's a convenient way of dismissing the subject," he said derisively. "But if you don't mind, we'll get things straight." He would not stop clowning. Eventually he took her elbow.

She would never again be able to find the way to that sunny hillock wedged in between overhanging cliffs, but she would always remember the spot, the light-green moss on the grey boulders, the hot, windless stillness, the bright purple harebells. . . .

They had reached it by devious paths. There had been a long, pointless conversation and she saw that Tulin was at the end of his tether. When he laughed, the corners of his mouth creased, almost like an old man's.

He went on talking and talking, but she lost the thread of his feverish, muddled thoughts.

He was lying in the grass and the tall harebells swayed over his head. Zhenya put her hand on his forehead. He closed his eyes, but suddenly moved away and said: "Richard is dead. He no longer exists. I can't do anything about that. Why do you want him always to stand between us? Why?"

She leaned over him.

"I don't know what's best. I'm only thinking of you," she said quite honestly.

She despised herself for saying it, but she really wanted to help him.

He gripped her shoulders.

"Oh, it's all nonsense really. . . ." He turned away and looked at the grey wall of rock. "Don't leave me!"

Still looking away, he embraced her, and she felt her shoulders growing weak. The air became very hot. And suddenly she realised that he had said the one thing that really mattered to her.

"I can still see him," Tulin muttered.

"Even now?" She lay down and pressed very close to him, looking into his eyes with fear and a desperate determination.

The jagged grey spurs of rock reared skywards like towers and the black fir-trees also looked as if they belonged to some ancient fairy-tale. And then the huge purple bells began to ring, as this magic land floated gently away into the soft grey blueness of the sky.

She wanted to stay in this place for ever. It seemed such a pity, so unnecessary, to leave it.

Everything had become tiny—the houses, the people, and all the worries of the past. Zhenya was striding across mountains and the sun was perched on her shoulder.

The men looked at her in a way that made her feel her breasts high under her dress.

"The way you walk!" Katya said suspiciously.

"What about it?"

"As if you were in a fashion parade."

Zhenya sighed innocently: "It's these high heels."

She was astonished at the power of her own feelings. It was a discovery. She was sure Tulin must feel the same and she never tired of asking him why he loved her, how he loved her, and how it had suddenly come over him, as though what he said would help her to probe the mysteries of her own heart.

And suddenly the whole picture had been ruined.

It was Katya who started it. That morning, as she watched Zhenya doing her hair, she asked the question she had been longing to ask: "Are you sure he's serious about you?"

Zhenya was sitting in her nightdress in front of the open window. The cool, fresh air played on her skin like soda water. It seemed to fill her nightdress, her body, until she felt as light as a balloon and a mere tap would be enough to send her floating away.

"Do you think he'll marry you?"

Zhenya laughed quietly.

"What does that matter?"

"You're rushing headlong towards disaster!"

Zhenya had always been amused by Katya's odd combination of sober reason and high-flown imagery. Of the girls in her year Katya had been considered the steadiest. She lived according to a strict timetable. Even when she went to the cinema it had to be the nine o'clock show, and no other. Tulin's behaviour had aroused Katya's mistrust. Obviously he had no intention of marrying Zhenya, particularly as she was being so silly about things, running after him like this. How could she behave with so little thought for the future?

"Don't you realise he has too many things on his mind just now?"

"He finds time for necking with you, doesn't he? Mark my words, men have no respect for women that throw themselves at them. They think that relieves them of all responsibility. You'd better keep away, if you want to get anything out of him except a baby."

By her own standards Katya was right and it was no use arguing with her.

"All this calculating common sense of yours," Zhenya said. "I can't be like that. You've got your whole life computed in advance."

She looked at herself in the glass. "What's a cameo? He told me I had a profile like a cameo."

"Yes, I have to be calculating," Katya said. "I haven't got your looks. I'm no cameo. And my father isn't an engineer either. I'd have got nowhere without will-power. You know very well that with a stomach like mine I have to be regular in everything." She swallowed her tears crossly. "My life's just one long diet."

Zhenya repentantly covered her with kisses and began doing her hair for her. Katya had rather a nice face, but it just didn't fit her character. It would have suited a sweet, featherbrained little typist, but on Katya it looked like a school frock on a grown-up woman.

But there was no putting Katya off the subject. She never left anything unfinished. At best, Tulin would turn Zhenya into a housewife. He was much too selfish to consider others. In this day and age one couldn't just obey one's feelings. One must think of the future.

"It looks as if my vocation in life is to be a nurse to others. You must be careful. He just doesn't need anyone, neither you nor anyone else."

It was that remark that really stung Zhenya.

Crash or no crash, the students had to get on with their practicals, hand in their reports, and prepare for their degrees. So once again the electric motors began to buzz and the rectifiers resumed their cheerful crackling. In the lunch-hour they would send someone off to buy peaches and go bathing, and Lisitsky quietly removed a couple of valves from the apparatus on which Richard had been working.

That morning Agatov held a conference to discuss the students' practical work. Tulin was present and Lagunov came in later.

Alyosha asked why the project was being closed down. Agatov chuckled.

"That has nothing to do with the matter in hand."

But Lagunov embarked on an explanation. He spoke to Alyosha in the confiding I'm-one-of-you tone that he considered essential when talking to the young generation. Soon they were in the middle of an edifying discussion about science and the character of the scientist. It was the kind of phrase-spinning that Zhenya could not stand. Lagunov said that in Stalin's time the work on the project would have been continued no matter how many lives it cost. "Or if they had closed it down, they'd have put the lot of you in gaol for sabotage. That's so, isn't it?" he added, turning to Tulin for confirmation.

Tulin nodded.

"You people don't appreciate the new age you are living in," Lagunov went on fatuously.

"What is there to appreciate in the fact that we're not arrested? That's just a normal state of affairs," Alyosha argued.

"Thank you very much." Katya bowed to him ironically. "We should all be very grateful to you, I suppose, for having achieved that."

But Alyosha was in a fighting mood. Since the crash he had begun to remind Zhenya in some respects of Richard. He would argue and get himself involved in things with a belligerence that he had previously ridiculed in Richard.

Agatov replied with a tirade against these young people nowadays who had things so easy, who had never been in a war. All this democracy was bad for them.

Tulin merely smiled absently and said nothing, but it was too much for Zhenya.

"Perhaps somebody ought to start a war to improve our education?"

Agatov whispered something to Lagunov. They both sniffed sarcastically and Lagunov stared at her curiously.

"If I were in your position I would be a little less coy?" Agatov told her.

Tulin heard what he had said but didn't stir a muscle. As if he were afraid to say a word. Alyosha went on arguing with Lagunov. "All right, but what about 'thirty-seven? How could you allow that to happen?" But Zhenya had suddenly lost all interest.

Fate had more than one blow in store for her. While she was working in the laboratory she stumbled over a crate and tore one of her new stockings. Quivering with vexation, she began to dismantle a circuit and jerked one of the wires so violently that it snapped. Agatov noticed it, of course, and made a fuss. But Zhenya returned in kind.

"What does a wire matter anyway! You've no consideration for people. Something terrible may have happened to me for all you care!"

Agatov was taken aback. What could have happened to her? Zhenya pulled up her skirt and lifted her leg under Agatov's nose.

"I've torn my stocking. Have you ever worn kapron stockings?"

Vera Matveyevna shouted at her to apologise at once.

"All right," Zhenya said and burst into tears.

Vera Matveyevna took her under her wing like a sitting hen and marched her off to her corner of the laboratory, where she produced some darning materials in a little leather case.

"Your Tulin's a coward!" Zhenya told her. "He's just an egotist."

Vera Matveyevna showed her how to stop the ladder, then said to her: "We women, are inclined to overestimate our worth. We can give a man a lot, but not all by any means."

There was neither envy nor jealousy in her words. It was something of which Zhenya had no understanding, something women acquired when they were over forty and could speak calmly of men and their ways.

"I once read my son the story of the Sleeping Beauty," Vera Matveyevna went on. "When I came to the end he wanted to know what happened afterwards. So I told him they got married. And what happened after that? Well, what could I say that he would find interesting? I don't suppose that prince had much of a life. She probably turned out to be a quarrelsome, backward sort of creature. After being asleep all that time! The good part of it was while he was trying to reach the castle."

Tulin was casually affectionate. It was quite clear that he had no time for anyone, including Zhenya and her love. She caught herself admiring his hands. That horrified her. So to crown everything, she was a loose, immoral woman. She had sunk to the level of those wretched, seduced creatures for whom she had always felt a pitying scorn. She no longer had the feeling that men were staring at her in admiration. Her legs seemed thick and ugly and she became painfully aware of a pimple that had broken out on her chin.

She had imagined that her love would be quite different from other women's. But what a cheap little affair it had turned out to be!

And Richard had assured her that Tulin was the man of the future. What a joke!

They were lying in each other's arms and she could feel him—his cheek, his belly, his legs. But it wasn't enough. She wanted to be able to feel his back, the nape of his neck. She wanted him all round her, she wanted to be swathed in him.

"This is the only real thing," he said. "The rest just doesn't matter."

"I thought you didn't need me any more."

"You're all I need. I need nothing else."

"A woman can give a man a lot, but by no means everything," she said didactically.

"There are a lot of women about, but to me you're—you're *Zhenya*, that's what you are."

So he needed her. It was as simple as that. Words were no use. She had felt that as soon as she threw the door open and saw his eyes leap to meet hers and felt his dry, trembling lips on her hands and face. She had tried to explain but suddenly it didn't seem to matter any more. And yet for some reason she wanted him to talk. When he talked she began to disbelieve him, but when he said nothing she wanted him to talk. Why was this so?

She laughed. Tulin kissed her on the shoulder and she laughed again, feeling the pleasure her laughter gave him.

She must still be just a girl if a kiss had such importance for her.

"There is nothing higher than this," he repeated stubbornly.

"But it doesn't satisfy you," she said gently.

He gave a quiet laugh.

"Does it satisfy you?"

"Oh, I'm just as bad. I'm ambitious. I want you to become a celebrity. I'm just an ordinary, narrow-minded woman really. Remember how you promised me you'd tame the thunder? Remember what you were like then?" She wanted to stir something in him. "Ever since then I've felt the only man I want is one who can control the thunder. No one else will do. I want your picture to be in all the papers. I want you to win prizes."

"What if I never win any prizes?"

"If you stop winning them for one minute I'll go away and leave you. I can't live with anyone but a prize-winner. Wife of a prize-winner—how grand! I shall clean your little badge every day, I shall make sure it's always on the jacket you're wearing, and on your pyjamas at night. And in winter I'll pin it to your overcoat, and when you come I'll put it back on your jacket. I'll be busy morning, noon and night."

"And to think I actually used to dream of something like that!" Tulin said quite sincerely.

"Why take that attitude? We can go to Moscow. We can complain to the Central Committee. They'll look into it. They'll soon be calling you up themselves. You see if they don't. . . ."

"No, you're missing the point."

By the light of the moon he seemed very pale and much thinner. His eyes were quick and restless.

"I want to explain everything to you."

Once he began talking he grew calmer, his mind seemed to settle down. Zhenya watched him admiringly. She wanted to tousle his hair but checked herself and started listening to what he was saying.

". . . I was always either trying to get a diploma, or my degree, or do research on something. A benefactor of humanity! I was always just something attached to my brain. And my brain was just a computer. When I go out for a walk now I look at the sky. I see the clouds floating by and I think they look like old galleons. It's the first time I've seen them like that, not dipoles, not space charges, but galleons. I want to be free, so that I can see galleons. My brain has just about dried up. I always had to be solving this or that. It's worse than slavery. I was chained to it, like a galley-slave. But I've had enough. To hell with it! When I read other people's work I envied them. I don't want to envy them any more. That was the yardstick I used on myself—how much had I done, how many articles had I written? Why can't I just live, go to the cinema when I like, fall in love, and not feel all the time that my work is hanging over me? Stop getting at me like this. I want to be like everyone else, I don't want to worry about the fate of humanity. I'm just an ordinary man. What do you think a man is—an end or a means?"

"A means," she said, guessing wildly.

"That's what Krylov says. But can't you see that man is an end in himself? Man is the highest good, everything exists for him. Neither you nor I will ever live on this earth again. We only exist once. So why should I cheat myself out of all the simple human joys? If I were a genius.... But the most I can do is beat the next man to it by six months or so. If I don't solve the problem, someone else will. Hundreds of people are working on the same thing. There are plenty of scientists nowadays. Take Altynov. What does it matter to you whether he can solve elliptic functions or how many articles he has written? What matters far more to you is that he's a good soul, an honest chap, that he's kind to people—that's what really matters, the human side! Only machines can be evaluated according to their power, their productive capacity...."

He stopped to think and she waited patiently, as women always wait for men when they are carried away by their thoughts.

Perhaps he's right, she was thinking. Who am I to judge him? He knows better than me. Though he doesn't really know anything. He doesn't know what he wants. But he'll never be able just to take life as it comes. He'd be finished without me, it'd be the end of him.

"...When a man lives for the present, he does more for the future, because he's more human. Understand?"

Zhenya nodded happily.

"Of course, I do. Whatever you tackle is bound to succeed."

He eased himself up on his elbow and looked into her face.

"You didn't understand a thing." His voice became dull. "It's all so elementary, yet no one seems to understand."

She tried desperately to argue:

"We're all working for the future. We've got to have something to aim for. Our work, specially if it's creative, serves society. You've got talent, and suddenly you.... If only I had talent! You're committed to individualism. Of course, in our society talent ought to be given ... certain conditions.... But we must be prepared to make sacrifices if we're called on to do so, if it's for the sake of progress. ..."

She could not find the right words. She was a poor hand at arguing on such subjects. It was easy for him to put her off and she could find only a few dismal clichés.

She felt that here, before her very eyes something irrevocable was happening. He was tearing out of himself the very thing that gave him a soul, that gave meaning to his life, the Tulin that she loved. And she could do nothing to influence him.

"What are you thinking about?" he asked.

"About you, of course. What else?" she said bitterly. "You're the sole end and purpose of everything."

It was not long before Tulin had a telephone call from Moscow. When he came with Zhenya to tell Krylov the news, he was radiant and excited. It looked as if he was in luck. He was to be given a job—touch wood!—on a sputnik project. The chaps were doing all they could for him. It was the project of the age. He could make good in no time.

Krylov was sitting at a desk heaped with reels of film, oscillograms and tables. He was carefully drawing little boats, dozens of little boats, hundreds of them.

"So the old man's got you in a corner, has he?" Tulin asked.

Krylov gave a forced smile and rubbed his red eyelids.

"When are you leaving?"

"Tomorrow. The request for me will come through today. I'll be flying out tomorrow."

"Leave me any stuff you've got on the detector."

He looked firm, but Tulin was not convinced.

"So you're going to soldier on? Think you'll manage it?"

"It's a matter of searching. It takes patience," Krylov said.

Tulin winked at Zhenya.

"Patience—the great virtue of all donkeys. No, I was only joking. I still love you, you old plodder." He perched himself on the arm-rest of the chair, placing one arm round Krylov's shoulders and the other round Zhenya. "Can't be helped. The rules of the game say it's now or never."

"But suppose I succeed in working this thing out?"

Tulin gave a faint whistle.

"You may succeed on paper, but not with the people at the top. The commission has closed down the project and they'll see it stays closed. Their decision will have been confirmed by people even higher up, who won't want to look silly either. And who's going to let you stay here pottering around anyway? If you don't go back to Golitsyn, they'll pack you off to somewhere in the back of beyond."

"What the hell has this got to do with the people at the top!" Krylov exclaimed exasperatedly.

"Oh, but of course! You are concerned only with pure science. But there's really no such thing. However, let us suppose that we are surrounded only by angels yearning for progress. Even so, you will have to start all over again. You'll have to fit out an aircraft, get a group together."

"You ought to help Sergei Ilyich," Zhenya said.

"Am I refusing? When that time comes, you can count on my help. Why not? But I rather think I'll be fishing you out of yet another mess instead."

Krylov tried to get up, but Tulin's weight kept the chair firmly anchored to the floor.

"I warn you..." Krylov began thickly, but Tulin cut him short.

"By the way, how did your reunion with Natasha go off?" he asked smiling.

Krylov could find nothing to say. So he was beholden to Tulin even for Natasha. There were so many things for which he was beholden to Tulin.

He managed to get up and say: "I warn you ... I mean, I want you to know. If you leave now, I'll never take you back."

At first it simply didn't register with Tulin.

"How do you mean? You won't take me back where?"

Krylov looked at Zhenya and hesitated.

"I mean, if I get this straight and you want to come back on the project."

Only then did it dawn on Tulin what he was trying to say. He burst out laughing. It was so amusing, so absurd, so fantastic. He held his sides with laughter. Zhenya laughed, too, and even Krylov grinned sheepishly.

Tulin jabbed him in the ribs.

"You old crackpot! Don't let things upset you!"

When they reached the street, Tulin looked back. Through the open window he saw Krylov sit down at his desk and butt his head between his hands, and for a second he actually felt as if Krylov had rejected him. Zhenya said something and the sound of her voice reminded him of their talk coming back in the lorry in the rain, when they had known nothing about the crash, and it had seemed to him that he held the future in the palm of his hand.

Chapter Four

The plane was due to leave at 17.00 hours. Yuzhin and Golitsyn were strolling together in the airport garden. Lagunov and the other members of the commission had gone back to Moscow to report two days ago. Yuzhin had stayed on to inspect the airport's servicing facilities, Golitsyn to give some advice to the aerologists.

They crunched along the seashell-strewn paths past fading rose-bushes, and looked forward to seeing the damp, cool forests round Moscow, where the mushroom-gathering season was in full swing. Golitsyn could hardly believe that in a matter of a few hours he would be home. A glance at the timetable told him it was so, but he could not get used to the idea, as Yuzhin had. Like most of his generation, Golitsyn lived by two different geographies. One was the geography he had learnt at school, derived from contour maps and the narratives of the great explorers, with its meridians, its tropics, its continents where man was but a grain of sand lost among the deserts, its jungles, all the endless spaces of the earth. The other was the geography of aerodromes, air services, jet aircraft, where thousands of miles were compressed into hours and a man could leaf through countries like the pages of an atlas. Golitsyn had flown into Berlin a year ago with his hat still damp from Moscow rain.

Speeds that bore no comparison to one another were calmly accepted in everyday life. It took Golitsyn as long to travel up from the suburbs to his institute as it would now take him to reach Moscow.

They were walking towards the airport building, chatting about these things, when Krylov came pounding up. He pushed his way through the group that had gathered to see them off and pointed the fountain-pen he was still clutching in his hand at Golitsyn.

"Statistics!" he exclaimed delightedly. "Statistics show that the impulses are of rare occurrence. It's all quite simple. One in ten million. Of course, we missed them. Look how it works out."

He grabbed Yuzhin's newspaper and began scribbling in the margins. The ink blurred on the paper and Yuzhin couldn't make anything out, but Golitsyn took Krylov's pen and started underlining and correcting and Krylov took his pen back, and they argued and interrupted each other, each trying to take possession of the newspaper.

"May I ask just what you are trying to prove? That there were no deviations?"

"That's right," Krylov agreed enthusiastically. "The impulses are so few in number that they couldn't be registered on our instruments."

"But you must agree that is extremely odd," Golitsyn said. "You are arguing that they exist on the grounds that you have no record of them."

"That's the whole point! Statistically they do exist. But they couldn't appear in our records."

Golitsyn looked at his blissful face and sat down on a bench. He had a stabbing pain in his chest. There were tablets in his pocket but he was loth to display his weakness in the presence of so many people.

Reproachful looks were cast at Krylov.

"What's going on?" Yuzhin whispered angrily to Krylov. "Why cause all this fluster? You could have put your idea down in writing."

A loudspeaker requested passengers to board the plane. Yuzhin took Golitsyn's arm and walked with him on to the airfield. Krylov walked beside them talking all the time. At the ramp they halted. Yuzhin made his good-byes and climbed the ramp.

"Arkady Borisovich, it's time we were going."

Golitsyn and Krylov stared at him blankly.

"Oh, yes," Golitsyn said. "Just a minute."

And he walked away with Krylov past the aircraft, over the sun-drenched concrete of the runway.

"Disgraceful!" Agatov said. "The fellow must be insane. He's worrying the old man for nothing. I'm going to have a word with him."

"I'll do that," Yuzhin said.

He walked back down the ramp and caught up with them.

"Forgive me, Sergei Ilyich, but it's time for us to go aboard."

They eyed him thoughtfully for a time. Golitsyn took hold of one of Yuzhin's buttons.

"Let's assume this is so," he said. "I'm willing to assume that it is. But how significant is the fact that there are so few impulse zones?"

"I think that increases the possibility of active intervention," Krylov replied.

"But they are more difficult to locate."

"Arkady Borisovich!"

"Wait a minute," Golitsyn said crossly and, suddenly becoming aware of Yuzhin, the airfield and the waiting aircraft, was so confused that he even forgot to play his doddering-old-man trick. "This is very important, General. I'll have to stay behind."

"You mean he's hit on something?" Yuzhin asked.

Golitsyn frowned impatiently.

"It must be checked, of course."

"But people are expecting you, Arkady Borisovich."

"I'll come by the next flight."

Yuzhin looked keenly at Krylov. He was surprised that there was no note of triumph in Krylov's voice.

"Should I congratulate you?"

Krylov gave a little nervous laugh. "No, it's much too early yet. It's a tough job having Arkady Borisovich as an opponent."

"All right, all right!" Golitsyn cut in. "I've no time to spare."

Yuzhin asked about the ticket and luggage, but Golitsyn looked at him as if he were proposing a game of dominoes. They dismissed Yuzhin with impatient good-byes and faces that were equally absorbed. There was an amazing likeness between them now. Golitsyn's face wore the same expression of eager curiosity as Krylov's, as though they were associates and not opponents. Yuzhin looked back as he climbed the ramp, and wondered how anyone could become so completely oblivious of his surroundings.

As he sank into his cushioned seat, he was still thinking of the mysterious power that had taken possession of their thoughts and feelings. He couldn't help respecting it. It lifted them to a plane from which both Lagunov and Yuzhin, for all their power, and even Krylov's own life, seemed of little importance. They had their own values, their own conception of happiness. It was out of this world, yet for this world, this ancient, insatiable thirst for knowledge, the urge to create that was one of the mainsprings of life itself. Why did it mean so much to Krylov? What prevented him from seizing the chance of forgiveness and, perhaps, even recognition and all its advantages?

Chapter Five

Tulin sent a wire from Moscow and Zhenya started packing. The practicals were nearly over. Katya was going to visit her parents, Alyosha had decided to strike out for the sea, but Zhenya was going back to Moscow.

That evening she called in to say good-bye to Krylov.

"Well, how's it going? Shouting 'Eureka' yet?" Zhenya said, nodding at the paper-strewn desk.

Krylov stretched himself.

"Not a hope." Glad of the chance to make a break, he began doing knee-bends and swinging his arms about.

A few hours' discussion with Golitsyn had shown that his idea was quite a good one, but it was hard to calculate and prove that the deviations could be measured.

"I would have stayed behind to help you," Zhenya said. "But I've just had a wire."

"Well, how's he getting on?"

She noticed that he was quite unaffected by Tulin's new appointment and the considerate reception he had been given in Moscow.

"You mustn't think I completely agree with him," she said.

"I wonder if you can do me a favour," Krylov said. "Would you call on Pesetsky at the institute and give him this letter? He may be able to manage this equation."

Zhenya watched him as he laboured over the letter, the tip of his tongue showing between his lips. There was a row of empty yoghourt bottles on the edge of the table. An ash-tray stood on the floor by the rumpled bed. On the window there was an old coffee-pot that Tulin had left behind and a hot plate.

"Let me make you some coffee," she said suddenly.

Krylov gave a grunt.

She was good at making coffee. It was her sole domestic achievement. Krylov drank it, closing his eyes with pleasure. Zhenya smiled. She felt sad.

How wonderful it would all have been if she had fallen in love with Krylov! Strictly speaking, he was even nicer than Tulin in some ways. The girls in the met office were crazy about him, and as for Zoyechka in the restaurant.... But for some reason they were shy of him. They complained he was not so easy to chat with as Tulin. This land of love that she now found herself in was ruled by strange, inexplicable laws. Here was a wonderful man beside her, yet she couldn't possibly fall in love with him. Katya, for instance, said she could fall in love with Krylov, but not with Tulin. Yet with her, Zhenya, it was the other way round. Why?

"Everyone's leaving," she said. "Lisitsky says they'll be sending you off somewhere, too. You ought to do something about it, not just wait for the blow to fall. Would you like us to ask some of the people in Moscow about you?"

"Yes, of course," Krylov replied absently and Zhenya realised he was not in the least interested in what she was saying. Lisitsky had patronisingly dubbed him the "martyr of science". Alyosha stood up for him, but of late Krylov was usually discussed in condescending tones, as an unfortunate crank doomed to disappointment and failure.

On her way to his room to say good-bye she had felt ashamed of leaving him here alone with Richard and the work Richard and Tulin, all of them, had been doing together.

And now it turned out that none of these things—her shame, the talk that went on behind his back, Tulin's success in Moscow—

mattered at all to Krylov, they simply didn't exist for him. The realisation gave her a strange feeling of disquiet.

"But what you think about Tulin isn't right either," she said.

Krylov looked at her in silence. His round face was very kind and very tired.

"I want to talk him round."

He gave a shrug and began to walk up and down the room. "What for?"

She could see how much it cost him to talk of Tulin.

"We shall have fresh failures. We shall make many more mistakes."

She had never thought he could be so hard.

He thumped the table. Gestures came easier to him than words. "Oleg's no good for this kind of thing."

"Is it that you feel he's deserted you?"

"No. Worse than that! I just don't need him." Krylov lowered his head grimly. "He'd get in my way." He looked at her from under lowered brows. "I suppose you think I'm not being very fair."

"I can understand you, I can really," Zhenya said. "It makes me feel ashamed to be going away like this."

"That's silly," Krylov said. "Don't even think of it."

But what else could she think of? She walked down the street, then along the river and past the suspension bridge. She didn't think enough as it was.

Without knowing how she got there she found herself in the cemetery.

White crosses, little painted obelisks crowned with nickel-plated stars. Sun-scorched grass. Daisies in a green bottle. The mound, already settled, that was Richard's grave. The wire frames of withered wreaths. The photograph beginning to turn yellow under the glass. Blue mountains, forests, aircraft roaring over them, and higher still a crimson star, probably Mars. So the years would pass over this grave.

All men die, the warm sands grow cool and grey,
And yesterday's sun on a black hearse is borne away.

Someone had recited those lines to her on the skating rink in Moscow. In those days they had been just rather nice lines.

Soon it would be Moscow again, the Tverskoi Boulevard, seeing Tulin, getting her degree. Perhaps they would make a trip somewhere or go somewhere else to live. Things would happen in her life, but here everything would stay the same—the mountains, the sky, so close above, the scent of the grass. Whatever else happened, nothing here would change. And the dead were even more eternal than these larches, than the mountains, than the earth and stars, these small, sharp stars that looked as if they had been pricked in the sky with a needle.

What lived after a man when he died? She, too, would die one day. She just couldn't imagine that she would have a grave somewhere like this one, with a few withered bunches of flowers on it. It was as hard as trying to imagine oneself an old woman, like Vera Matveyevna, or even older.

Would you agree to see how you will die? That was what she had asked her friends. Richard had said something in reply. She couldn't remember what.

It would have been good to stay behind here and slog away with Krylov in that ill-equipped hotel room, until all hope disappeared.

She did not believe he would succeed. She scarcely thought of the result. It was the urge, the desire to seek that tempted her and seemed to promise some mysterious reward. She mustn't leave, she despised herself for leaving, for not being able to master herself, for not being what she wanted to be.

Chapter Six

Rolls of oscillograms, charts, Golitsyn's notes. Graphs, rough calculations, tables, Golitsyn's notes.

Krylov sat with his head between his hands, staring vacantly at the useless pile of paper.

The peaks of the graphs confronted him like battlements. Wherever he sought an entry, it was this wall that balked him.

A very long time ago (it seemed like centuries!) he had rushed off to catch Golitsyn at the airport. He had been jubilant with inspiration. There had been no happier man on earth. Trouble was in retreat. There seemed to be nothing that could spoil his happiness. Was it to be always like that? Happiness, a fleeting interlude, and all the rest, just a brain-racking search.

He felt he had never been so depressed in his life as he was now. He could overcome any trouble or sorrow, but now he was afflicted by a calm and lucid awareness of his own helplessness. This mental impotence was the worst torture of all.

To an outsider it might have seemed that he worked in the laboratory, went to the restaurant, joked with Zoyechka and listened to what was said.

"Zoyechka, how many more times are you going to bring Krylov the biggest cutlet?"

"You come off the sick list today, Krylov."

"Gagarin will be speaking on the radio today."

To an outsider it would appear that he had an appetite, that he liked showing off in his Polish sandals, that he was being very conscientious over exercising his injured leg.

In fact he did nothing all day but sit clutching his head in his hands, and that great useless head was the only thing that existed for him. And the brain inside it was just a wretched grey pudding that he had squeezed absolutely dry. What governed the formation of storm centres? Why didn't the peak discharges fit such and such an equation? Why was it impossible to calculate a normal circuit? And if so, what kind of circuit could be used? Why had other people got all the talent? Dan would have solved the whole thing in a flash. Dan would have found the answer. Dan had a way of seeing things in a different light from other people. That was genius. Krylov had often thought of Dan lately, of that gentle, absent-minded smile: "Sergei Ilyich will now tell us about an infinitely long flash of lightning, acting in an infinitely homogeneous environment on his infinitely sceptical colleagues." Dan had no weaknesses. It wouldn't have cost him so much to break with a close friend. The loneliness wouldn't have worried him because he would have had his talent to bear him up.

Man could achieve anything—a yogi could stop his own heart, Anikeyev had learned to play a Beethoven sonata, just for a bet, without knowing a note of music, but no man could make himself talented. Persistence? He had been ready to wait a year, two years for Natasha. He was ready to sit at this desk, over these papers for months on end. But what was the point? Sitting on his backside wouldn't do it. Talent was needed. Talent was all he needed. Position, success, even love, a man could obtain anything if he really wanted it—but not talent. He couldn't have that even if he killed himself.

What could be deduced from the fact that the zones where lightning originated were of a very rare type? Would it be like this all his life—a flash of inspiration, a lucky guess, then further frustration? Where was the joy, the satisfaction? The joy of creative work! The happiness of creating! They were the inventions of novelists. Laboratory assistants had an easy life. All they had to do was submit their calculations and say good-bye. No headaches, nothing to upset their evening's pleasure. All the technician had to do was test the circuit he

was given. Or take Alyosha. He would construct a curve according to
the points, but what did it matter to him that six of the points simply
wouldn't fit in anywhere? But he was a good chap. He was doing
his best to help. Now that Lisitsky had gone and the rest were sitting
on their luggage. now that everything had been dismantled, and every
report submitted, it would have been tough going without Alyosha.

"Anything else I can do?" Alyosha had asked, dumping a bag of
plums on the table. "What about a spin on the bikes? Sport's a
great healer, you know. All the great men have been keen on sport.
Or we could attend the local hop? Keeps the circulation going, too.
Any real fast music is as good as sport." With a stony expression
on his face, he demonstrated a few steps.

"Who's trying to trip you up, Sergei Ilyich? Any obvious diehards
to be dealt with?" Looking at Krylov with dedication in his eyes,
he adopted a boxing stance, as if the whole problem could be solved
with the aid of his fists.

"Diehards!" Krylov repeated the word with a dreamy sigh. "How
lovely it would be if there were! Then there'd be somebody to fight.
It's worse when the snag's up here." He tapped his forehead.

Alyosha dropped his fists. Being fit and on your toes was not much
use in a case like this. The local girls couldn't keep their eyes off
Alyosha's athletic figure. With his polished dancing style, his talent
for dalliance and ability to dress he could have put any of them in
his pocket. But what in reality was he beside Krylov? Just a nin-
compoop! He suddenly wished he was sitting there, in Krylov's
place, going through the mill. Let the others dance and have their
fun. He would sit up all night and every night, he would go about
unshaven, so tired he couldn't walk straight, dressed any old how,
with no time for dancing. So much would depend on what he
managed to think up. He wanted to be a lone fighter, with the people
round him all disbelieving and laughing at him. He wanted to make
a sacrifice, deny himself something. The things he had once ridiculed
now seemed to him, as he looked at Krylov, the only things that
really mattered in life. But to be able to suffer, you had to have
ability.

From the next room came the hum of a rectifier. Vera Matveyevna
was busy there. She was the only person who, in spite of everything,
was calmly completing her programme of measurements. Krylov
envied her. He envied Alyosha. He envied them all because they all
knew their jobs and were doing their jobs, and he was the only one
who was utterly incompetent.

He was hemmed in by curves and charts, he blundered among
them in despair. The curves expressed dozens of flights, and every
point was a cloud, a wind, an altitude, a roar of engines. Time and

again he roamed the sky, probing and delving among the clouds. Somewhere below lay the earth, with its billions of people, with all their passions and endeavours, which had no influence whatever over the laws that governed the clouds. It was a struggle in which no one else could help him.

When he got completely bemused he went off to the meteorologists to verify some of the flight data.

The chief meteorologist helped him dig up some old maps, which provided no consolation.

They walked out on to the square and ran into a milling crowd of passengers who had just arrived on the Leningrad plane.

Passengers and taxi-drivers all seemed to be shouting at once. The newcomers were enthusing over the warmth, the southern air and the mountains.

"This happens a dozen times a day and it's always the same," the meteorologist said. "The same old phrases. This human lack of imagination is enough to drive you up the wall."

He was stooped and narrow-shouldered. His yellow, sun-shrivelled face with its intelligent, mocking eyes reminded Krylov of Mephistopheles.

"What about a drink?" the meteorologist said.

They each had a glass of dry wine and a glass of sweet wine at a stall.

"Everyone drinks to something," said the meteorologist, "everyone's concerned about the future. But people really ought to live for.... Well, I, for instance, drink to blot out my memory." He winked at Krylov. "It's fine when you can't remember a damn thing. Memory is a punishment conceived by the devil." He emptied his glass and smacked his long lips. "We'd all be happy if we had no memories. Golitsyn and I, you know, we started together. Now he's a Corresponding Member of the Academy and I'm stuck in this hole, just a meteorologist. But what was the difference when we met—just a couple of old men."

A full glass appeared in front of Krylov. The meteorologist straightened up and craned his neck. He was tall and thin, and his arms flapped as if he wanted to fly.

"I advise you to give up this battle. I'm a fortune-teller. It's easier to tell fortunes than forecast the weather. Want me to let you into a secret?" One of his eyes became very round and began to wink. "The man who knows what no one else knows is dangerous! If you know the truth, you're dangerous! I, for instance, am no longer dangerous. Golitsyn wanted to recall old times, said he was sorry for me. But I've no regrets. I'm quite happy. I've done my bit. Tulin's thrown up the sponge, and good for him! Who are you going to fight anyway? The other side doesn't fight, you know. That's where the catch lies. I know that Lagunov of yours. No matter what you do, you'll be working for Lagunov and he'll reap the benefit."

"Let him, for all I care!" Krylov wagged a threatening finger at the meteorologist. "I don't mind if Lagunov becomes an Academician. Results? Results are never final. There's always another result that comes after. One day they'll find out more about the speed of charge generation in clouds and it'll be good-bye to our results. You've just got to press on. It doesn't matter whether you crawl on your hands and knees, but you've got to press on."

"Motion is everything, the aim nothing. Yes, we've heard all that before. But where does it get you? Tell me that. I fought like a tiger when I was young, thought I was finishing off injustice for good and all. But now I'm old and there's just as much injustice around as ever."

Music was coming over the loudspeaker in the restaurant. Every now and then a voice would interrupt to announce the flight departures: Tashkent, Alma-Ata.... Krylov was struck by the number of places one could fly to. Syktyvkar! Fancy being able to fly there! And the people here all had tickets and knew where they were bound for.

"You and I, you know what we are? We're sacrifices on the altar of science!" the meteorologist declared.

"That's it! Sacrifices!" Krylov replied joyfully and they exchanged tender kisses.

The pickled mushrooms slid elusively around his plate.

"You mustn't have any more, Sergei Ilyich," Zoyechka told him.

He wagged his finger at her. They wanted him to go back to that damned desk, did they? Well, he damn well wouldn't! He was going to fly to Syktyvkar! He was going to marry Zoyechka. And he'd take her to visit Natasha, so that she'd know who his wife was. Perhaps Zoyechka would make him talented. With impartial curiosity he watched himself split apart and become two different people. One was the Krylov who was still sitting poring over his desk trying to think of new ideas. The other was a wild young fellow who had just escaped and wanted to go dancing or go to sleep, and who eventually discovered that he could pull tables apart and bend plates and do things that made the furniture sway and sing in a dozen different voices, much louder than the music from the loudspeaker. Then a third Krylov appeared, who tried to put a party of foreigners in their place when they started making passes at Zoyechka, and who eventually got so aggressive that a first-class fight developed.

Alyosha appeared on the scene. Krylov felt he was doing fine with his straight lefts to the jaw, then he received a good punch in the eye, which sobered him up a little, and Alyosha and the meteorologist managed to haul him away before the militia arrived.

It was a calm starry night. He didn't want to go home. He was sick of figures and tables. But the meteorologist and Alyosha marched him along relentlessly, like guards escorting a runaway. He could have walked straight without them, of course, but he just couldn't be bothered.

There were nearly three thousand million people in the world and no one could help him. That was the bitterest thing of all. Everyone could put a spoke in his wheel, but as for helping him, even if they wanted to, they couldn't. Look at all those lovely stars! What a beautiful sky. But he'd got to fight it. He'd got to take on the whole sky alone, for the sake of all these people. Dear old sky! The sky belongs to me! . . . .

With much reproachful shaking of her head the manageress gave him a telegram. It was an urgent summons to Moscow.

He looked awful. There was a purple swelling under his eye and scratches all over his face. The girls in the personnel department exchanged glances. He was offered a job in the Pamirs, where a power transmission line was being carried over the mountains and the risk of lightning had to be studied with a view to providing adequate protection devices. He tried to explain to them that he couldn't go away until he had proved. . . . Intensity gradient . . . delta E. . . . The girls tittered disappointedly. Delta E! Somebody had wanted to pack him off to a godforsaken spot, but the head of the personnel department, a retired colonel, had said: "I don't like to see a lot of people crowing over a man when he's down." The girls said proudly they had been defending him. They had found him an interesting job, but now it turned out that he wasn't an unjustly persecuted hero at all but just one of those backsliders who would try any trick to get out of being sent to the provinces. Either they had invalid parents, or a wife who was a concert pianist, and here was this one with his delta E.

The personnel manager lectured him patiently on the state importance of the project, state interests, state discipline and so on.

"What makes you think you know more about state interests than I do?" Krylov was quite sincerely puzzled. "But the state will gain far more if I solve this problem."

They both stared at each other in astonishment and the personnel manager went off to report to his superiors.

Say what you like, Agatov knew how to make himself useful. He was the chief witness. He had foreseen everything, he had warned Yuzhin. He helped Lagunov to draw up his conclusions and prove his case. He advertised himself as a faithful disciple and supporter of Golitsyn. He was placed temporarily in charge of the group and the winding up of its affairs.

In Lagunov's presence he praised Golitsyn to the skies. Lagunov took it calmly but Agatov knew that he was making an impression. He waited, waited with patience and skill. Eventually, when they happened to be alone together, Lagunov asked about the state of Golitsyn's health. Various institutes were being merged into a single department of atmospheric electricity. Wouldn't the organisational period be too much of a burden for the old man?

The creation of such a centre was something Golitsyn had dreamed of for years. He had always been trying to prove the need for it. Agatov realised that Lagunov was thinking of putting the old man on the shelf. What a swine, he thought.

With a regretful sigh he said: "You're probably right. That amount of work at his age would be bound to cause some damage."

"It's likely to be rather a sticky business, but we're relying on you," Lagunov said.

For a moment Agatov felt sorry for his master, but, after all, there was nothing he could do about it. Such was life. If he didn't take the job, someone else would.

On his return to Moscow, Lagunov recommended him to the Ministry as temporary head of the department and secretary of the organising committee of an international symposium. Agatov did not refuse.

The features of his pale face, which had once looked as though someone had rubbed them out with an eraser, had since the crash acquired prominent shape and now seemed to be carved out of marble.

His chin jutted forth heavily, his lips were firmly set, even his hair seemed to be growing thicker over his narrow, deeply furrowed forehead.

In the past few weeks he had actually grown taller. His jacket was too short for him. "We're relying on you," he sang to himself, repeating Lagunov's words. They were music to his ears, a whole symphony, complete with drums and trumpet calls.

He felt as though he were standing on an invisible pedestal, from which he had a magnificent view.

Before him stretched a spacious private office, very neat and business-like, with a separate table for telephones, one of them directly connected with the sanctum sanctorum.... Spacious conference tables covered with dark-blue baize, secretaries moving swiftly to and fro, a tapping pencil calling the meeting to order, queues in the waiting room, backslapping, toasts, introductions, friendly handshakes.

He saw a world of plans. Plans that had been approved, that were novel, grandiose, striking, effective and overfulfilled, plans that pleased everyone, that pleased the President of the Academy, and spheres even higher, people right at the top. He saw a world of Academicians out of touch with real life and needing energetic organisers capable of selecting personnel, distributing personnel, listening to other people's opinion, encouraging initiative, strengthening ties with production, supporting new ideas.

He would take part in solving problems that demanded drastic changes, breadth of vision, dealing with diehards, merging of institutes, removal of institutes to new areas, opening of new institutes, improvement of leadership.

He would eliminate parallelism in research, wastage of resources, all sorts of unnecessary barriers and stumbling blocks. He was ready to send people to the provinces, submit unbiased opinions, reject pure science, defend pure science, train personnel, hold symposiums, congresses, write obituaries, and rise to the occasion.

But as a scientist he would lose a little ground. It couldn't be helped, current affairs would take up too much of his time. Someone had to make sacrifices. He was prepared to sacrifice himself, and others, too. He would shoulder responsibility, eliminate friction....

No, he was not ambitious, he was not a careerist. He was not out for a high salary. All he wanted was to get away from these galvanometers and formulas and maximum zones, from this dangerous world of madmen who bragged of their mathematical curves and judged a man by the extent to which he could understand their charts and diagrams. He yearned to flee from all this to a place where there would be no more erroneous calculations or fruitless experiments, where he would be out of reach of colleagues who spoke at seminars, safe from what was said at those seminars.

Safe from Krylov and his ilk.

They would ask if they could see him. He could refuse.

Or he could hear what they had to say with an amiable smile and fob them off with a promise.

Or he would send them on to some other department and prepare their reception with a phone call: "There'll be a certain individual coming over to see you shortly. He's rather a hopeless case, I'm afraid."

And if they didn't apply to him, they could be summoned. And they'd have to wait before he saw them, thirty minutes, forty minutes. . . .

He walked round his desk—one of the smart, modern kind, without any drawers—to meet Krylov. "So sorry to have kept you waiting. I just don't have a minute to breathe." He motioned him into a chair —foam rubber, red upholstery, very modern, like all the rest of the furniture, symbolical of the new style of management. "Now what's the matter? Not been in another crash, I hope? So you don't like your new appointment, Sergei Ilyich. I should be more happy in a laboratory myself, but we've all got our duty to do, we're soldiers, you know. What progress are you making? Nothing so far? Too bad! I'm afraid you'll have to accept the appointment then. I'd be glad to help, but it's out of my hands. No use putting the matter up to Academician Likhov, I'm afraid. Only make matters worse."

How affable Agatov was, how amiably apologetic, how sympathetic! Unfortunately, he would have to make this known to the Party Committee. Public opinion would have to have its say.

Krylov had to sit there and listen to him and plead. How much can a man stand? Far more than he thinks. He can stand a great deal. He can stand everything, and more besides.

That evening Bochkaryov and Pesetsky came round and they discussed the situation. They were not organisation men, not psychologists, not politicians. They knew nothing at all about the law, but Pesetsky proved that any sly trick was ultimately nothing more than the best choice out of a number of possible alternatives. Damn it all, couldn't people who were physicists and mathematicians put it across this Agatov fellow! Careful and highly scientific analysis of the problem revealed the following line of action as the most promising: Krylov—Anikeyev—Likhov. Krylov at once rang through to Anikeyev in Leningrad. After a lot of humming and hawing at great expense to himself, he established the fact that Anikeyev, like Bochkaryov and Pesetsky, could see nothing immoral in his request. While unable to vouch for the success of the operation he felt that Krylov himself knew what course of action to take.

The circuit was made. Krylov received a summons from Likhov.

Once again in the presence of Agatov and the head of the personnel department he repeated his case. This time he didn't bother about the impression he was making because he had little hope that Likhov would appreciate what he was trying to say. His exposition was coldly lucid, without a trace of emotion. Before him sat not Likhov but an old man with a shaven head, and hairs growing out of his ears.

Likhov asked one or two pertinent questions. He was easy to talk to and Krylov became animated. He enjoyed expounding the details, got into an argument and, when Likhov tried to bring in Langmuir, snorted impatiently: "Oh, come off it! Langmuir, Langmuir! As if Langmuir couldn't make a mistake. What your Langmuir says about this is just rubbish."

"Indeed?!..." Likhov's fingers rapped the table and his ears turned purple. Agatov knew that Likhov was quick-tempered and harsh and he looked forward with relish to the retribution which was bound to come because Krylov was quite obliviously begging for it. Even now he was leaning across the table, drawing his own curve and Langmuir's curve on Likhov's pad.

"You see the difference!" he bawled. "Two orders. Can you understand that?"

But instead of turning him out of the room Likhov scratched the back of his head in irritation, then said with a wink: "But Arkady Borisovich knows what he's doing, too."

"He does," said Krylov.

"Anikeyev told me about you." Likhov paused for a minute, then added: "Agatov has also given me his report." Again his tone of voice gave no hint as to what side he was on.

"Are you sure you will find the solution?"

Krylov settled back in his chair with a sigh.

"No, I can't vouch for that."

"You're quite right not to. And what if, in spite of everything, we do send you to Kirghizia?"

"I won't go."

"What will you do?"

"I'll just go on plugging away at this problem."

"And you won't get anywhere."

"I shall go on until I do get somewhere."

Likhov turned to Agatov and said: "I was at the experimental factory yesterday. The men were getting their wages. There was a pile of notes on a table and each man came up and took what was due to him. Krylov, do you think there is a possibility of proving this thing?"

"Yes," Krylov said.

Agatov shook his head warningly.

"By the way, Yakov Ivanovich," Krylov said enthusiastically, rummaging among his papers. "I've found out why the detector didn't work."

Agatov turned away. His lips seemed to disappear into his pale face.

"Why?" he breathed meekly. Krylov lifted his head and Likhov gave him a keen look, and, because they were both surveying him in silence, Agatov lost control and burst out: "What's it got to do with me? Why tell me?"

Yuzhin, Krylov, and now Likhov and the head of the personnel department—the number of people who might be suspicious was increasing. It kept on increasing.

"I won't keep you any longer," Likhov said in a tone that brought Agatov leaping to his feet.

They watched him slink to the door.

The telephone rang. Likhov listened for a moment and said: "No, not yet. Wait a minute." He put down the receiver. "There's a problem my grandson can't manage. And I can't do it either."

It was a problem for children of fifteen about a cotton reel being pulled by a thread. They tried it together, but it baffled them both. Likhov lost his temper.

"This is scandalous!" he boomed at Krylov. "Scandalous! And you undertake to refute Golitsyn."

He turned to the head of personnel: "Very well, we'll try him out. I'll go bail for him. Some people say it's a risk. But it's more of a risk when people won't try than when they will."

In the anteroom Agatov was waiting for Krylov.

"What did you find out?" he asked.

"The power supply was cut," Krylov explained.

Agatov nodded wretchedly.

"Yes, that's possible, I suppose." He changed the subject. "Likhov's furious because I've been pushing your case. But I'm glad I've managed to give you a hand. I'm with you heart and soul, you know."

When he got into the street Krylov realised what speed the cotton reel would move at and rang Likhov from a public telephone.

"Good man," Likhov growled in his deep voice. "My grandson got it himself. By the way, since you've rung up"—he breathed heavily over the wire—"I wish you luck. . . ."

Krylov knew what he had left unsaid. In spite of various pressures Likhov had decided to back Krylov. It would be a nasty knock if Krylov let him down. And the fact that he hadn't said so only made it harder for Krylov.

Chapter Seven

Every day, at the same hour, just as it was beginning to get light, the old and withered maple-tree that grew by the window began to sing. It always woke him up. Scores of birds that had gone to roost amid the scanty yellowed leaves broke into a chorus. The leaves trembled in the windless air as the birds sang. Their voices trilled on different notes but all together they made a harmonious choir, to which each contributed his own part. They swayed on their branches in time to the music, as musicians do. The maple-tree stood in the yard with a high brick wall behind it. The greyish-brown balls of fluff with their yellowish-green breasts looked like spring leaves and the tree seemed to be breaking into leaf. After a time the birds flew away and the maple-tree relapsed into an empty, motionless silence.

After a hasty breakfast Krylov sat down to work. The month's respite Likhov had given him was nearly over, but at last it looked as if something had begun to move. The idea had come suddenly and he was afraid of letting it slip. He was not going to be fooled this time. He put all thought of rejoicing out of his mind. All this talk of inspiration and seeing the light was just fiction.

Yet, without admitting it to himself, he rejoiced inwardly. It was a break-through, everything was coming easily. He calculated and wrote as fast as if someone were dictating to him. Pesetsky put off his own work to help him with the calculations. The whole thing had become so clear and obvious that it was hard to see what they had been struggling with so long. The fact that the zones in which lightning was generated were extremely rare actually made it easier to influence them and offered greater opportunities of doing so. The flights must be continued with the apparatus aimed at areas where lightning had just struck. The facts fitted together like tiles on a roof. The rest of the building was a mere skeleton, but, at least, the roof was on.

When they had worked their brains into a state of coma they would put on a Bach recording, sit back with their feet on the table and listen, smoking blissfully. The music was majestically austere. There was no embellishment, nothing superfluous. A clear, unembroidered theme was repeated again and again, and every time it was different. Everything it had to say seemed to have been said, but no, there was yet another turn to be taken, fresh strata to be unearthed. The simplest things had a profundity as inexhaustible as beauty itself. It was like physics, they told each other. Every elementary particle was infinitely complex. The perfection of this music reassured them. Perfection was what they needed now, the perfect culmination.

Zina would call for Pesetsky in the evening. She was in love and happy, and Pesetsky, a confirmed bachelor, was talking sheepishly of getting married. Krylov stood at the window and watched them walking away across the yard with their arms round each other.

He had a long way to go before evolving any real theory. Only the approaches, certain basic principles were emerging, but even this was an advance. Only now was the task ahead revealing itself in its true dimensions. Up to now they had been blind men trying to hit a target. It was amazing that Tulin should have been able to find the target at all at that stage. He must have had exceptional powers of intuition, unusual insight. It was a miracle that they had been so near the truth without really knowing where they were.

He now saw the crash in an entirely different light. The detector's power supply had been cut off. Would the detector have helped them if it had been functioning properly? Isn't it always useful to have a compass? Of course, if Richard had been able to bale out with the drums, they might have found out something.

Now Krylov realised what they really needed and what they had previously failed to understand. At last it was possible to formulate certain vital questions concerning the nature of lightning. And after all, what really mattered in any research was to formulate the question properly.

The most powerful installations for producing artificial lightning were not capable of making a spark leap more than about fifteen yards. Yet nature could produce lightning that travelled tens, even hundreds of miles. For millions of years the clouds had been casually generating enormous, incredible voltages, and squandering them as casually. He felt he might one day lay his hands on sources of electric power no one had yet contemplated.

Because he knew how this and many other things could be investigated.

Richard's thesis, which Golitsyn had passed on to him, contained several interesting alternative circuits for a storm-detector. Krylov had made use of them. He had also used some of Tulin's ideas and Golitsyn's objections to them, and also the work done by the French scientist Duras, but what had emerged from all this was something quite new, of which no one yet had any conception. He, Krylov, was the only man in the world who knew what to do. And how to do it! He was the first!

An aircraft would take off and the heavy violet clouds, bulging with thunder and lightning, would begin to pale and turn silver, then float away into the heights and melt to nothing in the sunny blue. When he had listened to Tulin talking in this vein he had always felt slightly embarrassed, but now he enjoyed recalling these fantastic visions. Perhaps he was becoming something like Tulin. He went over to the mirror. No, oddly enough, it seemed to be just the same Krylov as before. The same small, unexpressive eyes. How very strange! Yet this man had the great power of one who commands the truth. Yes, perhaps there was a certain radiance in those eyes, after all. Almost invisible, must be infra-red.

People were walking along the street with their umbrellas up as if nothing special had happened, just as they had walked last year, ten years ago. His neighbour, a sailor's wife, flirted with him unsuspectingly and asked him round to tea. Zina was reading Leskov. They were playing Mussorgsky on the radio. It was as if he had suddenly slipped back into the distant past. How strange that these people hadn't the faintest idea of the joys that lay in store for them.

At last the day came when he took his folder of proofs to Golitsyn. The old man was busy with some delegation or other and received him hurriedly, yet managed to exhibit the restraint characteristic of a man of the old school. Very good, but it would all have to be checked and tested, of course.

There were many weak spots but, for some reason, as he found them, he felt irritated not with Krylov but with himself.

Finding other people's mistakes—that's all you're good for now. You can keep abreast of the journals, take the chair at a conference, receive a delegation, read books, but what does it all amount to? What's the point in all your reading and note-taking? Look at Krylov. He doesn't know a tenth of what you know, yet he has ideas. They may not be up to much but you'd be glad to have them. You simply refuse to admit that you're old and no use for anything except helping others. Or are you going to annihilate Krylov once again? Yes, you're still capable of that. For that you have both the erudition and the energy. How many times have you told yourself it's too early yet to consider yourself old? Yes, we know you can still drive a car and show off your learning, but you won't create anything new. No one knows yet that you're barren of ideas. But perhaps everyone has known it for a long time? Just an old fogey! He suddenly remembered that people used to speak of Volkov like that. And that brought it all back—Petrograd, the Forestry Institute, Volkov with his polecat coat hanging bell-like over him, the spring sky with its curly clouds, the rickety table standing amid the melting snow, and the first experiments with a radiosonde. In spite of all Volkov's predictions the sonde had carried out its programme. And he remembered himself, a beaming, floppy-haired youth in a waistcoat, prancing about like a young goat beside the radio set. How gleefully he had waved the radio message from the sonde in Volkov's face! And Volkov had just sat there with a drip at the end of his red nose.

Yes, how ruthless you were at that moment! Youth is always ruthless. Now you've had a taste of it yourself, now that it's too late to make amends.

No one remembers Volkov any more, except you. The names of your idols mean nothing to the young people nowadays. Smurov, Molchanov, they're just so much ancient history. If you showed Krylov that radiosonde and told him that was what you got made a professor for, he'd simply roar with laughter. The method of measuring ion mobility that you had such a struggle with he simply dismisses with a "How else?"

You used to be a luminary in the mathematical world, but now the equations you provided the answers for can be solved by students.

Did you ever seriously believe you were destined for immortality? No one is. Remember the Plato and Ovid of your school days? Who reads them now? In another century or two no one will be able to understand what we loved in Blok and Vrubel.

A little earlier, a little later, that's the only difference. What's the difference between a marble sculpture and a snowman? Longevity? And yet Newton is immortal. And so is Mendeleyev. But you are not in that class. And it's time you resigned yourself to the fact.

He thought of the conference hall of the Academy of Sciences and his report at a plenary session on the nature of lightning. Truth had seemed to dawn, had seemed to be within his grasp, yet again and again it had slipped away. What was left? Nothing. For a time his work was referred to, then those that had referred to it were referred to, and only the table remained. And after that the table was reduced to a single figure that was included in a new comprehensive table. Zero point seven three. Nobody nowadays knew who had arrived at that figure. It stood in a long column with the others, two figures after a decimal point, just part of a very long table. Yet even that was something, something achieved. The catch was that even when a man had been happy he always looked back with a sigh.

But all the same the young people nowadays were a strange lot. He rang Krylov and invited him round to his house. He wanted to talk to him about other things besides the work. About the present age, about the way a man's life could be judged by what he passed on to his pupils. The best possible use must be made of experience. . . .

"Well, what do you think?" Krylov asked before he was inside the door. On hearing the reply he gave a quick laugh, put his hand over his eyes, stepped across to the window and waved to someone outside. He heard nothing more of what Golitsyn was saying. Golitsyn looked out of the window. On the other side of the street stood Pesetsky, Zina, the laboratory assistant, and another, very beautiful young woman. They were making expressive gestures. Krylov shifted impatiently from one foot to another. Perhaps this was the fashion nowadays, Golitsyn told himself and smirked at his own touchiness. He handed the folder back to Krylov and arranged to go with him to see Yuzhin the following morning.

To give him his due, Lagunov had not left a single loophole in the report he had drawn up for the Minister.

When Lagunov had finished reading it, the Minister went on turning over the pages of his copy.

"Of course, it's easy enough to ban things," he said finally. "But the problem remains. You can't ban that."

"But the head of the project, Tulin himself, has stepped down," Lagunov replied.

The Minister fixed an expectant eye on Yuzhin. Yuzhin said nothing.

"Well, that settles it then," said the Minister.

His disappointment was completely unexpected, yet so natural that Yuzhin found himself wondering why he hadn't thought on the same lines, then remembered that he had, but had put all such thoughts out of his mind.

Lagunov was looking pleased because at last it was all over and the Minister had agreed with the commission's conclusions.

And a damn good thing, too, Yuzhin told himself, eyeing Lagunov with distaste. I'm darned glad to be shot of the whole wretched business. After all, why should he quarrel with Lagunov merely for Krylov's sake, and let himself in for all kinds of trouble besides? He would have to bear the brunt of the charges that would follow. Yes, thank God, the whole thing was over and done with.

Lagunov overtook him as he was leaving the building.

"The drinks are on you this time, General."

Yuzhin smiled sourly. Lagunov was right in a way. The commission's decision had acquitted the Board and Yuzhin of all responsibility. Everything was blamed on Tulin's method, and, since Tulin's method had been scrapped, the rest could be quietly buried and no questions asked.

". . . and no questions asked." It was Lagunov's voice.

It gave him a start. He halted abruptly and clicked his heels.

"Good day to you," he said sharply, gave a salute and walked straight to his car without looking back.

Golitsyn and Krylov's arrival in his office stirred up all the old feelings of disquiet. The whole business was supposed to be over and done with, and here were these two again. He was particularly irritated by this new alliance: Golitsyn—Krylov.

He decided to have a dig at Golitsyn. "I must say you change your point of view at remarkable speed, Arkady Borisovich," he observed.

Golitsyn bristled up. "I'm very sorry, but I should first like to know what I am to understand by 'point of view'. You seem to regard it as something stationary, as some sort of constant. It may be so with statues but not with living people. There is such thing as the process of cognition. Thought develops, I don't change my views, I develop them. Krylov's basic conception is a very bold one, very audacious and"—he lifted a warning finger—"entirely legitimate. It deserves to be thoroughly tested."

"So you made a mistake?"

Golitsyn tossed his head with dignity.

"In the world of science it is no disgrace to admit one has made a mistake." He gave a little smirk of triumph that baffled Yuzhin completely. "In this particular case we will be dealing with work on an entirely different qualitative plane. Here we will be going right to the root of things."

His explanation was lucid and impressive. Yuzhin had noticed that the bigger the scientist the simpler his explanations.

"But why didn't you see all this before?" he burst out. "You've only got yourselves to blame."

"But, good heavens, man, how could we? Sergei Ilyich has only just succeeded in proving. . . ."

Yuzhin's face became inscrutable, almost wooden.

His uniform was beginning to feel tight round the chest and waist. He told himself he must have it let out. The layers of fat were accumulating like the annual rings on a tree-trunk, and the young, clean-cut Yuzhin inside them was finding it increasingly hard to breathe and get about.

"Your thought processes and your scientific ideas are obviously going great guns," he remarked caustically. "But we can't chop and change like this."

The fact that Golitsyn, apparently, thought it quite natural to say one thing one day and something else the next, and was even proud of it, got under Yuzhin's skin. There was something unjust about it. He couldn't see quite what, and he couldn't see either why he, and not Golitsyn, should feel embarrassed, as embarrassed as he had felt during his interview with the Minister.

"We can't stop now," Krylov said cheerfully. With his jutting cheekbones and hair growing down the back of his neck he looked rather like a long-lost traveller who had just reached civilisation. "We've got to get on with the testing as soon as possible, you know." He was looking at Yuzhin as though they were all in this together and his objections were not really meant to be taken seriously.

Yuzhin fumed. They were both a pair of nuts, and it was time someone brought them to their senses. He set about the task without pity. With the greatest ease he proved to them that they were too late, they were flogging a dead horse. An order was an order. How could he go back to the Minister now?

Golitsyn's face saddened and he looked depressed. Krylov also seemed to emerge from his trance. He screwed the cap on his fountain-pen and put it away in his pocket, then he began to look not at Yuzhin's face but at his uniform. This was irritating. Yuzhin suddenly had a vision of what he must look like to Krylov. The uniform began to feel even tighter, and Yuzhin felt he was not saying what he wanted to say, and this made him even more furious. But now he was a prisoner of his own words and had to go through with them. He felt as if he had known all the time what he was going to say, even before he had kept silent when the Minister asked about Lagunov's report. But no matter how far he looked back he couldn't make out when the whole process had begun. Suddenly he remembered how Tulin had sat in this armchair and talked him round and the memory gave him fresh resolve.

Start flying into thunderheads again? Take more risks?

Golitsyn maintained a confused silence. Evidently neither he nor Krylov had considered this side of the question. But Yuzhin reminded them of it. Neither had he forgotten Golitsyn's speech to the commission.

"We shall go about the job systematically, stage by stage..." Krylov began.

"Yes, we've heard all that before. But you'll get no help from me this time," he said. "If I'm ordered to, we'll discuss the matter—and not before."

"But to whom can we appeal? Where can we get support?" Golitsyn asked.

Krylov rose slowly to his feet. There was a terrible weariness in his face, his boyishly full lips had suddenly become drawn and scored with wrinkles.

"I'm not going to appeal to anyone!" He slammed the folder down on the table and his voice rose to a shout. "I've had enough! I've done my bit! Now you can do what you like about it!"

"Sergei Ilyich!" Golitsyn cried.

Krylov stepped into the middle of the room and stretched himself as if he had just thrown off a great burden, and Yuzhin realised that Krylov was not bluffing, that this was not just a pose. He was quite capable of walking out on them. This young fellow judged things by his own yardstick. He acted in the open, without worrying about what impression he was making. He was like Yuzhin's friends, the men he used to fly with, like he himself had once been, in his front-line days.

"Washing your hands of the whole thing is the easiest way out," Yuzhin said. "But you can't expect me to fight your battles for you, Sergei Ilyich."

Krylov looked again at Yuzhin's uniform, then went back to the desk. The sleeves of his jacket were too short as usual, but the jacket now seemed baggy as well.

He picked up the folder and, without raising his eyes, said: "You've got a lot of medals and they were all won in action. You must have had a lot of guts in those days. And now there's not even any shooting."

He walked to the door. Yuzhin watched him go.

Golitsyn began to apologise for Krylov. Yuzhin felt he had to say something, so he said the institute ought to be told to give Krylov a few lessons in how to behave.

Yuzhin went home on foot. He left early, saying he had a headache. It was cold and sunny. The street was crystalline in the autumn air and the gleam of rain-washed windows. He could see far. People's faces looked fresh and their eyes sparkled.

It was a long time since Yuzhin had walked the streets in the daytime with nothing to do. Young men strode past him with their hands stuffed into the pockets of their short overcoats, bright-coloured scarves wound carelessly round their necks. Yuzhin felt the weight of his air-force greatcoat on his shoulders.

He started going over in his mind when and for what he had been awarded his medals, but for some reason could remember only the regimental mess and his flight mechanic who liked to recite: "Up the line's the farthest they'll send you, and a bullet o' lead's the most they'll lend you." Then he remembered his first dogfight over Luga and returning to base to find it already occupied by the Germans. He had brought his plane down on a cart track, got hold of some petrol somewhere and taken off again in search of his regiment.

In the regiment he had been considered brave. But he knew, if anyone did, that bravery was not just a knack. It was something that had to be produced from scratch every time. And bravery in war was not the same as bravery in civilian life. He cursed Krylov mentally in the hope of relieving his feelings, but no relief came. Neither Krylov nor Golitsyn would ever get anywhere. They were not the right type. They didn't know how to talk to people in authority. Krylov had plenty of guts, of course. . . . It suddenly occurred to Yuzhin that even while the commission was sitting he had felt a secret sympathy for Krylov. Yes, a secret sympathy. He had even congratulated himself on keeping it so, on being able to suppress his personal sympathies. In reality, it had made things much easier for him. Convenience always looks like the truth at first. If he had trusted his feelings from the start, it might have pulled him through. How could you expect to be trusted when you didn't even trust yourself.

Eventually Yuzhin came to the conclusion that he had been letting himself slide of late. He was surprised to find himself indulging in so much introspection. He had never gone in for that before. He had thought of his job, of his children. And what else? Of his friends, his wife, of course, but he had never thought about himself. There had never been time, and there hadn't seemed to be any sense in it anyway. Yes, that was how life went on, until one day you realised all of a sudden that you had never considered how you were living it. You could spend a whole lifetime jawing about things with other people, and yet find no time to commune with yourself. No time, no desire, or perhaps—not enough courage.

Chapter Eight

The folder lay on the table wrapped up in a newspaper and Krylov did not touch it.

He had imagined that this folder containing the answer to so vital a problem would be snatched up, that everyone would want to see it, that it would make a sensation. He had seen himself being chaired across Red Square or, at least, getting a bonus of an extra fortnight's pay.

His report was listened to, he was congratulated, and that was that. There had even been offers of help, but he had no idea what to ask for. He was like a runner who covered the distance well, then found that he had no one to hand the baton to. To be quite honest, he had never seriously considered taking over the leadership of the group. He had merely wanted to solve the problem. He had solved it. Now let somebody else do the worrying.

Ada was staying in Moscow. She was on holiday and on her way to the Crimea. She had brought him a letter from Anikeyev, who was inviting Krylov back to the institute. He promised to arrange everything with Likhov.

Ada seemed to Krylov more beautiful than ever. She had softened a little. Her eyes had a new blueness, like the blueness of melting snow. She no longer tried to teach and instruct, and Krylov was very glad to see her. She suggested that they should go to the Crimea together. He hesitated, not knowing what to reply. He didn't really know what he was waiting for. Sometimes he fancied there would be a knock at the door and someone would come in and take that wretched folder, and then, at last, he would be free.

The guests were arriving for the symposium. Golitsyn was busy from morning to night and Krylov had nothing to do. Ada cautiously advised him to go and see Likhov.

"But why the hell should I?" Krylov flared up. "Why should I make myself cheap? If they're not interested, neither am I."

"Who are 'they'?"

He looked at her obtusely, then laughed at himself.

It was Sunday. It had been raining all the morning. Ada decided to tidy up the room. She threw out old magazines and newspapers and the room became bigger and more comfortable. When she was dusting the desk she wiped Natasha's photograph carefully, without asking any questions. With a towel for an apron she worked quietly and efficiently, joking about men's slovenly habits, and Krylov expatiated to her on how women held up the development of the human race. They tied up industry with their demands for jewellery and handbags. And as for their hats? A new fashion every year. And cosmetics. . . .

Ada laughed at him and her eyes shone under her disarranged hair. She was touchingly domestic, nothing like the austere, beautiful statue, in whose presence he had always felt like a visitor to a museum. And suddenly it occurred to him that Ada had waited for him even more devotedly and unselfishly than he had waited for Natasha. And it must be just as sad for her as it was for him. In fact, he had treated Ada just as Natasha had treated him, except that in Natasha's case he himself was to blame, whereas Ada's only fault was that she loved him.

"Why don't you go south?" he asked and, as usual, began clumsily correcting himself. "I mean to say, I'm very glad you're here, but you're wasting your holiday."

"Weren't you thinking of taking a holiday too?"

"Me? I've got to be at the symposium. . . . And Pesetsky has asked me to his wedding."

"I've got a sick aunt in Moscow," Ada said. "Let's go to the Tretyakov Gallery. I haven't been there for ages."

How terribly complicated life was, especially if you took it seriously, he thought on the way to the gallery. Why used everything to be so much more simple?

"You know, I always used to be able to break away and take myself off, if I wanted to. I made mistakes but I did as I pleased."

"But if you break away this time, who will carry on your work? It'll be forgotten without you. I used to want to break away too, but now I know that nobody can ever be completely free."

They strolled arm in arm round the gallery, just as they used to in Leningrad, when Ada was "educating" Krylov, except that now she no longer explained things or lectured him. They just looked and shared each other's pleasure, if they both happened to like the same thing.

They stopped in front of Serov's *Girl with Peaches*. She sat there in the late-summer sunshine, posing unaffectedly for the artist, her face reflecting the colour of her loose pink blouse and giving off all the velvety, sunny warmth of the peaches lying before her on the tablecloth. She seemed to look thoughtfully at Krylov, just as she had looked at the millions of other people who had stood before her, lavishing upon each the purity and strength of her kindness. He felt the sunlight turning into the juicy sweetness of the fruit. He felt the taste of the sun, the mysterious workings of light, its gradual transformation. The warmth that radiated from this round-cheeked girl made him think of so many youthful joys that somehow he had missed. It also made him think of the invincible strength that kindness could command.

Ada gave him a quick glance and Krylov came out of his reverie. "Yes," he said, "that's how it's got to be. . . ."

Ada couldn't understand what he meant, but she refrained from asking.

He was not sent an invitation to the symposium. He thought it was an oversight and called on the organising committee. They passed him on to Agatov.

"We thought you had gone away," Agatov said.

"But I haven't."

Agatov smiled.

"So I see. But some people think, you know, that it would be better if you weren't there." He dissociated himself from the idea with a gesture. "They think you'll start complaining and there'll be too many foreigners around."

"D'you expect me to beg to be admitted? If you want to know, some people think you ought to go and stuff yourself!" He flung out of the room, slamming the door behind him.

In the corridor he ran into Voznitsyn, who took him aside.

"Something's afoot," he whispered. "I hear Yuzhin's been to see the Minister. Have you heard from Bogdanovsky yet?"

"Who's Bogdanovsky?"

"You mean you don't know anything then? He's looking for you. This is between ourselves, of course, but there's a letter signed by Likhov, Golitsyn and Anikeyev demanding that work on the project be restarted. If you talk to Bogdanovsky, remember that we have no objections."

"But what has changed? You knew before this that I had proved. . . ."

"The situation's changed, the situation!" Voznitsyn said cheerfully. "Everything will be all right. I told you it would long ago."

He dragged Krylov to a telephone, then gave him a lift in his car to the Board. The next three days were a whirl of conferences at long tables and in offices without long tables, of making up forms and estimates and memoranda, of clattering typewriters, buzzing telephones and visits to various establishments.

Voznitsyn clutched his head in despair when he heard some of Krylov's completely unguarded replies. Yuzhin winked approvingly. Bogdanovsky appeared on the scene and asked Krylov a lot of tricky questions, like a gypsy bargaining for a horse. Lagunov made rather a critical speech, but Krylov got up and asked him what positive suggestion he had to make. The point was that none of his opponents had anything positive to offer. Bogdanovsky seized on this argument and wielded it effectively against Lagunov and anyone else who opposed him.

"You treat thunderstorms like Mummy's skirts," Bogdanovsky declared, taking a final lunge at Yuzhin. "You think they'll cover up a multitude of sins if you hold on to them tight enough. Blame everything on Jupiter, that's your policy."

Yuzhin merely puffed out his cheeks and calmly laid himself open to attack, deliberately helping Bogdanovsky and Likhov.

Krylov was quite dazed at the skill displayed by the belligerents. On the third day he emerged from the final purgatory, limp as a wet rag, but thoroughly tried, tested, signed, affirmed and sealed.

"Congratulations," Bogdanovsky said to him, when they were left alone in his huge, uncomfortable, smoky office. "But I've been watching you and I can tell you this. You'll make a pretty poor administrator."

"That's just it," Krylov replied. "I don't want to be one. I'm sure I'll make a hash of things."

"So what do you intend doing? Just *taking part*?" Bogdanovsky asked sarcastically.

"Why didn't you show up right away, after the crash, and try to help Tulin?" Krylov asked.

Bogdanovsky sat on his desk staring at him impassively, his face with its prominent cheekbones as immobile as a Buddha's.

"Why didn't I? We have to help those who can help themselves. It's no good helping those who can't. It doesn't pay. Just a waste of time." He paused. "As an organiser, you fall a long way short of Tulin. But never mind, you'll learn. What is it that's worrying you?"

"We've let the group fall apart. There were some useful people in it. I don't know whether they'll agree to come in on this thing again."

"Never mind, we'll make them an offer. Every project has its ups and downs. We are working for the public good, we have to ignore personal feelings."

"But will these people want to ignore their personal feelings?"

Bogdanovsky frowned.

"If we asked people all the time what they want and what they don't want, we'd still be living in caves."

"That kind of progress doesn't appeal to me. I intend to ask people what they want!" Krylov snapped. "And anyhow I haven't yet decided. . . ."

Bogdanovsky was not used to persuading people, but he was even less used to having people argue with him.

"You will," he said. "You're cornered anyway. You can't escape your destiny. Incidentally, we shall be paying you a special salary."

"Why?"

"It won't do you any harm, young man. Disinterestedness sounds very fine, but it's not reliable."

Krylov looked at him keenly.

"I don't like your line of reasoning."

It was not the kind of thing that was usually said in this office but Bogdanovsky, to his credit, smiled understandingly.

"You're probably feeling a bit tired after all this unaccustomed strain." Then his smile vanished. "We shall have to work together.

I don't know the meaning of the words 'like' and 'dislike'. I need you and you need me. Is that clear?"

"Clear enough."

Whereupon Bogdanovsky decided that each of them had his own idea of what was clear, and that men like Krylov could not be forced because they obeyed rules of their own making.

Krylov turned round at the door.

"By the way, how did you get to know about me? And the whole situation. . . ."

Bogdanovsky cut him short. "I know what you mean. One of the women on our staff, Natalya Romanova, came to me and pushed your case for you. I was going to bury the whole thing after the crash. Then I had a look at the record."

"Where is she now?"

"Romanova? She's with a surveying party. One of my secretaries will tell you where that is."

At home Ada was waiting for him. She sat on the sofa in the twilight and he talked to her. He told her everything, about Natasha, too.

"So now you're all set," she said evenly. "Anikeyev's been on the phone. He's in Moscow and he wants to see you."

Krylov rang Anikeyev and arranged to meet him at the Moskva Hotel.

"I can't go with you. I've got my packing to do," Ada said.

"What's the sudden hurry?"

"My aunt's better now. I ought to be on my way."

"I won't go out this evening then."

She forced a smile.

"All right, let's go together."

On the way Krylov persuaded her to drop in with him to see Vera Matveyevna, in Gnezdnikovsky Street.

Two long rings and a short one. Vera Matveyevna's husband opened the door and took them into a room where two boys were doing their homework on the dining table. Vera Matveyevna came out from behind a screen. Her arm was still in a sling.

Krylov told her how things had turned out.

He made no proposals, but a sudden hush fell on the room. Both boys looked up together and Krylov saw anxiety in their eyes. Vera Matveyevna's husband buried his head in his newspaper.

"Yes, of course, that's very interesting," Vera Matveyevna said. "I would like to take part but I'm not in a position to."

She took them into the hall and, glancing over her shoulder, whispered: "You mustn't be offended, Sergei Ilyich. I'm simply afraid. When I remember what it was like.... No, I just couldn't possibly. I'm sorry, Sergei Ilyich."

"But, of course, I quite understand," Krylov said.

When they got into the street Ada took his arm and began telling him with exaggerated cheerfulness about the factory and how, before she left, she had called in at the technical inspection department, where Dolinin was now in charge. Did Krylov remember him? He had shown her the "Krylov Tester". Everybody called it that now. She had asked one of the practical students—an amusing young fellow—who Krylov was. The student had answered with a shrug that he must be some inventor or scientist. Of course, Dolinin had come down on him like a ton of bricks and the student had had to wriggle out by saying such things weren't on their syllabus.

Krylov sighed. Those were the days!

Anikeyev belonged to those days too. He kissed Krylov on both cheeks, then called him an idiot for not wanting to return to his institute. While he ate fried carp, he pulverised Lagunov, and over coffee cursed Bogdanovsky.

"You're a very fierce person," Ada said.

Anikeyev set his jaw aggressively.

"I've too good a brain to be kind. Fierce people are useful. They stimulate progress. They overthrow authorities. You, Sergei, lack ferocity."

"I'll try to improve," Krylov said.

Anikeyev just couldn't get over the way this quiet, simple fellow had succeeded in smashing such a tremendous wall of opposition. He kept asking him how he had managed it, but Krylov had no explanation. He thought it had all happened by itself.

"Yes," Anikeyev said, "a man can do a lot, if he's got the truth on his side. He can do a hell of a lot...."

"Monsieur Krylov?"

It was professor Duras, whom Krylov had met in France. How he had changed! The lively youthful fat man Krylov remembered had given way to a sad and seedy individual, who looked as if he were suffering from some incurable disease. Duras told them that his son had recently died of radiation sickness.

"I was invited to the symposium," he said. "But I don't really know why I came...."

The symposium was due to open the following day and many of the guests were in the restaurant. They all had badges and little cards dangling from their lapels on which were written their name and country. There were people here who had known and argued with each other for years, without ever meeting face to face. They judged one another by a standard that did not depend on title, office or rank. The criterion was what a man had done, what mistakes he had made, what discoveries, what research he was at present engaged in.

"Doctor Regner would like to meet you," Anikeyev said.

Krylov had been following Doctor Regner's work for years and had a picture in his mind of a great, boisterous German with a fantastic imagination and an equally fantastic mane of hair. Anikeyev chuckled to himself observing Krylov's startled face as he shook hands with a flirtatious long-legged blonde, who immediately took a photograph of him.

When Krylov returned to his table, only Duras was sitting there. Anikeyev and Ada were dancing.

Krylov asked Duras what he had been doing lately. Duras suddenly threw up his hands and shook his fists over his head.

"It is all senseless. Can't you see! The world has gone wrong. At any moment someone may press a button and it will all be over in a few minutes. All our science, all our academies and colleges. Everything will be erased from the face of the earth. All the leopards, the children's nurseries, the picture galleries, the missionaries, everything."

"Well, we can do without the missionaries," said Krylov. "Why bother about the missionaries?"

"Yes, and all the symposiums too. We, along with our grandchildren and our great grandchildren, will all become neutrons and electrons and whizz about according to Heisenberg's laws, and Heisenberg himself will whizz about with us." His eyes blazed with a macabre gaiety and he reached forward as if to press a button. "The world is full of madmen and one of them will find his way to it. And then all the wise men of politics and all their predictions will be reduced to dust! The Madeleine—to dust! The whole history of mankind will end at this button, the final, culminating point of history."

"Do you really believe this button can't be destroyed?"

"It is too late. It exists. Try to destroy Ohm's law, Maxwell's equation. They have been discovered. They belong to mankind. We can't get rid of them, no matter how we try."

"But this button of yours isn't a law!" Krylov exclaimed.

"It is more than a law! It is God! It is the modern religion. We all walk beneath the sign of the button. We must go down on our knees and pray to it. It should replace the crucifixes in the cathedrals. Yes, there is no other God but Button. What can you offer instead? The button reduces everything to absurdity—lies and achievements, courage, even cynicism itself. How can you take life so calmly? Are you all blind? Are you deaf? Can't you see that the world is out of joint? You think it's because of my son? No, my son was my own personal tragedy. Sooner or later we must all pass away, but there has always been the future, something to work and suffer for. Now there is nothing. The future has been stolen. . . ."

The stumbling, feverish torrent of words began to exasperate Krylov. He liked Duras. The Frenchman was a brilliant scientist and it was painful to see this penetrating mind corroded with fear. Couldn't he see that it was easy to pile horror upon horror? At the beginning of the century the bogey had been entropy, the heat death. There had always been panic-mongers. Religion had excelled in painting horrific pictures of the end of the world.

"But there is no religion," Duras argued. "We have destroyed our faith. What's left instead? Nothing. Where is our moral support? At one time we at least had faith in the immortality of the soul."

"God can't deal with your button, that's true," Krylov said. "It's better to believe in man. The main thing is life, not the threat to life." They were speaking English and Krylov had difficulty in finding the right words. He wanted Duras to understand him. "The tragedy is that humanity discovered nuclear energy too early, before the world was liberated from capitalism. The progress of society can't keep up with the progress of science. In about two hundred years from now I dare say our fears will seem laughable."

"You think there will be anyone left to laugh?"

"Yes, I am sure there will," Krylov said emphatically. "It's always easier to deny than to affirm. My dear Duras, I didn't take part in the war. But I know that, even when you're surrounded, you still have to go on fighting till the last. And after all, you and I aren't surrounded. We've got strength on our side, there are more of us. We have greater resources, greater numbers."

"I could argue that point," Duras said, "but I don't want to win this argument, I don't want to change your opinion. What I want to understand is where your optimism comes from. What it rests on. . . ."

He broke off, looking at Ada who was walking back to the table with Anikeyev.

She walked with her head high, equally attractive to old and young. They forgot their arguments and smiled as they looked at her.

"Still at it?" Anikeyev said as he came up. "You lack frivolity. With science racing ahead as it is we've got to learn to forget serious things sometimes."

Golitsyn and Likhov emerged from somewhere at the back of the restaurant.

Anikeyev hailed them.

Golitsyn asked Krylov how he was getting on.

"Fine," Krylov said. "I'm building up a wonderful group."

"Who's in it?"

"Just myself. But it's a good solid organisation." To himself he thought, at least I've got Richard.

Likhov said something to Duras in French and Duras gave Krylov a surprised, thoughtful look.

"Oh, I nearly forgot," Golitsyn said. "I've had an application from Mikulin. Do you remember Mikulin, who took his finals this year?"

"Alyosha?"

"Surely you don't expect me to know whether his name's Alyosha or not," Golitsyn grumbled. "At all events, he's asked me to give him a reference. Perhaps you will grant my request and accept him?"

"I'll see what I can do," Krylov said.

It was just beginning to rain. A few leaves were scattered on the asphalt. The street was cold and deserted. They were walking past the old Manège Building.

"Hasn't this evening reminded you of anything?" Ada asked.

"No," Krylov said. He was wondering whether Duras would have understood where his optimism came from if he had known that after their conversation he, Krylov, was thinking of how to persuade Altynov and Lisitsky to return to their group.

But suddenly he remembered that evening with Tulin and Ada. They had entered the square from the other direction. And they had met Zhenya and Richard there. Someone had had a transistor. He could remember the tune.

So here we are again, he thought, and looked up at the clouds hiding the night sky. They would have to start all over again, in a different way, in quite a different way. Or perhaps they would be going on from where they had left off, but it would still be quite different.